REVIEWS

"A unique, deftly scripted, and extraordinary novel by an author with a distinctive narrative storytelling style that will hold the readers dedicated attention from beginning to end, "Farewell My Life: Buona Notte Vita Mia" is an impressive and unreservedly recommended addition to both community and academic library Contemporary Literary Fiction collections. One of those rare novels that will linger in the mind and memory long after the book itself has been finished."—*Mid-West Book Review*

"The author knows her characters very, very well; this shows in the consistent and very individual way they act. This is not a plot-driven story; it's character-driven. In this book, the characters are the jam which holds everything together. The best example of this is Grace, the talented violinist, who, simply, jumps off the page. I loved her."—*Wishing Shelf*

"This is not your typical mystery; it's for fans of thrilling action and historically-inspired events…Contra to the status quo of the genre, the men are the romantics – though in a deranged manner – and the women showcased are the core strength of the novel."—*BookLife Prize.*

"The author…adeptly summons the era in all its manners and details with her descriptive prose…Her omniscient, third-person narrator effectively flits through the heads of various characters, offering momentary glimpses of their inner lives."—*Kirkus Reviews*

Farewell My Life

(Buona Notte Vita Mia)

✠✠✠✠✠✠✠✠✠✠✠

Cynthia Sally Haggard

Spun Stories Press
Washington, D.C. 20036

This book is a work of fiction. Names, characters, places, and incidents are either products of the author's imagination or used fictitiously. Any resemblance to actual events or locales or persons, living or dead, is entirely coincidental.

Published by Spun Stories Press and KDP.

Designed by Cynthia Sally Haggard

Cover image: Thinkstock.

Manufactured in the United States of America

ISBN: 9781092730754

Dedicated to the memories of
Theodore William "Ted" Bogacz (1943–1992),
my first husband, who taught me much about
modernity, the Great War of 1914–1918, and shell shock,
and
Nannie Jamieson (1904–1990),
my violin teacher at the Guildhall School of Music and
Drama in London, England

Table of Contents

Spoiler Alert

For reasons that I hope will become obvious, I have made the unconventional decision of placing the *Author's Note* at the beginning, rather than at the end of this novel. However, if you would prefer to read the novel first, please skip ahead as it does contain a couple of spoilers. (I hope you agree with my artistic decision.) The novel actually begins with a quotation from Vladimir Nabokov's *Laughter in the Dark*, appropriate, I think, for this dark and rather subversive work.

Author's Note

Writing about vanishing, dissolving and the crumbling of comfortable lives, assumptions, and civilizations, it seemed appropriate to end *Farewell My Life* on 9 November 1938 when *Kristallnacht*, the Night of Broken Glass erupted. This was a pogrom against the Jews living in Nazi Germany, carried out on the night of 9-10 November by paramilitary forces and German civilians. It is not known how many people died, but modern historians believe that it must have been in the hundreds, if not the thousands. Afterwards the Nazis arrested around thirty-thousand Jewish men and incarcerated them in concentration camps. The Final Solution had begun.

The Oster Conspiracy was one of around twenty attempts between 1934 and 1944 to assassinate Hitler and destroy the Nazis. It was foiled by the actions of Neville Chamberlain, who sought appeasement to prevent another war. I was fortunate in being able to find a recording from the BBC Sound Archives of Chamberlain's return from Munich on 30 September 1938.

The First World War cast a long shadow over the 1920s and the 1930s. Modernist ideas blew in on the winds of that devastating war, in which hundreds of thousands of young men perished. The figures are truly shocking. On the first day of the Battle of the Somme in 1916, around sixty thousand men in the British army died. Much has been written about this battle and the trench warfare of the Western Front, a line of trenches that ran through the flat lands of north-east France into Belgium. The Italian Front is less well known, but the slaughter was just as senseless. The Italians and Austrians battled around Asiago in the Veneto and across the Isonzo and Piave rivers, in rough mountainous terrain in the foothills of the alps.

In 1921, no man over the age of twenty-one remained unaffected by this war, and shattered survivors filled the streets of European capitals. During the war, a new illness emerged that we now call post-traumatic stress disorder or PTSD. In the 1920s, this illness was referred to variously as "neurasthenia" or "shell-shock." The overwhelming number of maimed or dead young men compelled a generation of young women in Europe to forgo husbands.

The Treaty of Versailles of 1919 forced Germany to acknowledge responsibility for causing this war and pay reparations of 132 billion Marks (equivalent to about 442 billion dollars in today's money). This sent Germany into an economic tailspin. The value of the Mark had declined during the war, going from about 4.2 Marks to the dollar at the beginning of the war in August 1914, to about 8.91 Marks to the dollar at the end of the war in November 1918. But this trend increased, beginning with the first reparation payments in June of 1921 and continuing in 1922 and 1923. By November 1923, the Mark collapsed and the government introduced Rentenmarks to replace the worthless currency, where one dollar could buy 4.2 trillion Marks, and people piled wheelbarrows full of cash to buy a loaf of bread. The new currency commissioner Hjalmar Schacht, appointed at the end of 1923, accomplished the miracle of stabilizing the currency at the pre-war rate of 4.2 Marks to the dollar. But the price was a program of extreme austerity and a high jobless rate throughout the 1920s. Most historians now agree that the rise of Adolf Hitler in the 1920s can be directly tied to the economic desperation of millions of Germans.

Nowadays, the 1920s is celebrated for its glamor and embrace of modernism, when young women shrugged off the restrictions of Victorian society, abandoning long skirts and tight stays for shorter, lighter modern clothes. Just how revolutionary this was can be gauged by looking at the archives of *The Washington Post*, where several inches of copy were spent in discussing women's clothes in much the same way that people discuss iPads or iPhones today. But 1921 and 1922, when much of *Farewell My Life* is set, occurred before the rest of the 1920s, before the freedoms of the flapper era took hold. Those were the days when women still had to worry about their reputations, when it was still common for girls to marry in their late teens. The period of the early 1920s is equidistant between our time and that of Jane Austen (1775-1817), but in cultural terms it was much closer to her time.

Perhaps the trickiest issue had to do with Angelina, and the way in which she lived her life and earned her money. Her choice of career reflected the relatively limited options experienced by a woman born in 1888. Such women worked in typing pools, or as telephone operators, or as nurses. But they wouldn't have had access to more interesting careers such as being a doctor, lawyer, or architect, principally because women were barred from obtaining university degrees. For example, in the 1880s and 1890s, the University of London had a policy of allowing its female students to do all the work for a degree, without actually conferring the degree.

Another barrier was that banks would not allow women to apply for loans. Any woman who wanted to open her own business was obliged to find a "patron," who, in return for sexual favors, might advance her the cash. Aspects of Coco's story in *Farewell My Life* are based on the true story of Coco Chanel (1883-1971). Etienne Balsan, Chanel's first patron, relished her sexual favors but refused to help her earn her own money. Boy Capel, her second patron, saw behind the lovely profile, and appreciated her talent as an entrepreneur.

She ran her first business, ladies' hats, from his bachelor pad in Paris.

Like Coco Chanel, Angelina was a kept woman to a wealthy patron, a woman who kept her patron happy in part by her performance in bed. Although it seems hard to believe that such a woman would not have told her daughters anything about sex, that was a topic of conversation no one talked about openly. Before television and the Internet, the more sordid realities of life like sexual abuse, substance abuse, teenage pregnancy, and abortion were clouded in silence. Many blamed Angelina for not being a good mother, but she would have been blamed much more had she actually broached the topic of conversation about what a young woman's wedding night entailed.

Angelina's medical condition and her doctor's treatment of it is based upon that of Karen Blixen (1885-1962), who is better known as the author Isak Dinesen. In the early 1920s, the standard treatments for abdominal pains and pelvic infections were still mercury and arsenic because doctors had nothing else to hand, penicillin not being discovered until 1928, and antibiotics not available until the early 1930s.

Another tricky issue was Russell's relationship with Grace. The bible doesn't forbid a relationship between half-uncle and half-niece, but many of my early readers balked. The thorniness of this issue and the secrecy it entails forms the spine of the first part of the novel, and comes back to bite Russell near the end. And so I elected to keep it, instead of making things easier for myself by having, for example, Angelina be Russell's cousin, rather than his half-sister (as one reader suggested).

After the Franco-Prussian War of 1870, many from the east streamed into Berlin, including Jews, Hungarians, and Russians. So many Hungarians lived in Berlin at that time that it became known as the unofficial capital of Hungary. This is why I decided to make the Berlin landlady a Hungarian woman, rather than a German woman. I chose the name *Varga* (which means shoemaker) because it is easy to pronounce for English-speaking audiences. After the Communists overthrew the czar of Russia in 1917, Russian émigrés flooded into Berlin. It is true that previously wealthy Russian aristocrats fled with nothing but the clothes on their backs, and so the scene in which Violet and Grace encounter a Russian grand duke waiting tables would not have been uncommon in 1920s Berlin. Amongst those Russian émigrés coming to Berlin were the Nabokov family, including the celebrated novelist Vladimir Nabokov (1899-1977), who wrote a number of novels during his time in Berlin, including *King, Queen, Knave* and *Laughter in the Dark*.

It is true that Berlin had a drug culture. It is also true that there was a dancer called Anita Berber (1899-1928) who created dances based on her drug-inspired fantasies called the Morphine dance or the Cocaine dance. The activities and the settings I describe in the nightclub scene were true. (Some things you just can't make up!) By the end of the 1920s, Berlin had acquired a solid reputation for homosexuality, avant-garde art, left-wing politics, jazz, and erotic cabaret. It is well-known that Adolf Hitler hated the place and after his ascent to power in January 1933, was determined to destroy the city's culture.

I timed the early part of this novel to coincide with the movements of the well-known violin pedagogue, Carl Flesch (1873-1944), who held master classes at the Hochschule Für Musik, starting in February 1922, but who left in 1923 when the German Mark crashed. (He taught at the Curtis Institute in Philadelphia.) Returning to Berlin in 1928, he left for good in 1933, when Adolf Hitler came to power. Josef Wolfstahl

(1899-1931) who makes a cameo appearance in the scene where Grace plays in a quartet with Charles and Mabel Phelps, died at a young age of an operation that went wrong. My violin teacher, Nannie Jamieson (1904-1990), with whom I studied at the Guildhall School of Music in London, England, studied with both men in Berlin in the late 1920s and told me many stories about her time there.

I dedicate this novel to her memory and that of my first husband Theodore "Ted" Bogacz, who died tragically young in 1992 and taught me everything I know about the Great War.

Cynthia Sally Haggard
Spring 2019

About the Author

Cynthia Sally Haggard was born and reared in Surrey, England. About 30 years ago she surfaced in the United States, inhabiting the Mid-Atlantic region as she wound her way through four careers: violinist, cognitive scientist, medical writer, and novelist.

Her first novel, *Thwarted Queen* a fictionalized biography of Lady Cecylee Neville (1415-1495), the mother of Richard III (whose bones were recently found under a car-park in Leicester,) was shortlisted for many awards, including the 2012 Eric Hoffer *New Horizon Award* for debut authors. To date, sales have surpassed 38,000 copies.

Cynthia graduated with an MFA in Creative Writing from Lesley University, Cambridge MA, in June 2015. When she's not annoying everyone by insisting her fictional characters are more real than they are, Cynthia likes to go for long walks, knit something glamorous, cook in her wonderful kitchen, and play the piano. You can visit her at **www.spunstories.com**.

It was the obscure sensation
of everything's being suddenly turned the other way
round,
so that one had to read it all backward if one wanted
to understand.
It was a sensation devoid of any pain or
astonishment.
It was simply something dark and looming,
and yet smooth and soundless,
coming...

LAUGHTER IN THE DARK, *Vladimir Nabokov*

PROLOGUE

Once upon a time, there lived a girl in a mountain village in northern Italy named Teresa. She was the most beautiful girl in that village, which had a checkerboard for its main square. The village was called Marostega and was located in the Veneto, that region of Italy that claims La Serenissima, Venexia, as its capital.

Teresa married my father and had three daughters, Giuseppina, Luisa, and Angelina.

After her death, Father married again. Mother was the second wife, and she gave Father two sons. I was the youngest. In those days, my name was Domenico.

One day Father told us we were going over the wide, wide ocean to America. Mother made a huge bonfire, everything she could find that had belonged to the first wife, a pile of old-fashioned cotton dresses with large skirts, nipped-in waists, lace collars and cuffs, straw hats with wide ribbons, shawls of fine wool, even sepia-tinted photographs. I stood with my siblings, our eyes reflecting those flames. The heat of the fire melted the ice, sent by a February storm. My half-sisters' tears congealed into crystals, making their eyelashes stick. "Mama's gone," whispered Angelina as everything dissolved into clouds of ash picked up by swirls of freezing gusts that scattered the first wife's remnants into the cold February air.

I had just turned four.

Part I

The Lost Mother

Fall 1921

✠✠✠✠✠✠✠✠✠✠✠

Chapter One
Georgetown, Washington, D.C.
Friday, 2 September

Angelina led a life which required her to fib.

"How do you amuse yourself?" a stranger would ask.

"I do a little dressmaking," she would reply. "It has not been easy, with all the good men taken by the war."

She took pleasure in illicit trysts, in the veils and shadows of secrecy, until one day, this world began to crumble.

"Someone is talking about us," he said, standing by the window of the apartment he had chosen for her, in the West Village of Georgetown. The late afternoon sun slanted over his head, throwing his high cheekbones and the sharp bridge of his nose into relief, illuminating his thick, corn-colored hair.

Angelina was bending over the wet bar, mixing up a Mary Pickford. "Who?" she said, mainly for something to say. She was used to gossip and disapproving glances. People were so jealous, especially other women, even married women. One would think that women who had everything might be willing to help their less fortunate sisters, but that had never been Angelina's experience.

"I don't know."

Something about his voice caught her attention. She came around and handed him his drink. "You do not know?"

"No." He sipped without comment. Normally, he would wind one of her curls around his pinky finger, or smile, or make some remark to show that he appreciated what she had made for him. But not today.

The back of Angelina's neck stiffened. This was not good, something was worrying him.

Finally, he said, "A scandal would hurt my wife, and I cannot do that to a good woman."

She stood there, silent. If his wife was a good woman, what did that make her? She had known Scott McNair since he was a college student, well before his marriage, when she had been recently widowed, with two little girls to support. She had become complicit in satisfying his needs in return for money, jewelry, and clothes in the latest fashions. She expected him to terminate things once he married, but his wife did not like the pleasures of the marriage bed.

He put his drink down. "You do see that, don't you?"

She did not see at all. Why now? Why would a bit of gossip scare him off? She stared up into his face. Was there any way to plead her case? But his face, usually so open, was closed against her.

"I will give you something to cover your expenses for the next several months." He opened his billfold and dropped a wad of cash onto the mantle.

She could not move. She felt like a leaf dropped from a tree, curled up, and dead in the frosty air.

He went to the hatstand and took his hat. "Believe me, Angie, if I had any choice—" He hesitated for a long moment, his blue-gray eyes fixed on hers, and then the landlady banged a door downstairs.

He fled.

She waited for a second, five seconds, then went to the mantle, counting out the money. Five hundred dollars. At least he was generous, but it was not going to last forever. She stuffed it into her bodice, then twitched the drapes aside to survey the street.

He was gone.

✠✠✠✠✠✠✠✠✠✠✠

A few days later, Angelina found herself in Shepherd & Riley's bookstore. She needed to get something for Grace, who would be seventeen in a few days. She turned the pages of the volume in her hand. Perhaps *The Awakening* was not right for her dreamy daughter. It was expensive, and Angelina had money worries now that Scott had jilted her. She listlessly closed the book, trying not to think about him. As she pushed it back into its place the hairs on the backs of her arm prickled. Was someone watching her? Slowly, she turned.

He looked like a lover, with thick black hair for caressing and generous lips for kissing. But it was those dark eyes that caught and held, never letting go. *Bellissimo.*

He came forward, smiling.

"Mrs. Miller?" He took off his elegant Panama, balancing it gently in his long, tapering fingers.

Angelina started as she studied his face. No, she had never seen him before.

"How do you—?"

"Russell. At your service." He made a little bow that seemed both odd and old-fashioned. Angelina could not recall any man bowing to her, at least not recently.

She tilted her head to look up at him, showing off her slender neck. "Should I know you?"

He stared at her for a moment, his smile fading.

She moved closer. "We have met before?"

He glanced at the door, then scanned the bookstore, expertly taking it in, as if used to evaluating the shape of rooms, the placing of furniture such as bookcases, the position of windows in relation to the door.

Angelina followed his gaze, but all she could see were bored housewives in straw hats, and summer-colored dresses. They had open books in their laps or in their hands, pretending to read while staring at him avidly from the corners of their eyes.

"They have rich husbands," she remarked.

He turned back towards her, his hat still held lightly in the tips of those long fingers.

"Your life is not as predictable as theirs?"

Angelina raised her face to his and smiled. He was not merely good-looking.

"May I offer you tea?"

Intrigued, she accepted his arm. How glad she was she had chosen to wear a new frock, the olive-green silk, which set off her sherry-colored eyes. The brown high-heeled shoes drew attention to the hem, which was fashionably short at mid-calf. The brown cloche hat, trimmed with quail feathers, gave her extra height, for she was not tall. Angelina could not help smiling into the hard eyes of the left-behind women as she passed them on her way out into the street. *La gelosia*. How resentful they were.

He chose the nearest hotel, the Metropolitan on Pennsylvania Avenue, picking a table in the middle of the restaurant away from the windows and the noisy traffic outside. He selected a chair for Angelina, helping her into it before taking the opposite one, which gave him a good view of the door.

Angelina sat upright on her overstuffed seat, knees together, brown leather purse on her lap. She sensed there was some purpose here, some reason to meet her. Yet he said nothing. After offering her a cigarette from a monogrammed silver case, which she declined, he lit his from a matching silver lighter and smoked in silence for several moments.

She was just on the point of asking him again how he knew her name, when he tapped his cigarette ash into the ashtray and began, telling her that he had fought on the Italian Front in the recent war. Why was he telling her this? Did he want to boast about his war record? But no, he did not go into details, just narrated the bare facts. He spoke in a well-modulated baritone, which had an almost musical lilt to it, his eyes gazing into the glowing tip of his cigarette, or the bone-china bowl of his teacup. Perhaps he was telling her this in order to explain why he was studying to be a diplomat at the newly opened Georgetown School of Foreign Service. She stared at his closed face with its unreadable expression. Why would he be telling her that he had just begun to study there unless he wanted her to understand he was a pacifist? Perhaps he hoped this would distinguish him in some way. Finally, he raised his eyes.

"Mrs. Miller, please tell me about yourself."

Angelina sat still for a moment. "My husband died some years ago," she remarked quietly.

"Did you remarry?"

She laughed softly. "The war took all the good men away."

"Do you have children?"

Angelina, hesitating, sipped her tea. "I have two little girls."

His eyes locked onto hers. "How do you amuse yourself?"

"I do a little dressmaking," replied Angelina. "It has not been easy."

His face tightened into an expression of disapproval. He sipped his tea. "Do you have brothers or sisters?"

"I have two sisters."

His smile lifted a kind of heaviness that clung to him.

"Louisa married at sixteen, a lawyer who lives in New York City. Josephina is married to a doctor in Philadelphia."

He brightened."Do they have children?"

"Oh yes." Angelina made a face. She was not close to her sisters or their families—they would not receive her.

"Louisa has three girls, Josephina has three boys, and a girl named Paula, after *Zia* Paulina."

He leaned forward, his eyes fixed on her face. "How is —?" He paused. Angelina had the curious feeling he was about to ask after Zia Paulina, but that did not make sense. At that moment, the waiter appeared, and she glanced at her watch.

"*Dio!*" she exclaimed. "How time does fly. I promised Violet I would be back by five."

He rose to his feet as she stood, his face making some silent appeal. Perhaps he wanted to see her again. Angelina flashed a smile as she turned to go.

"Come to supper tomorrow, at seven."

He hovered, hat in hand, as if waiting. Angelina stopped suddenly, dumping her purse and gloves on a nearby chair.

"*Scusi.* Of course."

He stared at her for a long moment, then smiled.

Angelina rapidly opened her purse, took out an old envelope, and scribbled her address on the back using the stub of a worn-down pencil.

He examined the address, then scrutinized her.

Angelina's cheeks warmed. "You will come?" She picked up her purse and gloves.

He made her his little bow and waited while she hurried off.

Angelina took the Bridge Street cable car in the direction of Georgetown, taking a seat near the front as her stomach was having one of its moments of discomfort. The doctor had assured her the condition was nothing sinister; it was due to the difficulty of bringing Grace into this world, or perhaps that string of miscarriages following her birth. She leaned back in her seat and closed her eyes, allowing her thoughts to flow and distract her from the pain. Something about him touched her deeply, something that plucked at a memory. She was in Pennsylvania Station, New York City, twenty-three years ago. It was October 1898, and Angelina was waiting with her sisters. She was uncomfortably warm in the thick cotton dress worn on the long journey from *Italia*. She gazed around the station, bewildered by the crowds of people coming in and out. She had never seen so many before, they reminded her of ants crawling into and out of the anthills back home on the farm. Before she had time to think, a train arrived. Louisa took her by the hand and led her into the carriage, while Josephina asked the porter to help her with their luggage. The train puffed out of New York, and she fell asleep. She awoke to the sound of her sisters' voices, heard the word *Papa*, and sat up.

"*Dov'è Papa?* Where is Papa?"

They exchanged glances. Angelina gazed around the compartment. Strangers avoided her stare.

"Where are they?"

Her sisters looked at each other.

Ordinarily, Angelina would have stamped her foot or screamed. But there was something about their silence that stopped her. How could that happen? How could you live elbow to elbow with your family for years, for ten years, for all of Angelina's life, and then vanish? Where were her father, stepmother and two younger half-brothers? Had they said *'addio'*? Angelina did not think so. In that moment, the future stretched blank before her, like a white sheet strung along a clothesline.

"Where are we going?"

"To live with Zia Paulina." She was Papa's younger sister, married to a wealthy lawyer.

"Georgetown." She tried out the unfamiliar name on her tongue. "I thought we were going to Chicago." Another unfamiliar name. Papa's relatives had been clamoring for him to come join them in Chicago. That was the reason why he had taken his family to the United States, an ocean away from Marostica, the little village in the Veneto where the Paganos had been tenant farmers for centuries, because the *padrone* had seized the land and now they had nowhere else to go.

The memory faded. Try as she might, she could remember nothing more. The cable car clanged, jerking her out of her reverie. It was about to cross the bridge into Georgetown. Angelina hurriedly gathered her purse and gloves; the next stop was hers.

She walked north on Montgomery for four blocks before turning east onto Beall Street. It was September, still warm, so Angelina was careful to walk slowly as she did not want to ruin her clothes with sweat stains. The thick air was redolent with brick pavement, and box hedge, mixed in with the harsh odor of petroleum fumes as an occasional motorized taxicab spluttered by belching dust.

Finally she was home, the modest house on Beall Street, where she lived with Zia Paulina and her daughters Violet and Grace. She opened the door, stepped inside, and tapped her way up the dark wooden staircase. The top floor had three bedrooms: a large front one for Zia Paulina, a large back one for Violet and Grace, and a small, dingy, middle one that was Angelina's. She knocked on the door that faced the stairs and, after waiting a moment, opened it.

Grace was propped up on her bed, reading, while Violet sat on a low upholstered chair in the corner, where light from two windows fell onto her mending. Next to Grace, on a low nightstand, stood a statue of the Holy Mother, given to her by the nuns of the Convent of the Visitation. Angelina averted her gaze, made uncomfortable by evidence of her daughter's religiosity. She wished Zia Paulina did not encourage Grace to be so fanciful; it was not going to help her to cope with the real world. Next to Violet's bed was a pile of fashion magazines.

"When do you have your recital, *Graziella*?"

"Tomorrow night."

"Why do you ask?" said Violet.

"What time is it?" said Angelina.

"Professor Burneys wants us there at half past six," replied Grace.

"But a lot of people will be playing, won't they, Gracie?" put in Violet. "The Taussig sisters will sing, then there's Leo Smoot. He always bangs away at that piano for a while. It will probably go on for three hours at least."

"When are you playing?" said Angelina.

"I'm last," replied Grace.

Smiling, Angelina turned to Violet. "I think you should go with your sister."

"Why? I went last month. I'm tired of listening to sweet and serious, I want something jazzy you can dance to."

"Because she needs someone to walk with her."

"I was planning on spending the evening here, sewing." Violet gave her mother a look. She was making Grace a dress in honor of her sister's birthday—and usually, Angelina would have given into her wishes.

"I want you to go with your sister," she repeated.

"Why don't *you* go?" countered Violet.

Angelina hesitated.

"Who is he?"

"*Violetta!*" exclaimed Angelina. "That is no way to speak to your Mamma!"

Violet rose, folded her arms, and stared at her mother with a pair of bright blue eyes.

Angelina stared back, her sherry-colored eyes the exact same size and shape as her daughter's.

"Well?" asked Violet, after a pause.

"Mr. Russell is an excellent young man, a diplomat. I have invited him here for dinner."

"Aren't we going to meet him?"

"Of course you are. But not right away. I would like to know him a little better." Angelina left before Violet could ask more questions.

Grace put her book down. "He must be someone, Violet," she observed. "Otherwise, Mother would not have invited him to dinner."

Violet raised her eyes heavenward. "He's taken *her* fancy, that's obvious."

✠✠✠✠✠✠✠✠✠✠✠

"Thank you, Lucinda." Angelina tapped her way down the narrow wooden staircase the following evening as Zia Paulina's housekeeper disappeared into the kitchen bearing a large bouquet of golden marigolds, yellow Belladonna lilies, and white roses. Mr. Russell, immaculately attired in black tie, was evaluating the contents of the front parlor. Angelina turned, the silver beading of her green cocktail dress swaying, and tried to see it through his eyes. It was filled to overflowing with furniture. A loveseat faced the window, two armchairs sat by the window across from each other, and two more squatted further back in the room. These pieces of furniture were surrounded by several occasional tables covered in knickknacks.

She glanced at him. No doubt the furniture told a story of a family forced to abandon a large house, for a smaller one. Well, she did not want his charity.

"What would you like to drink?" she said.

"Whiskey and soda, but not too much whiskey, please," he replied.

While Angelina made his drink with ice, a generous dash of whiskey, a spritz of soda water, and a twirl of lemon, Mr. Russell crossed the room to study the portrait of Zia Paulina that Zio Luca had commissioned forty years ago, back in the 1880s, when she was his young bride.

Did he know Zia Paulina? Angelina handed him his drink, and then made the exact same drink, without the alcohol, under his watchful gaze.

"You do not drink?"

"It is not good for my stomach," she replied.

"Are you seeing a doctor?"

"He treats me with the mercury and the arsenic. I have a box of little pink pills."

As she rattled with nervous laughter, he winced in sympathy.

"I thought you said you had children."

"We are alone this evening."

Russell turned away, took an abstemious sip, and immediately put his glass down.

Angelina was not usually tongue-tied, but it was becoming clear that Russell was harder to reach than most men. Men usually liked it when you dressed up for them, gave them your undivided attention, and fixed their drinks expertly. But as the silence lengthened and stretched, Mr. Russell threw out subtle hints he did not want to be here. It did not make sense.

Just as she was on the point of asking him why Zia Paulina's portrait interested him so much, Lucinda appeared, announcing dinner.

Angelina had set the table with Zia Paulina's damask tablecloth, matching napkins, and best silver, selecting the tall candles that glowed in their silver sconces. Now, sitting opposite Mr. Russell, she hoped she had done something right. Lucinda's cooking was delicious, pumpkin soup, fried fish, and ice-cream topped with fresh strawberries, but Mr. Russell ate sparingly and did not say much. The only time he smiled was after sipping his wine.

"Where did you get this? It's a Bardolino."

Angelina started. Most people wouldn't know about that kind of wine, as you could only get it in the Veneto, the region around *Venexia,* where Angelina and her family came from. It was almost impossible to get anything like that nowadays, now that prohibition gripped the country by its throat.

"You are from the Veneto?" she asked.

"I fought on the Italian Front," he parried.

There was a pause as he swirled the wine around in his glass.

"It's hard to get decent wine these days," he remarked. "How did you manage it?"

"We had supplies," she said. Dr. Jackson, who treated her for stomach cramps, knew she liked Italian wine.

Angelina looked at him again, this time veiling her gaze through her lashes. "Where are you from?"

He studied his wine. "I was born in the United States."

"*Davvero?*" Angelina leaned forward to study his expression, but he kept his face averted. "So you do not know the Pagano family?"

"No." He drained his glass. She offered him more before going downstairs to make Italian-style coffee. When she came up the stairs from the basement kitchen, he was sitting in front of their boudoir grand, playing something from memory. It was something that Angelina had heard before but could not put a name to, the sort of thing Grace would know.

He rose instantly, accepting his coffee.

"Do not stop," she exclaimed. "I did not know you were a pianist."

"I'm not," he replied, stirring his coffee.

"But you play—*magnificamente*."

"I am out of practice."

"Do you have a piano in your lodgings?"

"Not yet." But he smiled. Taking the opportunity, she put down her coffee, and cranked the gramophone player. As the music took hold, she sashayed across the floor, her rope of pearls chinking.

He hesitated. She secured his hand. He drew back. She put her other hand on his shoulder. Again, he withdrew. They danced awkwardly, Angelina wondering how it would feel to be in his arms.

Just as the gramophone wound down, a female voice said, "Come on, Gracie, don't be such a slowpoke. Let's go meet this paragon."

Mr. Russell froze. He scrutinized Violet, then Angelina. Violet was a taller version of Angelina, her oval face framed by golden curls, not chestnut, her eyes blue, not brown.

Russell's lips were just framing an expression of disapproval when Grace stepped around Violet. His pupils expanded, making his dark eyes look even darker. There was something almost greedy in this look he bestowed on Grace.

Violet came forward. "I'm Violet Miller. And you are?"

"Russell. At your service." As he made his small bow, Violet's eyes widened. Then his eyes locked onto Grace again. The child looked charming in Zia Paulina's cast-off ivory-colored frock overlaid in lace, which came down to her ankles. The candlelight suffusing the room caught her nutmeg-colored hair, making it gleam.

"You didn't tell me your daughters were exquisite young women."

"Whatever have you been saying to Mr. Russell, Mother dear?" remarked Violet. "Didn't you tell him I was eighteen?"

Angelina swallowed and lowered her head. Violet was her best friend, her loyal supporter, but she wasn't the most tactful person in the world. Couldn't she see how much it hurt to have a potential suitor figuring out the mother's age from the ages of her daughters?

"This is my sister Grace," continued Violet. "She turns seventeen tomorrow."

Grace took one tentative step forward and gave Russell her hand.

Slowly, gently, he brushed his lips over the back of her hand, making a gesture that again was both odd and old-fashioned. Angelina watched, her shoulders slumping, but she forced herself to curve the corners of her pressed-together lips upward into a smile.

"Mr. Russell is a diplomat," she remarked. "He has come to take up a position in the District." She ushered everyone into the front parlor.

"Are you a diplomat?" Violet sat down on the loveseat next to Angelina.

He smiled, amused at her directness. "I am studying at the Georgetown School of Foreign Service. I have to know about international trade, law, and political science, as well as diplomacy. The State Department is eager to have us once we graduate, because Georgetown is the only school in the country offering a foreign service course."

"How do you know Mother?"

"I met her in Shepherd & Riley's." He coughed. "How do you amuse yourself?"

"I sew. I want to be a fashion designer and have my own shop in Georgetown."

"I didn't know you wanted to own your own boutique." Angelina lowered her head. Why was she telling Russell this when she had not told her mamma?

"You have been preoccupied," replied Violet. "I've talked with Auntie P., and she's agreed to find someone to help me."

Angelina's cheeks burned. "You might have asked me, *Violetta cara*."

There was silence.

"Would you like coffee?" Angelina turned to Grace.

"Yes, please," she murmured.

"We've just come from Professor Burneys'," remarked Violet as Angelina poured, "where Grace played her violin."

He put his coffee cup down and addressed Grace directly. "I am passionate about music. I would love to hear you play."

Grace cast her eyes down into her coffee, reminding Angelina suddenly of one of Raffaello's *Madonnas*.

"You look tired, Gracie," put in Violet. "You had a long evening." She turned to him. "Grace was supposed to be playing the Brahms *A Major Sonata*, but the pianist didn't show. She had to switch gears, and do some insipid Mozart instead."

"I know that Brahms sonata," he remarked. "The cross-rhythms are not easy for the pianist, but if you would like me to try—"

A sudden change took place. From lying back in her seat wreathed in her own thoughts, which often gave her an otherworldly quality, Grace actually raised her head, and looked straight at him for the first time.

"I was so disappointed I couldn't play it this evening."

A dazzling smile radiated over his face.

Sighing, Angelina led the way into the back parlor, where the baby grand stood. He sat on the piano stool and began to wrestle with the Brahms, while Grace took her violin out of its silken wraps, placed it on the piano, put rosin onto her bow, and massaged the fingers of her left hand.

Eventually, he turned to her and played the D minor chord so she could tune her violin. Then Grace placed her instrument under her chin, raised her bow, and they began. He played the wistful opening, which Grace replied to with a descending phrase of sweet sadness. He continued, and she replied. For many measures they conducted this sweetly musical conversation until Grace interrupted with a fiery outburst, introducing a surprising passion to her playing.

Angelina was not knowledgeable about classical music, preferring popular songs and the Italian folk music of her youth, but she could see that Russell was unusually good. He played with a lightness of touch that allowed him to bring out the rhythms from the thick texture of the piece, making it interesting in a way Grace's normal accompanist did not. Unfortunately, the Brahms sonata was darkly passionate. Unfortunately, they both played it extremely well. Angelina clenched her porcelain coffee cup in her slender fingers as she flicked her eyes from one face to the other. Grace wore her usual dreamy look, but her cheeks were tinged with a faint pinkness. Russell's dark gaze never left her. How he managed to play those fistfuls of notes without glancing at the music, Angelina would never know.

Her stomach wound itself into a knot as the piece continued. It couldn't be true—it wasn't true. She could hardly bear to think about it. This had never happened to her before, she had always been the one to attract male attention. But men did not look at her in the way he was gazing at

Grace. They looked aroused, or bored, or amused, or cynical. But not tender, not with that soft expression.

What would happen if he returned and asked permission to be Grace's suitor? Well, she would not stand for it. *Per l'amor di Dio*, for the love of God, Grace was only seventeen, and it was the height of rudeness to abandon the mother for the daughter. If he did return, she would see that he was sent away.

Finally, the sonata ended.

No one clapped.

Russell sat still for several moments, then rose and softly closed the piano lid. He took his hat from the hatstand and bestowed one last, long look upon Grace.

"That was miraculous." He placed his Panama on his head, and hurried away.

"What a dangerous man," Angelina remarked as soon as Russell shut the door behind him. "His behavior was unnerving. Look at the way he eyed Grace."

Grace glanced up from the task of putting her violin away. "I thought his manners were charming and very correct."

Angelina stared. Grace was not given to speaking up.

"He wasn't quite what you'd hoped for, was he, Mother dear?" remarked Violet.

"I was trying to help *you*," said Angelina, her cheeks warming.

Violet folded her arms and gave her a look.

"I'm never going to invite him again." Angelina weaved unsteadily on her high heels as she made her way towards the stairs and the privacy of her dingy room.

"You won't have to," replied Violet. "He'll be back."

Chapter Two

Wednesday, 7 September

"I am engaged to be married." Sanford Jackson went into the minuscule entrance hall of the modest house on Beall Street and took his hat off the hatstand. "We can't go on seeing each other. I think you should have another doctor."

Angelina's cheeks prickled as the color drained from her face. This could not be true. Dr. Jackson had become a good friend, treating her chronic abdominal pains, supplying the fine Italian wine. Men always provided. It could not be true Sanford was abandoning her as well.

She came closer and placed one hand on his chest. "Why?" she asked softly, endowing that word with all the seductive energy she possessed.

He glanced at her and hastily averted his eyes. "I don't want my fiancée hearing rumors. It's taken me two years to get her family to agree to the marriage. I've tried to be discreet, but Georgetown is a village, and people talk." He backed away.

Angelina panicked. "I cannot lose you too," she blurted out.

He paled, his gray eyes turning the color of rain-washed slate. "So, it's true." He put his hat on his head.

She moved to the door in one graceful motion, her pink silk kimono floating out behind her, exposing her drawers, stockings, and *Miracle Reducing Rubber Brassière.*

"Would you please re-tie your sash?" he snapped.

"What?" The silken kimono settled around her in concealing folds, but his expression remained pinched. She must make his mouth relax. She curved her lips just so, causing that dimple in the corner of her cheek to emerge. "If it bothers you so much, why don't *you* retie it?"

He put his hand on the door handle. "You have a boyfriend, don't you, who's provided you with a love nest on Potomac Street."

Abruptly, she stilled.

"It's true," he said again.

Angelina twisted her hands together. This was bad, very bad.

He grabbed her by the shoulders and shook none too gently. Then he yanked her sash, tying it so tight it hurt.

"I'm about to open the door," he snarled. "Don't you want to appear respectable in front of your neighbors, for the sake of your daughters?"

Angelina stiffened. She had forgotten they were standing in Zia Paulina's front parlor. Where was everyone? The silence was reassuring; Zia Paulina had not returned yet from Philadelphia.

Sanford turned to go, but Angelina put a hand on his shoulder.

"Who has talked?"

"Some new fellow."

"Mr. Russell." She had no idea if this was true; the name dropped from her lips like stone.

"That's it. You know him?"

"How does he look?"

"Tall, dark, and handsome, a snappy dresser, the sort that would appeal to the ladies."

"How did you meet?"

"I saw him in the Indian King. He was lunching there with a fellow named Hammond, asking questions. Your name came up, and he wanted to know where you lived. I told him you lived on Beall Street. He told me he was positive he'd seen you on Potomac Street, going out with a rich fellow who owned a Pierce-Arrow. I told him he must be mistaken. He smiled, said he didn't want to ruin the reputation of a lady. Hammond laughed and said it seemed they weren't talking about a lady. I told them to mind their own business." He glared. "I was wrong, wasn't I?"

Stomach clenching, Angelina sagged against the wall. *Cieli*, Russell had seen her driving around in Scott's Pierce-Arrow. And Hammond was Scott's lawyer, who must have warned his client to drop her. That was how she lost her patron and friend. In that moment, she saw her fingers wrapping around Russell's neck.

He gave her a hard look and went to the door.

"But Sanford—"

"Dr. Jackson."

"You cannot abandon me now."

"Mrs. Miller, you are a dangerous woman."

He was opening the door, slipping out of her life. She came closer. "When will I see you again?"

He pushed her away. "Don't you understand what I've been telling you? I could lose my license, my future wife, and be prosecuted if it was known I was—seeing a patient." He closed the door behind him.

She yanked it back open.

"Sanford!" she called. But he was gone—vanished just like that. Angelina turned to close the door, just as a horse-drawn cab rounded the corner. She was not quick enough to escape the notice of Zia Paulina.

"Angelina?" she said, a steely edge to her tone, as she got out of the cab. "What do you think you are doing?" She turned, nodding to the cabman who followed, depositing her bags in the front parlor.

He grinned, making eyes at Angelina, before accepting his money and leaving.

As soon as the cabbie shut the door, Zia Paulina swept up the stairs, towards her bedroom at the front of the house. Angelina followed, fingers clenched so tightly the knuckles turned white. When she had married Perry Miller all those years ago at age fourteen, going to live with him on the farm outside of Rockville, Maryland, she never imagined she would return to Georgetown. But Perry's unexpected death eleven years ago had left her destitute, and she was forced to sell the farm at a loss. Angelina did not like to think what might have happened to her, or her daughters, if her aunt, her father's youngest sister, had not insisted they come live with her.

Zia Paulina was now in her mid-fifties, with iron-gray hair and brown eyes that resembled Angelina's. She always dressed in an intimidating way: high-necked blouses, skirts that brushed her ankles. Only a few people were allowed into her bedroom, and fewer still were invited to sit in one of those comfortable chairs that squatted by the window. These people included Angelina's eldest sister Josephina, when she was in town, and Violet—but not Angelina. And Zia Paulina did not ask Angelina to sit now but stared up at her from her position on the vanity stool.

"You have had a lover here."

Angelina was shocked. Her aunt had never spoken to her so directly before. Well, not since her discovery that she was pregnant with Violet.

"No."

"No? Explain to me who Sanford is."

"He is Dr. Jackson."

"The doctor who treats you for stomach cramps?"

"*Sì.*"

"*Davvero?*" Paulina Pagano Barilla rose. "Are you going to stand there, Angelina Pagano Miller, and deny that Sanford Jackson is your lover?"

Angelina stared back. "I do not have a lover."

"Do not lie to me, Angelina. How else do you explain your evident agitation and your disgraceful attire? Why, you look like a whore."

Angelina flinched. At least she used the English word, not the Italian one that hurt so much. But she was not speaking Italian at all. She was measuring each word out in English, making everything seem so cold and judgmental.

"Angelina, I do not understand you. How could you be so irresponsible? Don't you care about the effect this is having on Violet and Grace?"

Angelina turned away. Why was everyone criticizing her for being a bad mother? Her daughters were now eighteen and seventeen years old. They were grown women; they could take care of themselves. When Angelina had been their age, she had to cope with two young children, and no one had cared a bean about her.

"Of course I care."

"Then why don't you show it?"

She looked at the floor. "I need money."

"Angelina, how could you say such a thing to me?"

"You do not listen. I told you not to sell the house on Second Street."

When Zio Luca died back in 1905, Zia Paulina had put her money into stocks to draw a quarterly income. She had never complained about money when Angelina returned to Georgetown at the end of 1910, two young children in tow. Then the Depression and her declining quarterly annuity had driven her to seek a less expensive house. It was Lucinda, who had known Zia Paulina since her arrival in Georgetown, in 1885, as a young bride, who had found them a small house near Herring Hill, in the less fashionable East Village, east of High Street.

It was true Angelina had not been happy about the move, arguing that it would be better to sell some stock. But Paulina disagreed. She was never comfortable with a fancy lifestyle and had assumed the role of wealthy matron only to support her husband; Luca Barilla was a lawyer with a well-heeled clientele, and appearances mattered. Paulina had spent her entire married life wearing clothes she did not like and living far above what she had been used to as a girl on a farm near Marostica. The Depression gave her occasion to live more modestly, and she had seized that opportunity, reasoning that Violet and Grace were sure to marry soon and that she would not need such a large house.

"I had a perfectly good reason for selling that house," she said now.

"But we were so happy there," replied Angelina. "Josephina, Louisa, and I grew up in that house. I thought Violet and Grace should live there too, in a good part of town. Here, it is squalid—"

Paulina felt a surge of warmth as she turned to glare at her niece. What was Angelina saying exactly? Was she complaining about their colored neighbors? Surely not. And in any case, what right did she have to complain when her life was so tainted?

"That is good coming from you," spat Zia Paulina, "who sells herself to any man for a price."

Angelina stepped backwards.

Her aunt jabbed a finger at her. "I know all about your sordid dealings, and don't think I don't. But now, I've had enough. I want you to leave by the end of the month."

Paulina had been longing to ask Angelina to leave, ever since she reappeared in Georgetown back in 1910, a young widow with two little girls, and gossip began to circulate about the kind of life she was leading. At first, Paulina had ignored it for Violet and Grace's sake. The girls needed a good home, and she was determined to give it to them. Now that they were grown, she was just waiting for Angelina to put a foot wrong. This incident with Dr. Jackson was her opportunity.

"But I am your niece. I have nowhere else to go," said Angelina.

"I think you do. I gather that one of your boyfriends is very generous."

Angelina brushed a hand over her cheek. "How did you know?"

"People talk. They gossip constantly about *you*. How do you think that I have felt all these years, trying to hold high my head, when your behavior is the subject of so much comment?" Paulina, sitting down at her vanity, opened a jar of cream.

"I want you gone by the end of the month."

"I will take my daughters with me."

Paulina looked up.

"*È vero*, it's true." insisted Angelina.

"Let me make something plain, Angelina Miller. The only reason why I have put up with your disgraceful behavior for the past eleven years is because the last time you threatened to do that, it carried some weight. Grace and Violet were only six and seven years old. You used my love for them as a weapon, to manipulate me into countenancing your behavior and keeping you in my home."

"Violetta will come with me. We are as close as sisters."

"Violet is fair-minded, but she does not approve of your behavior. But the person I am most concerned about, is Grace."

"Graziella does not notice anything, she thinks only of her violin."

Paulina banged her glass jar on the vanity, causing a heavy silver brush to clatter to the floor.

"Has it never occurred to you why Grace disappears so often? I will tell you why. Because she finds your behavior so painful. She is a sensitive child who cannot bear such sordidness. You will leave by the end of the month."

"Then you lose Grace and Violet."

"Miss Pauline!" Lucinda called up the stairs. "You have a visitor. Mr. Russell is here."

She went to the bedroom door and opened it. "Please ask him to wait in the front parlor."

"Mr. Russell?" said Angelina.

She turned. "Is he another boyfriend?"

Angelina stared at the floor, red spots appearing on her cheeks.

"Whom does Mr. Russell wish to see?" said Paulina to Lucinda.

"He's asking for Miss Grace."

She turned to Angelina. "Go to your room and get out of those disgraceful clothes. I don't want to see you until you are properly attired."

Angelina walked to the door. "*Prendo Graziella e Violetta,* I'll take Grace and Violet."

Zia Paulina narrowed her eyes. "I don't think so." She shut the door quietly after her niece and moved over to a full-length mirror that stood in a corner by the window. The blouse she put on this morning was already wrinkled, so she found a fresh one. She poured water from a jug into a bowl, dipped her hands into its refreshing coolness, and gently patted her gray curls so that they fell around her face in a more decorous fashion. After scrutinizing herself for another moment, she descended the stairs to the front parlor.

Her first impression was of a tall, well-dressed gentleman standing before the portrait that Luca had commissioned of her all those years ago. A first anniversary gift. The young man stood silent, dark eyes thoughtful. He had placed an elegant Panama on the hatstand; a large bouquet of flowers adorned the loveseat.

"Mr. Russell," she said.

He turned and regarded her. Now that she was facing him from a few feet away, she could see what a handsome man he was. Despite his name, he seemed a typical northern Italian gentleman, the sort of young man she had admired as a girl when living in the Veneto. Perhaps Russell was not his real name. Italians were so badly treated these days, many took refuge in Yankee names. In fact, he bore an uncanny resemblance to Domenico Lotto, the handsomest man in the village of Marostica, who had inspired fourteen-year-old Paulina to dream that he might choose her as his second wife. What did Grace think of Mr. Russell? Did he inspire similar feelings?

"*Per favore.*" She indicated that he should sit.

He chose an easy chair by the window and automatically crossed one elegant leg over the other.

She perched upright on the edge of an armchair. "You did not come here to see Mrs. Miller?"

Russell shook his head.

"Why not?"

Mr. Russell took a pink silk handkerchief from his breast pocket, patted his forehead, and dexterously returned it to its original position.

"I brought a bouquet of flowers for Miss Grace. I understand it is her birthday, and I thought—"

He was interrupted by the front door opening.

✠✠✠✠✠✠✠✠✠✠✠✠

Surprise, surprise. Violet gazed at Mr. Russell, standing in the front parlor with a large bouquet of pink roses, talking to Auntie P. She was returning from Miss Bernice's, where she'd taken Grace, so that she could have a final fitting for the frock Violet had made her as a birthday present.

"Mr. Russell has come to call," remarked Auntie P.

Violet, smiling, looked at Grace.

Grace blushed and looked at the floor.

"Do I have your permission to give Grace her present?" he asked.

Auntie P. examined the rather showy bouquet in silence for a long moment. "Seventeen pink roses, one for each year of Grace's life. That is rather romantic, Mr. Russell."

"My feelings for Miss Grace are—" He reddened.

She handed it back. "Grace is very young and is not accustomed to this kind of attention. She is also a fine violinist with a rare talent. I think she should develop that talent. Do you not agree?"

Nothing fazed, the young fellow glanced over at Grace, who was staring at her shoes. His expression softened.

"I agree, and I am happy to help in any way I can. I was going to ask Miss Grace's permission to borrow the piano part —"

"You are a pianist?"

"Only an amateur." He paused. "Do I have your permission to call again?"

"No," said Auntie P.

Grace looked up. "He really helped me with that Brahms sonata last night."

Auntie P. stared. Violet could almost hear her calculating the consequences. On the one hand, he must be very good if Grace wanted to continue playing with him. On the other hand… "Would you like Mr. Russell to come visit you?"

Grace hesitated. "Mr. Russell said he would be willing to practice the Brahms piano part, so we could play it again."

His dazzling smile lit his dark eyes.

"Do you have a piano, sir?" said Auntie P.

"I've just arranged for Steinway to move one into my lodgings."

Uh-oh. He never hesitates. Violet took in his cream-colored linen suit. It had not a speck of dirt on it. *What are we letting ourselves in for?*

"Where are you lodging?" said Auntie P.

"On Bank Street, with Mrs. Olivia Rittenhouse."

Sounds like he's made of money to lodge there. Violet stared at the pink handkerchief peeking out from his breast pocket. It perfectly matched the color of the roses.

"I know her slightly," said Auntie P.

And we would be visiting that good lady soon. Violet eyed Mr. Russell's pink roses. They were large, with floppy pink petals that hid a center the color of honey.

Sighing, Auntie P. turned to Grace.

"Do you want to accept Mr. Russell's present, child?"

Grace's cheeks became pink as she took in the pink roses, wrapped up in a pink satin ribbon, with a card attached. She looked at him.

"This is for me?"

"Yes."

He managed to imbue that word with all the longing and passion he could muster.

Grace slowly put out her hand, and he gently placed the bouquet in her arms.

Their gaze held.

Uh-oh. But he met her only yesterday. Surely Gracie didn't like him as much as that?

Auntie P. cleared her throat.

"Grace, you may give Mr. Russell the piano part to practice. And I will see you, sir, back here on Thursday afternoon, September the twenty-second," she remarked, naming a date that was at least two weeks away. "But not before then. Is that understood?"

Mr. Russell smiled, head inclined, the perfect gent.

He drew the piano part delicately out of Grace's fingers. "Until then."

Raising his hat, he vanished.

Auntie P. sank into her favorite armchair, looking fagged out. She greeted Lucinda and ordered her customary cup of tea.

"A lot has happened since you went away to Philly," remarked Violet, sitting next to her. "Mother says she's unhappy about the way Mr. Russell has behaved."

Auntie P. gave Violet a sharp look as Lucinda brought tea and a plate of cookies up from the basement kitchen.

"She says she doesn't like the way he looks at Grace," explained Violet, pouring the tea.

Auntie P. turned to Grace. "You're very quiet, child. What do you think? Was the young gentleman improper?"

"No," said Grace. "He played the piano with great sensitivity. He was able to follow everything I did, without banging away and overpowering me."

"I see." Auntie P. sipped her tea. "Did you like the way he looked at you?"

"I didn't notice," replied Grace. "I was concentrating on playing the Brahms sonata—"

Violet burst out laughing. "What do you mean? He could scarcely take his eyes off of you—"

"That's not true." Grace rose. "I'll go practice my violin now."

She drifted upstairs to the back bedroom. Presently, sounds of tuning followed by scales and arpeggios wafted down to the front parlor.

Auntie P. looked at Violet.

"How did Mr. Russell behave towards Grace?"

"He *behaved* like a gent."

"What about your mother?"

"He seemed to forget about her completely once he saw Grace. Naturally, Mother is rather upset."

"I wonder what Grace thinks about him."

Violet shrugged. "I really think this is all about her violin. The only pianist Professor Burneys could find for her was Leo Smoot, and he's not up to it. I think she fell for Mr. Russell's piano playing."

"Hmmm." Auntie P. nibbled her sugar cookie. "I hope you are right. It would be a great shame if her dreams of being a concert artist were derailed by a persistent young man."

✠✠✠✠✠✠✠✠✠✠✠✠

Grace drifted upstairs to the back bedroom and began her practice with scales and arpeggios. She glanced at herself in the mirror. How quiet her face seemed. It bore no sign she struggled to concentrate.

Usually, she liked being here in the peaceful bedroom she shared with Violet, with its white-washed walls, wooden floorboards, and two narrow beds. Thoughts swirled as indescribable emotions stirred. Grace stopped, and put her hand on some music, the first thing that came to hand. It was the "Siciliana" from the *G Minor Sonata*, by Johann Sebastian Bach. It was her favorite piece, a stately dance in 6/8 time with the distinctive dotted rhythms that conveyed an air of quiet poignancy. As she picked up her violin and bow and closed her eyes to drink in the music, his dark eyes fastened onto her face, as if thirsty for something.

She shook her head and continued to play. Gradually, his face was replaced by others, by other men, the ones who devoured Mother with their eyes and made comments with their moist lips as she sashayed along a Georgetown street, her hips describing gentle arcs, her high heels making light staccato taps.

Grace didn't want that from Mr. Russell, but weren't all men like that? Didn't flirting always lead to unpleasant overtures? Grace never flirted and never would. She put her violin and bow on her bed, touching her warm cheeks with her cold fingers. She wanted to be as pure as Our Lady. When she was twelve, she'd knelt before her in chapel, dedicating her life to music because that was how she could express her passionate nature without sullying herself. She never thought she would meet a gentleman who could move her. The back of her neck prickled. What should she do?

"*Ave Maria, gratia plena, Dominus tecum,*" she murmured under her breath, crossing herself. She glanced at the statue by her bed. The Holy Mother stood in a rose, whose scalloped edges curved around her like a wave. A willowy S-shape, she held a lively baby boy in her arms. Sometimes, Grace could almost hear her. Today, she was silent.

She let out her breath in a sigh and hunched her shoulders. Was it truly so difficult? All she wanted was to play a challenging sonata with a pianist who was musical enough to know how to do it, without having to exhaust herself in various explanations. Grace picked up her violin and bow, courage rising. She wasn't going to deny herself that pleasure.

✠✠✠✠✠✠✠✠✠✠✠✠

On the day that Zia Paulina had invited Russell to come rehearse the Brahms sonata with Grace, Angelina loitered near his lodgings on Bank Street. She took a clean handkerchief out of her purse and dabbed at her hairline. The thought of meeting him again made her cringe. But he was not only hard to reach, he was hard to read, and Angelina needed to know what was going on behind those dark eyes. But what should she say? He had an unerring ability to unsettle her. Angelina unfolded her handkerchief and dried her clammy hands. Somehow she must gather courage. He was just a young man interested in her daughter; she must get used to it. A sound made her turn, and there he was, coming down the steps, humming something under his breath.

"Good afternoon, Mr. Russell," said Angelina, taking his arm. "Would you escort me to Beall Street?"

He looked away as he acquiesced.

As they turned the corner into Second Street, his continued silence unnerved her. Ordinarily, she would have employed feminine wiles to ease the tension, but that annoyed him.

"I hope you are not going to make a habit of calling on Grace," she blurted out.

Against the tips of her fingers the muscles of his arm locked up. "What do you mean?"

"I mean that you should keep away from my daughter."

He shook her off, disengaging his arm. "You have no right to ask that of me."

A sudden rage surged through her. His male vanity, his cool assumption that he could do as he pleased, made her boil. "You have no right to worm your way into our family!"

He made a disgusted sound in the back of his throat, turned, and walked down the street.

She hurried after him, determined to have her say. "Mr. Russell!"

He turned, and glared at her. "Why do you insist on making a public spectacle of yourself? Have you no pride?"

She took his arm again as they crossed High Street, where horse-drawn carts competed with smoke-belching motorized vehicles. They doglegged into Beall.

"*Voglio parlarvi di mia figlia,* I wish to talk with you about my daughter. I want your promise that you will see no more of her."

He set his jaw. "*Amo, adoro vostra figlia;* I love, I worship your daughter."

She jerked her head back. "You are Italian."

"I speak four languages," he replied. "Italian, German, French, and English. How do you think I got into Georgetown?"

"You told me you were born in this country," she said. "But no non-native speaker pronounces that sentence the way you do, with the correct intonation."

He glared at her and took his arm away. "I will love your daughter until the day I die."

"You are a liar and a fraud." Angelina raised her voice. What would happen if she stirred the pot? "I know who you are."

Russell went still.

"You *are* Italian."

He folded his arms. "Who am I?"

She squirmed. She could not say—yet.

He walked on.

She hurried after.

"I intend to marry her," he said, without turning around.

"Not if I have any say in it."

"What makes you think she will listen to you? You have nothing to offer her. I have enough funds to provide for a wife and family. I could take her to Italy, to Venice. She could perform with the best musicians in the world."

"You are not marrying her."

"How are you going to stop me?"

"You will have to walk over my corpse."

Chapter Three
Thursday, 22 September

Angelina arrived on Russell's arm, out of breath and with untidy curls. Zia Paulina frowned, her look scouring Angelina from head to toe. Angelina had chosen a cream-colored frock with a handkerchief hem, which she'd accented with a red belt to show off her slender waist, red high-heels, and vivid red lipstick. In one hand she carried a sequined red purse.

Silently, Russell gave his hat to Lucinda and immediately made for the piano in the back parlor, leaving Angelina standing by herself in the front parlor, her cheeks warming. How had that gone so wrong? She should not have spoken so plainly, she knew better. One had to charm them first before making requests. But he should not have been so rude to her, especially as he *was* Italian, despite his name, and native-born Americans discriminated against Italians, believing them all to be dirty, servile, and crude. She fished a comb and mirror out of her purse. There must be some way to get rid of him. Angelina peered in the mirror until she had done her hair to her satisfaction.

The back parlor was double the size of the front parlor, and there, the family spent most of their time. It had a large brick fireplace, which warmed them in winter, and a small screened door, which caught any breeze coming by in summer. It was large enough for a dining-room table and full set of chairs to be placed in the back part of the room, opposite a side door that led downstairs to the large basement kitchen, where Lucinda cooked by day and slept by night. Towards the front of the room was a baby grand, surrounded by a sofa and easy chairs. Today, Violet had taken the eight chairs that normally went around the dining table and arranged them around the room—because all of their friends and acquaintances would want to meet Grace's new pianist.

Angelina chose a seat at the front of the room that gave her a good view of Russell and lit a cigarette with shaking hands. Footsteps slowly stepped their way down the wooden staircase, and Grace appeared carrying her violin and bow, Violet following with the music stand.

Russell rose, took her hand and hesitated, his shy smile mirroring Grace's. After a pause, he lifted her hand to his lips and would have kissed it, or made some gesture of possessiveness, but fortunately, Zia Paulina came into the room.

"There is one passage here," he said, sitting on the piano stool, "where we have to be together."

Grace bent over him as he pointed to the cadences at the end of the *Vivace*.

"I need to see you," he said. "We have to catch each other's eye."

"Where would you like me to stand?"

"I need you to turn slightly so that I can see you."

"Like this?"

"That's good."

"Where would you like me to put your music stand, Gracie?" said Violet.

"I don't need it. I can play it by heart."

His smile illuminated his face. "Can you really my Grace?"

Angelina cringed and took a long inhale on her cigarette.

They practiced the second movement for a while. Angelina observed her daughter. What was going on? Grace had made no effort to dress up for her visitor. She wore no makeup, no jewelry, and was attired in her oldest, most shapeless dress, faded linen with a Peter Pan collar. But his eyes scarcely left her face, and his smile was both intense, yet gentle.

Angelina bit her lip. She could not fault her daughter's behavior because Grace was not doing anything. But how come he was so attracted to her when her clothes proclaimed she was making no effort? Angelina dressed in an eye-catching style because if she did not, men's eyes slid over her, off onto younger women. It must be Grace's extreme youth. He could mold her as he wished.

Eventually, the other guests arrived, and when they were all seated, Grace and Russell played the Brahms *A Major Sonata* all the way through. Professor Burneys arrived late, after Grace and Russell had started, but Zia Paulina quietly insisted he take her seat in the front row.

Afterwards, he shook Russell by the hand. "You're a fine pianist, sir. Delighted to make your acquaintance. I'm Professor Burneys, Grace's violin teacher." He turned to Zia Paulina. "Would you mind if I gave Grace a lesson? Now that she's found such a talented pianist, I'd like to make use of him."

She nodded her agreement.

"Grace, my child, we need to hear more from you in this passage." Burneys pointed to a measure marked *forte*, where the piano part displayed a swirl of notes. "Mr. Russell is very gallant, but look at all the notes he has to play. He needs you to give him more room."

Mr. Russell glanced at Grace, who was blushing, and composed his features.

Angelina seethed. Men were so irresponsible. Couldn't Burneys see that Russell needed to be *discouraged*?

"We need more passion, and fire, from the violin here, so that Mr. Russell can display his considerable gifts. Let's try from here."

They played the passage again.

"But don't you think," Grace said suddenly, "that the tone needs to be more veiled? Those sudden fortes don't sound right." She went to the piano and pointed to the music with the tip of her bow. "Could you play the "Vivace" again, and make the tone more *sotto voce*? It should be rich, but ephemeral."

"I'll try," he said smiling, and immediately played the passage, watching Grace's face all the while.

"That's it," she exclaimed, her face lighting up. "You've got exactly the right touch."

He picked up a pencil with his left hand and scrawled something on the music.

"I want you to hear this," she said to Burneys, who stood there shaking his head.

They played the "Vivace" again. "I like it," said Burneys. "The dynamics are not what Brahms marked, but you and your talented pianist give the music such an *intimate* quality."

Angelina narrowed her eyes and rose in her seat, but Grace, who was blushing furiously, said, "Let's try the last movement."

And so they spent another hour practicing, while Angelina scrutinized Russell, and Lucinda served iced tea, lemonade, sandwiches, and her specialty, sweet potato pie.

At the end of the hour, Burneys turned to Russell. "I have an idea for a new piece for Grace to play, but I'd like to see how you tackle it first." He placed the piano part of something on the music stand.

Russell glanced at it and played the beginning, which had a similar style. When he got some way in, Burneys stopped him.

"I'm out of practice."

"You play it well." Burneys patted his shoulder. He turned to Grace. "This is the Brahms *D Minor Sonata*, his most difficult sonata, but your Mr. Russell has the technique to handle it. Why don't you stand behind him, so that you can read the violin line from his piano part?"

Russell shifted slightly on the piano stool so that Grace could see the music better.

At the end of the first movement, Burneys rose and clapped Russell on the back.

"I'd like to invite you to my soirée next month. I think you, and Grace, should play the *D Minor Sonata*. What do you say Grace? Are you up for it?"

"It's such a wonderful work." Grace glanced at her pianist and beamed.

Angelina eyed Grace as she bent over Russell, turning the pages of music, while she talked about the various things she wanted him to do. She made a mental note to tell her daughter not to stand so close to him; Grace had no idea what men were like.

Zia Paulina, rising, ushered both men to the refreshment table. Angelina followed.

"Grace is lucky to have you as her pianist," Burneys said. "Where did you study?"

"I've had private lessons since I was a boy." Russell accepted a sandwich from Lucinda with a smile of thanks.

"Where did you go to school?" asked Burneys.

"I went to Northwestern, in Evanston, Illinois. Now I am studying at the Georgetown School of Foreign Service."

"When did you graduate from Northwestern?" asked Zia Paulina.

"In 1915."

"Were you active in the war?"

"He *says* he fought on the Italian Front," remarked Angelina, dangling a cigarette from her fingers.

"My wife is Italian," remarked Burneys. "Clara!" he called. "Mr. Russell fought on the Italian Front."

Mrs. Burneys came over, her face sad. "My younger brother was at the Battle of Vittorio Veneto, Mr. Russell. Perhaps you heard of him?"

Mr. Russell's hands shook. He put his plate of food down.

"He was only nineteen years old and was studying languages."

Mr. Russell cleared his throat and wiped his mouth.

"He wanted to be a doctor. His name was Federigo Lombardi." Tears ran down her face.

There was a long pause. "I'm sorry," said Russell. "I don't think we ever met."

"So many enlisted," she replied. "Where did you see action?"

He looked at the floor. "The Piave River."

"That must have been dangerous," remarked Burneys. "Weren't the Italians standing *in* the river, with the Austrians shooting down at them?"

"Your name seems familiar," said Mrs. Burneys. "Is it Nicholas Russell?"

He nodded.

Angelina inhaled deeply on her cigarette.

"I'm trying to remember where I saw your name," said Mrs. Burneys. "It must have been in the *Corriere della Sera,* the Evening Courier of Milano— "

"Wasn't Federigo in that battle?" Burneys turned to his wife.

"Yes." Mrs. Burneys fastened her gaze on Russell. "Weren't you awarded the Congressional Medal of Honor?"

He was silent for a long moment his face drained of color. "I was." He paused. "Pardon me, Mrs. Burneys, the memories are—painful."

She patted his hand. "It must have been awful."

"Not many people survive to collect their medal," observed Angelina, folding her arms and exhaling smoke.

He turned to her for the first time since arriving at Zia Paulina's.

"I was knocked out for quite some time, and it was only through devoted medical care that I'm here today."

Angelina bit her lip. *Merda*. How unfortunate that Grace's unsuitable suitor should now appear to be a knight in shining armor. Would they never be able to get rid of him? She lit another cigarette. Even Zia Paulina was impressed.

"You won an award for gallantry?" she said now, handing him some lemonade. "Why didn't you say so before?"

"It's not something I care to talk about, Ma'am. War is a terrible thing. Too many people die, and the destruction is horrendous."

"Is that why you're studying at Georgetown?" asked Grace, who had come over to the refreshment table silently, listening intently.

Mr. Russell's taut face relaxed into a smile. "I hope to become a diplomat and do whatever I can to prevent war."

"That's what I think." Grace took a step towards him.

Shortly afterwards, Mr. Russell left with Professor and Mrs. Burneys.

One second after Lucinda shut the front door behind them, Edith Taussig sank onto the loveseat. "A decorated military hero!" She closed her pale blue eyes dramatically.

"You are *so lucky* Grace!" remarked her identical twin Frieda.

Angelina grimaced. The Taussig twins had the same thick flaxen hair, pale blue eyes and long limbs. They both liked to sing, with Edith taking the soprano part and Frieda the contralto. Angelina met them at the Burneys' shortly after Grace became his student. They were a little older than Violet, perhaps twenty years old.

"I'm not lucky," said Grace.

"He's not exactly paying attention to anyone else," remarked Frieda.

Grace reddened to the roots of her hair. She twisted her fingers together.

"Oh, look, she's blushing," said Frieda. "So you like him after all, huh?"

Angelina examined her daughter's lowered face. *Cristo Santo.*

"What I wouldn't give for a young man like that." Edith Taussig picked up her purse and gloves.

Angelina turned to stare at her. Why did Edith look so sad? Her family was rich, and it galled Angelina that Violet and Grace were the recipients of their hand-me-downs, their charity. Edith and Frieda, co-heiresses of their father's estate, were bound to marry well one day.

Angelina and her family waved goodbye to them; the other guests melting away soon after.

"Grace, dear," said Zia Paulina. "You look exhausted. It is time you went to bed."

Grace rose, but before going upstairs, she made sure her violin was safely put away. Her violin was more important to her than any person. Violet had complained to her mother on more than one occasion that Grace would get up in the middle of the night to check it was safe in its case. Tonight, Grace moved more slowly than usual as she went through her nightly ritual, and there were smudges under her eyes. Finally, she wished everyone *buona notte* and drifted upstairs.

"He made quite a splash," remarked Violet. "He's the cat's pajamas when it comes to fashion. It would never have occurred to me to accessorize an off-white linen suit with a gray silk handkerchief and tie. Look at what it did to his eyes —they had an almost velvety quality."

Zia Paulina laughed. "I can see he made quite an impression on *you*." She sat in her favorite armchair by the window.

Violet shrugged as she took one corner of the loveseat, smiling in a self-deprecating way. "You had only to add to this a story of gallantry, and the ladies were positively swooning."

"I had no idea he was awarded the Congressional Medal," remarked Zia Paulina. "That is quite an achievement."

"It is strange that he was reluctant to talk about it," said Angelina. "Men usually like to boast."

"You are right," said Zia Paulina. "He seemed upset."

"I wonder," said Angelina, sitting on the loveseat next to Violet, "if he is mentally fragile."

"What do you mean?" said Violet.

"He fought in the war," replied Angelina. "He might fall apart, fly off the handle, go off the rails."

"Do you think that is likely?" asked Zia Paulina. "He seems very civilized to me."

"We do not know him," remarked Angelina.

"That is true," said Zia Paulina. "It does worry me that he is so taken with Grace. It seems too sudden."

"I do not think he is suitable for her," said Angelina.

"Why not?" said Violet.

"He is too old."

"He can only be in his late twenties," said Violet.

"He says he graduated in 1915," said Zia Paulina. "That is six years ago. He must be about twenty-seven. That is not old."

"He is too old for her," stated Angelina.

"Perhaps you mean she is too young for him," said Zia Paulina. "And I do think that is an issue, especially as Grace has led such a sheltered life. I am surprised he is not more concerned. He must know he has to wait until she is ready."

"Suppose he cannot wait?" said Angelina.

"I watched him closely today," said Zia Paulina. "And I could not fault his manners. He was gentlemanly, very attentive to Grace."

"*Beh*." Angelina shrugged dismissively. "They are all like that in the beginning."

This remark earned her a pointed looked from Zia Paulina. "I do not think you should compare your situation with Grace's."

Angelina swallowed.

"I am concerned about the effect this is having on Grace," continued Zia Paulina. "She told me she was just interested in having a good pianist to play with. But Mr. Russell clearly has other ideas."

Indeed, he does. Angelina restrained herself from drawing another cigarette out of its packet and lighting up, as Zia Paulina disapproved. *And what is worse, Grace is beginning to soften towards him.*

"Grace is really getting too old to be spending so much time on that violin," she remarked. "She should start thinking about marriage."

"Angelina." Zia Paulina gave her a hard stare. "I am surprised to hear you say that."

Angelina clasped her arms across her bosom. "This is a man's world. Grace is going to have to struggle if she persists being a violinist. She should learn how to run a household."

"You never wanted to learn to run a household! You would not hear of such a thing when I tried to teach you."

"I know." Angelina held her head up, and gave her aunt a cool look. "But I was quite a bit younger than Grace is now. I do not see a future for Grace as a concert artist; I think it will be too hard for her. She needs to think about marriage. We should help her be more presentable; she needs lessons in deportment."

"Gracie could make more of an effort to sit up straight," remarked Violet. "She has a tendency to slouch."

"Angelina, the world is changing. I think Grace and Violet should develop their talents so that they can make their own money and not have to rely solely on their husband's income. I do not think it is good for women, especially good-looking women, to be so dependent on men."

Angelina stared back at her aunt, willing herself not to crumple into the loveseat. At this remark, Angelina felt the full force of her aunt's disapproval. But this was important. She made herself hold her head up.

"It is a man's world. Grace is too good-looking not to be swept up into the marriage market, and I do not understand why you are missing such an opportunity. Grace could marry well, like Josephina and Louisa."

"This matter is closed." Zia Paulina said in her majestic way. "Grace has more talent in her littlest finger than ever Josephina or Louisa had."

"I do not agree that the matter is closed," said Angelina. "You said yourself that Grace is very sensitive. This world is too harsh for her. With the right husband, she would be safe, and happy. She should focus on making the right marriage."

"And waste her God-given talent?" Zia Paulina's voice was hard. "I won't hear of it."

"She can do so much better than Russell," said Angelina. "You should get rid of him, it would spare us all a great deal of unpleasantness."

"And how do you propose we do that?" asked Zia Paulina. "Professor Burneys thinks he is a wonderful pianist, and Mrs. Burneys is grateful for his efforts on behalf of her brother. This will be all over Georgetown by tomorrow afternoon. It would be unpardonably rude to snub him now."

"I wish I had never seen him. I do not like the way he eyes Grace. He seems obsessed." Angelina rose, put her gloves on, and picked up her hat. "If I had any say in this matter, I would forbid Grace to see him."

Violet exchanged a look with Zia Paulina. They seemed surprised.

"*Perché*?" said a soft voice.

Grace stood halfway up the stairs, dressed in her nightgown.

Angelina went to the bottom of the stairs. "You are not marrying Mr. Russell."

Grace's eyes widened. "Who says I am?"

"*Signor* Russell."

"Angelina!" Zia Paulina hurried forward. "That is enough. Can't you see how exhausted Grace is? I think you should go."

Angelina turned to her daughter. "Remember this, he is *not* good for you. *Lui è malato ed ossessionato,* he is sick and obsessed."

Chapter Four

Saturday, 24 September

"Good morning." Mr. Russell lowered his newspaper as Grace wandered down the stairs of the small house on Beall Street and into the front parlor, her eyes unfocused from heavy sleep. It was Saturday, two days since Zia Paulina's party, and Grace was on her way to her weekly violin lesson with Professor Burneys.

"Are you ready?" he asked gently.

She nodded as she put her straw hat on. Why was he here? Grace didn't remember inviting him to escort her to her violin lesson. On the other hand, she wasn't surprised to see him.

"Would you like me to carry your things?" he asked, rising.

Silently, she handed him the leather portfolio that was full of music. She kept her violin.

He put his hat on and offered her his arm.

She buried the tips of her fingers in the crook of his arm.

"Now," he said as he shut the front door behind him, "which is the best way?"

"We go left on Montgomery."

They wandered through Georgetown in silence for a while, their steps echoing on the brick sidewalk. The heat of his body drove through the tips of her fingers. His male aroma and the musky perfume that overlaid it assailed her nostrils, mixing with rose, jasmine, brick, and box hedge, as the rising sun warmed everything, releasing their odors.

Grace half-turned her head away. Should she be doing this? She'd never been this close to any man. When Violet and Grace arrived in Georgetown, Zia Paulina sent them to a girls' school run by the nuns from the Convent of the Visitation, situated on the corner of Fayette and Third. From time to time he shot her searching glances, but said nothing. What was he thinking? Should she say something? Violet always said that Grace needed to speak up. She drew in a deep breath.

"I guess Professor Burneys wants us to play the first movement of the *D Minor*?"

"I believe so."

"I haven't worked on it, I was so tired yesterday."

He stopped. "Are you too tired to walk? I can get a cab."

She shook her head; she shouldn't allow him to spend money on her.

"Do I look tired?"

"No," he said. "You look wonderful."

She clenched her fingers around the handle of her violin case, willing her cheeks to remain cool. They turned into Dunbarton Street, passing brick houses with their black or dark-green shutters. It was not yet nine o'clock, and drapes still hid the rooms from public view. If only he would speak. Her hands grew clammy.

"I don't know what to do," she remarked. "I don't feel up to playing the Brahms today, but it will be a waste of your time if I don't."

"It will not be a waste of my time."

She stopped and gazed up at him. What did he want? His dark eyes held her.

"Mr. Russell, don't you think I'm too young for you?"

His eyes flashed as his face hardened into a mask.

She lifted her chin. "I've no conversation, no opinion about anything, and no judgment, due to my lack of experience."

His features softened. "Grace—"

"You must find me very boring. I don't know what to say."

"Grace!" He laughed so hard, he had to mop his eyes with his handkerchief. Then he glanced at her and stopped suddenly.

"What is so funny?" asked Grace.

He was silent. "You are a remarkable young woman," he said at last.

Was he mocking her? She peered closely up to his face.

"Most people assume they are delightful and fascinating to listen to. It shows great humility not to assume that."

"But—" She hesitated. "I don't understand."

"I see that," he said, smiling down at her. "Have you had a good look at yourself in the mirror recently?"

"I look in it every day to do my hair. But I'm usually trying to do it as quickly as possible so that I can begin practicing my violin."

He laughed again. Then he took her hand and kissed it. "Have you any idea how breathtakingly lovely you are?"

She was unable to reply.

"You must have noticed young men looking at you."

"I try not to notice. I don't want to get involved in that sort of thing."

He gave her a sharp, probing look. "Why not?"

She looked down. "It's too painful."

"Painful?" He gently tilted her chin with the tips of his fingers.

Something about the way he looked at her caused tears to appear. "You don't understand."

'But I do." He lowered his voice. "*La tua madre?* Your mother?"

Her hands shook. Did everyone know?

"Let me tell you how I met your mother," he said, offering her his arm again. "She reminds me of someone I used to know well at Northwestern University. That person was the wife of one of my professors there, and she was very kind to a shy young man. I believed she'd moved here during the war. Your mother looks almost exactly like her, especially from the back." He laughed softly, causing Grace's lips to curve into a reluctant smile. "That is why I followed her into Shepherd & Riley's bookstore. Your mother noticed me and introduced herself. I could see at once she wasn't the person I believed her to be, but she was pleasant and friendly, and so I invited her to tea at the Metropolitan Hotel. We sat and chatted for a bit, then I was obliged to leave as I had an appointment with Father Walsh." He turned to her. "He's my professor here, at Georgetown University."

Grace nodded as they turned a corner, past a well-tended garden where drowsy roses raised their heads to the warming sun.

"As I left, your mother invited me to supper at your home in Beall Street."

"That's what I thought," said Grace. "Mother saw you as her—friend."

His jawline tightened.

Grace drooped. Oh dear, it was so difficult to talk about her. When they were little, Mother told her daughters that she worked as a companion because, she explained, men didn't like to be alone. Grace used to be puzzled at what Mother could possibly find to say to fill the many hours she spent keeping gentlemen company. After all, she only came to life when she was talking about clothes, and surely that wouldn't interest them? Now that she understood what Mother had been doing, she couldn't find the right words to describe it.

And that raised another question, what had she been doing with Mr. Russell? She glanced up at him.

He reddened as he met her gaze.

"Grace," he murmured. "She gave me a formal four-course meal, I played piano, she made coffee, and then she wanted to dance to a popular song. I went along to be polite."

"Mr. Russell—this is awkward—Mother is not happy—She told me never to see you again."

The force of his glare thrust her back on her heels.

He bent towards her. "What are you thinking, Grace?"

"I don't know." She frowned. "It's very difficult, being seventeen."

"Indeed it is." He laughed, as he gently brushed away tendrils of her hair with the tips of his fingers. "But, Grace," he said as they turned into Congress Street where Professor Burneys lived, "I want you to know me, so you can make up your own mind. I would like us to spend more time together."

She wrapped her fingers around the handles of her violin case and bowed her head. "I don't know if I should."

He squeezed her other hand. "Do you have any objection to my taking you to your violin lesson?"

✠✠✠✠✠✠✠✠✠✠✠

She had only spoken to Russell three times, so it was not surprising he had never discussed his relatives, never mentioned if he had a mother or father. Angelina tossed her frocks onto her bed in the back room of her apartment on Potomac Street. Did it mean his relatives were dead? She hoped not. It was October the first, still warm, and she needed clothing that would stand up to the heat and humidity. She wanted to cut *una bella figura* in front of the registrar of Georgetown University on Monday so that she could find out more about the man who insisted—no, threatened—that he was going to marry her daughter.

Angelina shook her head as she looked at the dresses carpeting her bed in vivid shades of red, gold, green, or electric blue, their colors accentuated with beading, and plenty of gold and silver trim, which made them sparkle in the afternoon sun. The registrar was going to be an elderly or middle-aged Jesuit who would not take kindly to vibrant colors. The only dress that was suitable was a powder-blue one that had been Scott's favorite, but it had a plunging neckline. She rose, put her frocks in a shopping bag, stuffed some hats and shoes in another, and set off for Beall Street, hoping Violet would be there to advise her.

✠✠✠✠✠✠✠✠✠✠✠

"It's too low." Violet examined the plunging neckline of the powder-blue frock. "But I could sew on a white collar that would cover you up to the neck."

"You are so clever, Violetta. I knew you would come up with something." Angelina sat down on the low chair in the back bedroom that her daughters shared, while Violet rummaged through her sewing basket.

"Where is everyone?"

"Mr. Russell found some tickets to a concert and invited Auntie P.—and Gracie."

Angelina clenched her slender fingers around the arms of the chair.

"Why are you so upset with him?" Violet began pinning the collar to Angelina's frock.

"I suppose Zia Paulina thinks I am jealous."

"Well? Aren't you?"

"I am not." Angelina rose and paced, her high heels clacking on the wooden floor.

"He jilted you."

"He was unpardonably rude. But that is not what bothers me."

Violet paused in her pinning to give her mother a look.

"*Guardatelo!* Look at him!" exclaimed Angelina. "Graziella only met him on September the sixth. It is now October the first—less than a month—and he is squiring her around Georgetown, inviting her out to concerts, establishing himself as her favorite pianist."

"He is very taken with her."

"I do not trust him."

"Why not?"

"Something does not sit right, it does not smell right. He told me, for example, he was born in this country. But I am sure he was born in Italy."

"How can you tell?"

"We have spoken Italian together. His Italian is flawless, and he pronounces it with the accent of the Veneto."

"I wouldn't know about that," remarked Violet, returning to her pinning.

Questo era vero. That was true. Angelina's elder daughter, with her golden curls and blue eyes, was an all-American girl who almost never spoke Italian, preferring the jazzy vernacular of her peers. "Why did he go to the trouble of meeting me? He wanted to meet me because he has been following me around."

"How do you know that?"

"Because of all the gossip he generated." Angelina stared at her hands, trying not to think about Scott. "He caused me many difficulties."

Violet averted her gaze as she threaded her needle and started to sew, making small, even stitches.

"Who did he think I was?" Angelina frowned as she stared out the window.

"Didn't you say once," said Violet after a pause, "that you had some relatives from the Veneto who were in this country?"

"There was Papa's second wife. But I never wanted to see her. L*a mia matrigna era una vera e propria stronza*. My stepmother was a real b*tch."

"Mother! That's pretty strong."

"She was hateful."

"You're sure there wasn't anyone else?"

Angelina sat down, Violet leaned forward. "I never heard from Papa again after I got here," Angelina said slowly. "I always thought he went back to Italy."

"That's strange," said Violet. "Why wouldn't a father keep in contact with his daughters?"

Angelina drooped in her seat. "*Non lo so*. I do not know."

There was silence for a long moment, then Violet rose. "Why don't you try this on?"

Angelina put the frock on and stared at the stranger in the mirror.

"I look so matronly."

"Good," said Violet.

"What about my shoes? They are in there." Angelina pointed to a shopping bag.

Violet rummaged. "Too glamorous," she remarked. "You don't want the registrar to categorize you as one of the seven deadly's."

Angelina laughed, feeling suddenly lighter.

"I've got a pair of brown shoes that are badly scuffed," Violet offered.

"I am not used to this, I am going to feel so old. Which hat do you think I should wear?"

Violet took out Angelina's hats. One was decorated with an orange satin ribbon, held in place by a silk flower. Another was a large-brimmed straw hat, trimmed in brown grosgrain. The third was powder blue with a small brim and matching powder-blue veil. "These are too dainty," she decided. "Why don't you wear Grace's straw hat, the one with the faded ribbon?"

"Will she mind?"

"If she notices, I'll lend her one of mine."

"I should give Graziella one of my hats," said Angelina. "She has not had a new one in ages. Perhaps I should leave these hats and let her choose? I should also clear out my dresses and let you choose which ones you want. I am not going to need these fancy clothes any more."

Violet looked up sharply. "Why ever not?"

"I am getting too old for that sort of thing."

"Are you serious?"

"Maybe you should be the one to find *l'uomo affascinante,* the charming man."

Violet rolled her eyes. "The men I've met don't interest me. They expect me to act like a dumbbell. They hate it when I ask questions."

Angelina laughed. "When you turn those bright blue eyes on them, they find you intimidating. Men want their women to be baby-girls and sexy."

"I want to be myself. If a fellow can't accept me as I am, then he's not good enough."

Angelina studied Violet. She wanted both of her daughters to be happy and secure, and in this man-made world that meant marriage. But Violet was shrewd and had much more practical knowledge of the world than Grace. If any of her daughters had a chance of making it alone in this harsh environment, it was Violet.

"I wish I had thought of that when I was your age. I always thought it was my place to please men, and look where that has led. This affair with Russell and Graziella has woken me up. It is time I did something else."

"I've been telling you that forever, but I never thought you'd listen. What do you plan to do?"

"I have to make money. I thought I would become a translator."

Violet beamed. "That's wonderful."

"My Italian needs work. But first, I must rescue Grace."

"He's pretty determined."

"I know. But someone has to stand up to him. It is right it should be her mother."

"I don't know if I should like to cross swords with him," remarked Violet. "Have you noticed how he stares at you? It's unnerving."

"Someone has to stop him." Angelina picked up her shopping bag. "I must find out who he really is. I smell a trickster, a fraud."

Chapter Five
Monday, 3 October

Early Monday morning, Angelina set out for Georgetown University where she was directed to Father Findlay's office.

"Come," a deep voice said after she tapped on the door.

A sinewy Jesuit with hollowed-out cheeks sat behind a large desk, his blue eyes hard. What was wrong? Angelina had carefully put on the powder blue dress—ruined forever by its high, prim collar—the ugly scuffed shoes, *and* the straw hat with the faded ribbon. Didn't she look poor enough to suit his tastes? She considered for a moment. *Naturalmente,* she should not have made up her face. Perhaps the expertly applied eyeliner and lipstick clashed with the implied poverty of her clothes.

The silence lengthened. Angelina moistened her lips. "I understand a young man registered to take courses at the foreign service school."

"What of it?"

"His name is Nicholas Russell. I believe I am his long-lost relation, and I would like to contact his relatives."

"Why don't you ask him about it?"

Angelina looked at the floor. Why had she expected them to make things easy for her? "May I sit down?"

He indicated a seat.

She sat, fiddling with the handles of her purse. Eventually she said, "He wants to marry my daughter."

He appraised her narrowly. "You don't look old enough."

Angelina gave her tinkling laugh. "Ah, Father, you are kind. But, indeed, it is true."

"You are opposed to the marriage? What about your husband?"

"My husband is dead."

"But surely it would help you. If the young man has money enough to provide for your daughter, maybe he can provide for you too."

Angelina looked at her shoes, her cheeks scalding. She wasn't used to looking poor, and the last thing she wanted was Russell's charity.

"My daughter is very young."

"Is your daughter of age?"

"No. She has just turned seventeen."

"Well, Mrs.—"

"Miller."

"Mrs. Miller, what is your problem? If your daughter is a minor, she cannot legally do anything without your permission."

Angelina pinched her lips together. She might have known a Jesuit would throw out something she had not thought of.

"Do you know who I am talking about? Have you met him?"

"What did you say his name was?"

"Nicholas Russell."

He studied her for a long moment. Then he rose and went to a steel file cabinet. Moments later, he returned to his desk with a slim file.

"I don't recognize his name. Let me see if I interviewed him." Father Findlay riffled through the file. "No. Father Walsh did the interview. That makes sense as he is the director of the School for Foreign Service. I advise you to see him."

✠✠✠✠✠✠✠✠✠✠✠✠✠

Angelina sat outside Father Walsh's office on an uncomfortable wooden chair that bit into her back, making an effort to sit up straight with her knees together, her hands in her lap, and her eyes on the floor. But it was hard not to notice male stares and the occasional snigger. She toyed with her gloves. She had not been a good mother to her daughters. When she returned to Zia Paulina's house in Georgetown at the age of twenty-two, she wanted, more than anything, her own money. But she did not have marketable skills. She could not type, or do shorthand, or take dictation. And so, she had taken the easy way out, trading her charm, intelligence, and sexual favors for money. But society did not look kindly on women like her, women from the demimonde who satisfied the unmet needs of respectably married men. She never understood why since plenty of these so-called respectable women, the ones who scorned her the most, were carrying on with men they were not married to. They were not so different from Angelina, but maybe that was beside the point. She should have paid more attention to her daughters.

She put her gloves inside her purse. At least Violet had forgiven her, but she could not get anywhere with Grace. The child avoided her, preferring to play her violin to talking with her mother. Angelina sagged in her seat. When had that started? It must have been when Grace was about ten. Angelina remembered what life had been like at the age of ten, for that was when she had been taken from her home in *Italia* to travel on that huge ship to the United States. Ten was the age when you started to notice things. Grace never said anything; she simply disappeared.

Angelina rummaged in her purse for a tissue to wipe away tears. If only Grace knew how proud she was. Everyone thought highly of Grace, not only because she played her violin beautifully but also because she always behaved perfectly, like a lady. How Angelina longed to be closer to her daughter. She lost her own mother at age four and had missed her all her life. If she half-closed her eyes she could remember Mamma bending over her, feeding her with the grapes they picked, dangling the delicious fruit teasingly over her daughter so that Angelina gurgled with pleasure. She remembered being enveloped in her mother's gentle arms, her scent of bergamot. After her death, life became harsh, and hard. Perhaps the worst thing of all was that Angelina had never taken her place anywhere. She did not belong with her hated stepmother or with tiresome, if kind, Zia Paulina. She was not American, and she detested speaking English. She was not comfortable in her life and had not been so for a long time.

She glanced at her watch. Two hours had passed, and Father Walsh had not appeared. She emptied her purse, methodically organizing it. Time ticked on. She retrieved a piece of paper and wrote notes to herself on it. Finally, after about three hours, she heard a firm step, and a youngish man appeared decked out in Jesuit garb.

Angelina rose to her feet.

"What can I do for you?" he asked, unlocking his door.

She gave a brief explanation, emphasizing her concerns for her daughter. While she talked, he examined her closely.

"There isn't much to tell," he said, ushering her into his office. "Mr. Russell interviewed last February. His credentials were excellent, and we accepted him."

She forced a smile onto her face.

"He's been attending my classes three times a week and has never missed a class. What he does with the rest of his time, I can't, of course, say."

"Does he list next of kin?"

Father Walsh went to the steel filing cabinet, retrieving Russell's file. "He lists one brother. That is all."

She took a scrap of paper from her purse.

"That's odd," he said, perusing the file.

Angelina's head jerked up.

He snapped the file shut.

"What's odd?"

"I am not at liberty to tell you. You must understand, we are obligated to guard our student's privacy. I cannot give out names to people with whom I am not personally acquainted."

Angelina stared at him without blinking. Did Russell have a brother or not? She was sure he did, as that was what Father Walsh had said at first. So why was Father Walsh hesitating? She dropped her gaze. "Please, I am most concerned for my daughter's sake. Can't you tell me anything?"

"Very well. I can tell you that Russell's relation is studying to be a priest."

"Would it be possible to write him a letter?"

"Well, I suppose there's no harm in that. I suggest you direct your inquiries to the abbot at the Seminary of St. Francis de Sales in Milwaukee, Wisconsin."

Angelina carefully wrote this information down and looked up.

"Is Mr. Russell doing well at his studies?"

"Very well," said Father Walsh. "He will almost certainly get a position with the State Department, he's one of my best students." He held the door open for her and added, with a smile, "You should rejoice, Mrs. Miller. He will be able to provide for your daughter."

✠✠✠✠✠✠✠✠✠✠✠

"He has a brother." Angelina shut the door to the small house on Beall Street, took off Grace's old hat, put it on the hatstand, and gave Violet back her shoes.

"I'm so weary," she said as Violet came back up from the basement with an unopened bottle of prosecco from their store of liquor, and a plate of cookies. "I had to wait all day to see Father Walsh."

"Who are you talking about?" Zia Paulina came slowly downstairs.

"Mr. Russell." Angelina sank into a corner of the loveseat. The sound of Grace's violin wafted down the stairs as she played something that began serenely but soon grew more and more passionate.

"Mr. Russell's brother is studying to be a priest," said Angelina over the ascending violin line.

"Don't you know his name?" Violet poured a glass for Zia Paulina, then handed around a plate of cookies that were warm from the oven.

"Father Walsh wouldn't tell me." Angelina sipped her wine. "He said he was obligated to protect the privacy of his students."

"Fat lot of use that is," observed Violet.

"I managed to persuade him to give me his address. Apparently, he is studying to be a priest at the St. Francis de Sales Seminary in Wisconsin. Father Walsh told me to contact the abbot."

"That's surprising." Zia Paulina nibbled a ginger snap. "Is Mr. Russell religious?"

"I do not know." Angelina gave her glass to Violet for a refill.

"I had a talk with him yesterday afternoon," remarked Zia Paulina. "I paid a call on his landlady, Mrs. Rittenhouse, and she told me he had taken the entire top floor of her house. Then he came in, so I asked him about his parents. He told me they were both dead."

"How convenient," muttered Angelina. "Did he mention his brother?"

"No," said Zia Paulina, her forehead creasing. "And I have to say I felt he was being evasive about something."

Angelina sat up.

"What?" said Violet.

"I don't know," replied Zia Paulina. "What he was lying about is quite beyond me."

"You thought he was *lying?*" said Angelina and Violet in unison.

"Yes," said Zia Paulina. "Heaven knows why."

"So he can marry Grace, of course." Angelina put her glass down. "Whatever it is must be something that would prevent him from marrying her."

"But why would he want to marry Grace?" said Violet. "What advantage would she bring him? After all, our family isn't fancy, and we don't know anyone with cash or acclaim."

"Maybe it does not matter to him she is not rich.Maybe he is simply obsessed," said Angelina. "I thought he was following me around, perhaps he was following her."

"Did you ask him where he was born?" said Violet.

"He told me he was born here, in America," said Zia Paulina slowly, "but there I think he was not telling me the truth."

"Because?"

"He seems so Italian. He made coffee for me using a machine he had bought in Italy. But more to the point, his Italian is flawless, with exactly the correct intonation."

"That is what *I* said!" exclaimed Angelina.

"When I remarked that he carried many Italian customs with him, he replied that he'd fought in Italy for two years."

"Very pat," said Angelina, folding her arms.

"Except you felt he was being untruthful," remarked Violet.

"Who was lying?" asked a soft voice.

"Grace!" exclaimed Zia Paulina. "I thought you were practicing."

Grace wandered down the stairs, sank onto a chair, and looked at her relatives with an expression of resignation.

"I suppose you're talking about Mr. Russell."

"Indeed, we are," sighed Zia Paulina.

"Don't you have anything good to say about him?"

"Mrs. Rittenhouse told me he was the perfect tenant," said Zia Paulina. "He pays his rent on time, keeps his apartment clean, makes his own coffee in her kitchen. And he cleans up after himself."

"How nice that he knows his way around the kitchen." Grace's gray eyes lost their usual ethereal quality, coming to life. "He could teach me how to make perfect coffee."

"Does he have any friends?" asked Violet.

"No," said Zia Paulina.

"No girlfriends?" asked Angelina.

Grace worried a hangnail with the tip of her finger.

"Mrs. Rittenhouse told me that he behaves like a perfect gentleman."

"He is a perfect gentleman," declared Grace. She turned to her mother. "Violet said you visited Georgetown University today."

"I met with Father Walsh, his professor."

"What are his prospects?" said Zia Paulina.

Angelina hesitated. "Father Walsh told me that Mr. Russell was one of his best students. But," she wagged a finger at Grace, "that does not alter the fact that he is lying about his past. I found out today that he has a brother. Did he ever mention that to you?"

"No. But I never asked."

"Listen to me, Graziella," said Angelina. "Mr. Russell is lying about something. It must be something that would prevent his marriage to you, or he would have mentioned it."

Grace folded her arms, and, for the first time, got a stubborn look on her face that reminded Angelina of the way Papa would look when things were not going his way.

"We have not discussed this," remarked Zia Paulina.

"Then we should discuss it now." Angelina shifted to the edge of her seat. "I have caught him in a lie."

"Dishonesty isn't good," remarked Violet. "You want to know where you stand with a fellow."

"It depends on what he is being evasive about." Zia Paulina turned to Angelina. "Apart from his possible lies, what are your other objections?"

"He has an unhealthy obsession with Grace, and I do not think he can wait," she replied. "Grace is not ready."

"I agree with you there. He does seem impatient," said Zia Paulina. "But on his side, he is impeccably dressed, he is gentlemanly, and he is very attentive to Grace. I think he genuinely cares about her."

"That's what I think." Grace lifted her head.

"He seems rich." Violet nibbled at a raisin cookie. "He's got money to burn on a Steinway and an apartment in an expensive part of Georgetown."

"He must have a sizable income," remarked Grace.

"And we do not know how he got it." Angelina sipped her wine. "His money might be tainted."

"I still don't understand why the fellow would lie," said Violet. "What does he have to lie about?"

"He is proud and ambitious," said Zia Paulina slowly. "Perhaps he is ashamed of his origins. Perhaps he comes from Italian peasant stock, like us."

"Grace," said Angelina. "You must be on your guard. There is something suspicious going on."

"Are you going to forbid me from seeing him?"

"No," said Zia Paulina. "But for heavens sake, be careful, child."

"You should not trust him, Graziella," said Angelina. "Listen carefully to everything he says."

"I don't want to be a spy."

"No one is asking you to be a spy," said Zia Paulina. "We just want you to be careful."

"He might break your heart," remarked Angelina. "Men have roving eyes."

"What am I supposed to do?" Grace burst out in an uncharacteristically forceful way. "He asked my permission to escort me to my violin lesson, and I told him yes. Are you saying I shouldn't walk with him?"

Zia Paulina slowly rose and took Grace's face in her hands. "Do you want someone to go with you?"

Grace lowered her lashes. "I don't think so," she said quietly.

"Pay attention, *cara*," said Zia Paulina. "If he makes improper advances or makes you feel uncomfortable in any way, I want to know."

Grace nodded.

"Dio!" Angelina expelled air in a gust of frustration as she moved into the tiny foyer to pick up her hat and gloves. "I will write to the abbot of St Francis de Sales tonight. I must find out more about him."

"Speaking of letters," said Zia Paulina, and here she hesitated for a moment—long enough for the others to fidget and look at each other. "I just received a note from your sister Josephina, enclosing a letter she received from Jerome Pagano."

"From Girolamo?" Angelina moved eagerly back into the front parlor. "*Perbacco*, I forgot all about him."

"Who's he?" asked Violet.

"My half-brother. He is a year younger than me."

"Josephina writes that she had not heard from him in years, and then he sent her this letter, informing her that Franco had died."

"Papa dead?" Angelina sank onto the loveseat, trying to take this in. Slowly, she realized she had been waiting all these years for Papa to speak to her again, to tell her what she had done wrong. Now, he was forever silent.

"He died of a heart attack in Chicago."

"Chicago?" Angelina stared at her aunt. "I thought he went back to Italy."

"What makes you think that? Didn't you know I sent a card every Christmas to Chicago?"

Angelina was silent. How come she hadn't known?

"I remember how happy he was when he married your mother, Teresa, in 1882." Zia Paulina's voice broke. She cleared her throat, and continued. "I haven't seen him in years. The last time was just before I left Italy, in 1885. That would be thirty-six years."

"I had no idea he was here." Angelina stared at her hands. If she had known, she would have tried to visit. Except he would not have been pleased to see her. Angelina turned to her aunt. "I was always fond of Lamo. I suppose I must get used to calling him *Jerome*, his American name."

"But you haven't seen him in over twenty years," remarked Zia Paulina.

"I know. But I never forgot the time when my stepmother punished me for ruining her dress. She caned me with birch twigs. He tried to take my place. He was always kind to me when I got into scrapes with that bitch—"

"Angelina!" exclaimed Zia Paulina.

Angelina made a face. "I mean my dearly beloved stepmother." She rose. "Did he say anything about Nico?"

"Nico?" Violet looked up.

"He's Lamo's younger brother."

Zia Paulina frowned. "I don't think so. How strange. I hope everything is all right."

✠✠✠✠✠✠✠✠✠✠✠

It seemed as if all of Georgetown had come to Professor Burneys's soirée to hear his star pupil and her exciting new pianist. Angelina clasped her hands in her lap as Russell walked on stage behind Grace. What would a stranger make of him, a handsome young man, elegantly attired in black tie, who sat down, turned a gentle smile in the direction of her daughter, and played the D minor chord for her to tune her violin to? Angelina gritted her teeth.

The *D Minor Sonata* began sweetly, with an airy theme developed by the violin. Not more than a minute passed, however, before the violin found itself entangled in a passionate debate with the piano. Grace, however, managed to imbue this sonata with her dreamy personality. Russell, taking his cue from her, dexterously lightened the force that he applied to the piano keys and slowed his speed.

The second movement theme emerged as if in a haze, with her double-stops sounding smooth and richly passionate above his background murmurings. He started the third movement with an insistent theme that dissolved into a virtuosic descending flourish that announced her theme. In this movement, she seemed to find her way through the dense three- and four-note chords with ease. Her closing double-stops went up and down dreamily, perfectly in tune. The fourth movement opened in a stormy fashion, with his triplet figure followed by her ardent theme. Again, she played the quieter sections with a dreamy quality to her tone, which made the contrast with the stormy passages even more dramatic. In the middle section of the sonata, she wound the theme up smoothly from a quietly meditative state into a fervent exclamation. The closing section started with a strong bottom chord from the pianist, which led to more fire from the violin. But even here, she allowed for some sweetly quiet moments.

As the sonata closed, Angelina clenched her hands so tightly together, her manicured nails bit into the flesh. There was something about the expression on Russell's face that told her he was making a private vow to win Grace, whatever the cost.

There was a pause, then the room erupted into cheers.

Russell's face was radiant, washed by some strong emotion; Angelina could almost see the tentacles of energy creeping towards her daughter. Perhaps Grace noticed it too, for she turned scarlet as she took her bow.

Russell disappeared backstage, returning to present her with an enormous bouquet of red roses. Angelina's face tightened as Grace crimsoned up to the roots of her hair. Then he moved closer, put a hand on her arm, and whispered something in her ear. It was his stance as much as anything that disturbed Angelina.

He already looked like Grace's husband.

He continued to act like that for the rest of the evening, lacing his fingers through Grace's as he introduced her to Father Walsh, caressing her hand with his thumb as Professor Burneys congratulated him, insisting that she sit down while he went back and forth to bring her sandwiches and refreshments. All Georgetown looked on in amusement and a great deal of anticipation.

Finally, Angelina could stand it no more.

"How is your brother, Mr. Russell?" she said, as soon as she was able to get to him. "I understand he is studying to be a priest."

His face hardened; he glowered at her. "How dare you pry into my personal affairs," he whispered.

"I am not prying," retorted Angelina, not whispering. "I am merely trying to find out information about my daughter's suitor. As her mother, I have a right to know who you are."

Russell clenched his jaw as his face paled. *Bene.* Somehow she had found a way of getting under his skin.

"Angelina," said Zia Paulina in a low tone. "You are making a scene and upsetting Grace."

Angelina turned. Grace looked stricken.

"*Graziella, cara,*" she said. "I did not mean to hurt *you.*" But Grace turned away.

Zia Paulina steered Russell towards the refreshment table. The other guests eddied around Angelina, their faces averted, as if she were a piece of furniture, while Grace drooped beside her, awkwardly holding an empty plate. Several times Angelina tried to think of something to say to her daughter, but the words dried on her lips.

She turned to the refreshment table and saw Russell standing there in front of Zia Paulina, his hand to his heart, his eyes glowing darkly. Worst of all, her aunt was leaning towards him, her hand on his arm, the tilt of her head making her look almost flirtatious. Angelina took a step towards them but was stopped by the appearance of Professor Burneys carrying a leather portfolio full of music.

"Grace!" He pecked her daughter on the cheek. "I'm so proud of you. You did wonders tonight." He eyed Angelina and turned back to Grace. "Shall we go and speak to your magnificent pianist?" As Grace dipped her chin, he chuckled.

Angelina trailed behind, wondering how much of a part Burneys had played in promoting the romance. Had he suggested that Russell escort her daughter to her violin lesson? Now he was clapping Grace's suitor on the back and shaking his hand vigorously.

"That was a wonderful performance, sir. You inspired Grace to reach new heights. She played like an angel, didn't she?"

"Indeed, she did."

Grace relaxed into an answering smile, her usually quiet face becoming more animated.

"I have great plans for Grace," remarked Burneys. "I think she is ready to consider a solo career."

Grace straightened up, looking taller and more confident. She lifted her face as if meeting the warmth of the sun.

"I want her to study the Brahms concerto," continued Burneys. "But first, I think she should tackle the Beethoven concerto. What do you think?"

Russell grazed her with a dark smile.

"Beethoven is not kind to his solo violinist with those broken octaves at the beginning. However, I am sure Grace can handle it. Her intonation was flawless tonight."

"What a cruel thing to do to a violinist, but so typical of Maestro Beethoven." Burneys rummaged in his portfolio and handed Grace some music. "Broken octaves are hard to get in tune. Here are some special scales to practice."

It was insupportable. Angelina had to leave.

"Graziella." She pecked her daughter's cheek. "I must go. Come and see me on Sunday, after Mass. I have some things for you and Violetta."

Grace narrowed her eyes and looked away.

Angelina skewered Russell with a look as sharp as a dagger's thrust before sweeping out.

✠✠✠✠✠✠✠✠✠✠✠

Angelina seethed as she walked west towards her apartment in the West Village. Things were slipping beyond her control. It had been a little over six weeks since Grace had set eyes on Russell, and somehow that disagreeable fellow was getting to her. Under his gentle assault, she was softening. Angelina cursed herself under her breath for not paying more attention to Grace, for not arming her with the tools for dealing with predatory men. What was she going to do?

Angelina was so engrossed in her thoughts, she did not notice that her footsteps led her onto Bank Street. She looked up as she arrived in front of Russell's lodgings. Whatever was she doing here? If he found her, he would surely think she had some malign intent. She must leave. Angelina turned, retracing her steps, when she heard soft jerky steps coming from the other direction. A figure wandered into view, and tensed, perhaps seeing her standing there in the shadows. He scanned the quiet street in an expert fashion before moving swiftly and silently to a tree, which stood about thirty feet away from her and provided cover.

Angelina walked back to the tree, which stood directly in front of his lodgings, and stared. It was Russell. What had happened to him?

"Mr. Russell," she said softly.

He slowly peered around the tree.

"Damn," he muttered, coming out into the open, standing under the lamp that lit his front door.

"Why are you acting like that?"

"Like what?"

"You were acting strangely."

"I have seen things you cannot imagine."

Angelina folded her arms. "You think it is a good idea to marry my daughter," her voice rose, "when you are one step away from the insane asylum?"

"Angelina, don't exaggerate. Do you think I would have got into Georgetown if I couldn't function properly? Sometimes the war gets to me. That is all."

"*Per l'amor di Dio*, for the love of God she is only seventeen. How could you be so selfish? Have you considered that she might not *want* to be married to a war veteran?"

His face hardened into a white mask as he turned to open the door to his lodgings.

"If you do not stop seeing my daughter, I will write to your brother." Angelina had penned a letter already to the abbot, but so far she had received no reply.

He stopped, his hand on the doorknob.

"He is at the St. Francis de Sales Seminary in Milwaukee, Wisconsin." Her voice echoed up and down the quiet lane. It was nearly midnight, and the windows of nearly all the houses were dark.

"You wouldn't do that," he remarked in an undertone, laced with an edge of menace.

"You have not told your brother about Graziella, have you?" she said in her high, penetrating voice. The echoes reverberated.

"Angelina—"

"Why not?"

"Angelina." He came towards her, his voice low. "Keep out of this."

"Why?"

"You don't know my brother."

"How do you know that?"

He stopped dead, his face draining of color. She had got under his skin again. But why this glimmer of fear in his face?

"Why do you hate me?" he said. "What have I ever done to you?"

"You have caused me a great deal of inconvenience," said she, her bell-like voice projecting into the rapidly cooling air. "You spread gossip."

"I did not," he whispered, his voice low. "I was only asking questions."

"About me?" she said, coming closer. "Now why would you be so interested in me? Why were you following me around?"

Out of the corner of her eye, Angelina saw a drape twitching. She smiled. He was under a door light with her, for all the world to see.

"I wasn't following you around." He glided back towards the shadowy street.

"You were," she exclaimed, now in full performance. "You talked to Hammond and Dr. Jackson. You kept asking for Angelina Miller or Paulina Barilla." She emphasized each name. "But not Violet, or Grace."

"Angelina," he hissed. "Shut up."

A sudden thought occurred to her. "How strange," she said, raising her face to the waning moon, which had the effect of projecting her voice still further, "that your brother has a different last name than you."

His fingers clenched around an iron railing that edged the small garden in front of his lodgings.

"Aha," she said jabbing a finger at him. "You did not know I had found that out. I asked Father Walsh, and he showed me your records."

He shot out of the shadows and grabbed her arm, his steel fingers sinking into her soft flesh.

"Leave me alone, you bitch," he spat, droplets hitting her face.

Angelina grimaced and twisted away, but he clung on.

"I will leave you alone the day you leave my daughter alone," she screamed to the accompaniment of twitching drapes.

Chapter Six

Sunday, 23 October

"Graziella!" Angelina's smile filled her face as she rose and gave her younger daughter a peck on the cheek. The last time she'd seen her, the tensions between them had spilled over at the Burneys' soirée. How wonderful that Grace had actually showed up.

"How long have you been standing there?"

"Not long." Grace glanced at the papers piled high on the table in front of her mother.

"I am working on an Italian translation," remarked Angelina. "*La Grazia* by Grazia Deledda."

Grace tipped her head back as she took in the room. She looked surprised. Of course it would be disorienting for Grace; Angelina had not had a chance to tell her about her new life. She would not be used to seeing her mother wearing glasses—or a pastel-colored summer frock with a gently scooped neckline. Angelina would look strange in pearl earrings and no makeup. Most of all, she would not expect her mother to sit in front of a heap of papers and apply herself like this.

"I have to make money somehow." The apartment was paid up until March, then Angelina would have to support herself.

The silence lengthened as Grace continued to stand there awkwardly. Angelina rose and put her glasses on top of her dictionary.

"Sit down, Grace. I have some things for you in the bedroom."

She returned with three shopping bags laden with dresses and accessories. Angelina pulled out a gray silk gown.

"This matches your eyes."

Grace squinted at herself in the mirror without smiling.

"You don't like what you see," exclaimed Angelina. "Graziella, you are beautiful. Don't you realize that?"

Grace touched her cheek. "Mr. Russell said something like that."

Cazzo, F***. He was spoiling things for Grace's future suitors by being the first in everything: the first to give her flowers, the first to take her out, and now the first man to tell her she was lovely. After their row, she was at her wit's end, as it was clear he was not going to yield over Grace. In the sleepless nights that followed, Angelina had resolved to deal with Russell through Grace. If only she could persuade Grace that she didn't need him. But she would have to move gently, or Grace would close her mouth and refuse to speak.

"Why do you like him?" she said now, as she propelled her daughter gently to the loveseat, and sat down beside her.

Grace fiddled with the cuffs of her blouse, and looked down.

"He's a good pianist."

Angelina leaned forward. "You don't have to tell me what you think I want to hear, Graziella," she said quietly. "I think you like him more than that. Why?"

"I think he really cares about me."

Angelina felt a surge of irritation, which she squashed. "Tell me what you mean."

Grace looked down as she twisted her fingers in her lap. "It was before the last soirée, when we were getting ready. Mr. Russell was there, and Mrs. Burneys was helping me. She lent me some ivory-colored shoes to match that ivory dress that belonged to Aunt Paulina. I was worried because I didn't want to look too pretty."

"You don't you want to look pretty?" exclaimed Angelina. "Why not?"

Grace gave a large, gusty sigh. "It's so frustrating when people pinch my cheek, and say all sorts of silly things. I'm an artist, and I want them to see that."

Angelina, surprised, appraised her daughter. Grace was so quiet that it was easy to imagine she was meek and could be coaxed into doing what others wanted, like making a great match for the family. But now, things were not so simple.

Of course Angelina knew she loved to play her violin, but she thought it was a hobby. Did her daughter really want to play to strangers? Did she really want to travel from one large city to another as a professional concert artist? Russell had said he had the money to take her to Europe, where she could play with the best musicians in the world. In that regard, he had read Grace more accurately than her own mother. Perhaps she would like to go abroad to study. Perhaps she had ambitions to own a priceless Stradivarius.

Angelina bent her head as she studied her hands with their perfect nails. It sounded so glamorous and adventurous, far more than she had imagined for her own daughter. But then, it was so much more than Angelina had dreamt for herself. When Angelina had been Grace's age, she had no plans beyond surviving day to day on a remote farm, with in-laws she disliked, an absent young husband, and two tiny children. Before her shotgun wedding to Perry Miller at age fourteen, Angelina had no dreams beyond returning to that farm outside of Marostica. Zia Paulina had tried to interest her in various things—voice, piano or guitar, embroidery, knitting or quilting, books, newspapers or language lessons. Nothing took.

Angelina continued staring at her nails, repressing tears. She was happy that her daughters had ambition, of course she was. But how she longed to have a piece of this changing world, a world that was becoming a little kinder to women, before it was too late. She let out a sigh. She should stop thinking about herself and focus on Grace. It went without saying that she would want a pianist of Russell's caliber. *But she doesn't have to marry him.* Angelina lifted her head.

"Did you tell Mr. Russell you wanted to be an artist?"

"Yes," said Grace.

"Wasn't he put off?"

"No." Grace lifted her head, her gray eyes sharpening with vibrancy. "He asked me if I wanted to be a professional, like Alma Moodie."

Dio! How in the world had Russell known exactly what to say to her daughter? Alma Moodie was four years older than Grace and had taken Europe by storm with her violin playing when she was only thirteen. She was Grace's heroine.

"Mrs. Burneys said I had the talent, and Mr. Russell agreed. Then he scrutinized the way I looked. He liked my ivory lace frock, saying that the long skirts gave me an air of dignity."

Angelina smiled despite her irritation. It was a family joke that Grace did not like short skirts. Again, Russell had an unerring sense about her daughter.

"Mrs. Burneys remarked that young women these days use makeup to make themselves seem older," continued Grace, "but I told them I wasn't a flapper. I'm not jazzy or hard-edged. It isn't my style."

"What did he say?"

"He agreed."

Of course. Angelina simmered, exasperated.

"Then I asked him if I looked like a serious artist, and he said I should have my hair done in a chignon, as it would make me look older. Mrs. Burneys wanted to give me makeup, but Mr. Russell said I didn't need lipstick. He recommended a little kohl around my eyes and a touch of rouge on my cheeks."

How had he become an expert on makeup? Angelina tried to imagine Russell dressing as a woman but failed.

"He was right," continued Grace. "When I stepped back to look at myself, I did look older and more sophisticated. Yet I looked myself."

"Did he say anything else?"

"I told him how much my violin meant to me, and he promised that I could always count on him."

Then he kissed your hand, I suppose. Angelina stifled that sarcastic comment as she rose and opened a shopping bag.

"Why don't you try this on?" She handed Grace a large straw hat trimmed in brown grosgrain.

Grace looked at herself in the mirror. This time she smiled.

"It suits you," said Angelina. "It is time you had something new to wear. I do not need these any more." She rummaged in her shopping bags, bringing out frocks, shoes, purses, and hats.

They spent a pleasant afternoon examining her wardrobe, while Celia Stephenson arrived with tea and cookies, staying to provide advice. At length, Angelina packed away her clothes in two suitcases, one for Grace and one for Violet, and asked Celia to call a cab.

"You know, Grace." She laid her arm around her younger daughter's shoulders and brought her face close, close enough so that their cheeks touched. "You have so much talent, perhaps you should study at a music conservatory. Would you like me to find out how to apply to the Institute of Musical Art in New York City?"

Grace's smile suffused her face.

"If you got in, you could live with Aunt Louisa."

"Would she mind?"

"Of course not. She would be happy to help you, Grace." Angelina kissed her daughter as the cab drew up.

It was hard to say *addio*.

✠✠✠✠✠✠✠✠✠✠✠

It was October the twenty-fifth, and the weather was turning cool. Violet shut Miss Bernice's front door behind her as she made her way down the steps onto Dunbarton Street and turned right to walk over to Mother's. She'd gone to Miss Bernice's early that morning to finish up the hem on Mother's new cotton frock and to get advice on what to make her for the fall. She shifted the wicker basket from one arm to another. Miss Bernice had given her several patterns for dresses and skirts, even finding a piece of leftover fabric that was large enough to make a dress. Violet peered into the basket. Yes, Mother's new dress was there, wrapped up in tissue paper. Violet was designing a new look for her, so the dress was not in her usual flamboyant style. Instead it had a jewel neckline, capped sleeves that came down to the middle of the upper arm, and subdued coloring. What would she think?

"I like it." Mother stood before the mirror, wearing the finished dress. It was made out of olive-green cotton, with a full skirt, cap sleeves, and a slightly dropped waistline, which Violet had outlined in a dull-gold belt. Dull-gold piping highlighted the jewel neck and sleeves.

"I adapted the design from one I found in Miss Bernice's copy of the *Gazette du Bon Genre*."

"It is the new me."

"Yes." Violet placed the wicker basket that contained all her sewing supplies on the floor. "Gone is the glamor puss."

Mother laughed.

"Miss Bernice had some leftover material that I thought you'd like for the cooler weather." Violet took out a length of fine woolen jersey, which was soft to the touch and had a good drape. While Mother looked at Miss Bernice's patterns and made her choice, Violet fished around in her pocket.

"I can't find my tailor's chalk. What's this?" Violet drew something out. "Oh, it's for you. Auntie P. got it yesterday and asked me to give it to you."

Mother smoothed the crumpled piece of paper and read it aloud:

> Dear Mrs. Barilla,
>
> I am sorry to bother you, but I think you should know that my tenant, Mr. Russell, has threatened to leave. He says he doesn't feel comfortable having lodgings near your niece, Mrs. Miller, especially as she makes a habit of walking past and glaring at him every day. It unsettles him.
>
> It's not right to intrude on a gentleman's privacy, and I'm not surprised Mr. Russell is angry and upset.
>
> I know it is a lot to ask, but I was wondering if you would mind speaking to Mrs. Miller. Mr. Russell is such a good tenant, I couldn't bear to lose him. As a widow, I'm sure you'll appreciate that.
>
> Sincerely yours,
> Olivia Santucci
> (Mrs. Blake Rittenhouse)

Mother smiled. "*Bene,*" she said. "I am succeeding after all."

"You're succeeding in upsetting him." Violet picked up a pair of scissors and began to cut out the pattern.

Mother put the note down. "He is lying about something. I found out his brother has a different last name."

"How did you find that out?"

"I worked it out of Russell."

"I bet he wasn't pleased about that." Violet began to pin the bodice.

Mother threw her head back, her tinkling laugh spilling out.

"What is his brother's name?"

"He wouldn't tell me."

"He must be his half-brother then."

"I suppose. We must get Grace away from him. He has to stay here for another couple of years until he completes his degree. I have already talked to Grace about applying to the Institute of Musical Art in New York City."

"I hadn't thought we'd be saying goodbye to Grace so soon." Violet rummaged in her basket for some pinking shears.

"Why do we have to say goodbye to her, Violetta? He should be the one saying *addio*. Perhaps we all should leave. You have learned a lot over the years by poring over fashion magazines and whatever Miss Bernice could teach you. But you could take classes in fashion design in New York—even be apprenticed to someone."

Violet glowed as she finished pinning the bodice. "I really will be able to have my own shop." She began cutting the fabric. "I wonder what will happen to us."

Mother leaned forward and patted Violet's hand. "You will be all right, Violetta. I just feel it in my bones. You will do whatever you set your heart on."

"How are we going to pay for it?" Violet started on the sleeves.

"I believe that Zia Paulina will agree with me about this. We could put our money together. I could find more work."

"It will be strange leaving Georgetown."

"You girls are both growing up so fast. I need to make sure you both start out on your best foot." Mother opened her dictionary. "Before Mamma died, I had a happy childhood in Marostica." Her voice became dreamy. "She was the kindest person in the world. I still remember how she would take us out for picnics, even though we didn't have much. She would make Pandora cake with her own limoncello, she would soak left-over risotto in almond milk and serve it with home-made preserves. We would swing down that lane together, Giuseppina, Luisa, and me in the summer frocks she made for us. She used to smock the bodices so that they would last longer—"

"Giuseppina is Aunt Josephina, isn't she?" Violet finished cutting out the sleeves and started on the skirt.

"Papa made us have American names. He made Giuseppina become Josephina, Luisa become Louisa, and Girolamo, Jerome. But I rebelled. He wanted to call me Angela, but I wouldn't do it."

"Wasn't there another brother?"

"Nico. I don't have such vivid memories of him."

"Why's that?"

"He was a quiet boy, rather like Grace. When I last saw him, he was only four years old. He's six years younger than me."

Violet unpinned the bodice pattern from the material. "Why did you leave Marostica?"

"It was Rosa's fault, she was so jealous." Mother's face tensed up. "Papa wanted a party to say *addio* to everyone before we left. Our family had farmed the land for centuries, so we were related to everyone in the small villages around and about."

"So if we were to go there now, we'd meet tons of relatives?"

"*È vero,* truly I never thought of going back there."

"Perhaps we should." Violet rolled the raw edges of the fabric and pinned. "What did Rosa do?"

Mother's eyes glittered. "We were to have new frocks, which was uncommon as Rosa skimped on our clothes. Louisa was trying on hers in the kitchen when Rosa came in and started screaming. I took Louisa's part and earned a beating. Papa was furious about the whole thing. He blamed it on us, saying he was tired of all the arguments we had with our mamma." Mother turned back to her work. "Rosa wasn't our mamma, of course. Our real mother was dead."

"But how would having a row with your stepmother cause you to be kicked off your land?"

Mother shrugged. "The *padrone* could do as he liked—we were only tenant farmers. I do not think he liked Papa, he wanted us gone." She paused. "Papa always hoped Jerome would become a lawyer so that he could sue and get our land back. But now he is studying to become a priest."

Violet rummaged in her bag, looking for more pins, then she drew out a fan. It was black, red, and white, displaying an elegant lady in a kimono sitting in front of her mirror, while her maid did her hair.

"That's where it is. I found it in your room at Beall Street, tucked in the back of the closet."

Mother's hand flew to her bosom. "*Cielo sopra,* that is Mamma's fan. Your Aunt Louisa saved it from the flames."

"What flames?"

"When Rosa became Papa's second wife, she celebrated by making a bonfire of all of Mamma's things."

"Why did she do that?"

Mother rose, wandered over to the window, and looked out. "*Non lo so,* I do not know." Absently, she plucked a pink rose out of a vase, and shred its petals. "All I remember is the bitter cold of a night in February, with snow on the ground, and air as sharp as a razor's blade. And then I remember the ashes, piles and piles of it, as the dust from that fire swirled up into mountain wind and scattered."

"You've never told me this before."

"It is too painful." Mother's voice broke. "There was nothing left of Mamma. Nothing at all."

Violet moved across the room and put an arm around her shoulder.

"What did Grand-mamma look like?"

Mother turned, the waning light showing the tears streaming down her cheeks, her face ravaged.

"She looked exactly like Graziella."

Chapter Seven
Friday, 28 October

"It's Mr. Russell. He wants to see you." The door opened, and Celia Stephenson's bobbed head appeared around it.

Angelina hesitated. It had been exactly a week since Professor Burneys' soirée, but she did not need to see him, she had other plans for Grace. All she had to do was discuss them with Zia Paulina. Perhaps she should not see him, and yet—

"Send him up, please."

"I'm going to spend this evening in Alexandria, with my sister." Celia turned, her silver sheath-like gown catching the light of the setting sun.

Angelina nodded, eyes returning to the text in front of her.

He knocked on the half-open door a moment later.

Angelina kept to her seat, looking at him over her glasses.

He stopped as he came in, gaze scanning her room, taking in everything in an expert fashion, just as he had when she first met him in the bookstore. At last, his eyes came to rest on her. After registering surprise for an instant, his expression softened into a smile.

He thinks I am dressed well enough to be his mother-in-law.

"I thought you might like a gift." He made his small bow as he produced a box tied up in red, white, and green ribbons from a modest canvas bag.

She stiffened. "*Perché*?"

He sat opposite her, unasked, placing the box in his lap, shoving the bag under the chair.

"If only you understood how much Grace means to me."

Angelina wasn't prepared for such a naked plea. She took off her glasses to scrutinize his face. What did he mean? He sounded like a drowning man clutching at a straw, and that straw was Grace.

"We do not have anything to discuss. Graziella is a minor and cannot marry without my permission. And I am not giving it. She has better things to do with her life than marry you."

"I disagree," he said with a degree of composure that made the backs of her arms prickle with unease. "I have plenty of funds, enough to take Grace around the world and finance her career. And I would hope that you would take an interest in being on friendly terms with your son-in-law and not cause trouble."

"This is what this visit is about." Angelina pushed her papers away. "You want to stay with Mrs. Rittenhouse."

"Mrs. Rittenhouse wishes me to stay with her. I come to you with a box of Italian pastries in the hopes that we might sweeten our relationship. Your dislike of me is so extreme, it is causing a great deal of comment. I thought we should try again."

"But I do not care about your opinion," retorted Angelina.

"You should," he remarked calmly, folding his arms. "It is not fair to put Grace in the middle of a—war."

"You speak as if you are already engaged to her."

"We plan to announce our engagement soon."

"But I do not give my consent."

"Mrs. Barilla does." He fished in the pocket of his brown jacket and drew out a letter. "She was good enough to share this with me. It's from my brother." He handed her the typed page.

`My Dear Mrs. Barilla,`

Thank you for writing to me. I appreciate how loath you are to part with your great-niece to someone you do not know. My brother and I have had many telephone conversations, and I think his love for Grace is serious.

"Zia Paulina wrote to him? How did she get his address?"

"She didn't tell you?"

Angelina shook her head and continued to read.

As for my brother, I can assure you he is the kindest man in the world, who would make any woman a fine husband. Ever since he was a boy, my brother has loved having animals around him. Cats, dogs, even horses, would come up to him to be petted. Thus, Grace would be in safe hands were she to marry him.

In closing, I would like you to know I am at your disposal should you have any further questions. I expect to be ordained at Easter and will be posted to Catholic University. I hope we will finally be able to meet soon.

Believe me,
Very sincerely yours,

Angelina peered at the scrawl of a signature, but could not make it out.

"I hoped we might put the past behind us, now that we're about to be related." He held his hand out for the letter.

Without thinking, Angelina handed it over. Sounds receded. Everything slowed, becoming waterlogged, as if she were sinking into a dank pool. How had this happened? She had meant to go to Zia Paulina to discuss Graziella, but had got behind on her translation. It never occurred to her he could pull this off. Why had Zia Paulina agreed?

"Please believe me, Mrs. Miller, when I say that I love your daughter very much."

His quiet voice barely intruded on her thoughts. What was going through Zia Paulina's head? *È vero,* truly she had been so adamant about Grace's career. Had Angelina's fears about Grace not being strong enough to survive in a man's world changed her mind?

"Why don't you join me in a drink?" His voice was soft and beguiling.

Scott used to like her to make him a drink after a day in the office. But how could she have so blithely mixed whiskey and soda for him when she should have been home with her daughters?

"I believe you have some left-over amaretto."

Her family had punished her for this. When had she last seen her sisters? Their faces seemed forever veiled in youth.

He returned from her tiny kitchen with the bottle and two shot glasses.

Zia Paulina visited them regularly and must have endured their well-meaning questions about her. But then she had to deal with all of Georgetown.

He poured a measure for both, and lifted his glass. "Let's drink to Grace."

On their many walks through the village, Saturdays for shopping, Sundays for going to Mass, Zia Paulina would be in front with the children, Angelina bringing up the rear in her flashy clothes, trailing looks and whispers.

They clinked glasses. Angelina inhaled the distinctive bitter scent of *mandorla amara* as she swallowed the sweet liquid.

Zia Paulina wore an aura of protection around her that extended to Violetta and Graziella. She would gently propel

Angelina's girls into various shops and while she was there people were polite, deferential even.

He found some plates, napkins, and forks, opened the box, and arranged the pastries on a plate. There were Venetian *baicoli,* Tuscan *panforte,* and some *bruttiboni* from Prato.

She was well-liked for her warmth and generosity, she never forgot people's troubles and often helped out from her own purse. But when Angelina was by herself, tagging along in Zia Paulina's wake, they eyed her unkindly and did not trouble to lower their voices.

"Mrs. Barilla assured me you were very fond of the *bruttiboni,*" he remarked, his tongue shaping the words with the faintest lilt of Italian.

Russell had been coldly disapproving, the smile fading from his face as he studied her.

Angelina took a bite. The almond-flavored cookies exploded in her mouth, enhanced by the lingering taste of the amaretto.

He used these family tensions to take control.

"You're hungry," he remarked, offering her another one.

Control over Grace.

"You must have forgotten to eat today."

It was her fault. She had failed her daughter in all ways. Now there was nothing she could do to stop him.

Nothing.

Niente.

Impotente.

Angelina gasped for breath, her stomach knotting.

He eyed her keenly. "*Buono*?"

"*Squisito,*" she replied, sinking back into her chair. She clutched the arms of her chair, trying to sit up. She opened her mouth to speak, but was overcome with dizziness and nausea.

Within minutes, she'd blacked out.

He sat still for many moments. When the silence was truly silent, he fished a pair of black leather gloves out of the canvas bag he'd shoved under the chair and put the amaretto bottle and shot glasses into it. He cleaned up the vomit, swept up the crumbs, and placed the pastry box, with its colorful ribbons, under the bed.

He listened again. There was no sound.

He went into the kitchen and found Angelina's bottle of pink pills, the arsenic and mercury treatment her doctor was giving her for stomach ailments, possibly syphilis. He went into the bedroom, placed the pink pills on Angelina's nightstand, and pulled down the blanket and top sheet of the bed.

He came back into the living room with the pink silk kimono he'd found under her pillow. Only then did he hesitate. He could hardly believe he'd snuffed her out. Cyanide worked as fast as lightning, as quickly as those medical books had promised. Of course he'd murdered people before, it was part of his duty as a soldier in wartime. But he'd never done the act quite so cold-bloodedly. And now he had to partially undress her to wrap her up in this kimono because he needed the authorities to believe she'd died in her sleep tonight.

He took a deep breath and swallowed. This was going to be hard, she looked so peaceful, so pretty, her chestnut curls enticing him into a caress. But he had to ignore that, he had to squash his sorrow and doubt. She shouldn't have interfered, she shouldn't have invaded his privacy, she shouldn't have threatened to expose him. Tightening his mouth into a thin line, he relieved Angelina of her shoes and frock, wrapped her in the kimono, picked her up, placed her in her bed, pulling the blanket and sheet back over her torso. He hung the clothes she'd been wearing on hangers in her wardrobe, then walked slowly around the quiet apartment, examining everything carefully, erasing it if necessary.

Finally, he took his gloves off, picked up the canvas bag, placed his hat on his head, closed the door softly behind him, and crept downstairs. Once outside he scanned the street, then stepped into the darkening evening, making his way to the C & O Canal.

✠✠✠✠✠✠✠✠✠✠✠

Violet wasn't crazy about that smoothy. Maybe she found his dark gaze unsettling. Maybe it was because she couldn't believe a fellow would be such a perfect gent. In any event, Violet came to see Russell as an inescapable part of her Saturday morning. She was a natural early riser; he was always there, always earlier than her, waiting to escort Grace to her violin lesson, while Grace struggled to get out of bed.

As always, this Saturday he rose from his seat, *The Washington Post* in his hands as Violet descended the stairs. By now, it was the very end of October, the twenty-ninth, and Mr. Russell showed no sign of going away. He was more stuck on Grace than ever, if such a thing were possible. As usual he was neat, his suit clean, his shoes shined, his hair brushed back from his forehead.

"Grace will be down soon." Violet answered the unspoken question that hung heavily in the quiet morning air.

Mr. Russell nodded and resumed his seat, disappearing behind his paper as she left.

The cool air of a late October morning kissed her cheeks as Violet strolled along Beall Street, admiring the leaves. She touched one pink-red leaf of a maple tree that drooped gracefully over the white planks of a picket fence. She had Mother's new dress in her bag; she'd visit this morning.

Violet crossed High and doglegged onto Second. What was going to happen next in the ongoing battle between

Mother and Mr. Russell? Mother had written to the abbott of that place in Wisconsin, but heard nothing. Was the silence ominous? Violet turned left onto Potomac Street. Mother didn't know the name of Russell's relation, his half-brother who was studying to be a priest. But shouldn't she have heard something? It was the last weekend in October, and Violet was sure Mother had written during that first weekend. Nearly a month had passed.

Mrs. Celia Stephenson, Mother's landlady, opened the door a chink, revealing one well-shaped blue eye surrounded by mascara.

"Your mother isn't up yet," she remarked, swinging the door open while her lips curved into a smile. "Would you like me to knock?"

She nodded, while Mrs. Stephenson ran lightly up the stairs, her sleek head bobbing. A moment later, she reappeared.

"She must be sleeping soundly, I can't rouse her. Do you want to go up while I make tea?"

Violet walked up the stairs and knocked on the door.

There was no reply.

She pushed the door and it opened silently. The apartment was quiet, too quiet. Violet went to the bedroom door.

Despite her knock, there was no sound.

She knocked again. "Mother?" Slowly, she turned the knob.

A lingering scent of bitter almonds coiled out. In the gloom of the room, she could make out a shape entwined in the bedsheets. She opened the drapes.

Mother lay on her back, wrapped in her pink kimono, her face youthful in its surprising quietude. Violet hurried across the room.

She placed her fingers around Mother's wrist, but there was no pulse. She bent over her, but there was no breath. She touched her forehead, but it was as cold as marble.

Violet sank to the floor.

There was a rattle of cups.

"Miss Violet?"

Violet opened the bedroom door. The morning light picked out everything with harsh accuracy.

"My God."

Mrs. Stephenson hastily put the tea-tray on Mother's bedside table, knocking over a bottle of pink pills.

"Has she been this way all night?" Mrs. Stephenson sank into a chair.

Violet gagged and disappeared into the bathroom.

✠✠✠✠✠✠✠✠✠✠✠

Later, she did not remember how she walked home, how she went upstairs to Auntie P.'s bedroom, or how she broke the news. Grace was out with Mr. Russell at Professor Burneys, and. Auntie P. would not hear of her being disturbed. They waited all morning, making plans. When she tripped in, Auntie P. broke it to her as gently as she could. Grace paled, but otherwise didn't react. She slipped away to practice her violin, and so Violet and Aunt Paulina left her in the house while they spent the afternoon making arrangements at the Birch Funeral Home, on the corner of Bridge and Jefferson Streets. By the time they came out, Aunt Paulina was looking yellow with fatigue, and so Violet persuaded her to return home while she placed calls to Philadelphia and New York.

✠✠✠✠✠✠✠✠✠✠✠

Grace dragged herself upstairs and slumped into the silent back bedroom, unable to think, unable to feel, the silence of absence washing over her. How drab everything seemed. How could she play her violin now? She looked around. Everything in the room squatted there, in a kind of nothingness. Grace couldn't bear it. Something was better than nothing, so slowly, she opened the case, and untangled her violin from its silken wrappings. Into that silence, she lifted her violin and bow, put her second finger down on the E string, gently put the bow on at the tip, and then built the quiet melody into a rising climax that dissipated into a rush of downward-moving sixteenth notes. There was a pause, and she repeated the music a tone higher.

Mother had gone. She was never coming back. Grace put the violin on her bed and walked around the room, rolling her shoulders and doing neck exercises. Mother wouldn't be around to make unpleasant scenes. She wouldn't be around to interfere with her growing friendship with Mr. Russell. Grace sank onto a chair and stretched her fingers. Certain issues were forever gone. She should be glad. Instead she felt empty. Bleak.

Tears pricked. Mother had been so vivid; now the world was too silent. Grace pressed her lips together and picked up the violin. She became so involved with controlling the ebb and flow of the music, the subtle speeding ups and slowing downs, that she didn't notice someone knocking. When, finally, she put the bow and violin on the bed, she heard it.

"Ma'am, I'm Officer John Ellis from the Metropolitan Police Department of Washington D.C.," he said, showing his badge. "May I come in?"

✠✠✠✠✠✠✠✠✠✠✠

Slowly, reluctantly, Paulina left Violet to make the phone calls, while she walked home, east on Bridge Street, north on Montgomery. All she could focus on was carefully putting one foot in front of the other. For the first time, the fact of Angelina's death began to seep in. Angelina had been only ten years old, a vulnerable child, when she appeared on

Paulina's doorstep all those years ago. Yet Paulina had never thought of her in that way, not since she had learned from her sisters that the reason Franco had sent them all to Georgetown was because Angelina had been so hostile towards her stepmother. Franco's note, which Josephina placed in her hands, explained that Angelina was ungovernable. Things had come to a head just before they left Italy, when Angelina had destroyed Rosa's best dress, ripping it to shreds with a knife. Franco wrote to his sister that his three daughters needed a woman to guide them into maturity, but with his first wife dead, and his second blocked by Angelina's hostility, it had seemed best to pass them on to his gentle, good-natured sister. He ended by telling her that he wanted nothing more to do with his daughters, that he trusted her to do the right thing by them.

Paulina clearly remembered reading her brother's note for the first time and not believing him. After all, family was everything. What did he mean by disowning his daughters? Was Angelina's bad behavior to apply to them all? But as the years rolled slowly on, as she could not get him to reply to news of his daughters' impending marriages, as it had been Luke who escorted first Louisa, then Josephina, and lastly Angelina, down the aisle, she slowly began to realize he meant it, and her feelings towards the girl soured.

She had not been very sympathetic when Angelina finally admitted she was pregnant. Paulina could still see her standing there, hanging her head, as tears rolled down her cheeks. She had been only fourteen, but the thought uppermost in Paulina's mind had been relief that she was to get rid of her troublesome niece earlier than expected, that she could pack her off to her in-laws who lived twenty miles away on a farm outside of Rockville, Maryland. Unfortunately, that did not last long. When it became clear, seven years later, that the young widow was destitute, Paulina had reluctantly invited her back into her home. *But you would never have done that if it had not been for Violet and Grace,* said the voice in her head. Well, who could blame her? Angelina's behavior had been disgraceful from the beginning, with all that carrying-on and the subsequent embarrassment it had cost Paulina. Still, she had a vague feeling that she had never done enough for the girl simply because she had never really liked her, blaming her for Franco's disappearance. Paulina placed her hand against a brick wall to steady herself. That had upset her a great deal, more than she cared to admit.

She stood still for a moment, breathing heavily. She had not been feeling well for about six months now, growing increasingly tired. This was partly the reason why she had agreed to that provisional engagement between Grace and Russell. She sighed as she resumed her plodding. How much longer did she have? She could probably make it through next spring, perhaps the summer. But after that, the future stretched into an unknowable darkness. It was such a relief to find that Grace had attracted a young man whom everyone thought highly of. Professor Burneys found him a marvelous partner for Grace's musical ambitions. Mrs. Burneys spoke about his compassion and evident love for Grace. Father Walsh was telling everyone that he was his most promising student, and that he expected him to rise high in the State Department. Her precious Grace would be safe in the hands of this devoted gentleman. He seemed so sincere, and there was something about the way in which he had made his declaration at Professor Burneys's soirée, his promise that he would keep Grace forever safe. It instilled such confidence.

She stopped again to catch her breath. Everything was beginning to seem like such a mountain to climb, and now that Grace was safe, she wanted to conserve her last energy to do something for Violet. Violet was not as strikingly beautiful as Grace, she was not as obviously talented, she was not as sensitive, but she kept the family together. She was the only one who had been able to get through to Angelina, and she had sustained her great-aunt through many difficulties. Paulina desperately wanted to make her dream of opening a boutique in Georgetown come true, before it was too late.

She turned the corner into Beall Street, walked up to her modest home, and opened the front door. A wave of queasiness washed over her. She had not eaten, the day's dramatic events driving all thoughts of food out of her head. There was the *Washington Star,* the afternoon paper, placed next to her armchair in the front parlor. Paulina sagged into her chair and picked it up.

DEAD WOMAN HAD A PAST.

DAUGHTER ENGAGED THE DAY HER MOTHER PASSES.

Underneath this headline on the front page was a large photograph of Grace standing beside Russell. Her eyes were blank; his smile was satisfied.

She pushed her chair back, moved to a dark corner of the room where a commode sat behind a screen, leaned over it, and vomited. When the heaving stopped, she took a handkerchief from her sleeve and slowly wiped her mouth. Somehow, she found her way back to her chair. The edges of her cheeks prickled with heat as she stared at the front page.

He had played her for a fool.

Her anger pooled at the bottom of her throat. He had not kept his promise. He had not got Grace's consent to the engagement, the expression on her great-niece's face told her that. Waves of guilt crashed over her, making her heart thud in her chest. She had betrayed Grace.

How could she have been so stupid? She balled her hands into fists and struck the arm of her armchair, causing a bruise to bloom on the side of her hand. What a foolish old woman she was, allowing a handsome charmer to beguile her into relaxing her guard. She went limp and bowed her head. It was the old story. She had become fond of him, enjoying their outings to concerts, enjoying their talks. She had taken pleasure in seeing Grace come out of her shell. She even just liked looking at him.

And where had that got her?

Slowly, she put the newspaper down and went to the bottom of the stairs. She did not have the energy to climb them, so she listened carefully to see if Grace was home. The house was quiet; probably Grace was asleep. She must be worn out, poor child. Slowly, Paulina returned to her armchair. If only she had been more skeptical, like Violet. There was nothing she could do now until Violet got home.

She must have dropped off, because she did not remember anything more until the front door opened.

"Is that you, Violet?" Paulina struggled to sit upright in her favorite armchair.

"Yes." Violet stuck her woolen gloves into the pocket of her peacoat, unwound her scarf, hung her garments on the hatstand, and placed her felt cloche on top. She walked into the front parlor, lighting the oil lamps that stood on side tables by the window.

"Have you seen this?" Paulina gave her the *Star*.

Violet took it from her and examined the melodramatic headline.

"Jesus Christ, he's hitting on all sixes, isn't he? And she looks like a dumb Dora."

Paulina flinched. She would not have put it that way. It seemed to her that Grace was in deep shock. Her anger flared.

"How dare he make such an announcement publicly, without consulting me." It was time to talk to Grace. She folded the paper so that she could not see the front page, placed it on the seat of her armchair and went to the bottom of the stairs.

"Graziella!" she called.

There was a soft reply, and Grace drifted downstairs.

"How do you feel about Mr. Russell, child?" She closed the drapes.

"He was wonderful," replied Grace. "While you were away, Officer Ellis of the Metropolitan Police came to question me about Mother. After he left, people with cameras and pencils crowded around the front door, shouting questions. I was so frightened by all the horrible things they said, but I didn't know how to make them stop talking. Then Mr. Russell appeared as if by magic. He sent them away."

Aunt Paulina shook her head slowly as she sat down. It was amazing how quickly word got around. She had no idea that going on that errand to the funeral parlor with Violet would leave Grace exposed to the attentions of the press.

"Did he say anything about an engagement?"

"He gave me this ring to wear."

Paulina and Violet bent over to look at Grace's left ring finger, which was now claimed by an amethyst and pearl circlet.

"He has good taste, I will give him that," Paulina remarked. "That is a beautiful engagement ring."

"An engagement ring?" Grace's mouth slowly opened.

"What did you think it was, Gracie?" asked Violet.

"Mr. Russell told me to think of it as a friendship ring."

Paulina's anger suffused her chest, making her cheeks scald. She took both of Grace's hands in her own.

"It is true that I gave a *provisional* blessing to your engagement with Mr. Russell, provided that he waited until you were ready and got your consent to the engagement. I did not give him permission to announce it to the press, and I made it very clear that the engagement was not going to happen soon."

"But Auntie P., why did you consent to *anything*? He's the kind who would take a yard if you gave him an inch," said Violet.

Paulina regarded her other great-niece. She had not yet told her how ill she was. "Because I want Grace safe," she replied carefully. She drew her handkerchief out and patted her hairline, which was dampening with beads of perspiration. *Cieli!* She was unwell today. "I do believe he cares about her and that he will help with her career." She was not sure where those words came from—they did not match her angry feelings at all. But there was a kind of truth to them.

"He was trying to protect me from all the nasty things they were saying," remarked Grace. "He told me this ring would protect me from gossip."

"Maybe we should give him this much cred." Violet opened her fingers an eighth of an inch. "But he's feeding you a line, Gracie."

"It was very neatly done. The consequence is this." Paulina jerked the pages of the *Star,* making them crackle, as she finally showed Grace the front page.

"Oh no." Grace drooped in her seat.

"Did you give your consent to this engagement?"

"No. I didn't realize—"

Paulina tightened her grip on the newspaper. Pages crumpled. "This announcement will be all over Georgetown by tomorrow. Everyone will be congratulating you, Graziella."

Grace covered her face with her hands.

Another wave of guilt washed over her. "*Graziella cara,* I am angrier about this that I can say. Think what this means. This fellow has done something that is going to have a profound effect on your life, and he has not even asked your permission."

"I can't get married." A tear ran down Grace's cheek. "I'd make such a hash of it."

"Gracie." Violet put her hand on her sister's shoulder.

"Whatever are you talking about, child?"

"I would never be happy."

"Why not?" asked Violet.

Grace covered her face again.

Paulina leaned forward, and gently tilted her chin up.

"I think you would make a lovely wife."

Grace stared back in surprise. "But I don't feel ready."

Paulina let go of her chin, coughed, and glanced at Violet. "I am going to be frank, *cara*. Men are naturally impatient because they are thinking about the pleasures of the marriage bed. Has Mr. Russell behaved improperly?"

"He was going to kiss me lots, but I told him no."

"*Grazie al cielo*, it shows that you have more sense than your mother. Just remember, if you want to have any choice in this matter, you must not let him persuade you to have intimate relations, because if you became pregnant, you would have to marry him."

Grace's lips parted as her ears became red.

Paulina tensed her jaw. "Your mother had to marry your father more hastily than I would have liked, and as a consequence she was not happy in her marriage. Do not let that happen to you. As a woman, and the person with much more to lose, it is up to you to put on a brake."

"It won't be easy," remarked Grace. "He's very determined."

"Do you want me to act as a fire-extinguisher?" asked Violet.

✠✠✠✠✠✠✠✠✠✠✠

Next day, a Sunday, Mr. Russell was waiting in the front parlor as they returned from Mass. Paulina gave him a cold stare.

"I apologize," he said instantly, rising. "Of course I should have consulted you."

"Why didn't you?" said Violet.

"There wasn't any time. I was shocked by what I saw when I got here."

"Were you?" Violet sat in Angelina's place on the loveseat and stabbed him with her bright blue eyes, while Paulina sluggishly took the armchair by the window.

He coughed. "Grace was besieged by a horde of reporters asking impertinent questions. They were relentless—they were hounding her."

"You have played a neat trick, sir." Paulina's anger filled her chest. "I trusted you. Now, this is the talk of Georgetown. People were congratulating Graziella at Mass this morning."

He flushed. "I understand how angry you are." He looked directly at her. "But I wanted to protect Grace. I wasn't proposing we should marry now." He glanced over at Grace, who was twisting her hands in her lap. "I know that Grace is not comfortable with that idea. I thought we could have a long engagement. That way, she could be under my protection, and it would avoid any unfortunate gossip."

Paulina could not help herself. She immediately saw what must have happened, how he had somehow heard about Angelina's death, hurried over to the house to be with Grace, found the press asking questions, and stepped in to rescue her. Of course they must have asked him who he was, which had caused him to tell them he was Grace's fiancé. Everything he did had been to protect Grace. Her face lifted into a faint smile. "I see."

"Please believe me, Mrs. Barilla, when I say that I love your niece very much."

His eyes looked as frank as a mountain stream. She relaxed back into her seat. "I know that. Why do you think I allowed you to court Graziella?" She indicated the easy chair.

He sat.

Grace lifted her head and placed her hand on the arm of his chair. He laced her fingers within his.

"It would do Grace good to get out of town," remarked Violet.

Mr. Russell shot her a sharp look.

"Professor Burneys came to see me yesterday evening," said Paulina slowly. She had been on the point of going to bed when Grace's violin professor had knocked on the door. He had seen the newspaper and become very concerned about the effect this would have on his favorite pupil. Even in the depths of her guilt over Grace, Paulina had not contemplated leaving town. But Burneys had convinced her it would do the family good to leave.

"He tells me that Professor Carl Flesch will be holding a series of violin master classes in Berlin, Germany, starting in February."

Grace sat up, her head erect. Then she glanced at Russell and slouched in her seat.

"We think Grace should leave as soon as possible, to settle in—to ready for the audition," put in Violet.

He paled. "Why does Grace have to go all the way to Berlin?"

"Because Professor Flesch is the best violin teacher in the world," replied Paulina.

"And it would get us right away from reporters into our beeswax," remarked Violet.

He was silent for many moments. Finally, he said, "Do you speak German?"

Zia Paulina shook her head.

He smiled. "I speak four languages, including German. I would be happy to tutor you all if you needed it."

"Well—" Paulina hesitated.

"There have been problems in Berlin," he remarked, "with the Spartacists shooting at each other." He paused. "How would you feel if I accompanied you?"

Paulina dabbed her forehead with her handkerchief.

"I have contacts in the State Department. I'd be happy to investigate the situation for you."

Paulina nodded absently, suddenly overwhelmed with fatigue.

"We're not bunnies, Mr. Russell," remarked Violet. "I could go to State and investigate myself."

Grace frowned slightly as she looked at her great-aunt. She rose.

He rose also.

"Mr. Russell," she remarked, "how would you be able to accompany us?" She walked to the hatstand and handed him his hat. "Doesn't it take a week to get there? You won't get that position with the State Department if you don't pass your exams."

He smiled and bowed slightly. "I could bring my work with me. It would be my pleasure to accompany you, and make sure you're safe." He put his hat on his head, leaned forward, and placed a kiss on her cheek. "My love," he murmured into her ear.

Then he raised his hat to Paulina and left.

Chapter Eight
Monday, 31 October

Violet lost no time. The very next morning, she slipped into a blue frock, pinned Mother's powder-blue hat onto her head and donned the pair of matching high-heels that were also Mother's. She stared at the mirror. Mother's face, drawn and pale, stared back. Violet could not believe Mother had gone, just like that. How could that happen? Had it anything to do with Dr. Jackson's treatments? At least the fact that she looked so much like Mother would keep her memory alive. She picked up one of Mother's purses and hurried downstairs. Better to distract herself by helping Auntie P. plan the trip to Berlin rather than sit at home and brood over Mother's sudden death. If she did that, she'd sob herself silly.

The State Department was housed in a grand wedding cake of a building that Violet disliked on sight. But she was soon ushered into a small office with a view of the White House. The inhabitant, a lean, young man was reading something in a large book that Violet couldn't make out because she couldn't decipher the script. He looked up and rose.

"Charles Phelps, at your service," he said, extending his hand.

"Violet Miller," she replied, shaking his firmly.

They sat, and Violet explained that her family wanted to go to Berlin. "Is it safe?"

His gray eyes studied her face. "Safe? What do you mean?"

Violet's cheeks warmed. "A *casual* acquaintance informed my aunt that there were gun battles in the streets. Is that true?"

His face cleared. "I see what you mean. It is true that two years ago the Spartacists were fighting each other, and some passers-by were hurt. But now the situation appears to have stabilized. Why are you going to Berlin?"

"My sister is a violinist. She wants to take lessons with Professor Flesch."

"I've heard the name." He pushed his book to one side and leaned back in his chair. "Yes, Herr Professor Flesch is very well regarded. I play cello myself, but my sister is a violist. I believe my parents are trying to arrange for her to study with Flesch also. When are you thinking of going?"

"Professor Flesch's classes start in February, but we want to be settled in by then. I think my aunt wants us to go as soon as possible."

Mr. Phelps picked up a long, silver pencil and rolled it between his elegant fingers. "Since the war, the State Department has required all U.S. citizens to travel abroad with passports."

"I've never heard of them," remarked Violet.

"It will take a few weeks to issue, and I'm afraid there's some paperwork involved." He rose and handed her his card. "I recommend that you return here at your earliest convenience with all the traveling members of your family."

Violet took the cable car back to Georgetown, but instead of walking back to Beall Street, something made her turn west and wander over to Potomac Street. Mrs. Stephenson was not in, and so she used Mother's key to enter the cottage. The apartment upstairs felt flat and hollow, Mother's absence draped over everything. In the bedroom, Mrs. Stephenson had stripped the bed and tidied, but hadn't yet done her weekly cleaning. Shutting the door, she listlessly looked around the small room crowded with its bed, nightstand, dresser, and armoire.

It was too quiet. The only sound was a gentle soughing from the trees outside. Mother had completely vanished, taking her bright vivacity with her. Violet sank onto the floor as the weight of silence pressed in. Then she saw it. Something white emerged from the shadows under the bed. It was a cardboard box that had been done up in red, white, and green ribbons. Inside were flaky crumbs. An indistinct shape remained under the bed—a screwed-up paper bag.

Violet sat there, frowning, looking at her finds. What did it mean? Did it mean anything? Tears came, and she drew a handkerchief from her purse. After a few moments, she took the box and the paper bag downstairs and left a note explaining that she'd taken some of Mother's effects and would be back later for the rest. Scrutinizing the card the police officer had given Grace, which gave the name and telephone number of a Detective Ecker at an office on D Street N.W. near Union Station, she walked to Bridge Street and took the cable car back to town.

When Violet knocked on Detective Ecker's half-open door, she saw a youngish man of around thirty with a beak of a nose, and arresting green eyes unpacking boxes of books, which he was arranging on shelves. Obviously, he was moving in, perhaps recently promoted. He looked up.

She introduced herself.

He shook hands. "I am sorry for the loss of your mother. I was just about to call on your great-aunt, Mrs. Barilla." He cleared a space on his desk. "There's going to be an inquest."

Violet's heart thudded at the back of her throat. "Mother's death was suspicious?"

"I don't know. That is what the inquest will determine."

"I saw Mother shortly before she died. She didn't look sick."

"The inquest will answer your questions. It is going to be in about ten days. You are all invited to come."

"I visited Mother's room just now and found this." She held up a cardboard box and a paper bag.

His face went rigid. "When did you find this?"

"Just now."

He frowned as he examined the box. Then he smoothed out the paper bag, but it had no writing on it.

He looked into her face. "Miss Violet, I am devastated. My officers should have found this evidence and brought it into the station. I take full responsibility, and I promise to make it up to you in some way."

She nodded silently, wiping the tears away from the corners of her eyes with the tips of her fingers.

"I will need to ask you some questions," he remarked. "Do you feel able to continue, or shall I call on you tomorrow?"

"Perhaps I should go home."

"Where do you live?"

"Beall Street, in Georgetown."

"I need to examine your mother's rooms immediately. Would you let me give you a ride home? It's on my way."

She nodded.

His car was a Model T. Pressing a button on the floor to start the car, he took off the parking brake, engaged the clutch, and pushed a lever next to his seat to get into low gear. As the car slowly gained speed, he took his hand off the lever so that it could enter high gear as they eased into the traffic traveling northwest on Pennsylvania Avenue, in the direction of Georgetown.

He was a good listener who asked many questions. Violet soon found herself talking to him about fashion and her plans to open a boutique.

"I suppose you think I'm hopelessly out of date." He ran his eyes briefly over his gray, three-piece suit, making a self-deprecating smile.

"You're wearing a classic, Detective Ecker. That can never go out of style." She leaned forward. "Just after the bridge, turn right on Montgomery and then right again on Beall."

They drew up next to a church. He braked and pulled the lever all the way back. Coming around to Violet's side of the car, he followed her across the street and into the modest house opposite. She took his hat and asked him to take a seat in the front parlor.

"Auntie P., Gracie," she called up the stairs. "There's someone I'd like you to meet."

There was a soft answer, and Grace emerged, clad in an old-fashioned black dress that reached to her ankles.

"It's all right." Violet ushered her into the front parlor. "He won't bite."

Ecker rose and introduced himself. "Miss Grace," he said, shaking her hand gently, "I am truly sorry for your loss, and will do everything in my power to see that justice is done."

Grace sat down without looking at him.

He turned to Violet. "I've already interviewed a number of people, and it seems things started to change for your mother once she met Mr. Russell. Can you tell me how you met him?"

He listened, jotting notes, as Violet described how she and Grace had been at Professor Burneys's soirée, and returned to find Mother with her new friend.

He turned to Grace. "What was your first impression of Mr. Russell?"

Grace folded her arms. "He was a gifted pianist who was able to help me play a difficult piece."

Ecker smiled into her closed face. "What was he like as a person?"

She tapped her foot."I don't know what to say."

"Take your time," said Ecker.

"He acts like a gentleman." Her voice was cold. "He's sensitive, attentive, charming, and highly intelligent. Father Walsh says he's one of his best students."

"I see." The paper crackled as he leaned in hard to jot something down with a stubby pencil. "How does he feel about you?"

Grace crimsoned and looked down.

"Did Mr. Russell want to marry you?"

Grace stared hard at a hole in the shabby Persian rug, as if by staring at it, she could make it speak for her.

"Did you want to marry him?"

Grace thinned her lips.

"There's been a tug-of-war over that issue," remarked Violet quietly.

"Between?"

"Between Mr. Russell on one side and practically everyone else on the other. It's not been easy for Grace. She's only known him two months, and he's very persistent."

Footsteps slowly sounded down the stairs, and Auntie P. plodded into the front parlor.

Ecker rose and introduced himself.

"I owe you an apology, Mrs. Barilla," he remarked. "I believed Mrs. Miller's rooms to be thoroughly searched, but Miss Violet found some items that had been overlooked. I take full responsibility for this, and I'm on my way to Mrs. Stephenson's so that I can search Mrs. Miller's room myself."

Auntie P. sighed as she sank into her armchair. "So many things have gone wrong since Angelina died. It is so unfortunate that all kinds of—details about my niece's life have made their way into the papers. I am concerned about her daughters."

"Are any of those details true?"

The lines of her face hardened into an expression of distaste. "It is true that my niece did not behave in a fashion I would have liked."

"Is that why she was living on Potomac Street, not here?"

"I had rules." said Auntie P. after a pause. "I knew the kind of life she was leading, and I told her I would not have any carrying-on in front of Violet and Grace."

Under his delicate scrutiny, Auntie P. talked about Mother, how she stumbled upon Russell in a bookstore and invited him to dinner, his growing friendship with Grace, and how opposed she was.

He glanced at his notes. "Where can I find Mr. Russell?"

"He lives on Bank Street with Mrs. Olivia Rittenhouse. Just around the corner from Mother, as a matter of fact," said Violet.

Ecker raised an eyebrow and rose.

"When can we bury Mother?" Violet handed him his hat.

"I'll try and expedite things so that you can bury her by the end of the week."

✠✠✠✠✠✠✠✠✠✠✠✠

Grace hesitated outside Mrs. Rittenhouse's front door. Was it proper to visit Mr. Russell in his lodgings? She didn't know even if they were engaged or not. Grace took a deep breath. One false step and she could ruin her reputation and become a fallen woman. Like Mother. As she turned to leave, Mr. Russell appeared, strolling along the street. His face lit up as his eyes fell upon her. He hastened forward.

"Grace! Is something wrong?"

Grace's cheeks warmed as she studied her hands. She shouldn't be here.

He scanned her face and quickly opened the door, gesturing for her to go up. Woodenly, she obeyed. He followed, his footsteps echoing on the wooden stairs. He opened the door to his sitting room and clasped her hands.

"You're so cold. You need something."

"Please, don't bother."

But he disappeared, returning a moment later with a cup of hot tea. He placed it in front of her and went to his dry bar. Unstoppering a bottle of bourbon, he poured a couple of drops into the teacup.

Grace sipped, but it wasn't too strong. It flowed through her, calming and warming. She put her cup down. "Detective Ecker paid us a call. He seems suspicious."

"And you came to warn me." He turned her hand over and kissed the inside of her wrist. Grace sighed as she let him stroke it.

"Grace." His voice caressed her, soft yet powerful. "What did he say to upset you so?"

She swallowed. "He was asking about Mother. Whether you'd had anything to do with it."

He picked up her other hand and grasped both now, chafing them with his strong yet sensitive fingers. "Look at me, Grace. What are you thinking?"

Grace forced herself to look into his face. "I don't think you did, but he—" She gulped back a sob.

"Grace." He wrapped his arm around her while she sobbed. What had come over her?

"I couldn't bear it if anything happened to you."

"Is that true?" He pulled away and gave her a probing look.

She stared at him through a film of tears.

"Dear heart." He gave her his cologne-soaked handkerchief and knelt before her, his smile lighting his face.

She dabbed her face with his handkerchief. "What are you going to say to Detective Ecker?"

He took the handkerchief from her and gently wiped her eyes "It seems that most of Georgetown already knows all the details."

Grace stiffened and sat up.

"I'll agree with the prevailing view, of course." He gave her his dark smile. "There is no point in denying that your mother and I didn't get on."

"But—"

"He will ask about us naturally. He will want to know if we would've been able to marry if your mother had lived."

She fixed her eyes upon his face.

"I will tell him that everything depended upon you." He stroked her cheek with the back of his finger. "That I have no motive because you would have done whatever you wanted." He kissed her cheek.

Grace slowly drew away and rose.

He rose also. "You've never seen my lodgings, my love. Do you approve?"

She looked around. He must have just ordered those white drapes with a pattern of orange and green leaves; they still showed faint creases where they'd been folded.

"Now that you're here, I'd like to show you something." He led her through a large bathroom and beyond into his bedroom. Grace hesitated as she took in the huge bed under its white velvet coverlet. But he walked right past it without looking and opened a door to one side.

Slowly, she followed, and stopped. She had never seen anything like it.

"It's a walk-in closet."

It held all his suits, hats, shoes, and shirts. Each item was meticulously arranged on hangers, in boxes, in drawers, and in cubbyholes. On the opposite side stood a full-length mirror and a dresser. Next to it were floor-to-ceiling cubbyholes that held shoes—lady's shoes. Grace caught her breath, then picked up one in gray suede.

"Would you like to try it on? It's your size."

She glanced at him. How did he know her size? "No, thank you." She put it back.

"What do you think of these?" He plucked three dresses from a rod.

She examined them. They were beautifully made in expensive fabrics, burgundy satin, brown velvet, and gray silk. How Violet would love to see these. But what were they doing here?

"What are these for?"

"They're for you."

Grace stared at him. "You can't be serious."

"I am."

She sank onto a plush velvet chair situated in the middle of the small space.

"Grace, you don't have many clothes. You need a suitable wardrobe for auditions and small concerts. I took it upon myself to find you a few things. Do you like them?"

Grace remained silent, speechless, as she fingered the gray silk that matched her eyes exactly. What did this mean? Was he paying for her to do something? Was she a doll for dress-up? Mother's voice intruded. *There's something unhealthy and obsessive about him.*

The silence lengthened. His jaw twitched several times. "Do you mind if I smoke?"

She shook her head.

He took a silver monogrammed lighter from his pocket and lit up. The silence held. Mother's warning sounded again in her head.

He compressed his lips as he played with his cigarette, patting it gently with the pad of his thumb so that ash fell into a chrome ashtray, which had a stylized mermaid undulating upwards from one corner. Grace's eyes gradually locked onto that mermaid. She was naked from the waist up, and her face and hair seemed familiar. The image blurred into a face—her face. She leapt to her feet. "I should leave."

He stubbed out his cigarette. "Grace."

She turned and walked quickly past the enormous bed, the bathroom with all of his intimate things, the front room with its dry bar, piano, easy chairs, and modern décor. She clattered down the wooden stairs and nearly bumped into a woman coming up the garden path.

She blinked in surprise. "Why, I do declare—it's Miss Grace." Mrs. Rittenhouse winked. "Have you enjoyed your visit, dear?"

Grace brushed past, her cheeks scalding, and made for the sidewalk.

"Grace." He came after her and reached for her arm. She shook him off and stepped away into the middle of the street.

"I need to go home. Alone. Please don't follow me."

"When will I see you again?" His jaw twitched twice.

"At my violin lesson, but not before." Grace turned on her heel and walked away.

"Grace!"

She kept walking, the cool air buffeting her cheeks. Mother was right. He was obsessed with her. A cold wind whispered up her spine.

Chapter Nine
Tuesday, 1 November

"Ladies, I have news." Detective Ecker took the easy chair in the front parlor, while Aunt Paulina sat opposite in her favorite armchair. Violet and Grace sank onto the loveseat.

He took out his notebook, glancing at Grace.

"I spoke with Mrs. Olivia Rittenhouse yesterday, and she reported an argument Mr. Russell had with Mrs. Miller. It occurred October twenty-first, near midnight, in Bank Street. Apparently Mrs. Rittenhouse was visiting a friend across the street. She and her friend heard the sound of raised voices and went to the window. She says she saw Mrs. Miller standing under a streetlight, shouting at a gentleman, whom she recognized as her tenant. She reported that Mrs. Miller seemed very agitated." He paused. "I'm afraid that what I'm about to say will be embarrassing."

Grace bent her face, twisting her hands in her lap.

Looking studiously at the typescript, Ecker recited:

Mrs. Miller: You have caused me a great deal of inconvenience.

Mr. Russell: I was only asking questions.

Mrs. Miller: About me? Why would you be so interested in me?

Mr. Russell: inaudible.

Mrs. Miller: You talked to Hammond and Dr. Jackson. You kept asking for Angelina Miller and Pauline Barilla. But not about Violet or Grace.

Mr. Russell: inaudible.

Mrs. Miller: Isn't it strange that your brother has a different name than you?

Mr. Russell: inaudible.

```
     Mrs. Miller: Aha! You did not know I
had found that out. I asked Father Walsh.
He showed me your records.
     Mr. Russell [shouting]: Leave me
alone, you [epithet deleted].
     Mrs. Miller [shouting]: I will leave
you alone the day you leave my daughter
alone!
```

Grace's cheeks radiated heat. How embarrassing that Mother shouted such things at Mr. Russell in public. He must have been mortified. Her body softened as she smiled inwardly. He must love her very much to have put up with this while never failing in his attentions to her. He'd even chosen those lovely frocks—

"I believe Angelina was trying to help." Aunt Paulina pressed a handkerchief to her temple. "I really wish she had found some other way of doing it."

"Does this sound like your niece?"

"Unfortunately so."

"Mother did have a way of going on the rampage," remarked Violet.

The detective spent the next several minutes going over Mrs. Rittenhouse's testimony point by point.

Finally, Grace looked up. "Do we have to go on and on about him?"

"Miss Grace, whenever we investigate an unexplained death, we have to consider that someone may have caused that death."

She stared at him, a cold wind whispering up her spine. "You mean Mother was murdered?"

"I don't know. But when investigating a *possible* murder, we have to look for potential suspects. We look for people who have the means, the motive, and the opportunity."

He cleared his throat. "The reason why your Mr. Russell features so prominently is that his lodgings were near your mother, who lived alone, which gave him the opportunity. And he is the only person I've met so far in this investigation who could've had a motive."

"Mr. Russell told me he had no motive," remarked Grace. "He said I would have grown up and made up my own mind."

Ecker examined the expression on her face, but Grace stared back, waiting for his reply.

"Your mother seems to have had a talent for needling Mr. Russell," he remarked.

"But that doesn't prove anything," replied Grace.

"Not as yet." His mouth tightened into a grim line.

Grace glanced at him and shivered. A vision of Mr. Russell walking to the gallows flashed through her mind. Her stomach clenched, and she leaned over, feeling suddenly nauseous.

"I won't press you now, Miss Grace," continued Ecker, "but if you think of anything else, do I have your promise that you will let me know?"

Though she turned her face away, she gave the smallest of nods.

"If you can remember the names of anyone else who may have witnessed their encounters, it would be a great help." He handed Aunt Paulina his card.

Grace rushed upstairs to her bedroom and vomited into the commode before wiping her mouth clean and throwing herself onto her bed. A coil of images circled as she closed her eyes, as if the contents of his walk-in closet, the hats, jackets, shoes, shirts and even those lovely, expensive dresses, separated from their drawers, cubbyholes, hangers, and floated free in a gentle breeze.

✠✠✠✠✠✠✠✠✠✠✠✠

Detective Ecker stood outside Mrs. Rittenhouse's cottage, waiting for Russell to appear. There'd been fingerprints all over the pastry box and the bag, but they were so badly smudged, he hadn't been able to get good copies of them. Everyone he'd interviewed had been cooperative, reporting the many confrontations Russell had with Mrs. Miller. Clearly, they'd had a stormy relationship, but that didn't mean he'd murdered her.

He frowned. The fact was he hadn't been able to find out much. His first week on the case had been a blizzard of meetings and phone calls. Unfortunately, this meant he hadn't had the time to find Russell. It didn't help that the fellow seemed to have gone to ground, making this the fourth time he'd walked over to Bank Street. The previous three times, he'd been forced to return to the detective bureau empty-handed because there had been some meeting to attend or a pressing matter to deal with.

Today, he insisted on clearing his calendar to ensure that he'd be able to track Russell all over the District if need be —this interview was too crucial.

He rang the bell again and as he did so, a figure appeared, walking slowly, almost reluctantly, along the street. He was a dashing, well-dressed fellow, the sort that would appeal to the ladies. Ecker smiled slightly. From the many descriptions he'd heard, this had to be Russell. He stepped forward and introduced himself, taking in Russell's dark eyes, thick hair, and handsome face. What did Miss Violet think of him? It didn't seem likely that she would fall for him the way her sister had. He seemed to be in a different world.

"I'm the detective in charge of the investigation into Mrs. Miller's death. I would like to ask you a few questions."

Russell remained silent, his eyes fixed on the detective's face. When Ecker proffered his card, Russell scrutinized it for several moments before opening the gate to the small front garden and nodding for Ecker to follow him up the stairs.

"How did you meet Mrs. Angelina Miller?" he asked, as Russell indicated one of the easy chairs by the window and took the other.

"She approached me in the bookstore," came the pat reply.

Ecker sat down. Clearly, the fellow had money to burn. He must have just ordered those white drapes with a pattern of orange and green leaves because they still showed faint creases where they'd been folded. It wasn't to his taste, but it looked modern.

"Why did she approach you?"

"I don't know," replied Russell after a short pause.

Ecker shot him a look as he took out his notepad. Russell was fixing his eyes on the floor, a tactic that accomplished liars sometimes used. But why would he lie about a seemingly trivial incident? He took out his pencil, found a blank page, and wrote some notes, remaining silent until Russell spoke.

"I don't want to speak ill of the dead, or damage the reputation of a lady."

"This is a police investigation, Mr. Russell. You're not at liberty to hide behind a gentlemanly facade."

"If you put it that way," said Russell, taking out a monogrammed cigarette case and offering a cigarette to Ecker, who declined, "I'll be frank." He lit his cigarette and inhaled deeply. "The woman was a whore."

Ecker looked up. Usually when people told a police officer they were going to be frank, it meant they were going to hide something. So this nugget of truth was unexpected.

"What do you mean?"

"She had no sense of pride or decency. She would stand too close to you, put her hand on your arm, part her lips—" He reddened.

Ecker gazed at him. How interesting that Russell wasn't bothering to hide a deep-seated dislike. "You mean she was hot to trot?"

"Yes," replied Russell, after a brief hesitation.

"You didn't care for her?"

"I took an instant dislike to her."

"Indeed?" Ecker raised an eyebrow, pencil poised over notepad. "How come you took her to tea at the Metropolitan Hotel and then accepted her invitation to dinner?"

"I didn't want to be rude to a lady."

"But you just told me she was no lady. Why would you care what she thought?"

"We were in a public place, and I didn't want her to make a scene."

"You think she would have caused some unpleasantness?"

"Yes."

"How could you know that, when you'd only just met her?"

"I think I sized her up pretty accurately. As it turned out, I was right. She had a habit of making unpleasant scenes in public places, causing me a great deal of embarrassment."

Ecker narrowed his eyes, but Russell stared back, unblinking.

"There's something that doesn't make sense," he said slowly. "If you didn't like her, you could've gotten rid of her. There must've been something about her that caused you to stay talking to her."

Russell compressed his lips as he played with his cigarette, patting it gently with the pad of his thumb so that ash fell into a chrome ashtray, which had a stylized mermaid undulating upwards from one corner. The mermaid was naked from the waist up, and its face and hair seemed familiar. The image blurred into Miss Grace's face. Hairs rose on the back of Ecker's neck.

He coughed and directed his attention back to Russell, who was patting more ash into the ashtray.

Finally, he said, "Perhaps I take too much pride in being a gentleman, and sometimes it makes me weak." He exhaled smoke in Ecker's direction. "I should've gotten rid of her, but she wasn't unattractive."

"But you just said you disliked her."

"I was new in town, I had no friends, and she promised me dinner," replied Russell with a shrug. "I thought I might be mistaken, and there was no harm in finding out if the lady improved on further acquaintance."

Ecker waited, but the fellow was good. He sat there, imperturbable, until the detective moved on to other matters.

While Ecker covered his meetings with Mrs. Miller's daughters, family, and friends, Russell allowed himself the slightest softening of the jaw. It wasn't obvious, and Ecker might have missed it if he hadn't been watching Russell so closely. Even his rows with Mrs. Miller didn't seem to faze him. He merely repeated what everyone else had said. Which left the question of why he was lying about that meeting in the bookstore, and why he stayed to dinner.

"Tell me, Mr. Russell," he said as he put his notebook away. "Do you think you would've been able to marry Miss Grace if Mrs. Miller had lived?"

Russell stubbed out his cigarette and immediately lit another. "Everything depended on Grace. I would've done whatever she wanted. We could have eloped." He slid his eyes towards Ecker. "There was no need for me to murder Mrs.

Miller, if that's what you're asking. I plan on working for the State Department. I'll be living abroad for most of my life."

"Meaning?"

"Grace would have achieved her majority and made up her own mind. As my wife, she would have been thousands of miles away from her mother."

Damn him. Ecker walked slowly along Bank Street. Russell was lying about something, but what? Was he lying about that meeting in the bookstore to cover up a crime? And why wasn't he bothering to hide his dislike of Mrs. Miller? Ecker shook his head. Nothing made any sense. But the fellow seemed sinister, and if Ecker knew anything about human nature, he'd be willing to bet that Russell was quite capable of murdering anyone who stood in his way. And it wasn't just because of the war. Despite his Yankee veneer, he was Italian, wasn't he? Didn't he come from a country of famous poisoners?

✠✠✠✠✠✠✠✠✠✠✠

Mother's funeral Mass was held on Thursday, November the third, at Holy Trinity Church, at the corner of First and Gay Streets in northwest Georgetown, attended by Mother's closest relatives—Great-Aunt Paulina, Aunt Josephina, Aunt Louisa, Violet, and Grace. Afterwards, they went over to Oak Hill Cemetery, tucked into a leafy nook of northern Georgetown, and said their farewells to her there.

Behind a blur of patterned black netting, Grace remained dry-eyed, unable to feel much of anything, while her sister sobbed into a lace handkerchief. Life had been reduced to a bitter, ashy taste. As a black-clad gentleman approached, Grace's heart skipped a beat. But it was only Detective Ecker.

"Miss Violet, Miss Grace." He raised his hat.

But Violet ignored him, tears trickling silently through her fingers.

He stood resolutely by, regarding her gravely. "I wanted to ask your permission to write to you while you are in Berlin."

"Is something wrong?" Violet's normally pink cheeks were pale.

"It may not be possible to hold the inquest before you leave. In that case, I'd like to notify you personally."

Violet looked at Mother's grave.

Detective Ecker's gaze never left her face. "Miss Violet, can you trust me to ensure that justice is done?" His gloved hand reached for hers. "You probably won't be there, but if you wish, I will write you and enclose my report."

Violet fastened her bright eyes on his face.

He smiled down as he continued to hold her gloved hand."Don't hesitate to call on me if you have any questions, or if you think of anything else. Otherwise, I wish you and your family a safe trip to Berlin, Miss Violet."

Violet murmured her thanks.

He touched his hat, nodded to Grace, and left.

Grace stared after him as he disappeared in the direction of Road Street. Had Aunt Paulina invited him? Then she turned to look at her sister. But Violet, normally so sharply perceptive, noticed nothing. She was too busy weeping.

✠✠✠✠✠✠✠✠✠✠✠

A week or so passed, Aunt Josie and Auntie Lou went back to their homes in Philadelphia and New York City. Pretty soon, it was the week before Thanksgiving. Then came Saturday, which meant that Mr. Russell showed at eight to take Grace to her violin lesson. Violet walked to the post office to mail state department documents to Aunt Josie and Auntie Lou. After that, she had a dozen errands to run in the village, and before she knew it, lunchtime had passed, and she was famished.

Violet turned back toward Beall Street, a basket of seasonal goodies heavy on her arm. By this time, the clouds were rolling in, a cold wind whipping the leaves. She pulled her felt cloche down over her curls, turned up the collar of her peacoat, and dug in her pockets for gloves. When she arrived, she ran up the steps.

"I received a letter this morning," said Auntie P. She was standing in the front parlor with her back to Violet. Facing her stood Mr. Russell, clad in black. His face was as white as his starched collar.

Violet closed the door quietly, for it was freezing outside, put her basket on the floor, and edged into the room. Auntie P. was so riveted by Mr. Russell, she didn't notice.

"It is addressed to Angelina." Auntie P. cleared her throat.

Angelina cara,

I wish I were writing to you under happier circumstances. If only I could see you in person! For what I have to say will shock and horrify you.

You remember, of course, my brother Nico. I believe he was four years old when you last saw him. When we came to the United States, Papa made us change our names, and that is how I, Girolamo, became Jerome, and how Nico, Domenico, became Nicholas. Nico fought on the Italian Front during the Great War, acting as a spy for the State Department, due to his fluent knowledge of both Italian and Austrian German. He needed a cover name for his activities and wanted to take the name Rossi, a common name in *Italia* as you know. However, State made him Anglicize it to Russell to avoid trouble from his peers who might be prejudiced against Italians.

It grieves me greatly therefore to tell you that your younger daughter's suitor, Nicholas Russell, is—*il tuo mezzo fratello*, your half-brother Nico.

"What do you have to say to that, sir?"

Mr. Russell's pupils contracted. His pale complexion turned even whiter. "You are right to be angry with me, Mrs. Barilla." He spoke so softly, Violet had trouble catching his words. "But let me explain so at least Grace can understand."

Violet searched the room. Grace was slumped on the bottom stair like a doll that has lost its stuffing.

He cleared his throat. "When I was accepted into Georgetown," he said, "I was delighted, not only because Georgetown is such a prestigious place to study, especially for an observant Catholic, but because—" He took a deep breath. "Because I was also hoping to reconnect—with my—family—here."

Auntie P. flushed brick red. "You are Franco's son."

He didn't take his eyes off of Grace's face. "I am."

"You *lied* to us."

He made the smallest of nods.

"Why?" asked Grace.

"Because everything went wrong. I meant to introduce myself to you, Mrs. Barilla." He turned towards her. "I went to the house on Second Street, but was told you'd moved to Herring Hill. When I finally located your home on Beall Street, I saw a woman coming out of this house who gave me pause. She dressed in a rather…eye-catching style."

Aunt Paulina sagged into her armchair. There was silence.

He coughed. "I wasn't sure what to do. I asked around and ascertained that the woman was Mrs. Angelina Miller."

"You followed her around," said Violet.

He flicked his gaze over.

"Did you follow her into Shepherd & Riley's?"

"Yes."

"Why?" asked Violet.

He cleared his throat. "She invited me to supper, and I accepted because I was hoping to meet you." He turned to Auntie P. again.

"But I was in Philadelphia, visiting Josephina."

"Unfortunately," he replied tightly.

Silence filled the room, and in that moment, Violet felt just a teeny, tiny bit sorry for Mr. Russell, or whatever his name was.

"Are you going to tell us what happened next?" she asked.

He sighed and glanced at Aunt Paulina, whose cheeks bloomed with angry red patches. "I will say as little as is necessary. I had hoped to like your mother more, but I ended up liking her less. I was just wondering how I could make my excuses and flee—"

"*Flee*, Mr. Russell?" Grace opened her eyes wide. Had he disliked Mother as much as that? He must have done. He must have seen what she did for a living. Grace hung her head as her cheeks blazed. Even her ears felt hot.

"None of this excuses your behavior, sir." Aunt Paulina scowled at him from her armchair. "How could you have imposed your attentions upon Grace?"

"You are right to be angry with me, Mrs. Barilla," he replied quietly. "But have you ever set eyes on someone and known, just known from the very depths of your being, that she was so right for you?"

Grace twisted her fingers tightly in her lap. *He really loves me, I can hear it in his voice.*

"How could you lie to Grace?" said Aunt Paulina. "You must have known that if you pressed your attentions, we would want to know who you were."

"Why didn't you tell me?" Grace looked up. She had trusted him, knowing implicitly that he would never do anything to embarrass her. He was a keeper of secrets. Her stomach wound itself into a knot. She hadn't known he would keep secrets from her.

Russell took a spotless white handkerchief from the breast pocket of his mourning suit and dabbed at his forehead. "There, I lacked—courage." He replaced his handkerchief, and gazed at Grace. "I could not bear—" He went so white, even his lips became white.

"Could not bear what?"

"I could not have borne it if you'd turned away."

"Why would I?"

"Because of who I was."

"You are Franco's son." Aunt Paulina's musical contralto was knife sharp. "Grace is Franco's granddaughter. You may not marry."

Grace's hands shook as she stared at them in her lap. His words reverberated inside her because she'd heard them before. Her memory drew her back to the afternoon before Professor Burneys's soirée, when all Georgetown had come to hear them play. They'd been eating sandwiches and drinking tea together, alone, in a rare moment of privacy.

"Do you feel nervous?" she had asked.

"I'm new in town, so I'm being judged," he replied. "Everyone's expectations are high. If I stumble and spoil your performance—"

"You won't," she'd said, looking at her plate.

"You have confidence in my abilities?"

"You are a fine pianist, Mr. Russell." Grace accepted another sandwich. "Besides, we play well together."

"Indeed, we do." He smiled and took her hand.

His hand felt warm and solid as she let her fingers lie there.

"Mr. Russell, you are very persistent in your attentions."

"I can't help myself." He kissed the inside of her wrist, sending a tingle flowing through it. Grace gently withdrew her hand.

"Who are you?"

Abruptly, he turned away and rose.

Her neck ached from playing, but she tilted it to look at him more closely. He continued to gaze out the window, his back to her.

"You don't have to say, if it makes you so uncomfortable."

He swung around. "Of course I want you to know."

She frowned. "But—"

"I don't want to scare you. The worst thing you could do to me would be to run away."

Grace stared at him. *Run away? Couldn't he feel how much she liked being with him?*

He sat down and took her hand. "Grace, do you believe that love is everything?"

She let herself drop into his eyes.

"Is it so wrong for two people to love each other no matter who they are?"

"No," she murmured. *Was it?* She racked her memory, but it was so hard to think when his eyes were upon her.

"Dio mio," he breathed. "You overwhelm me." His lips brushed hers.

And now, a month had gone by. They were in the front parlor. They had received a letter from his brother. And Aunt Paulina had just told her they couldn't marry.

"That can't be true," she said."It's not true, is it Mr. Russell?"

"My brother is studying to be a priest, and I asked his opinion. I believe his letter tells you that he consulted his Bible, and there is nothing in there to prohibit a marriage between a half-uncle and a half-niece."

"It is incest!" exclaimed Aunt Paulina. She turned to Grace. "You must think about your children, Graziella *cara*, it is not healthy."

He kept his dark eyes fixed upon Grace. "We may still marry. Lamo has promised me he will get a Papal dispensation. A priest may perform the sacrament."

Grace stared back. *Was that true? Could they still marry?* A kind of heaviness lifted and dissolved.

"You lied about something important," continued Aunt Paulina. "You are not the stranger you pretended to be, sir. You are my nephew."

Two spots of color flushed his cheeks. He averted his eyes. "I wish I had met you first." He paused and his eyes sought out Grace's.

"I know I have no right to ask this of you, but can you forgive me?"

Grace walked to the window and stood there, gazing out, her back to him. It was too much to deal with. She was his niece? No, she was his half-niece as Grandpa Franco had two wives. Her grandmother was the first wife, Russell's mother was the second. No wonder he'd lied to her. And now she held this all-powerful gentleman in her power. He wanted her forgiveness. But wasn't she furious with him?

"Didn't it bother you that you were so closely related?" Violet's voice intruded on her thoughts. Grace turned slightly to peek at him from out of the corner of her eye. "Didn't it occur to you that maybe you shouldn't be Grace's suitor?"

He passed a shaking hand over his hair. "Of course it did. I spent many sleepless hours wrestling with my con—"

"I am appalled by your behavior," interrupted Aunt Paulina "I forbid you from ever contacting Grace again."

He gazed at Grace, but she averted her face. He made his last plea. "I do not expect your answer now."

His voice was mellifluous. Memories resonated in her head. *Call me Nicholas, my love. Think of it as a friendship ring, something that will protect you from further harm. You need something, dear heart, especially as you're not in the habit of eating much. I wish I could soothe you. You are a young woman of exquisite sensibility, nothing your mother has done can ever mar that.* Not everything he said was double-edged.

"I know you will have to give a great deal of thought to this," he said.

"Indeed, she will." Aunt Paulina threw open the front door with a bang. *"Figlio di Puttana, vai a farti fottere!"*

Grace spun around. Her great-aunt had just insulted him in the worst possible way. She gazed into his frozen face.

There was a silence.

Slowly, like the reel of a movie coming to life, he jerked across the wooden floor, taking his hat and coat from the hatstand, making for the door.

He was leaving forever. She had to stop this.

As he passed through, his dark gaze lanced across the room. She took one step towards him, lifting her hands as if to touch him once more.

Their eyes met.

"*Buone notte, vita mia,* farewell my life." He touched his hat and was gone.

"Phew!" Violet turned to Aunt Paulina. "I'm so proud of you for sending that creep packing!"

Grace flinched. She hadn't known Violet disliked him so much.

Aunt Paulina smiled faintly as she drooped in her seat, her face gray.

"Your mother was right about him all along."

Violet's mouth turned down. "How sad she isn't here to witness this."

"How strange life is," remarked Aunt Paulina. "I completely misjudged Angelina. She showed a great deal of persistence in this matter, she really fought him over it. I didn't know that about her, I always thought she lacked application. If it hadn't been for her efforts, we wouldn't have found out about...him."

Grace kept silent. How powerful words were. They could destroy lives. She suddenly saw herself standing in the tumbledown ruins of a house, with broken pieces of brick, broken jabs of wood, broken stabs of glass around her. She stood frozen in the middle.

Devastated.

Part II

An Unsuitable Suitor

Spring 1922

✠✠✠✠✠✠✠✠✠✠✠

Chapter Ten
Hochschule Für Musik
Berlin, Germany
Wednesday, 18 January

Grace craned her neck as the taxi slowed to a stop outside a large beaux-arts building.

"Fasanenstrasse," said the taxi driver.

"Hochschule Für Musik?" inquired Uncle William.

"*Ja.*"

She got out and looked up. The building was three stories tall, with each wing defined by an impressive tower. Where did Professor Flesch hold his classes? Probably in one of those tower rooms with the high ceilings.

A sharp gust rattled old leaves and garbage. Using one hand to hold her collar up, Grace hurried behind Violet, Aunt Louisa, and Uncle William, clutching the handles of her violin case.

Professor Flesch was the most famous violin pedagogue in the world, and Professor Burneys had spoken with awe of his newly developed international school for violinists. The Vienna Academy of Music had wanted him, but he'd chosen Berlin instead. His violin academy was to rival the Paris Conservatoire.

Grace should be thrilled to be meeting the great man at last, but as she followed her relatives into the Hochschule, her courage failed. Why in the world would Professor Flesch be interested in taking her on as his student? Her repertoire was not extensive, her experience limited. Professor Burneys had never been able to provide her with chamber music lessons despite his efforts. Georgetown was just too small. Her heart squeezed, jolting uncomfortably in her chest.

A young woman met them in the entrance hall, then led them through a maze of corridors and up one flight of stairs. Grace had prepared three pieces to play from memory: the Brahms *D Minor Sonata*, the "Rondo alla Turca" from the Mozart *A Major Concerto*, and the "Adagio" from the Bach *G Minor Sonata* for unaccompanied violin. She'd practiced them faithfully every day for the past month, and now she was sure she couldn't play them before the most demanding teacher in the world. She was bound to forget something. What then?

But the young woman led them into a room that had large windows on two walls. Grace looked around and took a deep breath. She must pull herself together. She must somehow convey to the great man. how immeasurably she loved playing the violin.

A concert grand stood on a wooden dais, with a baby grand tucked nearby. Metal music stands and wooden chairs were strewn haphazardly across the large room. They were early, and no one was there. While Uncle William and Aunt Louisa went off to find someone to talk to, Violet tidied the room, arranging the chairs into neat rows and placing the music stands in one corner.

Grace walked around the periphery listening carefully. With the roar of the Berlin traffic muted to a distant hum by its thick walls, the room vibrated with a kind of hollow emptiness. Even her footsteps echoed on the wooden floor. There were no drapes, no carpet, nothing cushioned or soft that might muffle the sound. He would be able to hear everything.

Her shoulders drooped as she put her case down. She eased the thick mittens off her hands, massaging the fingers of her left hand to keep them warm and supple. She took the violin out of its case, closed her eyes, and tuned it, taking time to test the acoustics of the room. Settling the violin on her left shoulder, placing her chin in the chin-rest, she drew an arc in the air with her bow and began. The opening "Adagio" from the *G Minor Sonata* by Johann Sebastian Bach radiated across the room, with descending notes that flourished proudly from the monumental chords.

A thick silence resonated as she finished. Uncle William and Aunt Louisa stood in the doorway with a stocky man of middling size. He looked to be about fifty, with gray hair that grew well back from his forehead and eyes hidden behind thick eyeglasses. Something about him was intimidating, even unfriendly. Grace pressed her lips together.

"You must be Fräulein Miller," he said in excellent English. "I am Herr Flesch."

Grace's fingers squeezed the bow. How had she played? She couldn't remember. Had she done justice to that glorious piece of music?

Flesch cracked a smile. "Do not be nervous, Fräulein. You have talent. Did you bring a pianist with you?"

Grace shook her head.

Flesch gestured, and a thin young man appeared. "Herr Ritter will serve as your accompanist. Now, let us start. What have you brought for me to hear?"

They played the Brahms *D Minor Sonata*. Herr Ritter was technically fluent. He played each note at exactly the right time. But her performance wilted under his uninspired playing. If only Mr. Russell had been there. How magnificently he'd accompanied her at Professor Burneys's soirée, tossing off the cascades of notes that Brahms demanded of his pianists with virtuosic bravura, but without overpowering her violin line. By contrast, Herr Ritter was too loud, and she felt compelled to follow his ponderous too-slow playing, rather than recreate the piece in her quieter, suppler fashion.

When they reached the end of the piece, Flesch rose and came over.

"May I see your left hand?"

Grace held it up. Mr. Russell's pearl and amethyst ring nestled on her heart finger.

"Why have you come to Berlin to study with me if you are engaged to be married?"

"My niece is not engaged," remarked Aunt Louisa.

Flesch barely glanced at her. "I want to hear from Fräulein Grace."

"Mr. Russell is in America, studying at Georgetown University," said Grace tightly. "I have not seen him since November—"

"How can you be serious about the violin if your thoughts are elsewhere? I only consider taking on students who are committed to their studies."

Prickles of ice jostled up her spine. "I am serious about my studies. The violin means everything to me."

"When do you plan to marry?"

Violet leaned forward.

Grace's cheeks warmed. "I don't—"

But he cut her off. "You see, Fräulein, you cannot have a career as a violinist if you have a husband and children to care for. As one of a large family myself, I have always felt that children are the ultimate purpose of marriage."

Grace had heard such sentiments before, usually propounded by smug individuals with yards of children. But what about those who'd never had children, like Aunt Paulina? Did that make her marriage to Uncle Luke invalid? And what about Mother, who'd cobbled together a life as a rich man's mistress after the death of Father? Where did she fit in his scheme of things? Grace's cheeks warmed.

"If you are planning to marry soon," continued Flesch, "then I cannot take you on."

A stab of anger made Grace lift her head and stare him full in the face. "I am not planning to marry. I left America to come all this way to study with you. I only wore this ring for good luck." She wrenched Russell's ring off her finger and threw it into the end compartment of the violin case, where she kept rosin and some extra strings. "I will do anything to pursue my violin studies with you."

It was quite hopeless. He would never accept her now. He could easily have other students.

"Good," said Flesch. "Now we will talk about your playing." He went to the back of the room and conferred with two other professors. They must have come in while he was interrogating her.

Grace hung her head, her face growing hot.

"Fräulein Miller. These gentlemen want to hear you play. I think we should start with the Bach."

She glanced at them, but their expressions told her nothing. They drew up chairs and sat down near the front of the room. Grace stood where they could see her, and began. The dark architectural structure of the *G Minor Sonata* unfolded in slow gestures. It was one of her favorite pieces, but her nerves jangled up the performance. She tried to steady them by breathing with the music, but her stomach gurgled. Beads of perspiration formed on her upper lip. She clenched her bow to stop it from shaking.

"That is enough, Fräulein." Flesch held up his hand and then leaned over to talk to his colleagues. They spoke volubly with gestures, but Grace couldn't tell whether they were saying good things or bad. "We will hear the Mozart now, if you please."

She blinked. How in the world was she to switch gears from the dark gravity of the Bach, to the teasing, light-heartedness of the "Rondo alla Turca"? But there was no one to help her, so eventually, she closed her eyes and lifted the violin. The courtly eighteenth-century music filled the room, but it sounded so thin. If only she had a pianist to support her. Eventually, the stately dance of the first part of the music was interrupted by a Turkish march, which required Grace to coax darker tonalities out of the violin. She became so involved in trying to produce a sound that conveyed the smoldering passion of a banked fire, she didn't notice everyone was smiling until she finally came to.

Professor Flesch signaled for her to stop and picked up a pencil.

"You are holding the bow too tight. You must relax, or you will kill the sound." He handed Grace the pencil. "I want you to hold this as you hold the bow."

She tried to arrange her fingers and thumb around the pencil, but it was so light. How were they to stay on?

"Now bend and straighten you fingers, like this." He made her practice for a while, then picked up his bow. "I want you to do this." He made his hand walk up the bow.

"What if I drop it?"

"If you practice it over your bed, it doesn't matter if it falls. But you must practice this every day, to give you the confidence that you won't drop the bow, and more importantly, to give the strength and flexibility to do any bow stroke, in any part of the bow."

While Grace practiced moving her hand up the bow, he turned and said a few words to his colleagues, who got up, made stiff bows to her, and vanished.

"Fräulein," said Flesch, "you have a gift, and I can see you work well. I will take you on."

But Grace could barely hear his words as a chorus of female voices singing *a capella* sounded softly in her head. The sound pulsated, making his face shimmer. Through the haze, Uncle William said,

"Vielen Dank, mein lieber Herr Professor." He opened his wallet, but Flesch waved him away.

"This lesson is with my compliments. The Herr Direktor will make the necessary arrangements for future lessons." He turned to Grace. "I expect you back here, Fräulein, on Monday, February the sixth. The class starts at noon. I do not tolerate lateness."

✠✠✠✠✠✠✠✠✠✠✠✠

"This is most unsuitable." Aunt Louisa wrinkled her nose as they emerged from the U-bahn, blinking, into the whitish-gray light of a Berlin winter afternoon. Grace shivered as she breathed in the unfamiliar damp cold that somehow sank into her bones, even though the temperature was no colder than Georgetown. She could hardly believe the audition had gone so well. Now, she could give herself permission to spend her first afternoon in Germany tasting the city of Berlin with Violet, Aunt Louisa, and Uncle William, exploring the Nollendorfplatz area where Aunt Paulina contemplated taking rooms.

How disappointing that Great-Aunt Paulina wasn't able to be with them, but she wasn't well, still recovering from the six-day voyage. Wait until she heard what Grace had to tell her; she would be so delighted to hear that her great-niece had been accepted by the greatest violin pedagogue of the day —even if he had been unpleasant. Grace rubbed the empty space on her ring finger with her thumb. It felt naked and unprotected. A cold wind from the east bit through her stockings, chafing her ankles. It lifted grit, cigarette butts, and several pieces of trash. Grace looked around. Wasn't Berlin a prosperous European city filled with beautiful, old buildings? But it looked poor and drab. Everything was gray, from the crumbling buildings to the clouds that lowered over the city, heavy with snow.

Berlin seemed boring, until she encountered the inhabitants.

People stood. They loitered around the large square, Nollendorfplatz, bisected by the U–Bahn station. Many of them were respectably dressed women who looked like secretaries or receptionists. They seemed to be waiting for something. Grace turned her head and caught sight of a large clock. It was three o'clock in the afternoon. What were these women waiting for? A demonstration? A tram? But they weren't standing by a tram stop, and there was no distant roar to indicate a demonstration. She clutched the handles of her violin case. What was going on? Who were those men who slowly appeared and engaged these women in conversation? Grace's stomach twisted. No, surely not. Not that, not again.

"No wonder it's called Sin City," remarked Violet. Standing near the entrance to the U-bahn, a group of girls wore unusually short dresses that showed off their knees. Their only concession to the freezing weather were the feather boas that floated around their shoulders. As Uncle William emerged, they swung their purses and called out something in German. The tallest one bent down to adjust her garters, flashing a white thigh. She smiled at him from under her short bob.

Uncle William turned redder than a beetroot.

Grace came to a dead stop right in front of them. Is this how Mother had presented herself when she was a young woman? But Mother, even at her worst, had never looked like that. The worst had been dresses with deep décolletage, sequined purses, and high heels. In comparison with these girls, Mother had seemed respectable in her fashionable silk dresses that came down to the mid-calf. These were tarts. Mother had been a rich man's mistress. That was the difference.

Violet grasped her sister's elbow.

They strolled along Nollendorfstrasse. The Berliners slouched against walls and doorways as they passed, wearing caps, heavy shirts, pants, and boots. They smoked cigarette butts that appeared non-stop from their pockets. Between puffs, they stared.

Grace drew near to Violet and pointed with her chin. "Is that a man or woman?" She indicated an individual dressed in the garb of a workman, a cap pulled down over his head. A lock of bright hair spilled down his shoulder.

"A woman," hissed Violet.

Uncle William and Aunt Louisa looked at each other, telegraphing something in that silent way habitual to long-married couples, and continued on.

Grace came to a dead stop.

"Just keep walking, Gracie, don't be such a slowpoke." Violet prodded her sister in the back.

"How can you tell?"

"The hair, the small hands, and the curvy figure."

Grace turned away. Did she seem as strange to the Berliners as they seemed to her? She looked at her relatives. Uncle William was a tall man with bright blue eyes and hair that had once been golden. A successful lawyer, he wore his habitual three-piece business suit, topped by a black coat and hat. He'd been married to Aunt Louisa for twenty-one years and had come to Berlin to create more business for himself and his partners. Beside him, Aunt Louisa looked diminutive. Her dark-brown curls peeked out from beneath an elegant cloche the top of which came to just below his shoulder. Today, she wore a thick wool coat, but hers was accessorized with fox fur at the cuffs and neckline. She was the family beauty, acquiring at sixteen a husband who'd graduated from Yale Law School, and owned both a house in Connecticut and an apartment in New York City.

They came up to a building with large letters lit in garish colors. More girls hung around in short dresses, smoking. One of them eyed Uncle William and blew smoke in his direction.

At that moment, someone bumped into her. Grace took an involuntary step back.

The individual said something to her in German, drawing out each syllable in a languorous fashion. Her thick sable coat dragged on the ground, making her trip. Her rope of pearls twisted in some disarray around her throat. She gesticulated with her hands, raised her face to the sky, and opened her arms wide. Grace couldn't wrench her eyes away.

Uncle William, who understood German, coughed, and turning around, offered Grace his arm.

"Let's get a taxi." Aunt Louisa stood on her tippy toes and gesticulated.

They piled inside to the sound of raucous laughter.

✠✠✠✠✠✠✠✠✠✠✠✠

They returned to the hotel armed with brochures and news of Grace's audition.

Once Great-Aunt Paulina's effusions of delight had quieted, Aunt Louisa cleared her throat. "Nollendorfplatz is not suitable. The people one has to pass on the street are undesirable."

"It's not their fault there's no work." Aunt Paulina sipped the whisky Uncle William offered. "The mark is plunging, the value of their money shrinking, They have to survive."

"That may be so," countered Aunt Louisa, "but I wish to do a lot of entertaining. You can't expect smart people to come to that part of town."

"There's the Metropol-Theater on Nollendorfplatz," said Violet, perusing a brochure that showed a picture of it on the cover. "The neighborhood is full of cafés."

"It's too shabby. Why don't you come to Charlottenburg? It has lovely villas."

Aunt Paulina glanced at the brochure Aunt Louisa handed her, which showed photographs of several mansions. She shook her head. "I can't do that. It's too pricey."

"We would be happy to have you come live with us."

Aunt Paulina flushed, handing the brochure back. "It's kind of you, *Luisa cara,* but those mansions are too fancy for me. I wouldn't know what to do with myself."

Aunt Louisa sighed and tapped the brochure against the table.

Uncle William cleared his throat. "I made some inquiries, and I understand that there is a widow, a

Frau Varga, with rooms to spare, who lives near Nollendorfplatz. She lost her husband in the Great War. "

Aunt Paulina scrutinized the slip of paper with his notes on it. She raised her chin. "My dears, you must do as you see fit. I intend to visit Frau Varga myself tomorrow. I think her place will suit us very well. Her rates are very reasonable."

"Of course, they are," said Aunt Louisa, looking through her brochure. "The area is in a state of decay."

"There are many artists there," remarked Grace, looking up from the Nollendorf brochure with its advertisement featuring the Metropol-Theater. "We'll meet interesting people."

"Indeed, we will." Aunt Paulina patted her hand. "Especially now that you're a student of Professor Flesch."

Grace glowed.

"Look at this." Aunt Louisa gave her brochure to Uncle William. "Here's a mansion on Savignyplatz,, in Charlottenburg. I think it would suit us perfectly."

Uncle William glanced at the photos of the handsome residence and nodded. He turned to Aunt Paulina."Are you sure you wouldn't be more comfortable with us in Charlottenburg? There would be plenty of room."

Aunt Paulina flushed and shook her gray curls. "I thank you for your offer, but I would prefer something more modest."

Uncle William and Aunt Louisa gave each other a look.

"Don't worry, Auntie Lou."Violet linked her arm through her sister's. "We'll enjoy living in Nollendorfplatz."

✠✠✠✠✠✠✠✠✠✠✠✠

Frau Varga's second-floor apartment consisted of a dining room that doubled as a parlor, two bedrooms—one large, one small—a kitchen and a bathroom. Faced with three American ladies who agreed to pay in dollars, Frau Varga insisted on giving her own bedroom to Violet and Grace. They opened the door and looked in.

Frau Varga's room had two large windows that gave onto the street. In front of one of the windows was an oak vanity with several small drawers and a large mirror. The vanity stool was covered in faded pink chintz flowers that matched the large window drapes. Violet turned down the bedclothes of the large bed, finding starched linen sheets that had been carefully mended. On top was a thick down comforter embroidered all over with red, green, and white flowers. Opposite the foot of the bed stood a large oak armoire with an oval window in one door. In a corner opposite the window was a small oak washstand, worn with use. The top shelf held a large jug inside a matching bowl that had a chip in it. Both showed yellow cockerels crowing against a lush background of green leaves and white and red flowers. The bottom shelf held several colorfully embroidered linen towels, which had also been carefully mended.

Aunt Paulina took the small back bedroom that had a view of the dark interior courtyard, filled with washing lines, bicycles, and children's toys. She waved away Violet's offer of trading places.

"It's a slice of life," she said. "I can experience everything even though I don't speak German."

Violet retreated to their new bedroom and unpacked her sewing basket. "I'm so glad Aunt Paulina stuck to her guns and let us live here. It's not far from Viktoria-Luise-Platz. I can go to the Lette-Verein and take classes in fashion design."

Grace smiled at her sister. Violet hadn't sounded happy in a long time. She took her violin out of its case and stood by the window where light poured in so that she could see to clean the dust from underneath the fingerboard, the bridge, and on that part of the bow that faced the horsehair.

What would Mr. Russell think if he could see her now?

"Buone notte, vita mia. Farewell, my life."

Grace tilted her head as if she could actually hear him say those words. He had such a beautiful voice, so very expressive, and there was something about those words and the way he said them, that gave her the physical sensation of being touched, as if he were caressing her hair or cheek. During all the chaos that had followed his departure, those words played over and over again in her mind. She couldn't get rid of them, especially in the middle of the night when she couldn't sleep. Those enigmatic words comforted her in some strange way.

But wasn't he dangerously obsessive, as Mother had said? What about all those shoes, all those expensive dresses suspended in his creepy closet? Grace shivered as prickles ran along the backs of her arms. Was that a bad quality to have in a suitor, or a good one? Was it grounds for complaint that he'd taken the initiative to get her some new clothes? Or bought an ashtray that looked like her? Instead of being frightened, perhaps she should have been delighted. But suppose his obsessiveness prevented her from doing what she wanted?

She allowed her shoulders to relax. He wasn't like that. When she'd told him to focus on passing his exams, instead of coming to Germany, his only response was to mildly suggest that he bring his work with him. Then he'd brushed his lips across her cheek, calling her *my love*. Her heart thrummed. Was that so bad? She shook herself. He'd lied to her, she was furious with him. She wrapped her arms around herself. She should be furious with him. She shouldn't allow herself to draw comfort from the sound of his voice or remember with pleasure the way he'd accompanied her on the piano. She couldn't, she mustn't imagine how he must be now, alone, bereft, in Georgetown.

A tear ran down her cheek. Grace returned to her violin, and focused on getting the rosin off the wood.

Violet came over. "What's wrong, Gracie?"

Grace put her violin in its case and slumped onto Frau Varga's bed. Couldn't Violet see she wanted to be left alone? What was she to say? She couldn't talk about Mr. Russell, because Aunt Paulina had forbidden any mention of his name.

"Mother." Grace leaned forward to avoid looking into Violet's face.

"Really?" Violet sat next to her and touched her sister gently on the arm. "So you miss her, too?"

Grace considered. Did she miss Mother? If she half-closed her eyes, she could feel the softness of her cheek pressed against her own when they'd said goodbye that last time. Something about that gesture told her Mother loved her. Tears pricked. She hadn't thought of her for a long time. Somehow Mother had disappeared in the press of events surrounding her death and Grace's sudden departure from Georgetown. For the first time, Mother's voice intruded: *I am not prying. I am merely trying to find out information about my daughter's suitor.* Mother had been right that there was something odd about Mr. Russell. But why had she tormented him so? She'd inserted Grace into the middle of an endless war of divided loyalties, of emotional fault lines that jerked her this way and that.

"Well?" Violet leaned forward.

"I don't know," mumbled Grace. "Everything feels strange. What would Mother think if she could see us now?"

Violet looked away for a moment. "She'd be very proud."

"Proud?"

"She was always proud of you."

Grace gazed at her sister as she vainly searched her memory. Had Mother been proud? She couldn't recollect anything. Well, there had been that last time.

Violet leaned forward and touched her sister's knee. "Of course she was proud of you, you silly goose. She was proud of your talent and your good looks."

Grace fiddled with a corner of the colorfully embroidered comforter that sprawled across the bed. When she'd shown them around, Frau Varga had explained that she'd embroidered all the comforters herself in the style of Kalócsa, where she came from. His voice sounded in Grace's head. *Do you have any idea how breathtakingly lovely you are?*

Grace compressed her lips, but she wasn't quick enough.

"Whatever is wrong?" Violet peered into her sister's face.

Grace turned away, the hairs on the backs of her arms prickling as her neck stiffened. He was so white, even his lips were pale.

After Great-Aunt Paulina banished Mr. Russell forever, she cabled Aunt Louisa and put Grace on a New York-bound train that afternoon. A week later, after shutting up the house in Beall Street, she'd taken the same train with Violet. With Violet's help, Aunt Louisa organized everything for the trip to Berlin, as Aunt Josephina was unable to come due to Uncle James' poor health. Grace was grateful. She just couldn't seem to focus on dresses, hats, gloves, shoes, stockings, or finding clever ways of packing them into suitcases. It was all she could do to find the concentration to practice, for every quiet moment was inhabited with his presence.

As she sat on Frau Varga's bed next to Violet, memories crept like a series of photographic stills. *Buona notte, vita mia*. The expression of his dark eyes lanced through her. They were so magnetic, they could make her do anything. How had Mother felt when she looked into his face? When had she last seen him? A coil of fear slithered up her spine. Did he have the power to make Mother do his bidding? Is that why she reacted so angrily? What words had they exchanged that last time? What had he done?

Bile rose in Grace's throat.

No.

The kind and attentive man she'd known seemed so at odds with someone capable of… When Mother baited him, he'd been so controlled, so apologetic. It wasn't, it couldn't—

The door opened.

"*Guten Abend*, Fräulein Graatz, Fräulein Vi'let."

Grace jolted up as Frau Varga bustled in. Her cheeks stretched as she forced an answering smile onto her face. How glad she was to see Frau Varga! Short and diminutive, with swarthy skin, sharp black eyes, and thick dark hair, Frau Varga hardly ever stood still. She bustled around her house from morning to night, polishing every surface until it shone. When she wasn't expecting company, she wore a pink chintz dressing gown over her foundation garments, a set of lavishly embroidered petticoats, stockings, and corset. The amount of petticoat, lace, or ribbon that Frau Varga allowed everyone to see, Grace and Violet were quick to learn, was an accurate barometer of her mood. If she were depressed or grumpy, the dressing gown would be closed up tight. When she was feeling relaxed or happy, a bit of lace or ribbon would show.

"All Berlin is crazy about my legs," she warbled, as she attacked the non-existent dust on the nightstand.

Grace's face cracked as her smile widened. It was impossible not to be drawn in by Frau Varga's zest for life. Grace made a supreme effort and shut down all those poisonous feelings of doubt that lay coiled in the bottom of her stomach. *The world is not that bad. It cannot be with someone like Frau Varga*. She rose to her feet, humming the tune under her breath. Frau Varga must be in a good mood to sing that.

Frau Varga grabbed a wooden chair and set it under the window. *"I'll know that you still love me…"* She mounted the chair. A red ribbon and a froth of petticoat fluttered out, showing well-turned calves. She banged the blind. *"So long as your panties are hanging on the chandelier…"*

Grace paused. What had she said? Was it as saucy as she thought? She exchanged glances with Violet. They had been studying German vocabulary, but that Berlin dialect was almost impenetrable.

"Where are you sleeping tonight, Frau Varga? We've taken your bed." Violet hurried over to the window.

Frau Varga got off the chair. "Come." She led the way to the dining-room parlor and made gestures to show them that she intended to sleep on the foldout sofa. She dragged the sofa so that it barred the front door of the apartment.

"It doesn't look comfortable to me," said Violet. "You've got freezing drafts coming in through that front door."

"I am happy."

"But you don't have a headboard."

Frau Varga laughed. "I need not, Fräulein Vi'let."

"Are we safe?"

"Today, we have full of peace. But if anything happen," she added, "I swear at them in Berlinish."

"What could happen?"

"Fräulein Vi'let, two years ago, it bad. When *der Kaiser* deposed, people shot in the streets. They threw hand-grenades from the *Brandenburger Tor*. They waved red flags, they shouted slogans." She made gestures. "It crazy."

"Those were the Spartacists?" asked Grace. She remembered Mr. Russell trying to dissuade them from going to Berlin.

Frau Varga stared. "You heard in *Amerika,* Fräulein Graatz?"

"Could there be problems again?"

"Everything quiet now," replied Frau Varga, shrugging. She patted Grace's arm. "Worry not."

"I'm not worried as long as you're not," remarked Violet.

Grace frowned.

"Fräulein Graatz, worry not. Look!" She swept aside the bedclothes to show the knife that hid under her pillow.

Chapter Eleven
Monday, 6 February

Violet walked home from the Lette-Verein, as rapidly as she could. It was freezing, the icy air turning her legs red and chapped through the thin layer of her stockings. She must let Auntie P. know it was a waste of money. Things hadn't gone well since she arrived two weeks ago, when the director informed her she couldn't participate in dressmaking because her German wasn't good enough.

Violet glanced at the sky. It was only three o'clock, but already growing dark. How she missed the bright winter sunshine of Georgetown; these northern European winters were so much darker. Violet didn't think she had ever been so cold as she had been these past couple of weeks in Berlin. She turned up the collar of her peacoat. There must be a professional dressmaker in this city who would take her on as an apprentice. Today had been particularly trying. After two weeks of watching several placid young women clumsily attempt to make clothes, Violet was dying to get her hands on a length of wine-red organza that someone had brought in today. How she'd found it, Violet had no idea, because they were short on supplies. Violet was just twining the fabric through her fingers when a booming voice intervened.

"*Fräulein, Fräulein.*"

Herr Poppmeier, the director of the Lette-Verein, bristled, his big, beefy face going pink.

Violet snatched her fingers away.

"One has told me that you have had a drawing class never. Is true?"

Violet nodded.

"How can you to design if you draw not? You must classes to have." Herr Pompous patted the large watch that lay across his belly and bowed stiffly from the neck. "I, myself, will you teach."

Violet stifled a groan. Those Germans were so detail oriented. It could take months.

"*Fräulein*? You listen not. You must to have the system to draw—the dots, the lines, the form, to you make into the *sehr gut*—what is the word?"

"Dressmaker."

"*Nein, Nein, Nein*. That is the wrong word, *Fräulein*. You come not here to be the dressmaker. If that is your desire, you waste the time. No. What is the right word? *Ach, ja*. The fashion designer."

"How long will this take?"

"Hmm?"

"How long will it take you to teach me drawing?"

"Hmm. The full year."

"Why can't I make clothes and take drawing classes at the same time?"

"Because that is not the right thing to do. One must be systematic. You Americans are very—quick." And Herr Pompous droned on and on in this vein for several more minutes, while the muscles surrounding Violet's mouth locked up from the smile she pasted on her face. Eventually, he let her go, and she fled.

Now Violet marched briskly through shabby Nollendorfplatz, bisected by its U-bahn. A chill wind scattered dirty piles of leaves, newspapers, and cigarettes. Thank goodness it was only a short walk to Frau Varga's. As usual, the square was populated by colorful street people and many, many young men. According to Frau Varga, these men had no jobs to go to because the Mark was falling through the floor. It didn't help that they were returning war veterans.

"They cannot work," she explained.

"Why not?"

"They cannot think—*denken*."

"You mean they can't concentrate?"

She nodded.

Violet crossed the square, passing a restless young man. He was handsome, with pale blue eyes, blond hair, and regular features. But he couldn't sit still. He paced back and forth in the same small corner of the square, talking rapidly to some non-existent entity. He would crouch, jump, and declaim until his long-suffering wife or mother appeared to lead him back to their apartment. Many young men sat around, staring apathetically. But if you walked too close, they jumped violently. Many of them were amputees, who sat all day because it was so difficult to walk. Some of them had a peculiar stare of non-seeing.

As she passed through Nollendorfplatz, she saw a familiar figure clutching a violin case facing a circle of men. A man with a red face, leaning heavily on crutches, made loud smacking noises as Violet passed by. He nudged his companion in the ribs, said something loudly in German, and grabbed her arm.

Violet hurried forward.

"Go away," said Grace to one particularly disreputable-looking individual, who was jabbering at her in German. "Leave me alone."

The person eyed Grace malevolently and reached for her violin. Quick as a whip, Grace clutched it to her chest and began running.

Violet ran after her. "Gracie! Are you all right?"

She turned, her face wet with tears.

Violet put her arm around her, as if she were the young child she'd comforted all those years ago in Rockville, Maryland, before Auntie P. had come into their lives. She led her inside Frau Varga's, carefully shutting and locking the door.

"Fräulein Graatz," called Frau Varga from the kitchen. "Your master class good?"

"It was wonderful, Frau Varga." Grace brushed away tears and put her case on the dining room table. "He kept us there for over two hours. He made us all play."

"You eat?"

"I forgot," mumbled Grace. She opened each compartment of her case, checking on strings, rosin, tuning fork, and all those other things she had to have.

Frau Varga bustled out of her kitchen. "Something wrong?"

"Some people in Nollendorfplatz tried to snatch her violin," said Violet.

Frau Varga flushed. "Ach. The people here. The police, they do nothing. Nothing broken?"

Grace picked up her violin, turning it slowly in her hands as she scrutinized it. She tapped it lightly near its curvy edge. She tilted her head as she held it up to the light. "No."

"You must to eat, Fräulein Graatz. We cannot have you to collapse in front of the Herr Professor."

Grace smiled briefly. Then she picked up her violin and started to play.

Violet followed Frau Varga back into her tiny kitchen, where she had a two-ring burner. On one, she put some soup to heat. Violet filled a kettle from the water pump and put it on the other. Frau Varga cut thick slices of black bread and daubed them with butter. Violet heated the teapot with hot water from the kettle, then spooned in two teaspoons of tea. As they carried the tea-things out to the dining room, Frau Varga said, "You are the good helper, Fräulein Vi'let. Your mother taught you good." She set the tray down. "How is she?"

An image of Mother filled Violet's head. She wore that powder-blue frock with the plunging neckline. She was laughing because Violet had just remarked that the registrar at Georgetown University would categorize her as one of the seven deadly sins.

"Mother was—impossible." Violet turned away to brush aside a tear.

"Impossible?" queried Frau Varga.

Violet glanced up and hesitated. Grace appeared from the bedroom, where she'd stowed her violin.

Violet shrugged. "Mother would get bees in her bonnet about things."

Grace sat down and thinned her lips.

"Bees?" said Frau Varga. "In her bonnet? What does that to mean?"

"She was very determined," said Violet. She glanced at Grace. Grace stared into her teacup.

"In the past you speak of her."

Violet blinked. "She died suddenly."

"Oh. So sorry am I." Frau Varga patted her arm. "Mother you miss."

Violet swallowed, unable to speak.

"Fräulein Graatz, what of the mother?"

Grace froze, her teacup in mid-air. She flushed, then sipped her tea. "Mother was always nicely dressed," she said tonelessly. "Violet looks rather like her."

"Oh. She pretty. Fräulein Vi'let pretty, you think, Fräulein Graatz?"

Violet's cheeks warmed as Grace smiled faintly. Just then, the doorbell rang, and Frau Varga scurried off to answer it.

Grace put her cup down. "How is Aunt Paulina?"

"She was still sleeping when I left this morning."

"Is she getting better?"

"I hope so."

"Fräulein Vi'let, Fräulein Graatz, here is the auntie and the cousin," called Frau Varga. "More tea will I make."

As Violet straightened up from plumping the cushions on Frau Varga's shabby settee, she blinked. Two women stood there, looking like apparitions from another world. One was dressed in a bluish-gray suede coat trimmed with fox fur, and matching fur hat. The other was wearing a mahogany mink coat that swung out from the shoulders into sumptuous folds that fell to mid-calf. She stared out the window with her back turned. But when she swung around, there was Teresa wearing a new coat that must have cost several hundreds of dollars.

Violet looked down. She wore what she wore each day in Berlin: a black woolen dress, woolen stockings and pair of old clogs Frau Varga had leant her. She lifted her chin, stiffening as the scent of something expensive hit her nostrils. Why was her cousin here, splashing her finery around?

"Would you like to see Aunt Paulina?" Grace opened the door to Auntie P.'s room.

After exchanging greetings and inquiries about Great-Aunt Paulina's health, Auntie Lou came to the point.

"I'm concerned about the long walk Grace has to make. I think she should come and stay with us."

"Why, *cara?*" replied Auntie P. "She's not your daughter."

Violet narrowed her eyes. Why ask for Grace? She glanced at her sister, whose face was expressionless.

Auntie Lou moved closer to the bed and took a seat. "I feel I should do something."

Auntie P. plucked at her bedclothes. Violet helped her into a sitting position and took the other chair, leaving Teresa standing awkwardly at the foot of the bed alongside Grace.

"*Cara*, I have an obligation to Grace. I have to think of what's best for her. She doesn't know you well."

"Why don't you ask her?" She turned to Grace.

"I will. But first I'd like to know your reasons."

Auntie Lou played with the clasp of her blue-gray suede purse that matched her hat and coat. "I regret not staying in touch with Angelina when she was alive. And I am genuinely fond of Grace."

Auntie P. wheezed as she sank against the pillows. Violet leaned over and propped her up. Her skin was white with a yellowish tint. What a perfect opportunity for Auntie Lou to make her move. But why Grace specifically?

Auntie P. turned her head. "What do you think, *Graziella cara*?"

"I don't know," murmured Grace, looking down.

"Are you having any trouble getting to the music school?" said Aunt Louisa.

"No, thank you. I know the way there now."

"But my residence in Savignyplatz near Charlottenburg is much closer, only a shortish walk away. It is a charming mansion with wrought iron-work on the stairs and a kind of old-fashioned medieval feel that I'm sure you would enjoy, Grace dear." She paused. "Or Hans could take you there in the car."

Grace remained silent.

"There are many beggars in Nollendorfplatz," continued Auntie Lou. "You have to walk that way. Has anyone bothered you?"

Grace flushed.

"What happened?"

"Someone tried to steal my violin," whispered Grace.

Auntie P. sagged under the covers. "*Graziella cara*. It never occurred to me—"

"There you are. I told you this place was not suitable. Grace would be much better off in Savignyplatz."

"Auntie Lou," said Violet. "You can't do this. Grace and I have always been together. We're still recovering from Mother's death."

She stopped, tears pricking. She'd spent her entire life with Grace, couldn't imagine a day without her. True, her sister didn't say much, but she was always there. A memory intruded. Violet was standing in the kitchen of the farmhouse near Rockville, trying to make something for Grace to eat. She'd gotten a slice of bread and was trying to toast it over the fire. Grace sat on her haunches on the dirty floor, patiently waiting. There was a rustle and a squeak, and a mouse flew by, but Grace never flinched. She couldn't have been more than six, because that's when they left Rockville and moved to Auntie P.'s large house on Second Street in Georgetown.

Auntie P. turned to Grace. "Would you feel better if you went to stay with Aunt Louisa for a while?"

Violet folded her arms and looked squarely at Aunt Louisa, who returned her gaze with a smile. What was this about? There was something Violet couldn't put her finger on. But her place in Savignyplatz was close to the music school, and Grace wouldn't have to run the gantlet of beggars and unemployed men every time she went to the U–Bahn.

Grace twisted her hands and looked at the floor. Finally she said, "Perhaps I should."

"A wise move, dear." Aunt Louisa smiled and nodded her head.

Auntie P. beckoned, and Grace moved to the side of the bed. "You know, *cara*, you always have a home here, don't you?"

Grace nodded, looking forlorn.

"Louisa can do many things for you, child." Auntie P. took Grace's hand. "This could be the opportunity of a lifetime."

Grace nodded again, but her cheeks were stained with tears.

Teresa smirked and turned away.

"This isn't right," said Violet. "A family should stay together. I firmly believe that. No one cares as much about Grace as Auntie P. and me." She glared at Aunt Louisa.

"But Grace has had a nasty fright," said Auntie P. "I think we should accept Louisa's kind offer and see how Grace feels about it."

✠✠✠✠✠✠✠✠✠✠

Grace never realized before just how rich Uncle William was until she came to live at the rented mansion near Savignyplatz with its chauffeur, maid, and cook. Everything seemed much more sumptuous than even their apartment in New York. A filigreed iron railing wound up to the front door, which opened into a reception room with a wooden balcony and hooded fireplace that hinted at the medieval era.

"It's called Jugendstil here in Germany," explained Aunt Louisa as Grace looked around. "But it's more commonly known as Art Nouveau. Do you like it?"

"Yes." Grace sat down on a green leather sofa, which had a filigreed back that looped back on itself in a way that reminded her of the shape of an orchid or a calla lily. "It's very floral."

"Indeed, it is." Aunt Louisa rang the bell. "A cold collation, if you please," she said to the uniformed young woman who appeared. "And tell the maid to make up an extra bed in Miss Teresa's room."

She followed her outside to give more instructions, and as the murmur of voices continued, Grace studied the salon. The wooden floors were covered in thick cream-colored rugs. The walls were white, to set off the light-colored wood of the furniture and fittings. Scattered around the room in artful arrangements were easy chairs, occasional tables, another sofa, and a large cabinet that took up most of one wall, all done with calla lily-like loops that gave the room a light, sophisticated feel.

"Cousin Grace, they've fetched you!" Ella tucked a strand of yellow hair behind her ear and bent her tall frame over Grace. They pecked each other's cheeks and smiled.

Aunt Louisa and Uncle William had three daughters. Nineteen-year-old Teresa was the beauty, with her mother's poised, cool, and aloof manners. Twelve-year-old Adela was the spoiled baby of the family. But fifteen-year-old Ella was different. She wanted to be a writer.

"What have you been writing today?" Grace nodded towards a sheaf of paper Ella clutched to her chest with inky fingers.

"Shall I read it to you?" Ella sat down and immediately began.

Grace listened. Her cousin had a good ear for the rhythm of language.

"Did you like my description of Berlin? Did you know it's the most sinful city in the world?"

"What do you mean?"

"Haven't you heard? Everyone knows what goes on here." Ella lowered her lashes, hiding her pale blue eyes.

A reluctant smile tugged at the corners of Grace's mouth.

Ella leaned forward, blushing. "There are ladies of the night," she whispered, shielding her mouth with her hand.

"I expect there are." Grace remembered the prostitutes she'd seen the day of the audition.

Ella's voice sank to a pitch that was scarcely audible. "But not every city has gentlemen of the night."

Grace shivered. "Where on earth did you hear that?"

"I read it in a book."

The sound of female voices wafted towards them and then the door burst open.

"Are you coming to live with us?" Twelve-year-old Adela skipped in. She had dark curls surrounding a heart-shaped face, in which were set two dark-blue eyes. Was she going to be even more beautiful than Teresa when she grew up? Grace bent and kissed her cheek. She responded by performing a perfectly controlled pirouette.

"Where did you learn to do that?" asked Grace

"Herr Elsinore, the dancing master." Adela put her arms in front of her and struck another pose. "We're all taking lessons. Don't you dance?"

Grace shook her head.

"Don't you want to?" asked Ella.

Nineteen-year-old Teresa wandered in, divested of her sumptuous mink coat.

"Teresa went to a ball last night," remarked Adela.

"Why didn't you go?" Grace turned to Ella.

Teresa rolled her eyes and tittered.

"Because I'm not out yet. Mother says you have to be seventeen to be out. I'm only fifteen."

"It must be so romantic to go to a ball." Adela performed another pirouette.

"She wanted to go last night," remarked Ella. "She cried when Mother said that formal balls weren't suitable for twelve-year-olds."

"Grace doesn't even know how to dance," said Adela with a pout. "But I do. I could've danced with those gentlemen last night."

"Did you dance with anyone interesting?" Grace turned to Teresa.

"There was the prince of Liechtenstein," she murmured in a smoky voice.

"I thought you said he was a pimply-faced adolescent," remarked Ella.

Teresa thinned her thickly lipsticked lips and glared.

"Didn't you get anything?" said Adela. "I thought ladies received bouquets from their admirers."

"Adela, that was naughty." Aunt Louisa entered the room. "Please apologize to your sister and refrain from squabbling in front of company. It isn't seemly."

Adela jutted out her lower lip and muttered something that was scarcely audible. "She was rude, too." She poked Ella.

"Girls, girls!" Aunt Louisa clapped her hands. "If you don't behave like young ladies, I'll send you up to your rooms."

Ella rose and looked at her watch. "Goodbye, Grace. This is my time for writing."

"Isn't it a bit late to be doing that?" queried Aunt Louisa.

"I don't have time to do it during the day, what with all those social things you make us go to." She pecked her mother on the cheek and disappeared.

"Goodbye, Grace," said Adela, blowing kisses. "This is my time for dancing." She giggled.

Aunt Louisa beckoned. "It's high time you went to bed." She kissed her daughter on the cheek and gave her a gentle push. "I'm coming up in ten minutes. I expect you to be under the covers by then." Adela made a face and ran out of the room. Shaking her head, Aunt Louisa turned to her niece. "Grace dear, would you care for refreshments?"

"No thank you," murmured Grace. "I'm not hungry."

"You look tired." She turned to her eldest daughter. "Teresa, my love, show Grace her room."

Without a word, Teresa led Grace upstairs to a large bedroom that took up most of the side of the house. It was large enough to have French doors that gave out onto a balcony facing an interior courtyard. Yellow lamplight picked out the white marble statues and stilted trees currently buried under heaps of snow.

"Ma says you're to share my room." Teresa sat at her vanity and picked up a brush. Her vanity was the most beautiful piece of furniture Grace had ever seen. It, like the rest of the furniture in her room or downstairs, was made of light-colored wood, perhaps walnut, and decorated with those floral scrolls. Scrolls curled around the three-part mirror, the side of the oval table, and the drawers that peeked beneath white velvet drapes.

"Cat got your tongue?"

Grace studied the room, crammed with glorious things. Two huge armoires held Teresa's dresses. Scrolling shelves displayed her shoes. Filigreed half-open drawers spilled scarves, purses, jewelry, makeup, and silken underwear.

Where had everything come from? Grace didn't remember Teresa having to pack all that stuff into her trunks. She had way more clothes here than in New York, and they all looked very expensive. Grace frowned. Aunt Paulina had been talking about the falling Mark. *The only good thing about it, cara, is for people like us who have our money in dollars. It makes us incredibly rich, much more so than back home. But I'm not comfortable enjoying a life of luxury when so many are suffering. That's why I didn't want to live in a fancy mansion in Charlottenburg. It just doesn't seem right. You understand, don't you, cara?* Grace had patted her arm and told her not to worry. Now, she put her small suitcase on the floor. It held everything she had. "Where shall I put my violin?"

"How about under the bed?" Teresa laughed a long, mocking laugh.

Grace turned. There were two beds, done in that same calla lily design. One had a white velvet coverlet on it, and over it arched a wispy canopy. The other was made up more plainly. Grace sat on the unloved bed.

"There are rules, Gracie dear." Teresa wagged her brush in Grace's general direction. "No borrowing. I don't want to see anything touched. No dresses, no makeup, and certainly no jewelry. I don't want to see you taking anything."

Grace glared. "I'm not a thief."

Teresa rose and pinched her cousin's cheek. "Let's keep it that way, shall we?" She laughed as she switched off the electric light, plunging everything into darkness.

Chapter Twelve
Wednesday, 15 February
Morning

A couple of weeks passed. Gradually Grace found her routine, spending mornings at the music school, then afternoons and evenings at Aunt Louisa's mansion. Wednesdays was when she had her private lesson with Professor Flesch, which started on the dot of ten-thirty and lasted until noon. On this particular mid-February Wednesday, Grace drifted along the sidewalk, trying to remember if she'd packed everything. It was so difficult to find things when you'd just moved into a new place. As she turned left to go into the music school, someone came towards her. Violet.

"What are you doing here?" said Grace, as they pecked each other on the cheek. She abruptly clutched Violet's arm. "Aunt Paulina?"

"I left her sleeping peacefully." Violet paused. "Do you mind if I sit in on your lesson?"

"Of course not. But I'd have to ask Professor Flesch."

"Let's ask him then."

Grace led the way up the stairs to a corner room that had its door firmly closed. Behind that door, someone played a rising phrase over and over again. In the pauses between each performance of this melodic fragment, voices murmured.

"That's the person before me." Grace sat down on a wooden chair opposite.

"Who is he?"

"I don't know." Grace took off her gloves, put on the mittens Violet had knitted for her, gently massaging the knuckles of her left hand.

Violet sat down next to her sister. Grace glanced at her, but she said nothing, merely looking around with her bright blue eyes. The corridor extended the whole length of the palatial beaux-arts building. It was drab, dark, and visually unappealing, with wooden chairs scattered at intervals near the doors. Faint sounds of music drifted out under the closed doors of each room. There was a trumpet, a flute, a contra-bassoon, and a piano. Suddenly, the door to the corner room was flung open, and a diminutive young man with a shock of dark hair came out. He nodded and disappeared in the direction of the stairs, whistling under his breath.

Professor Flesch appeared in the doorway. "Guten Morgen, Grace-*chen*."

"Guten Morgen, Mein Herr Professor." Grace rose and indicated Violet. "Would you allow my sister to sit in on the lesson?"

He stared at her for a moment, but Violet could out-stare anyone. Finally, he cleared his throat. "You may enter on the condition that you make no sound. I insist on my students listening very carefully, and I can't have any distractions. Do you understand?"

"I understand," murmured Violet. Her mouth quivered at the corners as she silently took the chair indicated.

Grace placed her violin case on the floor, unpacked it, and went to stand in front of the grand piano, where Professor Flesch was adjusting a metal music stand to suit her height.

"Now, Fräulein, let us attack one of your weaknesses." Flesch put some music on the stand. He turned to Violet. "This is *The Preparatory Exercises for Shifting* by Otakar Ševčík. It contains fifty-six exercises and is ideal study material for the positions of the left hand as well as for shifting."

He picked up his violin to demonstrate. "A position is where one places the left hand on the fingerboard. Down by the scroll is first position." He moved his left hand down. "Up where the belly meets the fingerboard is fifth position." He moved his left hand up until the right edge of his palm touched the belly of the instrument. "Shifting is the movement one has to make to get from one position to another." He bent his left elbow as he shifted his left hand up and down. "One must keep one's wrist straight." He turned to Grace. "Like most violinists, you are familiar with first, third, and fifth positions. But now I want you to learn half, second, and fourth. You will thank me when you have some difficult passages to finger." And he went on, pointing out various things that he wanted her to remember.

Grace lifted her violin and began. Violet blinked. What was this boring music? She'd never heard anything like it in her life. How could Grace bear to play it? It consisted of endless repetitions of intervals, going up and down, requiring her to move her left hand up and down the fingerboard of the violin from several different starting points.

Flesch moved to a large leather chair positioned in the middle of the room, sat down, and placed the tips of his fingers together while Grace played. He looked extremely intimidating. Did Grace find him so? Violet glanced at her sister, but Grace was playing with her eyes closed. The exercises were so predictable she'd already memorized them.

The next item on the agenda was a study by Kreutzer. "Now, Fräulein," said Flesch. "This is *Étude* No. 2, the famous détaché étude. There are two important questions to consider in the study of détaché. First, in study, which part of the bow should be used for the détaché?"

"The upper half of the bow."

"*In study* Fräulein." He turned to Violet. "What do you think?"

"You should be able to do it anywhere in the bow," replied Violet. This bear of a professor would demand no less than perfection, expecting his students to study far beyond what would usually be required. Grace didn't seem to have figured that out yet.

Flesch stared at her. "That is correct," he said slowly.

"May I ask a question?" said Violet.

"Certainly you may, provided it has something to do with violin technique."

"What is détaché?"

"A good question." He turned to Grace. "Show your sister how to do it."

Grace played a few notes. "It means that you have to make a small space between each note, so that each one is detached from the other."

"Good. Now let us consider the second important question concerning détaché. In actual performance, which part of the bow is best suited to it?"

"The upper part of the bow, provided it is not too near the tip."

"And why don't you want to play too near the tip?"

"Because it leads to rolling motions of the upper arm and shoulder."

I hope he is impressed with how much she knows. Violet gazed at his impassive countenance. Since her arrival in Berlin, Grace had spent every spare minute studying up on the professor's tomes.

"And what is wrong with that?"

"It's unnecessary and makes you tired."

He cracked a smile. "Excellent. Now, let's start. First, I want you to play it slurred, to ensure purity of pitch for the left hand."

Grace lifted her violin and began.

This study was almost a bad as those horrible exercises she'd played at the beginning of the lesson. Now she was required to play an insipid tune that was annoyingly repetitive.

Flesch made her play it again, this time using détaché in the various parts of the bow, upper, middle, lower. Then he made her play it with a bouncing stroke, with one bounce per bow-stroke, then two bounces, then three, going up and down the bow, using a flick of the wrist to start the stroke, and relaxing the knuckles of the right hand to let it continue.

By the time Flesch abandoned the étude, Violet had a headache. The worst of it was that she couldn't get the annoying song out of her head. But Grace was smiling. Perhaps she was pleased to have found a professor who demanded as much of her as she did of herself. Violet glanced at the clock. Only half an hour had passed, and yet she felt as if she'd been sitting there all morning.

After that, things got better, at least for Violet. Professor Flesch skimmed the repertoire, wanting to hear the first movement of the Beethoven concerto, the last movement of the Mendelssohn concerto, the last movement of the Brahms *D Minor Sonata*. He picked up his violin to demonstrate, penciling in bowings and fingerings for Grace to follow, relentless in pursuit of perfection. Mostly, his face was set in an expression of stern determination. But as Grace played the "Siciliana" movement from J. S. Bach's *G Minor Sonata* for unaccompanied violin, his face softened. Was he pleased?

At the end of the lesson, he handed Grace a long list of things to practice. "Remember, Fräulein," he admonished as Grace dusted off the rosin from her violin and bow, "I expect you to practice no less than five hours a day."

"I'm staying with my aunt." Grace put her violin carefully back in its case. "She wants me to be involved in all kinds of social activities."

"Five hours a day of concentrated practice, and no less," repeated Flesch. "If your aunt does not understand, you must let me know immediately. I will talk to her about it."

Grace murmured her thanks as he opened the door and told her to be back on Monday at noon sharp for the master class. He managed a wintry smile for Violet.

Out on the street, it was another gray day in Berlin. Violet shivered as a cold wind from the east bit into her, because the woolen coat gifted by Aunt Louisa at Christmas wasn't warm enough.

"Let's get something to eat." Violet took Grace's arm.

"I'm not hungry," replied Grace. "Besides, I have to be back this afternoon for a quartet rehearsal."

"You didn't tell us you were playing in a quartet."

"It's only just started. Professor Flesch told me that I needed to play more chamber music."

"What time is the rehearsal?

"Two o'clock."

"We've got plenty of time. Listen to those bells." Violet turned towards the Kaiser Wilhelm Memorial Church as the noon bells chimed. "How can you possibly expect to play this afternoon after spending all morning with that bear of a man? You need some nourishment inside you."

"Didn't you like him?" They walked south along Fasanenstrasse towards the Kurfürstendamm.

"He's not my type. But what do you think? What is it like to be his student?"

"He's so exacting, he makes you realize how sloppy you've been. And he's been telling me about his ideas for putting violin playing on a more scientific footing."

"How can you do that? I wouldn't have thought it was possible."

"It is. You know those exercises I had to play first?"

"You mean those boring, tuneless things by the fellow with the unpronounceable name?"

Grace's pale face relaxed into a laugh. "Violet, you're irrepressible."

"You haven't laughed in a long time."

"And you haven't been funny in a long time."

Violet squeezed her hand.

"So, tell me more about those God-awful exercises."

"They were dreamed up by a violin professor some twenty years ago as exercise drills to solve technical problems quickly."

"Are they helpful?"

"Yes." Grace lowered her voice and looked around. "But I hate doing them."

"I'm not surprised. The fellow who dreamed them up must have been having nightmares." Violet scanned a row of shabby shops and cafés. "Here it is." They stepped out of the wind.

"Where are we?"

"Aschinger, a student hangout Frau Varga told me about. She said you could get a helping of sausages and a glass of beer for fifty pfennigs. But it probably costs more now." She peered at the board.

"I don't usually drink beer in the middle of the day."

"Nor do I, but you can't beat the price." Violet summoned a waiter in halting German. He showed them to a small table near the kitchen.

Violet took off her coat, basking in the warmth of the greasy, smoky interior. Grace stowed her violin against the wall, sitting in front of it so that it was impossible to snatch.

The waiter reappeared with two helpings of sausages and two beers.

Violet and Grace clinked glasses and sipped. It was good. "How are you getting on at Aunt Louisa's?"

"I know she's trying to be kind, but she's insisting on my going to all the teas and dinner dances Teresa gets invited to. I hate it; I never know what to say."

"I know it's not your thing, but it's good for you, Gracie." Violet patted her hand. "You've been too silent for far too long. It's good to talk, you know. It lets other people know what's going on."

"Can't they tell?"

"People don't have psychic powers."

"But they always have opinions about things. The trouble is, I don't." She leaned forward. "How are things going with you?"

Violet munched on a piece of sausage. "Frau Varga has been wonderful. She knows everyone. She introduced me to this French woman who's opening her own boutique in Berlin—Mamzelle Camille Boissard. Says she designed a beautiful wedding dress for a friend's daughter."

"Will you be able to quit that school?"

"I left a note for Herr Pompous this morning, just before I visited with you. Camille is going to take me on as her assistant next week."

A loud burst of laughter blew in from a nearby table. They turned.

A tall gentleman, impeccably dressed in a waiter's outfit, was looking down his nose at another man lounging in his seat. The waiter said something haughtily.

The customer smiled and took his time in replying. He drew out a packet of cigarettes, lit one, and blew smoke into the waiter's face. Then he slapped his thigh and rapidly said something else. The haughty waiter thinned his lips, swept the menu off the table in an elegant gesture, turned precisely on his heel, and left.

The customer burst out laughing, the same loud laugh that had first arrested Violet and Grace. He turned to a compatriot at the next table, gesticulated, and they both burst into loud raucous laughter.

"Miss Violet Miller?"

An American-accented male voice made her turn. A young man stood there. He was good-looking in a quiet sort of way, with regular features and melancholy gray eyes. It was clear he was American, because he was tall and had good teeth that were very white. Violet frowned up at him.

"I'm Charles Phelps, Miss Miller." He fingered his hat, cautious but confident. "We met at the State Department. I helped you organize the documents for your trip to Berlin."

Violet smiled. "Of course. Grace, you remember Mr. Phelps?"

Grace inclined her head. "Mr. Phelps, if you are with State, could you tell me about those gentlemen over there?"

"They're Russian," he replied.

"What are they doing here?" asked Violet.

"When Lenin took power four years ago, all the aristocrats and many of the intelligentsia left. That gentleman," he said, indicating the tall waiter, who was now carrying a plate of sausages, "is—or was—a grand duke."

Their mouths fell open. Both sisters turned to stare.

"They left with nothing but the clothes on their backs. Now they have no money. Nothing. They have to wait tables. Their women have to make a living by sewing, giving music lessons, or translating."

"Who keeps laughing?" asked Grace. The tall waiter had just set down a plate of sausages, enduring another gale of laughter from the man with the loud laugh.

"He's a communist. I overheard him tell his friend at the next table that he'd just received a telegram from Comrade Lenin. His merriment is on account of seeing Grand Duke Dmitri Alexandrovich waiting tables."

"It has a different tonal quality," remarked Grace. "I mean they're not speaking German?"

Phelps's eyes softened to the color of gray satin. "They are speaking Russian."

"You can understand Russian?"

He smiled down at Grace.

Violet looked at her watch. "It's getting on for two o'clock, Gracie. We must go back to the music school."

Grace rose, retrieving her violin.

"Perhaps I can accompany you?" He helped Grace on with her coat and offered his other arm to

Violet. "I play cello, and my sister is taking viola lessons."

"You play together?" asked Grace.

"We do when we can find a violinist." He glanced at Violet. "Your sister told me that you play very well. I wondered if you'd be interested in joining us."

"I'd have to ask Professor Flesch,"replied Grace. "He's already assigned me to a quartet for this afternoon."

He smiled. "I am also on my way to quartet practice at the music school. My sister asked me to fill in for the cellist, who has been taken ill. I wonder if it is the same quartet?"

They walked into the school and looked at the notice board.

"There," said Phelps, pointing to a listing. "You're in the same quartet as my sister."

Violet looked. Below *Second Violin: Grace Miller* was listed *Viola: Mabel Phelps*.

"Why are there so few German students?" Violet pointed with a gloved finger. "Most of these people seem to be either American or French."

"The Mark." He led the way up the stairs. "No German can afford to come."

The quartet was in a room on the top floor. When they arrived, two young women were already there, unpacking their cases. Mr. Phelps made the introductions. The diminutive brunette with the warm smile was Mabel Phelps, his sister. The tall blonde was a violinist called Céline du Bois, who'd come from Paris. Both women studied with Professor

Josef Wolfsthal, who would be coaching the quartet that afternoon.

"You must be the young woman who's studying with Professor Flesch," said Mabel. "That's quite an honor. He's very picky."

Grace smiled shyly and murmured her thanks.

Mabel and her brother fell into an easy conversation which Grace tentatively joined, while Violet studied the blonde standing quietly to one side. She was dressed stylishly in a pale blue dress of fine wool that matched the color of her eyes and clung to her perfect figure. Her light ashen hair was swept up into a chignon. She had small elegant hands sheathed in blue suede gloves, small delicate features, and a tip-tilted nose. As the others talked, she eyed Grace with great interest.

"Charles, you should tell everyone our news."

He glanced at her and reddened.

Céline laughed, a delicate tinkle. "Men are so easily embarrassed." She turned to Mabel. "Why, Charles and I are to be married. We are to make a formal announcement this evening."

Mabel paled. "Is this true?"

Phelps bit his lip.

"How can you be so ungentlemanly—" began Céline.

At that moment, Professor Wolfsthal entered the room. Violet stared. Professor Wolfsthal could not be more than twenty-five, with a round, clean-shaven face. He put his violin case down and glanced mildly around him. "*Mesdemoiselles, Monsieur,* I trust there is nothing wrong?"

"*Pas de tout*, not at all," replied Phelps crisply, turning his back on Céline to open the cello case, which had been left for him in the room.

"*Bon—laissons-nous commencer à jouer le quatuor à cordes*, good—lets start to play the quartet."

They played Haydn's *Opus 33, No. 6*, Céline playing first violin and Grace, second. It started with a sweetly graceful theme from the first violin, which demanded great control from the rest of the quartet, because they had to play softly enough so as not to overwhelm its serenity. Céline played well, but she couldn't stop looking at Mr. Phelps.

Professor Wolfsthal made some comments on Céline's playing, drawing his violin out of its case and demonstrating some passages to make his point. He produced a clear, light sound on the upper strings, which melted into intense warmth for the lower strings. He paused, glanced at Grace, and suggested that they repeat the piece with Grace playing first.

Grace flushed but quietly took Céline's place. She played mostly with her eyes closed, only occasionally glancing at the music. Her tone quality had an inner fire that made Céline's playing seem bland. She varied the ebb and flow of the timing, making Céline's playing seem wooden and boring. She somehow made the others enter more fully into Haydn's gently puckish world.

Professor Wolfsthal bent over Grace, suggesting fingerings and bowings, discussing dynamics, phrasing, and timing. Violet sat up in her seat. Clearly, he expected her to do much more. This had the unfortunate effect of keeping Grace in full view of Phelps, who, as the cellist, was seated directly opposite the first violin. Violet sighed. At least he was polite to his sister, Céline, and Professor Wolfsthal. But when he thought no one was looking, he gazed at Grace. Violet glanced at Céline. Her pale blue eyes were the color of ice.

After a couple of hours, Wolfsthal dismissed everyone for the day and left the room.

Immediately, Céline turned to Mr. Phelps. "Are you denying we're engaged?"

"You're putting me in a very difficult position."

"Your mother told me you would present to me a ring—"

"You willfully misunderstood me."

Céline glanced at her bare left ring finger as the color mounted into her pale face. "*Je ne t'aurais pas même si tu m'avais imploré,* I wouldn't have you even if you begged me," she spat. She picked up her violin case and left.

The door swung closed with a creak.

"Perhaps I should go after her," said Mabel.

"She's not worth your time," her brother replied.

"Won't her father be angry?"

He remained silent.

Grace picked up her violin case and made for the door. Violet followed.

He glanced up. "Please don't go, Miss Miller. I would like to explain."

They turned, Grace's hand resting on the doorknob.

"The du Bois family is distantly related to us, and over the years my father has become very friendly with Céline's. When Mother visited Paris last year, she met Céline and conceived the extraordinary notion that I should marry her. I met Céline only last month." He put his bow inside the cello case. "It is true that I was very taken with her. She is beautiful and elegant. But as I got to know her better…" He positioned the cello inside and shut the case. "This incident confirms my growing concerns." He flushed.

"I never liked her," offered Mabel.

"Although I've always observed the convention that a lady is never wrong, I could not let her get away with telling lies at the cost of my future happiness." He turned to Grace. "You do see that, don't you?"

Grace frowned as she opened the door. Violet could almost hear her asking herself why he was asking for her opinion. She clearly didn't want to get involved.

"Why is there this convention that a lady has to be right?" remarked Violet, pinning him with her stare. "It doesn't make sense."

Phelps's laugh eased the creases from his face.

Flushing, Grace glanced at Mabel, who smiled back. "Surely ladies are as likely to make mistakes as gentlemen?" she murmured.

He moved closer. "You don't think badly of me for exposing her dishonesty?"

Grace looked at Violet.

"Mr. Phelps," said Violet, "I wonder if you'd mind walking home with me. I'd like you to meet Great-Aunt Paulina."

Phelps reddened and turned away.

"Would you like me to walk your sister home?" Mabel smiled at Violet.

Violet returned her smile and gave her Aunt Louisa's address.

"Mr. Phelps," said Violet, when they'd walked awhile in complete silence in the direction of Frau Varga's, "I don't like to see Grace being trifled with. If it is true that you are engaged to Miss du Bois, you have no business flirting with my sister."

Phelps stopped dead. "I thought I had given you my assurances."

"But you are very taken with Grace. Isn't that so?"

"I don't deny it. I don't know your sister, of course, but I feel strangely drawn to her. She is a lovely young woman. And what a fabulous musical talent she has—" He broke off and smiled ruefully. "Forgive me, Miss Miller. I'm sure you can't find these observations interesting."

"Mr. Phelps, you should know that there's another gentleman. In fact, he considers himself to be Grace's suitor and has already gone so far as to buy her an engagement ring."

Phelps went still. Eventually, he said, "Thank you for telling me." There was another long pause. "She doesn't wear his ring on her finger."

"That is because her family had concerns about the engagement. We persuaded him to stay in America and continue his studies at Georgetown University."

"What were the concerns?"

"I'm not at liberty to say." Violet's cheeks grew warm. "But I can tell you that Great-Aunt Paulina sent him packing."

Phelps stopped dead. His gray eyes shone. "Is that true?"

Chapter Thirteen
Wednesday, 15 February
Afternoon

"Grace, dear. Where on earth have you been? Who is your friend?"

Grace's cheeks heated up. She hesitantly introduced Mabel Phelps.

"You must both stay and have tea." Aunt Louisa ushered them towards the large reception room. "Teresa."

Teresa languidly rose from her position on the green leather sofa with its floral scrolls and rang the bell for the maid to bring tea and cakes.

"How was your day?" Aunt Louisa asked.

"I spent an hour and a half having my lesson with Professor Flesch," replied Grace, putting on her mittens. "Then I had to spend the afternoon playing in a quartet he assigned me to."

"So that's what you were doing. I wondered where you were."

Grace glanced at Mabel. "Oh, dear, I forgot to tell you."

The corners of Mabel's mouth quivered.

Aunt Louisa made *tut-tut* sounds. "You mustn't be so absent-minded. How can you run a household and see to your husband's needs if you don't pay attention?" She turned to Mabel. "Do you play, dear?"

"I'm a violist. I'm taking lessons with another professor at the music school."

"Why not with Professor Flesch?" Aunt Louisa clicked her fingers for the maid to put tea and cake on the coffee table and leave.

"I only wish," said Mabel smiling at Grace. "But he takes only the very best. I was playing in Grace's quartet this afternoon. She's very good."

Grace smiled as she massaged the fingers of her left hand. "Professor Flesch said I had to practice five hours a day."

"But you need a social life." Aunt Louisa handed Grace the teapot.

"He's very insistent." Grace sat sideways on her chair, her knees together and handed around the tea. Not even one saucer rattled—that should please Aunt Louisa. "He said he would call and explain if you didn't understand."

"Dear me, how tiresome."

Grace pursed her lips. She would have to come up with a plan. Mabel's warm, brown eyes caught hers. She smiled.

"Don't forget the cake, Grace dear," said Aunt Louisa. "You don't want your guests to starve." She watched like a hawk as Grace handed around Anna-Maria's apple cake. No crumbs dropped onto that priceless thick carpet—she must be having a good day today.

"I suppose you didn't tell him that I've always let you have your mornings free to practice?"

"But I only manage to get three hours done in the mornings. I have to do five hours."

Aunt Louisa sighed and rose. "We'll have to discuss this some other time. We have to go to a ball tonight at the von Stosches."

"Oh, no." Grace felt her face sag. She had so much work to do. Besides, she had nothing to wear.

Mabel shook her head.

"Surely you haven't forgotten?"

"I haven't done my practice."

"That's because you've been at the music school all day. Don't be tiresome. You don't have to dance, but I want you to watch what goes on so that you know how to behave at a ball. Teresa, my love, where is the dress you picked out for Grace?"

Teresa rang for the maid, who came in with a dress composed of a golden mesh tunic over a matching satin gown. The neckline was high, making a gentle scoop around the neck. The sleeves came to the elbows and the gown had a short train. It was finished off with a spray of artificial flowers.

Teresa smirked as she handed it over. Grace furrowed her brow.

"This dress shows the influence of the Aesthetic Movement, with its simple lines," remarked Aunt Louisa. "Now go put it on and I'll find some jewels."

Grace turned to Mabel. "What do you think?" She stood and held the gown against her.

Mabel smiled and tilted her head. "You'll be no competition."

"What do you mean by that?" Teresa narrowed her eyes.

"It's yesterday's fashions, and it makes Grace look younger than she is."

"So it's perfect for her."

"What do you mean?" Grace glared at her cousin.

"Nothing at all, you little dumpling." Teresa pinched Grace's cheek. "It will act as the perfect foil for my dress." She held up a sophisticated olive-green confection that had the fabric draped across the bodice to make a plunging V. Below the close-fitting waist, the material draped into multiple skirts with handkerchief hems. Of course. Beside her, Grace would look like yesterday's roses.

✠✠✠✠✠✠✠✠✠✠✠

It was nearly ten o'clock before the chauffeur arrived with the Benz. The von Stosches lived in a villa on one of the many lakes to the west of Berlin, so it was well past ten-thirty before they arrived. Beneath the porte-cochère lit by a large overhead lantern, guests alighted from their cars swathed in thick furs, for the temperature in mid-February was below freezing. When the door to the Benz flew open, icy air gusted in. A servant dressed in a top hat and a quasi-hunting outfit handed them out: Aunt Louisa in gray satin and tulle, topped by white mink; Uncle William in white tie; Teresa in her sophisticated olive-green concoction, topped by that lavish mink coat with the hood; and finally Grace in the unthreatening gown, topped by Teresa's cast-off mink sans hood.

They followed the other guests into a brightly lit marble foyer where a large team of people dealt with their furs. Aunt Louisa made last-minute adjustments to Grace's attire, while Uncle William approached a servant to give their names.

"Mr. and Mrs. Philips from New York," he announced loudly in a heavy accent. "Miss Teresa Philips. Miss Grace Miller."

Mr. and Mrs. von Stosch stood with their daughter at the bottom of a staircase curving up to the upper floors. Mr. von Stosch was a Prussian who'd lived in America for many years and made a fortune in steel. His wife, Emmeline, was American and distantly related to the second president of the United States. They'd recently returned to Berlin and were holding a debutante ball in honor of the coming-out of their daughter Elise.

"Elise," said her mother, "I wish to present you to Mr. and Mrs. Philips, Miss Philips, and Miss Miller."

They shook hands, with Uncle William giving Mr. von Stosch a hearty handshake, for they were already well acquainted, Uncle William acting as a lawyer for Mr. von Stosch in complicated business transactions in the States.

"We've invited the cream of Berlin society to come see Elise," whispered Mrs. von Stosch to Aunt Louisa as she handed out the dancing cards.

Elise von Stosch was a long-limbed young woman, with thick golden hair that fell like a helmet around her face.

"So this is Grace." Elise spoke in a low breathy contralto that somehow didn't sound like her. "The name suits you. Your uncle says you have a talent for music."

Grace smiled. "Many people have told me so."

"Then you should come play at one of our parties." Her laughter glinted like steel.

Aunt Louisa murmured her thanks and moved into the ballroom, Teresa next to her, and Grace trailing after, her face warm. She should be able to think of a suitable put-down to that.

Aunt Louisa found an empty sofa and patted the space next to her. Grace obediently sat down and folded her hands, while Teresa took the place on the other side.

"Let me explain about these dancing cards." Aunt Louisa handed one to Teresa and the other to Grace. "It allows you to keep track of whom you've agreed to dance with." And she spent several moments explaining how to do it.

Grace drooped. Everything seemed so formal and artificial. A ball was supposed to be the best way for young women to find their future husbands, but how could you possibly get to know someone in this stifling environment?

She closed her eyes and thought about the ricochet bowing that she had to practice next week for the first movement of the Mendelssohn concerto. It was a cadenza-like passage where she had to play broken chords across the strings by flicking her wrist and bouncing her bow four times on a downstroke and four times on an upstroke. It created a sparkling, frothy effect, like champagne bubbles. Now, what was the best fingering for that passage?

"Sit up, dear, and hold your head high," instructed Aunt Louisa in low tones from behind her fan.

A youngish gentleman in white tie approached. His full mustache of blond hair dusted with red bristled around his mouth. "Count von Oldenburg," he intoned in a *basso profondo*, standing stiffly to attention.

Aunt Louisa and Teresa rose and curtseyed. Grace followed more slowly, trying a really deep curtsey just for practice. She managed not to wobble.

"Charming, charming," said the count. He bowed stiffly to Grace. "I would like to request the honor of this dance."

"Grace is just watching," said Aunt Louisa. "She doesn't know how to dance. My daughter is available."

"Grace looks graceful," he replied, chuckling. "She must dance. I insist."

"Go along, dear."

Grace gave him her hand.

"Not to worry, my pretty," said the count. "I will you show. Come."

He clamped her firmly around the waist.

"Lean into mine arms, *Liebchen*," he murmured.

Grace obeyed and found that her face was too close to his. He smiled down at her, his thick lips twitching. She pulled away, but he gripped her firmly.

"Don't—"

But he laughed and made her dance faster. At last, the music stopped.

"Next time, you will do better." He led Grace back to her seat. "So pretty." He pinched her cheek. Then he was gone.

Grace slouched down into the sofa. How she wished she could disappear.

"How was it, dear?"

Grace remained silent.

"You'll need to take dancing lessons."

Grace turned away.

"Miss Miller?"

Grace looked up.

Charles Phelps smiled down. He looked older and more handsome in white tie than he had at the music school.

"Who is this, dear?"

"This is Mr. Phelps, the brother of Miss Mabel Phelps. You remember she came to tea this afternoon?"

Aunt Louisa smiled and the introductions were made. Teresa presented Mr. Phelps with a limp hand, then Aunt Louisa rose, saying she wanted to take a turn around the room.

There was an awkward pause.

"Are you enjoying your time in Berlin?" asked Phelps.

"Tolerably well," replied Teresa. As she spoke, her gaze flickered around the ballroom, as if she were looking for someone. Finally, she leaned forward and, looking past Phelps to a young man dressed in well-cut clothes, said, "Who is that?"

He turned to look. "That's the Marquis de Chabrillan. His ancestral lands are near Grenoble in the French Alps, but he also has a career in international finance."

Her dark eyes glowed. "Would you introduce me?"

"Certainly," replied Phelps, thinning his lips.

Grace watched as he made the introductions quickly and efficiently. In her olive-green satin with its handkerchief hems, her hair held back by a matching silk band topped by a feather, Teresa looked exotic, alluring, and much older than her nineteen years. The young man smiled back at her as she replied to his questions in flawless French. Grace craned her neck as someone passed in front of her. Teresa smiled sweetly as she took his arm. They disappeared into the crowd of dancers. It had been such a long time since a young man had offered Grace his arm. She looked at the floor as tears pricked. What was Mr. Russell doing now?

"Would you care to dance?" Mr. Phelps reappeared, smiling.

"Violet isn't here," remarked Grace. "She doesn't come to this sort of thing."

"Then I'll dance with her charming sister." He held out his hand.

"I haven't had much practice."

"Don't worry." He steered her into a quiet corner. "We can practice here and when you're comfortable we can join the others."

They started dancing. It was a waltz in 3/4 time, easy to learn. Under his gentle encouragement, Grace relaxed.

"I knew you would get it right away." He drew closer. "By the way, you played beautifully this afternoon."

Grace smiled. "It's fun when you don't have to think."

"Indeed, it is. By the way, have I complimented you on your charming frock?"

"I don't believe so."

"It suits you to perfection."

Grace glanced at him. Was he mocking her? But his smile seemed sincere. The music came to an end.

He took her hand and kissed it lightly. "Can I count on another dance?"

"Yes," replied Grace. "But how shall I know which one?" She frowned over the card Aunt Louisa had given her.

Phelps took out a pen, and put his name down three times. "I'll find you," he said. "Don't worry."

Teresa glowered as Grace returned to the sofa. Aunt Louisa had vanished.

"Aren't you dancing?" Grace sat down as far away as she could.

"'Aren't you dancing?' What d'you think I'm doing?"

Grace shrugged and turned away, catching the bright blue eyes of a gentleman who was watching them thoughtfully. He seemed to be about forty, but his eyes had the same intensity of color as Violet's.

The gentleman came forward and bowed. "May I present myself? I am Herr Carl Graf von Lietzow. May I inquire into your name?"

"My name is Grace." She smiled up at him.

"A charming name for one as charming as yourself. Are you related to the von Stosches? You are American, I believe."

"Mr. von Stosch is a business acquaintance of my uncle's. You can see him over there. He's the tall gentleman with white hair and eyes of your color—" She abruptly stopped. "Oh dear. I suppose I shouldn't have said that."

"Why not? Perhaps you like blue eyes?"

"Your eyes remind me of my sister's."

"And where is your sister?"

"She's not here."

"She is unable to be here," put in Teresa.

"Ah. And this is?"

"My cousin Teresa."

"Good evening to you, Teresa. How are you enjoying your time here in Berlin?"

Teresa considered a moment. "It certainly has a lively social scene."

"Certainly? I should say. And what are you doing here in Berlin, Miss Teresa?"

"I'm here to find a husband." Teresa modulated her voice so that it had that same husky quality as Elise's.

"Do you have anyone in mind?"

She smiled at him slowly through her lashes.

He turned to Grace. "And you, Miss Grace, have you come to Berlin to find a husband?"

Grace massaged her hands. "I'm studying violin with Professor Flesch."

"How interesting. So, you're musical. I've heard of Flesch. He is very well regarded. How do you find him?"

"He's a very demanding teacher."

"So, you don't want a husband?"

"I have to practice five hours a day."

Von Lietzow threw his head back and laughed heartily. Then he clicked his heels together and held out his hand to Teresa. "May I have the honor of this dance?"

She smiled sweetly as he steered her onto the dancing floor.

Grace craned her neck and peered. What a good dancer Teresa was. She moved fluidly, never putting a foot wrong. And all the while she flirted, tilting her head, and looking up at him through her lashes. What a perfect countess she would make. She was so much more sophisticated, and she knew how to talk.

Grace looked at her frock and twisted her lips. It was pretty, but child-like. She slumped. She shouldn't have come. Everyone was just laughing at her. They would pinch her cheek, and no one would take her seriously. How could they? She was just a little girl—

"Miss Grace."

She looked up. The German count was back, Teresa on his arm.

"Now it is your turn."

Her cheeks fired up. They were playing a new dance called the foxtrot and she didn't know the steps.

"I can't dance."

"Why not? Have you gone lame?"

She shook her head.

"Perhaps you've taken a dislike to my company?"

"It's not that. I like your company very much. It's just that I don't dance well." Grace looked at Teresa. "Teresa is much more accomplished than I."

Teresa bit her lip and, in one swift movement, vanished.

Von Lietzow put his hands on his hips. "Young lady! Are you in the habit of fobbing off your admirers in this way? I saw you dancing just now."

Grace's cheeks warmed. "I don't mean to be rude, but I don't know the steps to the foxtrot. I would be a bad dancing partner."

"You should allow me to be the judge of that." His eyes twinkled as he held out his hand. "I'll forgive you, providing that you dance with me." Those blue eyes flashed. "Immediately."

Grace laughed as she gave him her hand.

✠✠✠✠✠✠✠✠✠✠✠

At least Aunt Louisa had insisted on Grace having her fair share of Teresa's room. She'd installed a vanity that matched Teresa's, an armoire with butterfly wing doors, and redecorated the unloved bed by winding white tulle drapes in and out and over a canopy carved to resemble a vine. Grace loved her portion of the room, and how could she complain as every day brought a present in the form of a dress, a piece of jewelry, a hat, a purse, or a pair of new shoes? When she asked

Aunt Louisa whether she should really have such nice things when so many were suffering, her aunt replied that they were helping out by buying their goods. Grace couldn't help enjoying her life of luxury. It made up for Aunt Louisa's fussy coldness and kept dark thoughts at bay.

Grace brushed her hair with a few strokes of a silver-backed hair brush, then put it down, for her long hair was all tangled up. She had a headache and her eyes were puffy from lack of sleep. She pulled the bell for the maid, who fixed her hair and helped her on with a two-piece woolen suit in chocolate brown, topped by a burgundy colored coat in soft felted wool with chocolate lining to match the color of the suit. It came with a soft floppy beret in burgundy, a jaunty brown ribbon sewed on its back. It was Grace's favorite outfit, ladylike but fun.

"Ask Hans to bring the car, please." Grace picked up the violin case. As she'd lost the morning to sleep, she must go to the music school, find a practice room, and try to do five hours.

Grace made her way downstairs, feeling disoriented. She'd never gotten up at noon before. The ball last night hadn't ended until three in the morning, making for an extremely long day, especially after the violin lesson and the additional quartet class.

She crept downstairs and passed the reception room when she heard voices.

"Where is the other young lady?" a male voice enquired.

Grace froze. Just then, Anna-Maria appeared. "Fräulein Graatz, your aunt wants you in the reception room."

Grace followed her.

Her eyes fell on Aunt Paulina. She looked pale, but at least her face had lost that unhealthy yellow sheen. Her expression widened into a smile as she saw Grace. But they had a distinguished visitor. Next to her sat Carl von Lietzow, dressed in a fur coat and hat, a pair of leather goggles in one hand. He rose and made a small bow. "Miss Grace, may I compliment you on your outfit? You look very charming this afternoon. Where are we going?"

His eyes fell on her violin case.

"Where *were* you going, Grace?" said Aunt Louisa.

"To the music school." Grace turned to her aunt. "I need to make up for lost time."

"But Carl von Lietzow has been kind enough to invite us to his villa."

"I thought both of you young ladies might enjoy a spin in my car." He included Teresa in his smile.

Aunt Paulina rose from her seat and came forward. "*Cara*." She hugged Grace tight and kissed her cheek. "I'm so proud of you. You've been getting a lot of attention recently." She smiled at Count von Lietzow.

"She's been getting too much attention," muttered Teresa under her breath.

"I sent an invitation." He looked around and picked up a large bouquet of white roses.

Grace looked at the art nouveau demi-lune. It seemed to be heaped with bouquets.

"This is my bouquet, with the invitation attached." Count von Lietzow showed it to Grace. *To Grace & Teresa*, it read. *I will call tomorrow to show to you my estates*.

Grace looked at the floor, her cheeks radiating heat.

"Grace dear. It seems you have acquired some admirers." Aunt Louisa picked up a garish mixture of orange, red, and pink roses. Tied onto the bouquet were a couple of ballet slippers made of gold and the following message:

Gnädige Fräulein:

Though you can't dance, you have my heart won.

A gift of dancing lessons for our next turn around the room, I send to you.

Grace put her violin case down. There was no signature. "I don't know who this is."

"But you danced with several people last night," remarked Aunt Louisa. "Where is your card? We can find out that way."

"Grace has probably lost hers," Teresa smirked.

Grace hung her head.

"Grace. It is important to know these things."

Grace's cheeks warmed as she examined the other bouquets. There was a box of six red roses addressed to Teresa from the Marquis de Chabrillan, but his note informed her that he'd had to leave for Évian-lès-Bains on a family matter. Lastly, there was a single white rosebud with her name on a card attached by a white satin ribbon. Grace turned it over.

You, who are innocent and lovely,

Happy is the man whom you choose.

I pray every day you will choose me.

An admirer.

Grace's heart thrummed. Had Mr. Russell sent this? It sounded like him. But how could he have known about the ball? She hadn't seen him in three months.

"Mr. Charles Phelps," announced Anna-Maria.

"I'm sorry to intrude—" His eyes found Grace's, and he came swiftly forward, folding his tall leanness into a bow as he kissed her hand. His melancholy gray eyes fixed onto her face.

"Mr. Phelps!" Aunt Paulina came forward. "Are you responsible for this?" She pointed to the white rosebud that Grace held in her hand.

He flushed and hesitated.

"Whatever possessed you to write to Grace in this vein? You've only just met her."

"I've had the pleasure of Miss Grace's company on three different occasions, at lunch, during a quartet rehearsal, and at the ball." He paused and gazed at Grace. "Grace is— She is very special."

Count von Lietzow frowned, his blue eyes going the color of ice.

"My family has money, and I—I stand to inherit a good deal," remarked Phelps. "Grace would want for nothing."

"What are your prospects, young man?" Aunt Paulina glowered at him.

"I'm a career diplomat. I've studied at Harvard and the Sorbonne. I am fluent in five languages, and—"

"Indeed?" Aunt Paulina cut him off, her face reddening. "If Grace married you, she'd be tagging around the world after you every couple of years. I've already saved her from that fate with another unsuitable suitor." She thinned her lips and glared.

Count von Lietzow smiled.

"Grace has a wonderful talent," remarked Mr. Phelps, turning to her. "I am fond of music too. I play cello, and my sister plays viola. Grace would be a wonderful—addition."

"You want Grace to be your chamber music partner?"

Mr. Phelps's soft gray eyes flashed. He set his lips. "It is much more than that, Mrs. Barilla. Much more."

"I find it hard to understand. It really is too much."

Mr. Phelps glanced at Count von Lietzow, who stood there frowning. "I would like your permission to call on Miss Grace."

"Understand me, young man. My duty is to protect my great-niece and consider her best interests. You are *not* to court her." Aunt Paulina plucked the white rosebud from Grace's hands. "Please take this away."

"But—"

"I mean what I say, Mr. Phelps."

Phelps set his jaw.

Aunt Paulina let out an exasperated sigh. She went to the hooded fireplace and tossed the rosebud in. It flared into a soaring flame that disintegrated into a heap of ashes.

Phelps's soft gray eyes met Grace's, his pupils contracting as his face whitened. Silently, he bowed to her and left.

Grace stared at the flames. If she squinted, she could just make out shreds of white petal disintegrating. Another face filled her heart. His dark gaze lanced across the room, piercing her soul. Tears pricked. She picked up her violin case. Maybe she could soothe herself by practicing the violin. But Count von Lietzow appeared by her side.

"I thought both of you young ladies might enjoy a spin in my car." He smiled at Grace. "Followed by tea at my villa in the charming village of Kladow on Lake Wannsee." He pinched her cheek. "Bring your violin, Miss Grace. I'm anxious to hear you play."

Grace glanced at Aunt Louisa, but she'd already risen from her seat. She kissed Aunt Paulina on the cheek. "Hans will take you home." Then Anna-Maria appeared and helped her into a new mink coat. Aunt Louisa glanced at her niece. "Come on, dear, don't dawdle."

To Kladow, therefore, they were to go.

✠✠✠✠✠✠✠

"Originally, this was my great-grandfather's hunting lodge." Count von Lietzow helped Aunt Louisa, Teresa, and Grace out of his car with a small bow. "My grandfather enlarged it and made it look like a miniature version of

Frederick the Great's palace of Sanssouci. Now I am modernizing the inside."

They wandered into an entrance hall where a large chandelier hung with a commanding air over a marble floor. Grace drew in a breath. The count turned right, ushering them into an elegant salon in the process of being painted a brilliant white.

"This is the formal reception room," he remarked.

Grace looked around. His villa was much larger than any other building she'd ever been in. A team of carpenters, plasterers, and painters worked on the walls, floors, and molding, and when he stepped into the room, the hum of activities stopped and they took their caps off their heads. He smiled and waved for them to continue. Several expensive-looking pieces of furniture lay scattered about the center of the salon, including two sofas and several chairs done in the old-fashioned style that reminded Grace of the furniture at the von Stosches'.

"Is there a swimming pool?" asked Teresa, smiling.

"I don't need one." They followed him into a bright yellow room. He strode over to the French doors and opened them with a flourish, letting in a blast of freezing air. Bright sunshine cast a brittle light over the ice-covered lake, making jagged patterns of tree branches against ice.

"Do you like swimming, Miss Teresa?"

"Indeed, I do."

"But not, probably, in the winter?"

Teresa smiled and tilted her head. "Is it cold here in the summer?"

"It's a very charming temperature."

"Well, then." Teresa moved gracefully away as he shut the French doors. "It would be an excellent way to start the day, do you not agree?"

He chuckled.

Above the fireplace was a marble mantle. Grace stood in front of it to study the design of apples and cherries.

"What do you think of the color of the walls, my dear?"

Grace turned. He stood next to her, his eyebrows going up and down while his mouth eased into a smile. Something about his expression made her feel lighthearted for the first time in a long time. She stepped around the room as the darkness of sorrow fell away, enjoying the color of the soft lemon walls.

"How about D-sharp?" Grace raised her eyebrows, almost laughing.

"Grace!" Teresa pealed with laughter. "We're not in the music room. Or hadn't you noticed?"

He glanced at Teresa with a polite smile, then turned towards Grace.

"Why do you say that, my dear?"

Grace bit her lip. Teresa rolled her eyes and wandered off to the other side of the room. Finding an elegant sofa, she sat down, crossing one pretty leg over the other.

He took Grace's hand. "I really want to know, my dear, why the color of the walls reminded you of D-sharp."

Grace shrugged. "It seems bright and gay. Perhaps a good place to entertain?"

He turned to a dark-haired gentleman who stood in the doorway, pencil poised. "Make a note of that. I think we should put a dance floor down here and have a bar in the corner. And a path from the French doors to the beach."

"Very good, sir," he said, noting it down with decisive strokes.

Grace's cheeks radiated heat. She scrutinized von Lietzow's countenance. Why take her opinion so seriously?

Why was he paying such attention to her slightest whim? "I didn't mean—"

"Grace doesn't know a thing about interior design, do you, Grace?" Teresa rose. "In my opinion, you should have plenty of bathrooms. I like to relax in a nice hot bath. Especially with the freezing winters you have here." She shivered and made a face.

He offered his arm and took her to see the newly installed bathrooms, pointing out the tiled floors, tiled walls, porcelain stoves, hot and cold running water, and the new water closets. Grace trailed after them. If only she knew how to make small talk.

At length, Teresa excused herself into one of the new bathrooms. As she turned away, he offered his arm and led Grace into a small room next door. The walls were painted a soft color between silver and gray.

"Which key?" he asked, smiling.

Grace scrutinized his face, but even his smile seemed serious. So she turned and took in the room slowly. "C minor. This is a somber room."

"I'll have my office here, then," replied von Lietzow, turning to his agent, who had followed at a respectful distance. "I need my desk here by the window, and I think your desk, Nordwitz, should go here, Weiss's desk here, and Weinberg's here."

Mr. Nordwitz made a sketch of the room, took careful notes, and asked a few questions.

"Your bathroom has only one washbasin." Teresa reappeared.

"How many do you think it should have?"

"Two would be good." Teresa favored him with a sidelong glance. "His and hers."

He chuckled and, offering his arm to Teresa, led them into a room that gave onto the central courtyard, where a fountain played softly in a French-inspired garden.

"That little garden is so charming," gushed Teresa. "I could sit here all day and sunbathe." She opened the French doors and disappeared outside.

Grace turned away and breathed in the room. Its walls were the color of a summer sky.

"The walls remind me of a day in Provence," he remarked. "What do you think?"

Grace closed her eyes. She could just make out the faint plashing from the fountain outside. "This room is *molto tranquillo;* it gives me a feeling of great peace."

He caught her hand and kissed it. "You are a lovely young woman." He gazed into her eyes. Then he turned to his agent and directed him to turn the room into his bedroom.

Grace turned to take another stroll around the room but stopped, catching the expressions on the faces of her relatives. Teresa glowered and bit her lip, but Aunt Louisa was smiling. Now why would that be? She couldn't be rejoicing in her own daughter's failure. A sudden thought struck Grace. Of course. That's why she'd been so kind. It was because she thought her niece could also hook an aristocrat for a husband.

Chapter Fourteen
Friday, 31 March

The beginning of the Brahms concerto sounded in Grace's head. Descending chords in octaves announced the appearance of the solo violin as if they were pillars holding up a massive building.

"Fräulein, are you lost?" A thin young man raised his hat.

Grace blinked. It was a bright sunny day and she'd slipped out of Aunt Louisa's mansion to have some privacy.

"I'm sorry I made you jump. Are you sure you know where you're going?" He bent towards her.

Grace didn't know, but she didn't want his help. She cast her eyes down and glided away. Now how should she finger that passage? Grace used her right forearm as a violin neck, so that she could study the various fingerings.

"Might I help you find something?"

A cool wind lazily lifted her nutmeg-colored hair. Puffy clouds scudded across the sky. A recent shower had left in its wake the clean smell of newly turned earth. Buds poked up from the soil and sunned themselves in the brightening spring sunlight.

"No, thank you." Grace briefly glanced into the gray eyes of a portly older gentleman who might have been a banker.

He raised his homburg and passed on.

One thread ran through her thoughts like a passacaglia. Aunt Paulina had ordered Grace to write to Mr. Russell so that she could return his ring.

"I've just received a letter from Mr. Russell's brother, which he wrote on New Year's Day. Unfortunately, it's taken ages to reach me. Would you believe it, but he has had the gall to apply to *il Santo Padre* for a dispensation—without consulting me? I cannot allow this to continue. *Cara,* you would be committing incest!"

Grace frowned. She thought Mr. Russell had vanished forever. "But if the Pope granted the dispensation—" Surely the Pope's word was final on such matters. How would she be committing a sin with Mr. Russell if the Pope agreed to it?

"Out of the question!" exclaimed Aunt Paulina, going red in the face. "I cannot allow Franco's son to court you. You must write to him at once and break things off. Send his ring back."

Grace had rarely seen Aunt Paulina look so angry, but she lifted her chin. "Why now?"

"*Cara,*" said Aunt Paulina. "Louisa tells me that Count von Lietzow is very interested. It seems he will propose to you soon. You cannot be the fiancée of two gentlemen. You must clear things up with Mr. Russell."

And so, Grace had taken Father Jerome's letter and walked out of the mansion on Savignyplatz, away from Teresa's glowering presence, her cousins' chatter, and Aunt Louisa's strictures, to a quiet spot where she could think.

Peace was a rare commodity these days. She reached a café on Mommsenstrasse, where an attentive waiter seated her near a sun-filled window, so that she could enjoy the flowers. In the last six weeks, Count von Lietzow had become a constant presence, appearing at Aunt Louisa's every other day. He had an easy charm, which made him at home wherever he went. He could discuss poetry with fifteen-year-old Ella, the latest Paris fashions with Violet whenever she appeared, play the *galant* to Aunt Louisa or Teresa, and engage in playful teasing with twelve-year-old Adela. His car was always at their disposal. They made many shopping trips and excursions to nearby beauty spots.

Grace tilted her head and his face came into view. He was kind and imaginative, and she liked him very much. They'd grown into an easy way of talking, which allowed them to speak about anything without getting too serious. He made her laugh. After she'd collapsed, giggling, at one of his remarks, he had the strange habit of taking her hand and kissing it gently while his blue eyes bored into hers. But he never said anything.

She put her head on her hand and frowned. What did he want? Surely Aunt Louisa was wrong. It was not possible, it could not be possible, that he actually wanted to marry her. If he did that, she would be Countess von Lietzow. How could she be that? She was young, ignorant, and foreign. She had no money. Her family came from humble peasant stock in Italy. Besides, he hadn't introduced her to any of his friends and relatives. How could he be thinking about marriage? No. He just wanted to be friends. He just liked hearing her play the violin and asking her thoughts about cars, books, politics, and plans for his new villa.

Grace had no idea why he asked her opinion on any of these matters, but—under Aunt Louisa's prodding— she made an effort to read so that they had more to talk about. It was true that he'd seemed pleased that she was improving her German by reading Goethe and by working to understand German politics.

The truth is, she wouldn't have understood these things if it hadn't been for the kindness of Charles Phelps. After Great-Aunt Paulina had dismissed him, she'd seen him again, a week later, when she'd visited Mabel. After that, he appeared at the music school at lunchtime with sandwiches, books, and the Berlin papers to discuss. They'd just finished *The Sorrows of Young Werther* and were now embarked on *Madame Bovary*. She was having a hard time understanding why Madame Bovary was so cruel to her husband.

"He's so kind to her."

Mr. Phelps had glanced at her and smiled. "But she's bored."

"Why? I wouldn't be bored if I were in her position."

"Are you sure?"

"It would give me more time to practice. Hours and hours without any tedious social engagements."

He'd patted her hand. "You know that my work for the State Department takes me to many countries around the world?"

"It sounds exciting."

He pressed her hand. "Would you like to travel?"

Grace leaned forward, pictures of exotic places crowding her head. "I've always wanted to travel. I'd love to come, provided I could bring my violin."

"Of course, you could bring your violin."

She sat back, closing her eyes with a smile on her lips. "It would be like a special kind of holiday."

He edged his chair around the café table so that it was touching hers. "Miss Grace, do you think you'd be happy traveling with me?"

"I don't see why not. You make me happy now." She sat up. "Oh, I forgot to ask you. Could you explain to me about the National Socialist German Worker's Party?"

He picked up her hand. "Grace, I have something I want to say—"

"Someone told me that their leader, Herr Hitler, is quite dangerous and that ever since he became chairman last July, the Storm Troopers have been attacking the other political parties. Is that true?"

Now Grace stirred in her seat at the café on Mommsenstrasse, taking her head off her hand. Why had he reddened and hesitated before replying?

Grace tried not to talk about Mr. Phelps, but yesterday his name had come up in conversation. Aunt Paulina's response had been puzzling.

"Has he been bothering you?"

"No. We just talk about books."

Aunt Paulina took both of her hands and leaned forward. "Remember this, *cara*. He is *not* to court you. You must keep him at arm's length. Be polite to him but do not allow yourself to become overly friendly, because he will definitely misinterpret your behavior."

"What do you mean?"

"You are aware of the discrimination we Italians face in America?"

Grace nodded. Mother had often complained about it.

"Mr. Phelps comes from an old Yankee family in Connecticut. They don't like young women without money and certainly want nothing to do with Italians. It is all very silly, but it is an unpleasant reality."

Grace looked down. Was that really true? Aunt Louisa had married into a Yankee family, and Mr. Phelps hadn't seemed put off when she explained that her father's family had been gentleman farmers in Rockville, Maryland, or that her mother's family were Italian.

"Thank goodness I was able to nip that courtship in the bud," continued Aunt Paulina. "It would have done you no good to have become fond of him. If you had married him, his mother would have made your life a misery."

Grace swallowed. "What about Count von Lietzow? Doesn't he mind that I have no money or that I'm Italian?"

Aunt Paulina's face relaxed into a smile. "He is a mature aristocratic gentleman who can do as he pleases. According to Louisa, he inherited his title when he was fifteen years old, but there was very little money left to go with it. I'm not sure why. He said he couldn't consider bringing a wife and family into such a tumbledown existence, as he put it, so his plan was to make money to refurbish his properties first, then marry after."

Grace frowned. "He told me that he traveled around the world."

"That's correct. After some time in the army, he became a business man and traveled everywhere looking for business opportunities. It was during this time that he discovered a love for music, art, and precious objects. He told Louisa that it took him years to make enough money to even consider making the repairs to the family mansion near Posen, in southern Prussia, or to the apartment in Berlin and the villa in Kladow."

"He seems rich."

"He is. According to William, he is a shrewd investor."

"He never married?"

"No. As he put it, his house wasn't in order. Just as he was about to hire laborers to start work, the Great War broke out. After that, there was a considerable amount of chaos in Germany. He decided to postpone the enormous project of repairing the Posen mansion until things settled down and focus instead on refurbishing Kladow."

Grace leaned against the back of her seat, imagining his life.

"He seems very fond of you."

"Of course he is. We laugh at the same things. But he's just a friend."

"He is a gentleman and you are very young. He is taking things slowly because he doesn't want to put you off."

"But he's so much older. He wouldn't be interested in marriage. He wouldn't be interested in marrying me, at the very least."

She covered Grace's hand with her own. "You're quite wrong there. Haven't you noticed how he lights up when you appear?"

Grace shivered. How would her career as a violinist develop if she became Countess von Lietzow? She would have to spend all her time holding balls and parties and setting her features into insincere smiles. She could never do that.

Grace took out a pen and a pad of paper. She must focus on Mr. Russell. His dark eyes gazed back faintly whenever she closed hers. So much had happened, they'd lost their power. How did she feel about him, now that she could compare him to Carl von Lietzow?

Grace tilted her head as the waiter set down a steaming bowl of milky coffee and a pastry. Slowly, she opened Father Jerome's letter and read it for the first time.

St. Francis de Sales Seminary
Milwaukee, Wisconsin
Sunday, January 1, 1922

My Dear Mrs. Barilla,

I thought I would take this opportunity of sending you my very best wishes for the New Year. I have finally been able to talk with my brother about his conduct, and I wish he'd had the courage to be more honest with you. Of course you are reluctant to consent to an engagement between your great-niece and someone whom you do not know. I would have the same misgivings, except that in this matter it is very clear to me that my brother is deeply in love. Indeed, I think his love for Grace is serious and a good foundation for marriage; for when I asked him why he loved her, he immediately spoke about his spiritual feelings, not her beauty, even though I understand she is a lovely young woman.

Grace looked up as her heart thrummed in her chest. She frowned and pushed her feelings away.

As for the objection that they are too closely related to marry, I have sent to Rome for a papal dispensation, which I expect to be granted for two reasons: First, Nico is Grace's half-uncle, not her uncle, and secondly, his war record is superlative. Should you give your consent to this marriage, a priest would be able to perform the sacrament.

In closing, I would like you to know I am at your disposal should you have further questions. I expect to be ordained at Easter and will be posted to Catholic University, in Washington, D.C. I hope that when you return from Berlin, we will finally be able to meet.

Believe me,
Very sincerely yours,
Your nephew
Girolamo Pagano

Grace glanced at the envelope with its liberal sprinkling of postmarks, a testament to its tortuous journey, and drew out her notebook. In her spare time, she'd gone to the Prussian State Library on Unter den Linden to read up on incest, to understand whom she might marry without committing a sin. She read her notes. One source argued:

> Because of the acknowledged derivation of the human race from the common progenitors, Adam and Eve, it is difficult to accept the opinion of some theologians that the marriage of brother and sister is against the law of nature.

According to another:

> These prohibitions relating to consanguinity between a man and the 'flesh of his flesh' are contained mainly in Lev., xviii, 7-13, and xx, 17, 19. Specific prohibitions are here made with regard to marriage or carnal intercourse with a mother, granddaughter, aunt by blood on either side, sister, or half-sister.

Grace read the third entry slowly.

> A man may not marry his: Mother, Stepmother, Wife's mother, Son's daughter, Daughter's daughter, Wife's son's daughter, Wife's daughter's daughter, Daughter, Wife's daughter, Son's wife, Sister, Wife's sister, Brother's

```
wife, Father's sister, Mother's
sister, Father's brother's wife.
```

In none of these was there anything about a half-sister's daughter, which is what she was in relation to Mr. Russell. Father Jerome must have looked into this and come to the same conclusion. They could marry. Grace re-read the letter to be quite certain of this. The problem about their being too closely related had been solved. If the Pope said they could marry, then it did not matter that Mr. Russell was Grace's half-uncle.

Grace sipped her coffee, took one bite out of the pastry, but pushed it away. Did she have to marry? She didn't really want to, at least not yet. But what about all the young men who wouldn't leave her alone? She couldn't even walk to a café by herself without being bothered.

Grace drooped. Could she forge a career as a violinist if she were an independent woman? If only she could hide behind a veil. What she most wanted was to play her violin without distractions. Perhaps if she married, she might have more peace. A husband would keep other young men from pestering her. Things seemed to be building in that direction. Perhaps she should decide now.

She half closed her eyes. What would life be like with each of her suitors? Marrying someone was like choosing a world. You not only got the gentleman you married, but all of his friends, acquaintances, and family. You got his preoccupations and his dreams. You got his professional life, too, and perhaps that was key, for as his wife Grace knew she would be required to support him. That was one thing Aunt

Louisa had made very clear—her violin would come second to her husband.

She shifted uneasily in her seat. All of her suitors had been so kind. Would they really get in the way of her career as a violinist? She remembered what Professor Burneys had said about her being ready for a solo career. How she wanted that glamorous life. But could she have it if she married?

She sipped her coffee. Perhaps the question was, how much would they get in the way? And there was another, even more uncomfortable question, what about love? It had been so long since she'd seen Mr. Russell, she could scarcely remember him. Mr. Phelps had regular features and melancholy gray eyes that made her want to draw near. They'd never kissed, but he had twirly brown hair she longed to stroke. She couldn't dismiss him so easily from her thoughts. And what about Carl von Lietzow (as he wanted her to call him)? He wasn't as handsome as Phelps. He had deeply cut lines etched into his forehead and around his mouth, and his brown hair was going gray at the temples. But his blue eyes brimmed with merriment, and how he made her laugh. He was an amusing companion who could make Grace forget her sorrows. He'd been a good friend to her and to her family.

Suddenly, Mr. Russell's dark eyes came into view. Magnetically, they drew her into him. Of course, he'd not written since that stormy confrontation with Aunt Paulina. Grace frowned as Mr. Russell's eyes became darker and filled with pain. She lingered, drinking them in. How much she missed them. How much she missed him. Her stomach knotted. She couldn't do it. She couldn't send his ring back. She couldn't cause him pain. What was she going to do?

Grace rose to her feet. A movement caught her eye. She turned. A young man standing outside amongst a crowd of shabby Berliners gesticulated. Grace wrapped her pastry in a napkin and handed it to him as she left.

✠✠✠✠✠✠✠✠✠✠✠

Aunt Paulina, however, was not to be put off. "If you marry him, you will lose your family. I can't speak plainer than that. People would be revolted and you wouldn't be received. You would bring shame and dishonor on the family."

Grace sat in Frau Varga's living room, tears trickling through her fingers. Thank goodness she was out.

Aunt Paulina touched her arm. "I blame myself for allowing this relationship to take root before we knew who he was. I am sorrier than I can say. But it must be done." She took a breath. "Do you have his ring?"

Grace nodded.

"Then I'll dictate the letter for you. You're not too upset to do it now?"

Grace wiped her face with her handkerchief. "I'll be all right." She uncapped her pen.

Dear Mr. Russell,

I am fortunate enough to have attracted the admiration of a distinguished gentleman here in Berlin. My relatives tell me to expect his proposal of marriage soon.

You were kind enough to bestow your attentions on me, but given the closeness of our kinship, I hope you see that any kind of union between us would be reprehensible.

Please consider our engagement to be broken. You extracted promises from me under false pretenses. Therefore, I enclose your ring.

Very truly yours,
Grace Miller

Slowly, Grace folded the page into threes, then she took his ring off her finger. She gave everything to Aunt Paulina.

"I know this is hard, *cara*," she murmured, kissing Grace's tear-stained cheek. "But believe me, I know what is best for you."

Grace let out a breath. Perhaps Aunt Paulina was right. There was something about Mr. Russell that was just a teeny-tiny bit scary. It would be a relief not to have to deal with the weight of expectation contained in those magnetic eyes.

✠✠✠✠✠✠✠✠✠✠✠

How could Grace have missed that he was madly in love with her? Charles Phelps left Pariser Platz and walked west in the direction of Charlottenburg, picking quiet residential neighborhoods so that he could think. Today was April the fourteenth, Good Friday, and he was to meet his family for the evening service at the Anglican Church of St. George's. How could she be so oblivious, interrupting his proposal of marriage with some question about German politics? What had he done wrong?

He leaned against a stone balustrade. It hadn't helped, of course, that her great-aunt had tossed his first declaration of love into the fire and had forbidden him to court her. How he wished he hadn't been schooled to be obedient towards his elders, because it had cost him time with Grace. He turned up the collar of his coat against the cool breezes from the east that were stirring the trees around him. What was it about her that was so compelling? Her cousin Teresa was just as lovely to look at, yet she left him cold.

He remembered the day he'd first met Grace in his office in Washington, D.C. She'd come in with her family, sat down, and stared at the floor, leaving her sister and great-aunt to do the talking. Never once had she lifted her eyes. How puzzled he'd been. Young women who were fortunate enough to possess those kinds of looks were not usually quiet. Usually they had been pampered and spoiled since birth and were adept at manipulating the men around them, like her cousin Teresa.

The first time he'd actually gazed into those expressive eyes was when he'd accidentally happened upon her eating with her sister. He'd gone there looking for his sister and, instead, had found Grace with her sister. As he looked into her eyes, he saw not the spoiled child he'd half been expecting to find, but someone who had the weight of the world on her shoulders. Yes. She looked sad. He was intrigued.

How wonderful it had been to give her her first dancing lesson. How easily they'd talked together. He smiled as he remembered. He could feel her waist and hand through the pressure of his fingers. He knew at that moment he was falling in love. The next day, he'd made his intentions clear to Mrs. Barilla, only to have her squelch them. The following week had been miserable, as dutifully, he tried to forget about her.

Then one day, he'd gone to the Victoria Studienhaus in Charlottenburg to visit his sister. This establishment provided an evening meal along with a room to rent for young female students. Mabel had been living there with other young ladies since she'd arrived in January. It had a reputation for propriety, and its rules were strict: Gentlemen callers were not allowed upstairs. So he was obliged to give his name to the concierge and wait. When she finally walked down the stairs, Grace came as well. It was clear they had become friends.

From then on, he found excuses to walk past the music school during his lunch hour and to spend more time with his sister. Naturally, Mabel was not fooled.

"I know why you're here," she said one day when he was waiting for her in the vestibule of the Studienhaus.

"I enjoy your company, too," he replied, giving his sister a peck on the cheek.

"But you love her, don't you?"

For the past two weeks, he'd been wondering what to do about the impasse with Grace, hesitating to confide his feelings as the whole thing was so embarrassing. But the situation was driving him crazy, he had to talk with someone. He drew away from the stone balustrade and walked quickly west. If he hurried, maybe he could catch his sister before meeting his parents.

✠✠✠✠✠✠✠✠✠✠✠

"I was on the point of proposing when she interrupted me with some question about politics." Charles and Mabel Phelps turned out of the Studienhaus and headed west to St. George's. "I don't understand what went wrong. Am I as bad at conveying my feelings as that?"

Mabel sighed as she wrapped her scarf more tightly around her. "Grace is naïve. She just thinks about her violin. It's the only thing she's really good at."

"I wouldn't say that."

"She doesn't read people well. She doesn't understand situations. You saw that yourself. She didn't pick up on your interest in her."

"But why not? Most young women are very sensitive about that sort of thing. If you display a flicker of interest, they're all over you."

Mabel put her hand in the crook of his arm. "But Grace is humble. She doesn't believe she's beautiful or talented."

Phelps turned to stare at her. "How could she possibly think that?"

Mabel shrugged. "Perhaps no one told her."

"What about her parents?"

"They're both dead, her mother just recently. Grace never talks about her."

Phelps passed a hand through his hair. "My goodness, I had no idea. No wonder she's so sad. It makes her different."

Mabel took his arm again. "Charles, everything about her makes her different. What are you going to do about the parents? You know they're not going to be happy."

Chapter Fifteen

Monday, 17 April

It was an unusually warm day for April, and so Mr. Phelps suggested that they wander around the English Garden, an area of Berlin's Tiergarten. The sunshine seeped into her woolen suit, smothering her with too much warmth. When he found a park bench near an English-style cottage, Grace sank onto the seat and slowly took off her jacket. Phelps had thoughtfully turned his back, so she straightened her blouse and skirt. If only she had perfume, a comb, or a handkerchief, anything to make her look more presentable.

"Do you mind if I take off my jacket?"

Her face relaxed into a smile. Thank goodness Mr. Phelps felt as uncomfortable as she did.

He returned her smile, settled himself next to her, and opened his copy of the novel.

Grace leaned against the curving back of the park bench. "I don't understand why Madame Bovary couldn't find something to occupy her."

"She has no particular interest in anything."

"But couldn't she find something to interest her? She's not unintelligent, or without taste."

He smiled. "She's interested in having an affair behind her husband's back. The intrigue and the risk involved help her to escape the boredom of provincial life."

Grace turned away, tears pricking. Perhaps Mother felt just as bored as Madame Bovary. Perhaps her life seemed just as empty. After all, when Mother was her age, she'd been responsible for two babies and had no one to assist her.

Mr. Phelps touched her arm. "Grace. Dearest Grace. Are you all right?"

"It's a painful story."

He turned her to face him. "My love, you're crying." He fumbled in his breast pocket and presented her with a neatly ironed handkerchief.

Grace buried her face in the softness of the fine linen, inhaled the musky scent of the eau-de-cologne, and swallowed hard. She must not think about Mother or she would sob like a baby.

"Grace, Grace." His voice sounded gentle and sweet. He brushed her hair back from her face and laid an arm gently around her.

She burst into tears. As soon as she could, she wiped her eyes and managed a weak smile. "You must think me very silly."

"I don't think that at all."

Grace gave Mr. Phelps his handkerchief. "I'm afraid it's very wet. I shouldn't have done that."

He gently wiped away the tears that continued to spill down her cheeks.

"What is wrong?"

She thinned her lips as her cheeks warmed. How silly she was. Why couldn't she control herself? Now he wanted to know what was going on. But she couldn't tell him about Mother. It was too embarrassing. She rose.

"I shouldn't waste any more of your time."

But he grabbed her hand.

"Grace! Don't go, I have something to say to you." He put his other hand over his heart and got down on one knee. "Will you marry me, Grace?"

Grace whipped around.

He clung onto her hand, stroking it and kissing it.

"I'm not good at expressing my feelings. But Grace, it doesn't mean I don't have them. I love you more than I have loved any other woman. No, that's not the right way of saying it. Grace, I'm passionately in love with you. I know you would make me happy. I want to spend the rest of my life with you."

What was he talking about? How on earth could she make him happy? She touched her forehead. It felt warm. "But I haven't done anything."

Mr. Phelps rose and gently sat her down on the bench close to him. He took both of her hands. "But you have. Just being with you is so refreshing. You soothe me."

Grace frowned, the not-quite-forgotten memories of Mr. Russell surfacing. "But marriage is a big thing. How can you be so sure?"

"I have come to know you through reading books. I see a lovely young woman with excellent moral principles, good intentions, and a kind heart who's suffered a great deal of sadness in her life. How I long to take you in my arms and comfort you."

He sounded eerily like Mr. Russell. But his soft gray eyes met hers, unwavering. How handsome he looked with his regular features, thick brown hair and melancholy eyes. And he didn't give her that faint frisson of fear that she sometimes felt with Mr. Russell. What would it feel like if he kissed her?

He gently took her in his arms and kissed her on the lips.

She closed her eyes, her heart thrumming.

"I'm the happiest man in the world," he murmured.

She placed a hand on his chest. "What about my violin?"

He took her hand and kissed it. "I make you a solemn promise, darling Grace that I will never get in the way of your violin."

"But what about your career? You will need me to support you."

"We'll go everywhere together, and you will bring your violin. I want you to play, dearest Grace. It is a part of you. You could entertain the guests at our receptions."

She withdrew her hand. She wanted to play, but would these guests appreciate her playing? Would they listen to her attentively while eating?

He squeezed her hand. "We'll have such a life together. I am not normally ambitious, but for you—" His words tumbled out as he told her about powerful connections he had in the State Department who would assure him of an influential posting, perhaps an ambassadorship, one day. He stroked her hand with his thumb and brought his face close to hers.

"I don't do this for myself. I need you, Grace. I need your support. I need—" He reddened. "I need your love." His voice dropped away to a whisper. "Nothing means anything without that."

Grace scrutinized his face, but his expression was serious, his gaze unflinching. He really did love her. He really needed her. It was all true. Unconsciously, she parted her lips.

He gathered her to him, kissing slowly, pressing her gently against him.

Grace inhaled his musky scent, a mixture of freshly-laundered shirt, starched collar, and male cologne that overlaid his own scent. She closed her eyes with pleasure and then pulled up short.

"Aunt Paulina. Whatever shall I do? She told me not to let you court me."

He took her hand.

"She told me that too. But Grace, this is about you and me, not your aunt. No one can stop us from marrying."

"What about your parents?"

"My father is on a business trip. He won't be in town for a few days."

"Then we must keep this a secret. I have to find some way of letting Aunt Paulina know."

"I can keep it a secret until my father arrives, but I must tell him then. You understand?"

She nodded.

He took her in his arms. "Don't you think," he remarked, making butterfly kisses over her face, "we should have a short engagement?"

✠✠✠✠✠✠✠✠✠✠✠

When Grace arrived back at the mansion at Savignyplatz, she had just time to change into her first cotton frock of the season, the olive-green one that Violet had made for her birthday, when Count von Lietzow appeared, his red five-passenger touring car polished so that everything sparkled in the sunlight.

Grace's relatives greeted him with smiles and urged her to go visit his villa without them. As they drove slowly west out of the city, hyacinths wafted their sweet scent from the bedraggled flower vendors who stood by the side of the road. As they picked up speed and passed Lietzensee on the outskirts of Berlin —"*Mein Heimat,*" murmured Carl von Lietzow as they passed—daffodils glowed in the sunlight. Finally, as they turned south near Pichelsdorf to edge around the western side of Lake Wannsee, through Gatow and Hohengatow to Kladow, apple trees unfurled their pink and white blossoms into the cooling breeze that came off the lake. He stopped in the middle of Alt Kladow in front of a square church.

"I thought I'd show you around. This is the nearest village to my villa. What do you think of it?"

He came around and opened the door. Slowly, Grace got out of the car, and raised her head to take in the church from top to bottom.. "It seems old."

"It dates back to the twelve hundreds."

Grace looked around. The scene before her was full of automobiles and people in modern clothes less shabby than the average Berliner wore. But how would it have looked back then? That road must have been a muddy track. Those people must have been garbed in long colorful robes and elaborate headdresses.

Carl (as he now wanted Grace to call him) took off his driving goggles and offered his arm. He had an immense number of suits for every occasion. Today he wore a beige one in light wool, accessorized with a narrow tie in blue silk. It matched the color of his eyes and stood out against his starched white shirt. "You have such an interesting expression on your face," he remarked.

She shook her head. "It was nothing. I was only imagining what it must have been like then."

"But you have an intense imagination, don't you?" he said as they came to the village church. "I can hear it in your playing."

She smiled up at him. How sensitive he was.

He opened the gate for her, and they went into the churchyard.

She relaxed into another smile. The baroque church was charming. It was small, with a squat tower topped by a gently curved roof. That tower had a determined air. It sat there, attached to its church, and stared at her.

He opened the door to the dark interior and took her inside. "My closest relatives are buried here. Here are my parents, Carl-Friedrich von Lietzow and Caroline von Welchau. And here is Uncle Gotthard."

Grace peered at the tomb which told her that the occupant was Gotthard Maria Leopold Maximilian von Graslitz.

"Uncle Gotthard and Aunt Sidonie married the same day as my parents, May the third, 1881."

"Where did they marry?"

"In Prague. Graslitz and Welchau are the names of estates in Bohemia, now Czechoslovakia."

"I had no idea you had Czech relatives. I thought you were German."

He laughed and pinched her cheek. "Czechoslovakia has only been in existence for four years. Before the war, that land was part of the

Austro-Hungarian Empire. Czechoslovakia contains many Germans within its borders."

"I see." Grace frowned, trying to puzzle it out. How complicated everything was. It seemed as if a German person's ancestry was almost as mixed as the average American's.

"This village means a lot to me," remarked Carl after a pause. "I have a place in town, of course, and a large estate near Posen. But this is where I come for peace and reflection. It is my hideaway."

"It has character," remarked Grace, tilting her head to peer up into the dark eaves. "The church seems very forthright. Like its people."

He laughed and kissed her hand lightly. "I suppose you could say that." He nodded to someone who greeted him. "The renovations of my villa are complete," he remarked, shutting the church gate behind them. "Would you like to see them?"

"Goodness," said Grace. "That happened fast. I didn't know they were so far along."

"I encouraged them to get a move on," he said, helping her into his car. He came around the other side and slid onto the light cream seat. "I was wondering if you'd like to live in it."

She gazed at him. He made it sound so simple.

"Would you like that?" he asked, starting the engine.

"It is lovely." Grace turned away. She loved his villa, and its rooms seemed like old friends now that she'd seen them in the process of coming to life. But could she live there? Wouldn't it be too grand?

"I would be there, of course."

Grace's eyes flipped open.

He patted her knee. "I'm part of the—how do you say it in America? Ah, yes. I'm part of the package deal. You get me with the villa. Inside the villa, if you like. With you."

Grace burst out laughing. There was something so funny about the way he said certain things. His blue eyes would sparkle with mischief, his mouth would crinkle at the corners, and his eyebrows would go up and down.

"So it's settled then?"

Grace wiped her eyes, giddy with laughter. She liked him so much. Perhaps it would be nice to have a place to live in with such a good friend, one who would provide a quiet, restful place for her to practice her violin. "If you wish."

He took her hand and kissed it. "I wish it, very much."

Oh no. Her stomach dropped.

✠✠✠✠✠✠✠✠✠✠✠

Grace made her way slowly through the doors of the music school out onto Fasanenstrasse, thinking about the Brahms concerto. It had a long orchestral introduction, interrupted by the violin bursting in with big architectural chords. There was the problem of getting them in tune with the orchestra, for after that long wait, the violin pegs could have slipped a bit. How was she going to solve that problem? She'd only been practicing it a month, but already Herr Flesch had hinted that he might like her to perform it soon.

"Darling Grace, you look so charming today."

Grace came to with a jolt. Her lips parted as she looked up into the soft gray eyes that belonged to her fiancé.

Charles Phelps kissed her lips slowly and placed a ring around her heart finger, the finger that had felt naked ever since she'd been forced to send Mr. Russell's ring back.

Her gaze wobbled from the magnificent emerald ring set in gold to Charles' smart gray suit.

"I've told my parents. They want to meet you."

Her stomach knotted. She hadn't told Aunt Paulina. She'd been meaning to, but never found the right time. Beads of perspiration formed in the cleft between her lips and her chin, and a trickle of moisture ran down her back. Her brown woolen suit was creased. Her cream blouse was damp around the armholes. Her hair felt flat and greasy.

"I'm not presentable."

"Mabel told me you would say that, so I'm going to take you over to the Victoria Studienhaus to freshen up in her room."

"Your sister is so kind," she murmured, smiling up at him as the tension melted away. Would Charles's parents be like Mabel?

✠✠✠✠✠✠✠✠✠✠✠

"Just be yourself," Mabel said to Grace, as she helped her with her hair. But as Charles took her into the Hotel Adlon, Grace quailed. It was huge, grand, and cold. Freezing fingers crept up into the back of her neck and drifted down to settle around her shoulders like an icy wrap. What was she doing here? A bowing footman ushered them into the Phelps's palatial suite. Grace took a deep breath. She was a foreigner entering strange territory.

They were both tall. Phelps Sr. looked like an older version of his son, but age had made his face coldly austere. Mrs. Phelps was fashionably slim.

Aunt Louisa's voice filled her head. *Always stand tall, lift your head up, and smile.* Grace flicked a glance at Mrs. Phelps. She stared back. Her eyes were the exact same shape and color as her son's. But the soft silky quality of his gray eyes had become hard diamonds in her narrow face. Those eyes swept her from head to toe. Grace lowered her head.

Phelps Sr. came forward. "How do you do, my dear?" He made a movement with his mouth, which suggested a smile, but showed large white teeth. He led Grace to a chair. Charles took the one opposite.

"Charles tells us that you play violin."

"Yes." Grace's throat constricted. She coughed to clear it. "Yes," she said, a little louder.

"Can you do anything else?" asked Mrs. Phelps.

Grace blinked. Why was she looking at her with such coldness? Why didn't she smile? People usually smiled at Grace, but not Mrs. Phelps.

"I mean, can you paint, embroider, arrange flowers, speak a language, that sort of thing?"

Grace twisted her fingers in her lap.

"Grace has been learning German for three months," remarked Charles loudly, "yet she already speaks it well. She is a graceful dancer. And we read books and discuss politics together."

"What kind of books?"

"*Madame Bovary*," replied Grace softly.

"What?" exclaimed Mrs. Phelps. "That tale of moral perversion? I cannot believe you would admit to reading such filth!"

"Mother! It's a great novel. I chose it for her."

Mrs. Phelps folded her arms and turned the corners of her mouth down. "So, tell me, Miss—Miller isn't it? Tell me about your father."

Grace hung her head. "He was a farmer."

"A what, dear? I didn't hear."

"A farmer," said Grace a little louder.

"Oh. A farmer." Mrs. Phelps nodded her head. "And your mother?"

"Mother is Italian," whispered Grace, drooping in her seat.

"Italian," said Mrs. Phelps, too loudly. "How interesting." She shot a look at her husband.

"Mother," exclaimed Charles rising. "Grace is my future wife." In one swift movement he crossed the room, took her hand, and helped her out of her chair. The emerald ring flared green in the sunlight.

"There is to be no debate about this. I will not have you quizzing my fiancée. You're upsetting her."

Mrs. Phelps flushed. "You gave her that ring?" she hissed.

Charles put his arm around Grace's waist. "Grace is a rare jewel, like that ring. She will enhance my life."

"Look at her," said Mrs. Phelps. "She has no poise. She has no bearing. She has no conversation. How can you possibly expect her to organize dinner parties for you and say the right things to the right people?"

"Grace is just seventeen. She'll learn in time. Won't you, darling Grace?"

Grace lowered her lashes and bit her lip. Everything Mrs. Phelps said was true. She was no good at anything. She would be hopeless as Charles' wife. She wiped away a tear with the tip of her finger.

"Caroline," exclaimed Phelps Sr., "you've gone too far."

"Grace?" whispered Charles, kissing her cheek.

She gave him her hand. Mrs. Phelps stood there with her arms crossed, tapping one elegant foot.

"Charles has a brilliant future in front of him. His wife must be someone who can further his career. You do see that, don't you?"

Grace turned to Charles. "I don't want to ruin your life."

"So you won't marry him, then?" said Mrs. Phelps, coming closer.

"Mother! Grace is my fiancée. How dare you speak to her like that?"

"Charles," said Grace putting one hand on his chest. "How would I be able to help you? You know I have a lot to learn."

He kissed her hand. "Dearest Grace, you do help me. Just having you with me is a balm to my soul."

Grace gazed into his eyes. Whatever had she done to make him say such things?

"Believe me, my love, my life would be nothing without you."

Grace glanced down at his magnificent emerald ring that lay heavy on her finger. When she looked up, Phelps Sr. stood there with his hands in his pockets, his expression thoughtful. Mrs. Phelps had her arms folded across her body like a tightly coiled snake. Aunt Paulina's words sounded in her head. *If you marry Mr. Phelps, his mother will make your life a misery.*

Oh dear. What should she do?

Phelps Sr. came forward, smiling. He turned away from his wife and gave Grace a wink.

Chapter Sixteen
Thursday, 20 April

"Mabel said she couldn't come. She told me you'd understand." Violet sank into the chair opposite.

Grace sipped the milky coffee the waiter put before her. They were sitting in a quiet café on Motzstrasse, near to the boutique where Violet worked, and far away from Aunt Louisa.

Violet leaned forward. "Gracie, what happened?"

Grace's cheeks warmed. "Charles proposed and then took me to see the parents. It wasn't a good meeting."

"Oh, Gracie." Violet touched her sister's arm.

Grace turned away to hide the inevitable tears. A pale young man sat at the next table, gazing into his cup of black coffee. Every so often, the left side of his face contracted into a spasm. He placed his trembling hands on each side of his coffee cup and sighed. A crowd of shabby people hovered on the sidewalk outside, hoping that a kind-hearted waiter or patron would give them a leftover. Grace signaled the waiter and ordered three pastries.

Violet spoke. "But didn't Aunt Paulina send him away with a flea in his ear?"

"She told him not to court me, but a week later I saw him when I was visiting Mabel."

Violet rolled her eyes. "Let me guess. He was kind and attentive and you had no idea he was interested in you—until it was too late."

Grace's cheeks heated up.

"Gracie, I didn't mean to be cruel. But we've seen this all before, haven't we?"

Grace managed a small smile. "He does sound eerily like…you-know-who."

"And you, Gracie. What do you think of Charles Phelps?"

Grace looked down and massaged the fingers of her left hand. "I like him, but I thought we were just friends. I have no idea why he wants to marry me. I haven't done anything."

"So he popped a ring on your finger and took you to meet the parents and—"

"It was at the Adlon Hotel. Violet, I hated it, it was so foreign, so cold—"

"What did they say?"

"Mr. Phelp's father was polite, but his mother was so…" Grace screwed up her face."

"Mean?" suggested Violet, as she accepted a cup of coffee from the waiter.

Grace looked up, tears pricking. "She quizzed me about the family. Every time I said something, she repeated it. She said things like, *Oh, a farmer*, when I talked about Father, or *Italian, how interesting*, when I mentioned Mother. She sounded worse than Aunt Louisa on a bad day."

"Is *she* still interested in Céline du Bois?"

Grace nodded. "But Charles says she's a cold-hearted…"

"Rhymes with witch," remarked Violet.

Grace studied the battered wooden table, her cheeks scalding.

"What about Charles?"

"He's more determined than ever. Says his mother doesn't have the right to tell him who to marry."

"Phelps must be in his mid-twenties. Which means Ma Phelps has no say in the matter."

Grace leaned over her coffee cup. "Violet, I haven't told Aunt Paulina about this. I meant to tell her, but I kept putting it off. What do you think I should do?"

Violet leaned back in her seat and looked up at the budding blossoms, which hung over the café. "Perhaps you shouldn't do anything. You say Charles is determined to marry you, so let's see how he negotiates that with his parents. You said his father was polite."

"Yes. He told his wife off when she made me cry. And he smiled at me as we left and winked. I don't know what that's about."

"Sounds as though he has a plan to calm his snobbish wife and get her to agree to the marriage."

"But what about Aunt Paulina?"

"That's going to depend on what Phelps and his father say to her. I mean they're loaded with money, and if the men of the family are willing for your marriage to go ahead, I think she might drop her objections."

"Do you really think so?"

Violet pinched her sister's cheek. "It's possible. But the question is, what do *you* want Grace?"

Grace put her head on her hand and sighed deeply. "I dunno. I wish I didn't have to deal with this. I just want to play my violin, but life won't let me."

"Oh, Gracie." Violet put her arm around her sister.

There was a pause, then Grace looked up. "What did you want Mabel to do?"

"I'm planning my first fashion show. She agreed to model for me—now she can't."

Violet had been working at Camille's boutique on Motzstrasse ever since she quit the Lette-Verein, saying that Camille was teaching her everything she needed to know in order to open her own boutique when she returned to Georgetown.

Grace rose. "Why don't we go over to Camille's?"

"What about your violin?"

Grace tilted her head, considering. She really should practice; she never seemed to get in the five hours she'd promised Professor Flesch. On the other hand, she couldn't concentrate. She couldn't shake Carl's casual invitation for her to live at his villa. He hadn't pursued it, so it might have been idle chit-chat. But Grace's concentration had really been blown to bits by the arrival of Mr. Russell's letter yesterday. His words burned into her brain:

> *Grace,*
>
> *How could you be so cold-hearted? Don't you realize I've been unable to stop thinking about you, by day or by night?*
>
> *But no matter. All that is at an end, as you've made very clear. You don't want me, and I no longer want you. Don't expect to hear from me ever again.*
>
> *Yours faithfully,*
> *Domenico Pagano Russell*

Grace would never see him again. She should be relieved, pleased even, but she couldn't talk about it, even to her sister. Violet disapproved of him so much, she would only make Grace feel worse.

"Are you all right, Gracie? You've gone pale."

"I'm fine." Grace looked up and forced a smile. "I was just thinking that Professor Flesch seems pleased with my progress. Perhaps it's time to do something else, like model for you."

"Gracie!" Violet hugged her sister. Then she glanced at her watch. "We're going to be late if we don't go. The models are arriving."

Grace divided up her pastries, pushing them into eager hands as they left. Then the sisters wandered over to Modes Camille and went upstairs to the fitting room. Violet brought out a white satin evening gown, made on the bias. The lines of the dress were accented with black piping along the seams, which increased the technical challenge because they had to be perfectly straight.

Grace put in on, and Violet started to fit it, a row of pins in her mouth. As Grace watched her sister work, she thought about how much everything had changed in the past few months. It had been ages since Violet had made anything for Grace because Aunt Louisa had taken care of Grace's wardrobe, ordering from expensive boutiques. An image of herself standing on Miss Bernice's table while Violet fit her birthday frock filled Grace's mind. Was that the last time she'd made something for her? How simple everything had been in those days. How happy they'd been in their dreams.

Someone knocked on the door. A tall young woman with a shy smile that revealed crooked teeth stood hesitantly there. "I'm Greta," she remarked. "Frau Varga told me to come."

Violet looked at her watch. It was two o'clock. "What hours do you work?"

She turned beet red. "I have to work nights. But I can be here by late morning."

Grace glanced at her. Many young women were losing their jobs as receptionists, secretaries, and telephone operators. They had to keep body and soul together somehow.

Violet nodded and picked up a sleeveless white tunic.

"This will suit your long legs."

Grace followed Greta into the dressing room. While she took off the evening dress, Greta put on the tunic. She made a face as she looked at herself in the mirror. "Isn't it a bit short?"

Violet came in. "It's a tennis dress. The hem is twenty-three inches above the ground."

"I don't think I've seen anything this short."

"Women need to wear something that helps them to hit the ball hard. You can't play a good game of tennis in long skirts."

"Don't I need stays?"

"You can't breathe if you wear a corset."

"But, won't everyone see your under-things if you start jumping around?"

"You can wear it over cami-knickers. No one will see a thing."

Grace stood back to examine the dress. Violet had made a Greek key pattern outlined in gold to go around the hem.

"Don't forget to shave your armpits," remarked Violet.

Greta nodded and closed the curtains to the changing room.

The door opened and another woman stood there. "Zsa-Zsa told me you needed a model."

Coco was a rail-thin woman of indeterminate age with a striking angular face and dull red hair. Violet picked up the bathing suit. The green two-piece consisted of figure-hugging shorts made in a jersey knit that came down to mid-thigh and a matching scoop-necked top that came down to the hips. The color was a perfect match for Coco's eyes.

"What do you do for a living?" Violet ushered her into the changing room and measured her waist with a tape measure.

Coco gave a tired smile. "I'm an artist's model."

Grace went to the porcelain stove in the back and gently touched the kettle. It was hot enough to make tea; Violet must have just boiled it up. Behind the curtains, they continued talking.

"Do you like modern art?"

"No."

"Why do you do it then?"

"I have to."

"Where are you from?"

"Paris."

"Oh—do you know Mamzelle Camille?"

"No. But there are many people in Paris. It's a large city—I had ambition. I didn't want to spend my life being a shop assistant."

"I'm a shop assistant," remarked Violet. "I plan to open my own shop when I get home."

"But you're American. It is so easy to open a business and make money, especially now. I'm older than you. I had no money, nothing."

"Couldn't you get the bank to give you a loan?" Grace opened the curtains and handed her a mug of tea.

Coco twisted her lips. "Banks don't loan money to young women. In order to get the cash needed, I had to acquire a…protector."

Grace froze.

Coco looked down and examined her nails. She flushed. "There was only one thing I had to give in exchange for money."

Violet and Grace stared at her.

"There is no other way of getting a loan, as you call it."

"But how do you know he'll give you the cash?" Violet accepted her tea from Grace.

"You don't. I thought we were coming to Berlin so I could open my own fashion shop. I waited fifteen years for him to give me permission. But he forgot to mention he had a fiancée, a lady with money. He left me on the street with nothing. Not even enough to buy a ticket home to Paris."

Grace sipped her tea. It was hard to believe that someone could be that cold. What must it be like to be dumped by the roadside by a man you'd believed would care for you? She shook her head.

How could she be so naïve? This must happen every day to women. She only had to remember what Mother's life was like. After all, she had belonged to that same shadowy world. Grace swallowed as an agonizing thought swept through her. If Carl had not mentioned anything more about their conversation—if he had not spoken to her family after—then was it possible…that companionship at his villa was his goal?

"It's a man's world," said Coco as Violet finished pinning. She opened a parasol that was lying around, sashayed over to the chaise longue, reclining on it. Violet's bathing suit looked tastefully elegant on her. "They do anything they please. We women are just here to serve."

"Isn't that the truth?" said someone in a husky voice who stood in the doorway.

Coco turned and smiled. "Margot!"

Margot was an unusually tall woman with a muscular figure. Her black hair fell like a cap around her perfect oval face.

"Zsa-Zsa told me you needed a model for a cocktail dress." Margot's voice was breathy and low.

"Margot would be perfect," remarked Coco.

Margot smiled slowly, revealing perfectly even white teeth. "It would be an honor, Mamzelle Vi'let."

Violet brought out the dress. Grace's mouth opened. Violet was a true professional to have made such an amazing piece. It was made of black tulle over red satin, with a ragged tulle train that gave the dress a light feathery feel. It was accessorized with black velvet opera gloves and a pillbox hat of black satin covered by red tulle.

Margot looked sensational when she opened the curtains to the dressing room. She preened and took mincing steps in the pair of high heels she'd brought along.

"Are you a model?" said Violet.

"No."

"Why not? I'm sure you could find work."

There was a pause.

"Margot has just arrived," put in Coco. "I've been telling her she should get connected to a modeling agency."

"You should give it a try," said Violet. "You look good in that dress. You move well, and you know how to carry yourself."

Margot bent her head gracefully to one side as she fiddled with the tulle veil. "You think I'd pass in a top fashion salon?"

✠✠✠✠✠✠✠✠✠✠✠

Grace swept the bow across the strings as she played the opening chord of the *G Minor Sonata* for unaccompanied violin by Bach. The notes climbed up like a rare dark flower poking out of the soil. Today, Grace played the music dreamily, with more quietude and less overt passion, letting each note shine softly.

At the end of the performance, there was dead silence. She slowly took the violin from under her chin and bowed her head, the echoes of the magnificent music washing over her like the afterglow of a setting sun.

Someone touched her arm and kissed her cheek. Grace lifted her head. The bright blue eyes of Carl von Lietzow gazed back.

"You look magnificent when you play, my dear. Such spirit! Such feeling! You will be an ornament at any gathering." He offered her his arm. "I want to ask your opinion about some plants I'm having put in. The gardener is anxious to start on the garden now that the villa is finished."

Gathering, he'd said. Gathering. Grace wondered what he meant, but knew it was something very different from the concert hall she'd just imagined herself in. Slowly, she put her violin on top of the piano and averted her face. She sank to earth as she loosened her bow. They strolled through the French courtyard garden. Easter had been the previous Sunday, and Grace's family had been guests at Carl's exquisite villa. Now that spring was running on towards late April, the angular shapes of the branches were dissolving into mists of green leaves. A light breeze ruffled her hair. As usual, there was someone waiting unobtrusively to carry out von Lietzow's orders. Grace asked for jasmine vine, because it reminded her of Georgetown. Carl asked for lavender and silver thyme to set off the jasmine.

"Do you miss Georgetown?"

She looked at the jasmine she held between her hands. Its creamy petals gleamed in the gloom of a Berlin April day, Georgetown seemed so far away. "It's lovely here."

He smiled. "I had a talk with your aunt the other day."

Grace clutched the cachepot as she turned towards him.

"She was delighted with our plan."

"Our plan?"

"You surely have not forgotten our conversation?"

Her cheeks warmed. "You asked me whether I wanted to live in your villa."

"Liebchen, I'm asking you to marry me."

Grace dropped the cachepot, a shard of fear prickling up her spine, an image filling her head. She was with Count von Lietzow in his garden, but it was as if she were floating away through a tunnel that became the wrong end of a telescope, so that they stood on a scrap of ground outside the tiny village of Kladow, in the metropolis of the little city of Berlin, in the small country of Germany, as tiny pinpricks between the vastness of earth and sky. Her voice, when she found it, sounded tinny and off-key.

"I couldn't do that. My violin professor would never allow it."

He gazed at her, stunned into silence. Then he started to laugh. He laughed so hard, tears rolled down his cheeks.

Grace stared. But his laughter was so infectious, she laughed along with him. How he made her laugh! She liked him so much.

He led her to a seat and sat close, his thighs touching hers. "Surely you must have noticed my interest. I have spent a great deal of time in your company."

The color drained out of her cheeks. He was serious—only she didn't know about what exactly. She suddenly had a sense that there might be something worse than companion.

He patted her hand. "You look worried, Liebchen. What is it? You can tell your Carl."

Grace took a deep breath and straightened her spine. "I'm not suitable. I know nothing about being a countess."

"Do you think I don't know that? But I will be here with you. We will do everything together."

She stared him squarely in the eye. "My father was a farmer, my mother was Italian. My grandparents were Irish farmers who fled the potato famine and Italian peasants who were turned off their land by the padrone. Doesn't that bother you?"

He stiffened. "Is there someone else?"

Grace rose. "Aren't your friends and relatives going to be hostile?"

He took her hand. "My parents are dead. You know that, I showed you their tombs in Kladow."

"What about your friends?"

"I didn't want to frighten you before. But now, as my fiancée, you'll meet all of them, I promise."

"There's been a misunderstanding." Grace moved away. "It is true that my relatives warned me you might propose, but I didn't believe them. I couldn't see why a sensible man like you would consider someone like me to be your wife."

He hesitated. "Liebchen, I decorated my villa with you in mind. Why would I do that if I didn't think we would be living together some day?"

She remained silent, she must think. If she told him about Charles, what would he do? Mrs. Phelps' voice intruded: *Charles has a brilliant career in front of him*. She couldn't bring von Lietzow's wrath down on Charles, she couldn't be the cause of shattering his hopes and dreams.

"Don't you remember how we discussed which room you'd like to have for your violin practice?"

Grace's cheeks warmed. Carl had commissioned the architect to make it into a perfect oval. He had solicited her help in decorating it, giving it the plain whitewashed walls that she wanted, taking her on shopping trips to find things that reminded her of home. That voice inside Grace's head clamored to know if having this room meant that she could be his countess and have a career as a violinist. But Grace quashed it. Now was not a good time, she needed to prove to him that she could be a good wife before she began making demands—in case he changed his mind.

His tone became cold. "There is someone else."

She glanced at him. His normally mobile mouth was drawn into a grim line, his blue eyes the color of a winter sky. There was more to Carl von Lietzow than the friend who amused her. He was truly formidable. No wonder his servants scuttled around in that obsequious fashion.

Grace lifted her chin and matched his tone. "There is no one else."

He took her in his arms and kissed her with a gentle pressure that became slower and more sensuous as he hungrily sought her lips. She wobbled as he released her, feeling unsteady on her legs as some very strange sensations coursed through her. She shivered with pleasure. "*Mein Gott,*" he murmured at last. "I've been longing to do that for months."

He wrapped an arm around her waist.

"Don't worry your pretty head about teacups and flower arrangements. I have the necessary staff to deal with that."

She laughed, lulled by his familiar bantering tone. Perhaps it wouldn't be so bad.

He pinched her cheek.

"There is no reason to be terrified, Liebchen. Carl will protect you." He took her hand and kissed it, staring at her as he did so. "I take it there's no objection to me?"

Grace shuddered. His hands were large and square, his fingers stubby, with black hair scattered over their backs. How would it feel to have those hands roaming over her naked body? She tried not to think about Mr. Russell's elegant fingers or Charles' soft lips. "I am not good at making small talk."

"It is one of the reasons why I love you. You are yourself. You have no idea how precious that is." He kissed her cheek. "But you will gain in confidence, Liebchen. I know it. You are already different, not quite the shy flower I met in February."

Grace smiled. She must try to relax. After all, being his wife would be easier than being anyone else's. Great-Aunt Paulina, Aunt Louisa, and Uncle William would be delighted. Charles's parents would breathe a sigh of relief. Even Violet liked him. The only people who would not be happy would be Teresa and— But Charles must understand she'd done it for his career. Should she write to him and explain? No. She couldn't take that risk. What would happen if von Lietzow discovered their correspondence?

She looked up to find him studying her face.

"You bewitch me," he murmured. "I feel as though I can't do anything without you. Ah, that reminds me. I have a gift." He drew a velvet box out of his pocket. Inside was a ruby ring set in solid silver.

"Who can find a virtuous woman?" he said as he slipped it onto her finger. "For her price is far above rubies."

Grace looked up at him. How odd to have *three* engagement rings. Thank goodness she'd decided not to wear Charles' emerald ring today, because it was so heavy it got in the way of her violin playing.

"It is from the Book of Proverbs." He kissed her luxuriously on the lips.

The ring glowed deeply red as it squatted on her finger. That sealed it. She would never think about him again.

Chapter Seventeen
Friday, 21 April

"There's a gentleman here to see you." Anna-Maria's eyes were bright.

Grace sighed as she put her violin and bow carefully away in the case. Yesterday, he'd put that fabulous ruby ring on her finger; today, he would return in search of her company. Should she put the violin case under the bed in the room she shared with Teresa? No. It would be safer in his villa.

Grace allowed Anna-Maria to garb her in new clothes and do her hair. Today she wore an apricot satin dress that clung to her body. She still wasn't quite comfortable wearing such an outfit, but Aunt Louisa assured her it was ladylike. Anna-Maria placed a straw hat over her hair and tied it on with a matching silk scarf. At the last minute, she remembered to put on her ruby engagement ring. It, too, was so heavy it made playing the violin difficult.

Everyone smiled as Grace came downstairs. Aunt Louisa and Uncle William pecked her cheeks and wished her well.

Carl came forward, beaming, and offered her his arm. "I take it that you have no objection to my taking Grace out for the day?" An eyebrow rose with merriment. "She tells me she has no idea about how to be a countess, so I thought I should take the opportunity of teaching her how to count."

Aunt Louisa laughed her trilling laugh, while the men shook hands and patted each other on the back.

"Goodbye, Cousin Grace," called Ella and Adela, blowing kisses. Behind them, Teresa glowered silently.

Then they were gone, just like that.

He smiled as he helped her into his car. "I see you've brought your violin, Liebchen. That's a promising start."

Grace tried to relax as she smiled back. What was he going to do? But everything seemed perfectly normal as she entered his villa, except that his flunkies bowed and curtseyed, congratulating her and referring to her as Greffin Graatz. She was shown into her new practice room, made into a perfect oval because Carl said it reflected the contours of her face, and she practiced for a couple of hours while he worked in his office next door.

Just before lunch, they took a tour of the villa to see how the final touches were progressing, then had lunch in the new oval dining room, next door to Grace's practice room, which Carl said had to be the same size and shape for perfect balance and symmetry. It had a view of the garden, which was now carpeted in pink tulips.

Carl was in a good mood and made her laugh with various tales about his friends, most seeming rather eccentric. After lunch, he told her he had a surprise and led her through the practice room into a room she didn't recognize. It was his bedroom, or rather, theirs, because he'd had it fitted up in a particular pink and coffee-colored fabric that she'd admired. The molding around the ceiling, fireplace, and walls was painted cream to set it off. On one side of the bed was a negligée set in matching silken fabric.

Grace smiled and kissed his cheek.

"Liebchen," he said sitting down on the bed, "shall I take off your shoes? Those new shoes are very elegant." He fingered her satin shoes, dyed apricot to match her dress. "But perhaps they pinch?"

She laughed at the expression on his face.

He gently removed a shoe and tickled the inside of her foot. "Let me see, how many bones are in your feet?"

She giggled.

"Shall I count them for you?" He planted butterfly kisses on top of her stockings along the upper part of the foot.

"Are you ticklish?" He traced his fingers up her legs until he got above her stockings. He stroked the inside of her thighs. "Your skin is as soft as rose petals."

She closed her eyes and moaned.

He let his kisses wander down her neck towards her bosom.

"You are so beautiful," he murmured, undoing a button in the front of her dress.

Her eyes flipped open.

He leaned over her and took her hands. "You are my bride, Liebchen."

Grace got up on her elbows. "Have you wanted to marry me for some time?"

He took her into his arms and stroked her back. "Ever since I invited you to my villa." He drew back to look at her. "Do you remember your first morning here, when you told me this room gave you a feeling of great peace?"

She smiled.

"I fell in love with you then." He kissed her hair.

"But Teresa made fun of me."

"I know. Your cousin is also a beautiful woman. But I wanted you. She didn't interest me."

Grace arched an eyebrow.

"I know the type all too well, the flirtatious young woman who is oh-so-knowing, complete with husky voice and eyelash glances. You, on the other hand, were always yourself. I respected, admired, and quickly loved you for it." He kissed her hand.

"I had no idea."

He undid more buttons, lowering his mouth onto her lips and kissing her with exquisite slowness. She melted as something uncoiled within. His fingers trailed under the satin material of her dress until he found a nipple, which he massaged gently with his thumb.

She moaned.

"Liebchen?"

She smiled, her eyes closing.

He lowered his mouth and sucked her nipple.

She moaned, her head rolling from side to side. She had the strangest sensations under her belly.

He took her in his arms and peeled off her dress. "Shall I help you off with your camisole and petticoat?"

The strange melting feeling was making her very warm. She nodded. In no time at all Grace lay before him naked from the waist up, wearing only her silken drawers and stockings. She'd never been half-naked in front of a man before, yet it seemed the most natural thing in the world.

He took off his jacket and lay down beside her. He smelled of cigars, with a hint of brandy. "You are perfect. " He drew her closer, making butterfly kisses all over her body, until he got to her drawers. "Take those off," he whispered.

"But I couldn't do that."

"Why not?"

"It would be—rude."

He laughed and touched her face. "There's nothing wrong with nudity. You can show me anything."

She complied.

Slowly, he drew her legs up and smiled. Lazily, he let his fingers trail up her thigh in circular movements, increasing this strange feeling. Slowly, he inserted a finger. She coiled up, arched her back, and cried out.

He kissed her deeply. "How passionate you are." He fumbled, leaned over, and thrust something deep within, kissing her to still her screams.

"It's all right, Liebchen." He stroked her face. "It won't ever hurt like that again. Relax. It's what men and women do. We're making love."

Moments later, he was roaring in triumph. "You have the looks of a goddess." He panted hard and flung himself on top of her. "Forgive me, Liebchen, for being so impatient." He took her in his arms and kissed her face.

She grabbed the bedding and rolled underneath it. "I have to marry you now."

"You were going to marry me anyway, remember?" He grasped her waist. "I couldn't wait until our wedding night."

Grace hung her head, remembering what Aunt Paulina had said about men being impatient for the pleasures of the marriage bed. This was what she'd meant. This was what Mother had never told her. She blinked back tears.

He tilted her chin up with his fingers. "Dry your tears, Liebchen. We can do this, we're engaged. I'm going to marry you, don't ever worry your head about that. You have my ring as my promise. You will be my countess."

"When are we getting married?"

"Whenever you like, Liebchen. I leave it up to you to name the date."

Grace turned to look at the ruby ring that lay heavily on her left ring finger. She was his mistress now. She was no better than Mother. Her cheeks flamed.

But Carl grinned as he pulled the bedclothes back, exposing her nakedness to his avid eyes. "Perhaps it should be soon," he murmured as his fingers slowly found their way to that wet place between her legs. "Let me show you more things." He lowered his mouth.

✠✠✠✠✠✠✠✠✠✠✠

Two large trunks and a suitcase stood in the hallway. One trunk, made for gentlemen, was four feet long and two feet square. It was flat-topped, made of leather-covered wood with steel corners. Inside was a tray for each dress suit, a place for collars and for cuffs, a tray in which ties could be laid without folding, and compartments for toilet articles, a manicure set, and a silk hat.

The other trunk was larger but lighter, and made for the clothes of a lady. Both trunks had three hasps that closed tightly, with the middle one being locked by a key. They were brand new, and their burgundy colored leather glowed softly in the late afternoon sunshine. A matching leather suitcase stood beside the trunks, filled with his books and papers.

Russell paused as he came downstairs. So many people had stopped by to wish him well in the last couple of days: Professor Burneys and his wife, the Taussig sisters, even Violet's friend Miss Bernice. Of course, they'd wanted him to send messages and greetings to Grace and her family, but there was something about the way they squeezed his hand, looked him in the eye, or clapped him on the back that conveyed their concern for him, too.

Russell paced up and down Mrs. Rittenhouse's hallway. Being forced to say goodbye to Grace in December had been one of the most painful events of his life. The thought of never seeing her again, after everything he'd done to win her, had plunged him into despair. He didn't remember anything about his journey to Wisconsin, except the look on his brother's face when he'd arrived. Alarmed, Girolamo had insisted that he go on a retreat during the Christmas holidays.

The priest leading the retreat, known for his piety and compassion, was a friend of Lamo's. During a private counseling session, when Russell had told him he could never be happy again, the priest had gently suggested he find someone else to marry:

"Perhaps someone older, someone a bit more mature." Russell had murmured his thanks but privately found the thought of marrying someone else repellant. If he couldn't find love, he didn't want marriage. But the priest's words gave him an idea.

In his youth, Russell had been in and out of love with several women. Though Lamo knew this, Russell had never mentioned his many sexual conquests or his friendship with a medical student who'd enlightened Russell about a man's responsibilities to a woman in preventing unwanted pregnancies. During his college years, Russell and his medical friend had had many conversations about ethics and medicine, and gradually the young doctor had won Russell over to his way of thinking, pointing out that the Catholic Church's attitudes were old-fashioned and sometimes harmful. Despite these conversations, Russell continued to feel a strong emotional connection with the Catholic Church. He loved the quietude and sense of spiritual purpose. But his views about contraception, abortion, and suicide were a different matter. Russell never discussed his opinions with his brother because he did not think he would be able to bear the disappointment in Lamo's eyes or the weakening of the bond between them. And so Russell became adept at acting with extreme secrecy when conducting his private affairs.

And now, as the priest talked about how life did not always go the way one wanted it to go and counseled Russell to try and find happiness anyway, he wondered if the best way of forgetting about Grace was to find a New Woman, a female who made her own money and therefore didn't need to marry for economic security. Perhaps he should make an effort to enter the twentieth century.

Telling his brother that he would tough it out like a man and apply himself to his studies, Russell returned to Georgetown. It didn't take him long to find her. Elaine was twenty-two years old, the daughter of a federal bureaucrat. Her parents had been putting pressure on her to marry, she told him as they danced the foxtrot at a Georgetown dance, but she wanted to be independent.

Afterwards, he'd offered to walk her home.

"Aren't you going to take me to a hotel?"

Russell reddened.

"Don't you want to—you know?"

He blinked in surprise. It felt so strange not to be the one making the moves. "I've only just met you." He sounded like a shy, young girl.

She draped her arms around his neck. "Kiss me," she murmured huskily.

Russell did not remember much, except the illicit pleasure any man would feel in bedding a pretty young thing and the force of his release, which allowed him some measure of peace.

And that was the only thing that made his life bearable for the next several months. Despite her protests that he didn't need to worry about anything as old-fashioned as her reputation, he insisted on conducting a discreet affair at the Metropolitan, far from the prying eyes of Mrs. Rittenhouse and her neighbors.

He was grateful to Elaine for her willing participation in gratifying his sexual needs, but he wasn't happy. As time went on, he found himself more and more puzzled by the New Woman he'd acquired. She was a pretty girl with soft brown hair and blue-gray eyes, but she ruined her looks by shaving her eyebrows and penciling them in, by marcellating her hair, and by applying lipstick too thickly.

By the end of the spring semester, things soured when she asked him to marry her.

"But I didn't think you wanted to marry."

She draped her arms around his neck and brought her lipsticked lips close to his. Russell felt familiar stirrings of lust but resisted. He scrutinized her face closely. "What are you trying to tell me?"

She batted her lashes.

Russell folded his arms and glared at her. "I used protection."

"It didn't work."

"Are you sure?"

She smiled.

"Then you should go to a doctor and have it taken care of."

Tears trickled down her cheeks.

"I don't understand," said Russell. "You told me you didn't want a husband—"

"I love you," she wailed. "And I want to keep the baby."

Russell sighed in exasperation. He thought he had been safe shacking up with a New Woman precisely because she would be too independent to play the old trick and trap him into marriage. But it seemed Elaine had done precisely that. He reached into his billfold and counted out five hundred dollars. "Here. Take this."

"I don't want it."

"You're going to need it if you decide to go to a doctor—"

She slapped him in the face.

Russell stared at her. She was acting like a typical woman, instead of negotiating for more money.

"I hate you!" she exclaimed, dissolving into sobs.

"Elaine," he said gently. "I never promised to marry you. I would never have gotten together if you'd told me you expected me to marry you. I chose you as my companion precisely because you said you didn't want to marry."

She turned away, weeping loudly, her face covered in pink blotches.

Russell sighed and walked to the window. Women had been given the right to vote less than a year ago, and their new responsibilities gave them an aura of independence. But these New Women were like meringues: glittering and hard on the surface, soft and chewy inside. They seemed more sophisticated, but the reality was that they still wanted the same things.

"Who is she?"

Russell started and turned.

She came closer then recoiled at the expression on his face.

He picked up her jacket, draped it over her shoulders, and opened the door.

Then he'd paid the bill, gone home to Mrs. Rittenhouse, and re-read Grace's letter. Of course. How stupid he'd been. That letter didn't sound like

Grace; she must have been forced to write it. He must go to Berlin at once to find out how things were and whether she could forgive him for his ill-judged fury.

Now it was a week later, May the twenty-fourth, and he was waiting for the cab that would take him to Union Station and the train to New York, where he would board a steamer to the port of Kiel early next morning. He stood in front of the hallway mirror to straighten his tie and smooth back his hair, but all he saw was another face. Her face. A heart-shaped face, with a dimple to the right of her mouth when she smiled. Flawless skin that ran over the mound of pretty cheeks. Deep-set sockets that held a pair of lustrous gray eyes. Luscious lips that demanded his kisses. Every night before going to sleep, he covered that face with kisses. Until he remembered how she'd looked at him that last time. The time she'd lowered her lashes.

Lowering her lashes was like the lowering of a portcullis. It shut him out of her life. The pain in his chest was akin to a knife twisting. He gritted his teeth as he re-knotted his tie, and scrutinized himself in the mirror. Was he making a terrible mistake? Should he go to Berlin?

His brother's voice intruded into his thoughts. "Domenico, why did you lie to Graziella?"

They'd been sitting in Girolamo's room, which had a view of a snowy cloister.

Russell hadn't replied. Instead, he'd taken his cigarette case out of his pocket and lit one.

Girolamo, disliking cigarette smoke, cracked the window open.

The freezing air cleared his head. At last, he said, "I didn't think she'd understand. I couldn't bear to lose her, not when things were going so well—"

"What about Angelina?"

Russell felt the color drain out of his cheeks. He'd forgotten that no one had told his brother what had happened. Grace's family had just reconnected with Lamo after a silence of over twenty years. What was he going to say? His fingers trembled as he patted ash into the ashtray his brother offered him. Fixing his eyes on the floor in front of him, he murmured, "Angelina is dead."

"*È morta?* Dead? What do you mean, Nico? How did that happen?"

"I don't know," he said, keeping his gaze glued to the floor. "There is to be an inquest."

Finally, he glanced up. Lamo folded his hands and looked at his younger brother. His gaze was unwavering.

Russell's cheeks warmed. There was a pause as he patted ash off his cigarette butt and lit another. "This whole thing has made me wonder about Father."

"You've never wanted to think about him before."

Russell grimaced as his father's face filled his mind, wearing his habitual surly expression, the corners of his mouth turned down, his jaw tight with rage.

"I was never close to Father, but if I could put one question to him now—" He inhaled deeply. "I would ask him how he felt about his first wife Teresa Giardini."

"What makes you think about her?"

"I understand that Grace looks exactly like her. If her grandmother, *la nonna Teresa,* possessed one tenth of Grace's beauty, she would have been a lovely woman."

"Indeed." Lamo's face sobered. "I never knew her."

"I wonder what Father was like as a young man," continued Russell, exhaling smoke through his nose. "We only knew him as an older man, in his fifties and sixties. But what do you think, Lamo? Would he have been capable of passion?"

Lamo's face sank. "I don't know," he murmured. "He was a stranger to us. But I remember he had a fiery temper, which indicates a passionate nature."

"I wonder if he felt the way about Teresa Giardini that I feel towards Grace."

"Perhaps." Lamo folded his arms.

"But don't you see Lamo? If he was passionately attached to his first wife, he must have been devastated by her sudden death."

"That would explain many things," replied Lamo slowly. "Like his chronic sour temper, and the way he shut himself off from everyone, including our mother." He paused. "We haven't finished discussing this whole mess you've got yourself into, Nico. It was your duty to put things right with Graziella and her family."

"Zia Paulina refused to listen. She banished me before I could make amends."

Lamo held up a hand. "Think of the harm you have done to your soul and Graziella's. *Le bugie hanno una sorta di terribilità,* lies have a certain kind of awfulness. They are so corrosive. Domenico, do you really want to begin your marriage with a web of lies?"

Russell averted his face.

"You want her to respect you."

"I want her love." Russell looked up. "I would give anything for that."

Lamo sat down. "Tell me why you love Grace so much."

"She gives me such peace. It is heavenly just to be with her. There was a precious moment when we were rehearsing at her violin professor's house. Grace seemed so tired, I persuaded her to rest. She trusted me enough to lie down in the same room as myself, unchaperoned, close her eyes, and sleep. Watching her, I felt a kind of joy I have almost never felt."

Lamo's voice softened. "But she knows you have lied to her, Nico. You must ask her forgiveness."

Russell stared at his cigarette for a long moment, then looked up. "You think we could marry?"

Lamo opened his mouth as if to say no. Then he stopped, and scrutinized his brother.

"You seem different, Nico. Quite different. Now you remind me of the boy I used to know before the war."

"Is that true?" He felt his face ease into a smile.

Lamo returned his smile and promised to apply for the Papal dispensation.

Russell adjusted his tie again in Mrs. Rittenhouse's hallway mirror, and glanced at his watch. It was nearly six o'clock, and he would miss the seven o'clock train if the cab didn't come soon. Swiftly, he went to the window and parted the blinds. The street was empty.

Just this morning, Lamo had telephoned to say '*addio.*' "Are you well enough to go to Berlin?"

"Of course."

"Are you sure this is a good idea?"

"I must go. I must hear from those heavenly lips how she feels about me."

"What if she's changed her mind? What if she has another suitor?"

There had been dead silence, the color draining from his face as though his very life-force were ebbing away.

"Nico? Are you there?"

"*Sì.*"

"What will you do if she's changed her mind?"

"I wouldn't be able to stand it," he mumbled tonelessly, adding without thinking "I'd shoot myself."

"Nico!"Girolamo thundered down the line,"You must not think such thoughts! Promise me that!"

Reluctantly, he'd given his promise.

Now, feeling as though his feet were encased in boots of lead, he moved to Mrs. Rittenhouse's front door and stared through the colored glass. His brother was right as usual. He probably shouldn't go. But just as he was about to be overwhelmed by despair, his quick ear caught the clop-clop of horses' hooves coming up West Lane and halting just outside the door.

Russell hesitated for one moment, then opened the door and gestured the cabbie to help him with his trunks.

Chapter Eighteen
Thursday, 25 May

The day before the fashion show, Camille gave Violet the day off, telling her to spend the day in bed. But Violet wasn't going to spend her day off lying around like Teresa. Instead, she would relax by sketching the passers-by.

Violet put on her peacoat and cloche, walked to Café Tomasa on Motzstrasse, ordered a *caffee mit schlag*, and opened her leather portfolio. It was now late May, and bright sunshine alternated with cool breezes, sending threads of cloud across the sky A young woman of around her age walked along the street wearing chocolate brown gabardine that set off her fair hair and pale complexion. The circular skirt fell in soft folds to mid-calf, and the long-sleeved suit jacket came to mid-hip. Fastened just below the collar was a cape of matching chocolate gabardine, which fell in graceful folds that emphasized her long limbs. A crepe de chine hat completed the look.

As Violet sketched the suit, her mind roamed over the events of the past three months. Teresa had not snagged her German aristocrat and was now demanding that everyone leave Berlin to summer in Baden-Baden. On the other hand, Grace was engaged to Count von Lietzow, while Mr. Phelps had disappeared. Violet was not surprised. It must be humiliating to be outgunned by von Lietzow and cold-shouldered by Auntie Lou and Auntie P.

How would it feel to have a countess for a sister? Violet's hand stopped in the middle of a line. Carl von Lietzow was not stuffy in the way she'd imagined aristocrats to be. What was it he'd called her?

She tilted her head, bringing to mind a day recently when she'd visited his estate. He'd been charming and gracious, including her in everything, even though it was clear he was mesmerized by Grace.

At the end of the tour, refreshments were served. While Grace excused herself, von Lietzow came over.

"Why are you here in Berlin, Miss Violet?"

Violet looked up "I'm studying fashion design."

"Indeed?" he replied, handing her a glass of chilled white wine. "Why is it that I don't see you at the balls and social events your sister goes to?"

"I have to work."

"You could go, Violet dear, you know that," put in Auntie Lou. "I'd be delighted to have your company."

Violet smiled but said nothing.

There was a pause, then von Lietzow said softly, "You don't mean to tell me that you work for a living?"

Violet's cheeks warmed. "I don't mind working, as long as it gets me closer to my goals."

"And what are your goals?"

She lifted her chin. "I'd like to open my own dress shop when I return to Georgetown."

"Violet, dear!" exclaimed Auntie Lou.

But he smiled. "I am not offended, Gnädige Frau. I like to see a woman with spirit." He returned his gaze to Violet.

"This has demanded a lot of your time, hasn't it?"

"I work sixty hours a week."

"Violet!" said Auntie Lou. "There's no need to say that. You have relatives to help you."

"But you prefer to be independent, don't you Fräulein Violet? You must be one of those New Women they talk about so much now." He shook his head and chuckled.

Violet smiled as she opened her leather portfolio and took out another sketching pad. A New Woman. She liked that description. How could married women bear to be so dependent upon their husbands? Violet ordered another coffee and studied more passers-by. Even though it was warmer than the below-freezing temperatures of January, February and March, the mercury had not shifted much beyond fifty degrees. People wore their winter garments, the men nearly alike, with their thick woolen coats and bowler hats. The women wore fur coats that had good lines and fur hats that framed their pale faces. Set against the gray beaux-arts facade of Berlin—which looked remarkably like the pictures of Paris she'd seen in various magazines—they looked stylish.

Violet sipped her coffee and picked up her notebook. Who was that handsome man? He had an interesting profile, with deep-set eyes and a beaked nose. His clothes were different from the German businessmen who surrounded him, being less heavy. Instead of a bowler hat, he wore a Stetson. Violet frowned as she tried to get his face right. At that moment, he looked up. Their eyes locked. It was Detective Ecker.

"Miss Violet!" he exclaimed, standing up and coming closer. "I was hoping I would see you. May I join you?" He brought his coffee and paper over to the table and sat down. "You're looking very well, Miss Violet."

Violet studied her sketchbook. Had she replied to the letter he'd sent in February saying the inquest had been postponed yet again? Yes, and had received a short note in reply saying that he would arrive in Berlin after Easter.

"May I look at what you were sketching?"

She bit her lip. "I was sketching you."

He examined it quietly for a moment. "You have talent, Miss Violet. That really is good."

"It isn't finished."

"Would you like me to sit for you so you can finish it?"

"If you don't mind." Her cheeks warmed. Why was he was making her feel so self-conscious? No one else did. She picked up her charcoal. "Could you turn your head to the left? That way. No, that way." And she frowned with concentration as she finished the drawing.

Afterwards, he said he'd like to purchase it.

"I'm not that good."

"I think you are very good. But I don't want to press you. Just think it over."

She nodded, packed up her things, and rose.

"May I accompany you home, or wherever you're going?"

She blinked. "Certainly. If you wish it."

"I do," he replied smiling. "And might I carry your case?"

A few moments later, they strolled through Viktoria-Luise-Platz arm in arm, almost as if they were a courting couple. But that was odd, for she scarcely knew him. Besides, men didn't treat her that way. At least not when Grace was around.

"Tell me, why did you take up sketching?"

She sighed as she explained her disappointments with the Lette-Verein, how she'd apprenticed herself to a professional dressmaker, and was now holding her first fashion show.

He stopped.

"You have been busy, Miss Violet. You've only been here—let's see—less than five months, and you're already putting on a fashion show?"

"I had to work hard."

"I daresay. Would you mind if I came?"

"Not at all. But—I didn't know you were interested in that sort of thing."

He smiled.

Her cheeks warmed. "It's at Modes Camille Motzstrasse 70, next Friday."

"Is this where you are staying?" They were outside Frau Varga's front door.

"Yes. Auntie P. and I are staying with a charming and quirky Hungarian lady."

"Where is Miss Grace?"

"She's with Mrs. Philips, near Savignyplatz."

He raised his eyebrows.

"It's closer to the music school."

He nodded and returned the leather portfolio.

"Until next time, Miss Violet."

He touched his hat and left.

That had to be the oddest conversation she'd ever had. Violet opened Frau Varga's door. She'd never felt so uncomfortable in all her born days. But she enjoyed his company— Violet stopped and held onto the door. Did he know the results of Mother's inquest? Oh, no. Was that why he was here?

✠✠✠✠✠✠✠✠✠✠✠

Modes Camille had recently been fitted with floor-to-ceiling mirrors to show off the fashions to their full advantage. A long staircase led from the workshops above the showroom, turned, and gave out onto the middle of the showroom floor. The models were to parade down the stairs, walk along a center aisle made by the rows of chairs, pause at the back of the room for a camera shot, then turn and walk back along the aisle and up the staircase. Camille had invited various members of the press to attend and they were stationed in chairs set along the back wall with their notebooks and cameras. Twenty outfits were to be shown. Four had been designed and made by Violet.

As Grace was modeling one of Violet's outfits, she had been the first to arrive with Carl. When she'd mentioned it to him, he'd immediately suggested combining Violet's fashion show with their engagement party, so they could both be held on the last Friday in May.

"He's not stuffy," Violet remarked as Carl disappeared to get refreshments. "That's what I like about him."

Grace shook her head. He was the opposite of stuffy. Instead of learning about menus, flower arrangements, and etiquette, she inhabited his bed. She'd done many things she'd never dreamed of.

Mother must have known all about it; she'd held the interest of that wealthy patron for years. And yet here Grace was, standing in the middle of a boutique, having a polite conversation with her sister. Did Mother ever feel so disoriented, or did she glory in her hidden knowledge?

"Is this bringing you closer to your goals, *liebe Schwägerin*?" Carl returned and bussed Violet on the cheek.

Violet smiled and nodded.

"You interest me." He handed her a glass of champagne. "You are poor, yet it doesn't occur to you to marry money. You could, you know. You are very pretty, Miss Violet."

Violet thinned her lips. "I prefer to earn my own money."

"You're not interested in young men?"

Violet scrutinized his face.

"I am asking you a genuine question."

"I'm not uninterested," said Violet slowly. "But I want to study right now and learn something useful that will serve me for the rest of my life. Young men are all very well in their way. But I see no need to rush into marriage."

He laughed. "Truly, I see a New Woman before me!"

Violet flushed and smiled. "I shouldn't have any more." She handed him her nearly full glass. "I need to keep my wits straight to deal with the models."

"They must be an interesting assortment of people." His eyebrow danced in amusement. Then he took Grace's hand and kissed it. "Don't forget our party, Liebchen."

Grace and Violet hurried up the stairs. It was already eleven-thirty, and the show was to start at noon. Violet buttoned her sister into the evening gown and fixed her hair, then she helped Greta into the tennis dress. But where were Coco and Margot?

Grace and Violet went to the head of the stairs and looked out over the audience, picking out Aunt Louisa and Uncle William, Ella and Adela. But where was Teresa? There was Aunt Paulina, wearing her habitual ankle-length gray wool skirt, topped by a frilly blouse and long jacket. Grace and Violet glanced at each other, the corners of their mouths crinkling. Dear Aunt Paulina had no ambition to change with the times. But she was not alone. Most of the older ladies refused to raise their hems.

There was a flutter, and Frau Varga bustled in, wearing her usual colorful attire of black skirt and jacket covered with red, green, and white embroidered flowers. Several people dressed in a similar fashion, all speaking that unpronounceable language, accompanied her. Had she dragged the entire Hungarian community along? Frau Varga took a gander, gave a cheerful wave, and sat in the back row next to Aunt Paulina.

They craned their necks and finally saw Margot. Dressed in a purple cocktail dress with a fringed hem that showed off her legs, her hair pulled back into a matching headband with a jaunty feather, she put one hand on her hip and sashayed up the aisle to the accompaniment of wolf-whistles and catcalls.

"You've certainly made an entrance," muttered Violet, taking her by the arm.

When Margot came out of the dressing room, Violet's fabulous cocktail dress didn't look good.

Violet frowned. "Stand on that platform by the mirror."

"Is something wrong?"

"That dress is not sitting right. It doesn't fit around your derrière. That's odd, because I spent hours fitting it exactly. What's changed?"

Margot pouted, her plum-colored lips looking like ripe fruit. "It's not my fault."

"Your bottom is flat." Violet frowned, then her eyes widened. "Don't tell me—"

Margot scowled.

Coco ran up the stairs. "Sorry I'm late," she panted. She stopped dead. "What's wrong?"

"This is a man!" exclaimed Violet. "How dare you?"

Margot stepped off the platform and took mincing steps in the high-heels he'd brought with him.

"But you told me you needed someone tall and striking," said Coco. "That cocktail dress will be sensational. And Margot's doing it for free."

Violet sank into a chair and put her head in her hands.

"It's Violet's best piece. She's going to have to take it out of the show. Why didn't you say something before?" exclaimed Grace, going to her sister.

"Look," said Coco. "I've got an extra bottom in my bag. All Margot has to do is pop it on."

"I want a female wearing my dress." Violet raised her face. It was streaked with tears.

"Fräulein Vi'let, it is true I have the toolbox of a man." Margot fluttered his long eyelashes. "But I never wanted to be one. I love being a woman."

"You don't have much choice," remarked Coco. "You're not going to find anyone else, especially anyone who can carry off that glamorous frock."

Grace glanced at the clock. It was five minutes past noon.

"The toast of Berlin, will I be!" declared Margot. "I just need a bottom."

But where was Violet going to put him? He couldn't be in the same changing room as the other girls. "What about the other ladies?" asked Grace.

"Ladies?" Margot laughed his husky laugh. "You've got Greta the hooker and Coco the artist's model."

And I'm la grande horizontale. Grace turned away to hide tears. None of us are ladies any more.

✠✠✠✠✠✠✠✠✠✠✠✠

"To end the show, we are showing four outfits made by a new designer, Mademoiselle Violet Miller," said Camille. "The first item is an evening gown."

There was a pause as Grace uncoiled her spine and looked straight ahead. Slowly, she walked down the stairs.

"This is made of white satin. It has a long tubular silhouette with an inverted tulip hem," said Camille as Grace passed. She wandered down to the end of the aisle of chairs, attempting a more ladylike version of Mother's sashay. When she got to the back, she turned slowly around, trying out several different poses as the cameras flashed and popped.

"Mademoiselle Violet has used the technique of the bias cut for a softer draping of the material," remarked Camille. "All woven cloth has warp and weft threads that make a ninety-degree angle. When you cut on the bias, you cut across that angle at forty-five degrees to take advantage of the fact that the fabric stretches more in that direction. In this way, you can subtly accentuate the body's curves and do a softer draping of the material." She paused. "That technique was first pioneered by Mademoiselle Vionnet in Paris. She was known as the Sorceress with the Scissors."

There were laughs and murmurs. Then Grace walked slowly back along the aisle and floated up the stairs as the audience applauded. She came to the turn in the stairs and smiled at Greta. As Greta emerged, there were several loud gasps. Grace stayed behind to watch from the balcony.

"This dress, also designed by Mademoiselle Violet, is made exclusively for playing tennis. As you can see, the hem is very short, about twenty-three inches off the floor. This is to allow the tennis player the maximum amount of freedom in playing the game. Young women nowadays play a different game than their mothers and grandmothers, one requiring much more activity. This dress was designed to address those needs."

Greta walked steadily to the back of the room. The photographers spent an inordinate amount of time photographing her, asking for various different poses. One individual even had the effrontery to lie on the floor and shoot his camera up her legs. Finally, they let her go, and almost running, she made her way up the stairs, brushed past Grace, and disappeared.

When Coco appeared in her bathing suit, the audience gasped again. But Coco flashed a smile and, twirling Camille's Japanese parasol, sashayed down the aisle, swinging her hips provocatively. Once in front of the cameras, she did several poses, front, back, side, and then front again. Then she went towards the staircase, where she paused, did one final turn, and headed up the stairs to the sound of clapping and whistling.

Now it was Margot's turn. But before he could make his entrance, the door opened and Teresa wandered in. She looked as if she'd come straight from a ball, even though it was around one o' clock in the afternoon. She wore a pink evening dress decorated in gold embroidery with a matching triangular headdress that gave the outfit an exotic, Russian feel. Around her neck was a long rope of pearls. She was on the arm of an impeccably dressed gentleman with waxed sideburns.

The sudden appearance of these two glamorous people caused quite a stir, as seats had to be found for them. By this time, Margot had arrived at the turn in the staircase. He glowered. Eventually the audience settled down, and Margot minced down the remaining steps dressed in the cocktail dress of black tulle over red satin. Holding his arms out—which someone, thankfully, had shaved—he did a turn while the cameras flashed and popped, striking a pose so that everyone could see the back of the dress with its ragged black tulle train that gave the dress its light feathery feel. The audience burst into applause.

Grace leaned over the balcony, scrutinizing him. As far as she could tell, the dress fit perfectly. Taking ladylike steps, Margot minced over towards Teresa.

"Welcome to our fashion show, my lady countess," he said in his husky voice, bowing and smiling like a wind-up doll.

Teresa's gentleman-friend curled his lip, revealing crooked, stained teeth.

Teresa wrinkled her nose.

A flurry of titters ran around the room.

"This dress is also designed by Mademoiselle Violet," said Camille. "It is a cocktail dress with a matching hat. The hat shows red tulle on black to provide a contrast to the black tulle on red of the dress."

Margot came to, flashed a brilliant smile, and tottered towards the cameras. He turned slowly and walked back to the staircase, allowing the audience another view of the back of the dress. What else could go wrong? But Margot did one more turn to show off the back of the dress and then wandered up the stairs to more applause.

Grace expelled her breath in a long sigh. Violet looked pale, but she rose to her feet, smiling, to acknowledge more applause. A lean gentleman with a beaked nose and green eyes stood near the back, clapping heartily. He seemed familiar. Grace stared. Whatever was Detective Ecker doing in Berlin?

"Liebchen." Carl planted a chaste kiss on her cheek. "You look gorgeous in that dress. Why not leave it on for our party?"

Grace smiled and allowed him to sweep her away to the Hotel Adlon.

Chapter Nineteen
Friday, 2 June

Nicholas Russell wandered aimlessly along the Ku'damm. He couldn't stand it. What was he going to do with the rest of his life?

He'd arrived at the port of Kiel at dawn this morning, and purchased a train ticket to Hamburg. From there, he'd taken another train to Berlin, which rolled into the Berlin Hauptbahnhof at precisely noon. After checking into his room at the Hotel Adlon, he rushed downstairs, not even giving himself time to bathe his face, sure he could find out something about her there as the Adlon was the place where all the journalists gathered. As he entered the restaurant, his eyes tumbled upon a discarded newspaper. It was the *Berliner Morgenpost*, carrying a lead story about the wedding of Count von Lietzow to an unknown American beauty, which was to take place tomorrow, Saturday, June the third. He read it, his jaw clenched.

The article gushed on about the young lady's beauty and wondered about the dress she would wear tomorrow. The location of the wedding was unknown, but that didn't prevent it from speculating that the pretty village of Kladow where the count had a charming villa would be just the place. The piece ended with a description of their courtship: how his car had become a well-known sight around Berlin chauffeuring her American relatives and how he had decorated his new villa to suit her tastes. A large photo above the fold showed Grace standing next to Count von Lietzow, wearing a luxurious satin dress that molded her figure. The caption described a ruby engagement ring that had cost a fortune. Great play was given to the Biblical quotation about virtuous women.

Savagely, he threw the newspaper down. Lamo had been right. He'd come all this way to Berlin only to find that another had snatched her up. The thump of artillery shells and the rapid report of machine gun fire resolved itself into the sounds of a streetcar clattering by. He went outside into the fresh air of a northern European June, heaving with rage, his insides twisting, breathing in jagged drags of air. He wanted to howl in frustration. Instead, he lit a cigarette and made himself walk slowly along the Ku'damm.

Inhaling deeply, he felt somewhat calmer. It was clear she was going to marry her aristocratic suitor because her family would insist on it. He would go to her wedding on Saturday and then shoot himself. Or hang himself. Or take poison. He hadn't decided which. He was in such hell now that the promise of eternal damnation meant very little.

Eventually, he came to the Romanische Café, opposite the Kaiser Wilhelm Memorial Church. He stood still, taking in the scene before him, of people eating and drinking, reading and writing, conversing and thinking. The war had been over for less than four years, and Berlin was full of amputees begging on the streets, of gaunt young men startling at the slightest thing. Their fixed stares, pallid faces, and shattered bodies cast a pall like a gray shroud. Would the memories of that horror of a war never go away? Russell sighed and sat down. At least he wouldn't be here for much longer.

He ordered a black coffee and took a book out of his briefcase. Here was something that looked interesting: A. Einstein: *Über die spezielle und allgemeine Relativitätstheorie*. Perhaps it could give him a few hours of pleasure, as the author claimed.

He immersed himself in Euclidian geometry, sipping his bitter brew, until something made him glance up. A well-dressed young man passed slowly along the sidewalk in front of him. The smoke from his cigarette drifted lazily across.

He stopped. "You're American aren't you?"

Russell nodded.

The other held his hand out. "Charles Phelps. I work for the State Department."

"Nicholas Russell. I'm studying at Georgetown."

"Russell? I knew I'd seen you somewhere before. So you got into Georgetown. That's great."

Russell looked more closely. Of course. Phelps was the officer responsible for coordinating his efforts from Washington D.C. He'd met him during the war, when he was working as a spy.

"Would you like coffee?" Russell, signaled to the waiter.

"Thanks," said Phelps sitting down. "How long have you been here?"

"I've just arrived."

"Have you been here before?"

"No."

"Where did I see you last? It was Paris, wasn't it?"

"Yes. In 1919."

"Three years ago. It's hard to believe that much time has passed."

"I'd like to see Paris again," Russell heard himself say. "It was beautiful, despite the ravages of war."

"I remember how you always seemed to have some gorgeous girl on your arm." Phelps's smile didn't quite reach his melancholy gray eyes.

"I wasn't the only one." Russell forced a smile. "How long have you been in Berlin?"

"I got here in January."

"Is it different from Paris?"

Phelps offered a cigarette to Russell, put another in his mouth and lit up. "Have you noticed the prostitutes?"

"I was accosted right out of the train station as I was hailing a cab. What's going on?"

"The Mark. Things have gotten so bad that respectable women like secretaries and receptionists have to put in a full day's work and then stand around on street corners looking for extra cash."

Russell raised an eyebrow. "It's that bad?"

Phelps nodded. "Here, middle-class families let their teenaged daughters dance naked for tourists because they don't have any other means of support."

"Jesus."

"Makes you glad you live in America, doesn't it?"

Russell nodded. "I've noticed some very strange characters that hang out in front of train stations. Hard to tell whether they're male or female."

"One of the specialties of this city is kinky sex. You can have women, men, men-women, chains, or whips. Anything and everything goes."

Russell grimaced. "What are the authorities doing about it?"

Phelps smiled wryly "Let me see. There's a club called *Weisse Maus* that has naked dances that start at midnight. The club manager always introduces the performances by disclaiming any pornographic intent. He always claims *We're here for Beauty*."

Russell couldn't help smiling in response to Phelps's chuckle. "Are the performances any good?"

"Anita Berber is interesting. I suppose you've never heard of her?"

Russell shook his head.

"She organizes the naked dances at White Mouse. But what makes her special is that she recreates her drug-induced fantasies."

"Jesus Christ!" said Russell. "There's quite a drug scene here?"

"You could say that." Phelps chuckled again. "She takes everything—morphine, cocaine, hashish, opium. They say that she breakfasts on white rose petals swirled in chloral hydrate."

"Are you an admirer of hers?"

Phelps smoked thoughtfully for a moment and stubbed out his cigarette butt. "I wouldn't say I'm an admirer exactly. On the other hand, she's extraordinarily erotic. She does a morphine dance, and a cocaine dance. Her costumes are out of this world."

Russell opened his silver monogrammed cigarette case, took one out for himself, and offered another to Phelps.

"Thanks," replied Phelps, coming out of his reverie.

Russell fished a matching monogrammed lighter from his pants pocket and lit up. Both men inhaled in silence.

Eventually, Phelps stubbed out his butt and glanced at the book lying face down beside Russell's coffee cup. "Interesting?"

"Very." He showed the title to Phelps.

"On the Special and General Theory of Relativity," read Phelps, translating. "What's it about?"

"Measurement. A physics professor here in Berlin has just come up with completely new ways of measuring mass and length that involve time."

"Hmm. I didn't know you knew anything about measurement."

"Nor did I," replied Russell. He shut the book and turned to Phelps. "I heard you were getting married."

Phelps lit up again and inhaled deeply. "Do you have parents?"

"No," replied Russell, patting ash off of his cigarette with the pad of his finger. "Why do you ask?"

"They're the most confounded nuisance, especially mothers. My mother had her heart set on a girl from Paris because she comes from the right family, speaks French, and all that sort of thing. But she's a cold-hearted bitch. Then I met someone else, fell in love for the first time in my life. I had no idea what love was like until I met her."

"Goodness," said Russell. "What does she look like?"

"Mesmerizing." He paused on a long inhale.

"What happened?"

"I took her to meet the parents, and they were mean to her. At least Mother was. Mother is a snob and didn't like the fact that her future daughter-in-law has no money and is Italian."

"Italian?"

"Italian-American."

Russell stared at Phelps, the hairs on the back of his neck lifting. He inhaled, then broke gaze. Surely there must be many such young women. "What makes the girl so special?"

"I don't know. There's something about her. She brings a kind of quietness with her. I don't know how to explain it."

"What happened when she met your parents?"

"Mother did everything in her power to put her off."

"What about her parents?"

"She doesn't have parents. She has an aunt and uncle and a great-aunt. Grace's great-aunt doesn't like me."

"Her name is Grace," whispered Russell.

"Are you all right? You've gone very pale."

"I'm feeling a bit under the weather." Russell took out his handkerchief and dabbed at his temples. "Tell me more."

"Yes, well, I was determined to marry her, but Grace put me off because she wanted to talk to her great-aunt first." He took another drag on his cigarette. "She disappeared."

Russell't throat clenched. He sipped his coffee, now cold.

"I went frantically searching for her. In the end, I went to see Mrs. Barilla—that's her great-aunt—and she threw me out. The old dragon told me never to come back."

Russell bent his head as he stirred some sugar into his coffee and added cream.

"I returned to the Hotel Adlon last Friday to see my parents and found them standing in the lobby of the hotel staring at the guests arriving for Count von Lietzow's engagement party. He's the local aristocrat, his family has owned parts of Berlin for centuries. Anyway, imagine my surprise when Grace showed up as his intended bride. I couldn't believe it. I'm still in shock."

Russell turned and signaled to the waiter. "Ein Weinbrand, bitte." When the brandy came, he pushed it over to Phelps's side of the table.

"Thanks," said Phelps, taking a sip. "I needed that."

"Where do you think she was?"

"I asked around," replied Phelps, "and I understand that he would call for her every morning at her aunt's place near Savignyplatz. She never returned until the evening, sometimes not until very late. She must have spent her days shut up in his villa. With him."

Russell picked up his cup and sipped the sweet, cold liquid. But his hands were shaking so much, it splashed all over A. Einstein: *Über die spezielle und allgemeine Relativitätstheorie*. He half-rose to lean over and mop it up with a napkin. His legs gave way.

"Let me," said Phelps, using his own napkin. He glanced at Russell. "You look dreadful. Are you sure you don't need a doctor?"

✠✠✠✠✠✠✠✠✠✠✠✠

Weisse Maus had to be the oddest place he'd ever been in. Russell lowered the black mask over his eyes, and sat down next to Phelps. The room they were in looked strangely bourgeois with patterned wall paper, framed oils, and round tables covered with white tablecloths. Nearly everyone wore half-masks to conceal their identity, giving the atmosphere a creepy quality of illicitness. He looked at his watch. It was a quarter to midnight and the place was packed. He'd agreed to go see this bizarre slice of life because he needed the distraction and because Phelps needed his support. Poor fellow. His companion looked as miserable as he felt.

"Who comes here?"

"Berlin intellectuals. Traveling salesmen on expense accounts. Underworld kings with prostitutes in tow. Lesbian groupies. Elderly gentlemen from the provinces—"

Russell raised an eyebrow. "That's quite a list." He lit a cigarette.

Phelps smiled faintly. "It reflects the strangeness that is Berlin."

"You found a seat," remarked a breathy voice. Russell looked up at a tall muscular woman dressed in dark purple, a cap of dark hair held back by a sequined band with a jaunty feather stuck into it. She stood there, her cigarette dangling out of an elegant ebony holder, her long nails tapping their table.

"This is Margot." Phelps rose and pulled out the last remaining chair. "She's the prostitute I told you about. She'll do anything you want."

Margot sat, inhaling deeply on her cigarette. As Russell continued to scrutinize her, she turned her back on him.

Russell drew his chair closer to Phelps. "You know her?"

"Intimately," he grinned. "She'll take your mind off your troubles. I don't know how I would have survived the loss of Grace without her."

Russell looked at Margot again, but she continued to ignore him. He turned to Phelps.

"She—he can't get pregnant," hissed Phelps.

"Ah!" Russell sat back in his chair, and opened his cigarette case. "Do you recognize any of these people?"

Phelps craned his neck. "It's hard to tell with all the masks, but maybe they'll bring something that will give them away." He took a drag on his cigarette and gave a low whistle. "That looks like von Lietzow."

A wave of queasiness broke over Russell.

"It is von Lietzow," remarked Margot. "Do you know him?"

Phelps shook his head.

"I do," she remarked.

Both Phelps and Russell recoiled, but she ignored them, turning her back once again to scan the crowd.

A gentleman in white tie holding a walking-stick entered with a companion. He was wearing a half-mask, his companion hid underneath a voluminous black veil.

"The giveaway is that walking-stick topped by an eagle's head," remarked Phelps.

Russell beckoned the waiter and ordered a magnum of champagne with three glasses. He hoped it would settle his stomach. Damn, he couldn't see. Swallowing his distaste, he drew his chair closer to Margot to get a better view.

The club manager got up and made his infamous speech, assuring the clientele that the purpose of their visit was for Beauty and Beauty alone.

This observation was greeted with loud laughter, then the show began. A line of show girls in skimpy costumes paraded up the ramp to the curtained stage. They were greeted by a torrent of lewd comments, which Russell, with his quick grasp of street argot, was mostly able to understand. As the dance number began, Phelps leaned over and gave him a nudge.

The old coot had his arm around his companion, but not merely as a gesture of affection. The being under the veil was writhing, trying to move away. Von Lietzow tightened his grip, while his other hand disappeared under the netting. His fingers grasped at each button as he yanked them open. He freed a breast, exposing a dusky pink nipple that hardened in the cooling air.

"Jesus Christ!" Phelps coughed on his champagne.

Von Lietzow bent his head, and sucked.

"That's not—" Russell half-rose in his seat, then sat down again.

A sudden movement made Grace's veil slide to the floor, showing her tear-streaked face. Unlike the others, she wore no half-mask.

Pink, rose pink. Where had he seen that color before? Snow, blue snow. A drop of blood fallen onto icy snow, striking the snow like an arrow, dissolving into pinkness. Russell touched his nose. Blood spattered his fingertips. Had he been shot? There was a rat-tat-tat of gunfire behind him and he plunged ahead toward that icy current—

"He's servicing her like a whore!" hissed Phelps between coughs.

Russell blinked and jerked up in his seat. Tears blinded his eyes. Grace had been such an innocent flower, so easily embarrassed. He dragged his hand across his face and looked around the room. Everyone was busily swilling champagne, leering, and groping. Hands were disappearing inside bodices and up skirts, exposing nipples and naked thighs.

Russell retched and pushed his champagne away. He appreciated pretty women, but this was a meat market. Grace was alone in a sea of strangers with no one to help her. Her family was probably tucked up in their bourgeois beds, oblivious to her predicament. And tomorrow, Grace would receive a life-sentence for torture. For this was what it was. He half-rose in his seat, but as he did so the naked dancing came to an end, the curtain closed and the lights dimmed to a blackness.

When the lights came up, the stage was empty except for a large armchair. Sunk into one corner was a creature dressed in black, silver beading coiling over the sleeves of the garment.

"Anita Berber," murmured Phelps to Russell.

In one hand, she held a syringe. She held it up, gazing at it for a moment, and then in a theatrical gesture, plunged it into her arm. Everyone watched in complete stillness. Suddenly, she thrust her body into an arc, which she held for a moment, then she adopted another position. In this disjointed fashion, she moved from one ecstatic pose to another.

Russell, leaning in even closer to Margot, swiveled his eyes to where von Lietzow was sitting. Margot responded by patting his knee and planting a sticky lipsticked kiss on his cheek, but Russell was too enthralled to notice. Grace edged away from her fiancé, but he squeezed her in an iron grip with one hand, while he let the other trail up her leg and part her thighs.

Grace made a supreme effort and wriggled free, but as she twisted, her dress ripped. Underneath she was naked, except for her stockings.

The audience gasped.

Anita Berber snapped out of her trance and clomped down the ramp towards Grace, shouting obscenities.

Grace looked wildly around her. Von Lietzow grabbed her, but she shook him off with a look of fury.

Russell rose. He must get to her. Now. But Margot was in his way and the room was packed. Could Grace understand what Anita Berber was shouting? He hoped not.

The buzz of voices slammed into silence. With one vicious movement, Anita Berber grasped the fabric and ripped off what was left of Grace's dress. Eyeing her nakedness, she walked slowly around Grace, flicking her lightly on the buttocks with the ends of her whip.

"Very nice," she drawled. "Come visit me after the show."

Grace lifted her chin. *"Nein!"*

The dancer raised her whip. "You will come!"

Phelps leapt to his feet, pushing through the crowd. Now was his chance. Russell shadowed him, pausing to pick up a discarded cloak.

As expected, Phelps was knocked down before he could get to Grace.

Like a dancer, Russell sidestepped the fight, then he lunged at von Lietzow.

"You filthy pervert!" he roared.

Chapter Twenty
Friday, 2 June
Morning

Tomorrow she would be Countess von Lietzow. Grace stood in the middle of Aunt Louisa's reception room, undergoing the final fitting for her wedding dress. Her newly acquired finery had been packed into numerous suitcases that squatted near the door, waiting for Carl's chauffeur.

Aunt Louisa was not one for procrastination, so when Grace mentioned that they wanted to get married soon, she agreed at once and marshaled her considerable powers of organization to ensure that they could marry on the first Saturday in June. Gratefully, Grace let her deal with the florists, bakers, cooks, and caterers. She let her choose the linen and the Meissen porcelain, the silver flatware and the cake, even the bouquet. On one matter, however, Grace insisted on choosing for herself. This dress, which she designed herself with suggestions from Violet and Camille, was the height of fashion, suitable for a society wedding. It was made from heavy silver damask and had no sleeves, giving it a straight, almost severe silhouette. It had a plunging neckline, a low-banded waist, and long skirts that brushed the floor.

A gust of air stirred Grace's skirts as the front door heaved open into a gaping hole. Teresa stumbled in, her eyes bloodshot, her gown hanging off her thinning frame. All the women gasped, though no one rushed forward—they were too stunned. Someone had planted a strawberry mark on her neck. Her pink Russian gown was torn and dirty. Hanging onto the banister, she slowly made her way up the wooden staircase leading to a Juliet balcony that looked over the reception room.

Aunt Louisa appeared on the balcony running along the opposite side of the room. She recoiled. "You're ruined!"

"Don't be ridiculous." Teresa removed her triangular Russian headdress and tossed it in down. Grace flinched as it fell not a foot away.

"I don't like this gentleman you go out with," her mother answered.

Grace rose and held her arms out. Liesl, one of the assistants from Modes Camille, gently drew on a tulle jacket covered in beading.

"He's rich." Teresa sank languorously onto the floor. The wooden tendrils of the balcony gathered around her.

Gretl, the other assistant, finished doing Grace's hair in a low chignon, then arranged the short tulle veil so that it covered her face and hair. She anchored it with a feathered confection placed just above her left ear. Grace studied herself in the mirror. Her outfit was rich and sophisticated and made her look much older than seventeen. She smiled.

"I don't care if he's rich. I won't have my daughter going out with someone so unsuitable. Why, he looks like a drug addict."

Teresa raised her head. "And I breakfasted on rose petals swirled in chloral hydrate."

"What?" Aunt Louisa paled.

"I'm not taking drugs, Ma." Teresa hiccoughed. "You've no reason to get hysterical."

"You're drunk."

"I'm not."

"I don't like your attitude. Where are your manners?"

"You shouldn't talk to your mother like that." Uncle William shut the library door behind him and walked into the middle of the reception room.

Aunt Louisa peered down at him. "The sooner we get out of this place, William, the better. I don't know how Teresa got mixed up in such bad company."

"You shouldn't have paraded me in front of all those aristocrats, Ma."

"Don't be ridiculous, dear. Look at Grace."

She skewered her cousin with a bleary gaze. "Goody-goody Grace. Purer than the driven snow."

"Go to your room and rest." Aunt Louisa beckoned to Uncle William. "I want you to be in a fit state for Grace's wedding tomorrow."

Teresa stood up and swayed. "Count Carl won't mind. He's mixed up with drugs, gambling, and prostitutes too. Didn't you know?"

The color drained from Grace's face.

"Gracie, darling," she giggled. "How could you be so naïve?"

"That's enough!" exclaimed Uncle William.

Aunt Louisa rang the bell.

"Take her up to bed," she said to Hans, "and give her a sedative."

"I don't want a sedative." Teresa made a wobbly descent from the balcony and headed for the front door.

"You're coming with me, young lady." Uncle William took one arm, and Hans took the other. Their voices faded into the distance as they manhandled Teresa up the main staircase.

"Madam," said Anna-Maria, "Count von Lietzow is here."

There was a flutter as the assistants pinned the last remaining tucks, then left, promising that the dress would be delivered that evening.

Grace went to the bedroom that she'd increasingly had to herself as Teresa had gone her own way, her mood soured as the Marquis de Chabrillan, or indeed any suitable suitor, had failed to materialize. Uncle William must have put her in one of the maid's bedrooms, because the room was empty. Anna-Maria helped Grace into a green silk dress, which draped across her bust like a shawl, matching green leather shoes, and a dainty straw cloche trimmed with a green ribbon. Grace looked around the room she'd come to love as she picked up a green leather purse. Tomorrow, she would be married and have three different bedrooms in three different residences.

Carl looked dapper in a light-colored wool suit with high, narrow, notched lapels. He greeted her with a chaste peck on the cheek, handed her into his car, and they motored over to Kladow. He offered her his arm, and they strolled around looking at the newly decorated rooms. The formal reception room was a study in white, with tall white ceilings, newly painted built-in bookshelves, white Louis Quinze chairs, white demi-lune tables, and sconces and chandeliers made of silver. Bouquets of white flowers stood on the tables, spilled over the windowsills, and gleamed in the fireplace. A quiet hum of activity emanated from the direction of the kitchen and butler's pantry as the staff carried in cases of wine, cases of champagne, and boxes stuffed with delicacies.

Afterwards, they went their separate ways. By now, they'd developed a routine. As usual, Grace practiced for a couple of hours in her oval practice room while Carl worked in his office nearby. It was important to her to continue with her violin, even though these days she scarcely had any reason to play. Shortly after their engagement, Carl had appeared at the Hochschule while Grace was having her violin lesson, the Herr Direktor in tow.

"Your Excellency," said Professor Flesch, rising to greet his distinguished visitors, "if I might be so bold as to inquire, when is the wedding to be?"

"The first Saturday in June."

"Not long now," said the Herr Direktor with a smile.

There was a spate of male laughter.

"It's too long for me." Carl had pinched her cheek as he settled himself into Professor Flesch's chair.

There was another round of male laughter.

"The reason why I inquire, your Excellency, is that I had planned to have Fräulein Grace play at our annual concert in May," remarked Professor Flesch.

"But, of course, she will have many other things to do."

"What do you think, Liebchen?" Carl turned to her.

How Grace would have loved to play. But she didn't want to start off on the wrong foot by making too many demands. "I think it will be too much."

"Very well," replied Carl. "Some other time. Perhaps, after we come back from our honeymoon."

Professor Flesch had nodded and turned away. It was the last time Grace had seen him.

Just before lunch, Carl would come to see her in the practice room, and they would discuss the refurbishing of the villa or plans for their honeymoon and new life together. Carl had planned a magnificent honeymoon. They were to spend a week in Vienna, then take the Orient Express to Constantinople. Carl had an interest in the occult, Freemasonry, and Eastern mysticism. As he took her in to lunch that day, he remarked that the Grand Lodge in Constantinople was about to close.

"I'd like to acquire some of their manuscripts."

"Won't that be expensive?" Grace allowed him to help her into her chair in the oval dining room.

He smiled.

She looked at him as the butler served consommé in their new soup bowls. The dining room was painted in soft sage gray, so Carl and Grace had chosen Meissen porcelain to match, making a special trip to the pretty town outside of Dresden. The bowls had clean modern lines, with silver paint along the rims and a sage band to set off the middle. Grace waited until the butler left and turned to Carl. "The Mark is falling."

"Just so. That is why I invested in American Steel. It's the secret of my wealth, Liebchen."

"Aren't things getting bad?"

"That's why we're visiting Vienna on our way to Constantinople. We may need to live there for a while until things improve here." He shook his head. "That *Diktat* has been a disaster for the German economy."

Grace nodded. He'd explained how the punishing reparations of 132 billion Marks specified by the Treaty of Versailles in 1919 were devastating to the German economy, causing the mark to spiral downwards in value.

She sipped a glass of white wine. "I don't think you ever mentioned this, but what did you do during the Great War?"

"Ah." He signaled the butler to take away the soup plates. "I wondered when my Liebchen was going to ask." He wiped his lips with his napkin. "As a Prussian aristocrat, I trained as an officer and joined the army as a young man. I acted as an advisor to the British military in South Africa during the Second Boer War. By the time of the Great War, I'd been out of the military for several years. I was a businessman, you see. So I volunteered to drive an ambulance during the Gallipoli campaign. Funnily enough, that's how I became interested in Turkey."

The butler put down a dish of sole meunière.

Carl was a wonderful raconteur and was soon off, telling her tales about his time in that campaign.

He enjoyed telling her tales about his life, like the one about his grand tour in 1904, when he'd visited Egypt, taking the train from Berlin to Vienna, the Orient Express from Vienna to Constantinople, and then local transportation south though Syria, Lebanon, and Palestine to Egypt. Grace looked at him now as he recounted this tale about his time in Gallipoli. It seemed to have affected him not at all, unlike Mr. Russell's experiences on the Italian Front, which had marked him for life. She quickly put that thought away and leaned forward to hear everything.

Their routine continued after lunch. Carl would open the door to his bedroom, and they would disappear inside. Immediately the murmurs from the staff, the birdsong, the soughing breezes from the lake would cease, for he'd soundproofed the room. While today she waited for Carl to emerge from his dressing room, dressed in his priestly robes, Grace donned a diaphanous gown and veil and reclined on Carl's bed studying the Kama Sutra, because it was her daily delight to choose which position they should try next, and Carl was anxious to try all sixty-four.

As he appeared, she turned the lights down. Small candles glowed in their sconces set here and there around the room. Carl put on a record of people chanting, their voices a low hum, and they sat on cushions near scented sticks for their ritual smoke, using a hookah, which Carl had bought many years before in Turkey. As the substance took hold, she danced. The dance was slow and sinuous, something that Carl had invented for her, based on some Freemasonry rite. Grace was the goddess Isis, Carl was Osiris.

What happened next took on a dreamlike quality, as if she somehow weren't there. They would disrobe, and he would sometimes tie her to the bed with silken cords. Gradually, she became less unwilling, as in that muffled darkness she would close her eyes and imagine it was Mr. Phelps who was on top of her, Mr. Phelps who was devouring her with his glances, his hands, his lips, his tongue, and that lump of flesh between his legs. Gradually, she became addicted to the eerie atmosphere of the quasi-dark in the middle of the day, of the puffs from the hookah that quelled her anxiety and comforted the shards of her mind. Gradually she came to desire the frenzy that overcame him as he climaxed inside her and brought her a kind of pleasure–pain he called love. Grace would imagine the delighted smiles of her relatives when they heard about the engagement, kiss his cheek, and allow his bantering tone to lull away all her doubts.

By late afternoon, they emerged into the brightness of the spring sunshine, bathed and dressed as the Count and Countess von Lietzow. The butler served tea. At six o'clock sharp, Carl would drive her back to Aunt Louisa's on Savignyplatz so that she could spend every evening with her relatives and every night in her bed, because he said it was important to observe the proprieties. Or at least pay lip service to them.

But today was different because it was the last night of her freedom, and Grace felt disinclined to pay lip service to Aunt Louisa's sense of propriety, especially as she knew Teresa would be in a particularly vicious mood tonight. She'd accused Grace once of stealing Carl from her.

"We should do something special." Grace inhaled deeply from the hookah.

"Something naughty?" He squeezed her nipple between his stubby fingers as they reclined on his bed in the nude.

"I've seen so many strange people on the streets of Berlin. Then there was one of Violet's models who was a man really, but he made a very convincing woman. People say that the nightclubs here in Berlin are very interesting."

"Do they indeed?" He popped her nipple in his mouth and sucked.

She smiled and stroked his hair. "I'd like to learn some new dances."

"Anita Berber is good," he remarked. "But I don't suppose you've ever heard of her, Liebchen."

She shook her head.

He stroked her cheek. "She organizes the naked dances at Weisse Maus."

"Naked dances? Are they really naked?" Grace sat up, unable to restrain her curiosity.

He chuckled as he kissed her slowly on the lips. "Well, not quite. Almost."

"Can you take me there?" Grace had heard about such places from Teresa, who went on and on about the exotic locales and alluring costumes when Aunt Louisa wasn't around.

He coiled a tendril of her hair around his fingers and kissed her neck. "Time to go back to Mrs. Philips."

"But I'll never see it if you don't take me now. Tomorrow we're going to Vienna."

"I can always take you when we return to Berlin."

"But I'll be Countess von Lietzow. You can't take your wife there. It's not respectable."

He pinched her cheek. "It's never respectable to go there."

Grace was silent as his hands stroked her flank. Did being his wife mean that she would no longer have to worry about her reputation? "Does that matter?"

He chuckled.

"I really want to go."

"A strange place to go on the eve of your wedding."

What wasn't he telling her? Grace was determined to find out. "All the more reason for going." She used a cheap trick to get him to agree. She slid away from him on his silken sheets and parted her lips.

He laughed low in his throat as he surged towards her. "I can refuse you nothing." His lips crushed hers.

✠✠✠✠✠✠✠✠✠✠✠

Carl had found her an outfit, a waitress uniform made out of cheap materials and fishnet stockings. Next, he made up her face, outlining her eyes with kohl, applying a thick layer of lipstick to her lips. Lastly, he draped a black veil over her head and pronounced her perfect.

"You won't know anyone there, Liebchen," he remarked as they sat on the back seat of his new

Mercedes, while the chauffeur drove them to Friedrichstrasse. "But even if you did, they wouldn't know you."

"Are you sure?"

"People only see what they expect to see. No one would expect to see you in such a den of iniquity."

The car came to a stop outside a club called *Die Weisse Maus*. Carl concealed his eyes behind a half-mask and helped her out of the car.

The room they entered looked reassuringly ordinary, with its oil paintings hung against flowered wallpaper. But nearly everyone was wearing half-masks to conceal their identity. Carl ordered a magnum of champagne and looked at his watch.

"It's a quarter to midnight. The show starts soon."

"Who comes here?" Grace sipped her champagne.

"Berlin intellectuals. Traveling salesmen on expense accounts." He patted her knee. "Lesbian groupies—"

"Lesbians?"

"Women with women."

"But how?"

He chuckled, placing his gold-topped cane against the table. Its head was shaped like an eagle, its eyes glinted with rubies.

"Are there lots of prostitutes here?"

"What a question to ask your future husband." He pinched her cheek. "Yes, there are many prostitutes in Berlin. With the mark falling, even respectable women have to stand on the street corners, as you've no doubt noticed." He paused. "And no, of course, I don't know any prostitutes. I come clean to you, mein Liebchen."

Grace looked away and bit her lip. Teresa's voice sounded in her head. Of course, he must have had all sorts of women before her. How stupid she was.

He took her hand in his. "I have no need of prostitutes, or even mistresses, when I have such a gorgeous, young bride." He kissed her hand.

A balding man with a paunch rose. "*Liebe Damen und Herren*, the purpose of your visit to *Die Weisse Maus* is for Beauty and Beauty alone."

A gust of raucous laughter followed this observation, then the show began. A line of girls paraded up the ramp to the curtained stage that spanned one end of the room. Their bodies gleamed pure white in the dark, drab interior of the club. Exotically printed headbands held back their curls and short bobs. Fringed skirts concealed their hips. Dancing shoes encased their feet. They made their way to the stage by passing provocatively close to the patrons and sashaying their derrières, which made their fringed skirts part suggestively and their bare breasts jiggle.

They were greeted by a torrent of lascivious comments, which made Carl chuckle. Grace cringed as her cheeks radiated heat. She thought it would be more glamorous, less seedy. She thought the costumes would be exotic, beautiful even. This seemed so sordid. Perhaps it hadn't been such a good idea to come here. She should have listened to Carl, for he'd wanted to protect her from all this. As the dance number began, he wrapped his arm around her.

Grace was glad of the warmth because her waitress uniform was made of thin material and she was beginning to feel chilly. In the near black of the room, Carl's hands twisted a button open.

Grace flinched. "You can't do that here," she whispered.

Slipping closer, he squeezed her nipple. "You have beautiful *brüste*, Liebchen." He lowered his lips onto her. "They're becoming bigger." He thrust his tongue inside her mouth. Her body melted, and her veil would have slid to the floor if she hadn't struggled to keep it covering her. "I'm getting too excited," she whispered.

He drew back and smiled, letting his hand trail up her leg under the uniform.

"Don't." She pulled away.

He lowered his mouth and kissed her deeply. Grace writhed in his arms. Her veil slid to the floor.

"How many times did we do it today?" He stroked the bare skin above her stockings. "How I love my passionate Liebchen."

"Not here," she murmured thickly. She pulled away and looked around. In the dark everyone was busily swilling champagne, leering, and groping. Hands were disappearing inside bodices and up skirts, exposing nipples and naked thighs. The music had a rhythm and a beat to it that made her sway in her seat. She used the opportunity to edge away from Carl's roving hands.

A gentleman slouched in his seat, sipping champagne, his white tie positively glowing in the dark. He had dark hair, a well-cut profile, and dark eyes. Grace half closed her eyes, a memory tugging. Carl had said she wouldn't meet anyone she knew. She had no wish for anyone to see her like this, tipsy, high, glorying in that secret power that bound Carl to her. She should be ashamed, she should be horrified that she had become just like her mother. Instead, she felt understanding and compassion for the choices Mother had made.

Slowly, Grace lifted her lashes. A pair of dark eyes gazed back at her, then his pupils contracted as his face reddened. The lights went out, plunging everyone into blackness.

When they came up, they showed a woman in a clinging black dress, reclining in her armchair.

Carl, visible in the ricocheting glow of the spotlight, sucked on her nipple. Grace pushed him away and moved quietly to another chair. Next to the gentleman with the well-cut profile sat another familiar figure. Someone tall and muscular and dressed in Violet's cocktail dress—Margot! As Grace watched, Margot slid over to the gentleman and planted a languorous kiss, leaving plum lip print on his cheek.

The audience gasped as the woman artiste, in a theatrical gesture, plunged a syringe into her arm. Grace glanced over at Margot as the gentleman with the lipstick mark turned his well-cut profile into the sparse amount of light emanating from spotlight. Surely it could not be—it was—

Her skin crawled. What was Mr. Russell doing here in Berlin? With Margot?

The audience came to life as the artiste thrust her body into an incredible arc, which she held for a moment before adopting another pose. In this disjointed fashion, Anita Berber moved from one posture to another.

Grace glanced over at Mr. Russell. He glared at her with his dark gaze. On his other side sat a shadowy figure who also seemed familiar.

Carl bent over her, breathing heavily. Fumes of champagne rolled from him. He clasped her with one hand, while the other trailed up her leg.

Grace made a supreme effort and wriggled free, but as she twisted, the dress ripped. Underneath she was naked, except for her stockings.

The place erupted into catcalls and whistles. Anita Berber snapped out of her reverie and advanced towards Grace, shouting.

Grace clutched at her ruined dress, but the thin fabric couldn't cover her up. She shouldn't have come. Carl shouldn't have brought her here—

The place became quiet as Anita Berber arrived. With one sudden movement, she ripped off what was left of the dress. Eyeing her nakedness, she walked slowly around Grace.

"Very nice," she drawled. "Come visit me after the show."

Grace lifted her chin. *"Nein!"*

The dancer raised her whip. "You will come!"

Mr. Phelps leapt to his feet, pushing through the thick crowd. But it was Mr. Russell who arrived at Grace's side, pouncing on Carl.

"You filthy pervert!" he roared in excellent German.

Grace screamed.

Carl ducked.

"What are you doing?" Grace grabbed Russell's arm.

"Rescuing you from the devil, of course." He bared his teeth, causing the kiss upon his cheek to contract, almost as if it were kissing itself. "You look like a whore, just like your mother. What in the world has happened to you?"

Carl straightened up. "She asked to come here."

Russell spat accurately into his face. "Grace is an innocent flower whom you have destroyed."

Grace stepped between Carl and Russell.

"He's right. I asked to come."

"You're higher than a kite!" He jerked back, his face taut with loathing.

"I insisted on coming here."

"Then it's high time you left!" He grabbed her arm, his face taking on a greenish sheen.

"She's my fiancée. We're getting married tomorrow." Carl stepped forward.

Before Grace had time to react, Russell went for Carl in a frenzy, kneeing him in the groin, kicking him in the head. "Scum like you are not fit to live," he spat. "You've committed soul murder on the light of my life."

He threw a cloak over Grace and marched her outside.

"Take me back!" shouted Grace.

But his grip tightened as he frog-marched her towards Jägerstrasse.

Chapter Twenty-One

Saturday, 3 June

Violet could hardly believe her kid sister was marrying today and would soon become a countess. She was happy for Grace, but sad for herself. She rose from her bed, washing away her tears in a basin of cold water. Things were never going to be the same. They would lead such different lives, they were bound to grow apart. Quickly, she put on her workaday clothes of cotton shirt-dress, woolen stockings and Frau Varga's clogs and headed out to Modes Camille.

The day was just beginning to lighten as Violet opened the door. Aunt Louisa's voice intruded: *It is to be a short engagement*. In fact, it had been very short, only six weeks since he'd popped that ring on her finger, and now Grace was getting married. Why? Was von Lietzow beginning to panic? But what on earth did he have to worry about? Violet put her felt cloche on the hatstand. It had to have something to do with Phelps, although that little detail had been glossed over in Aunt Louisa's explanations.

"It's for the best, dear," she'd said. "Naturally, the Count is anxious for the wedding to go ahead, and it will give me plenty of time to pack up."

"You're leaving?"

"Why yes, dear. None of the fashionable crowd stay in the city during the summer. Surely you know that. We are going to summer at a spa, to give Teresa the greatest possible exposure."

She makes Teresa sound like a performer. Violet opened the shutters to let in the early morning light. She had to iron the outfits Camille had helped her make for all of the female relatives, because there'd been no time to do it before. She went to the steam ironing station. How was Grace feeling now? Had *she* managed to get any sleep?

Violet went to the rack of clothes and laid each outfit on the ironing boards scattered around the room. There was Auntie P.'s burgundy velvet dress, Aunt Louisa's powder blue chiffon with an elaborate lace jacket, Ella and Adela's matching powder blue cotton shirt-dresses. She went to the ironing station, but the irons were not quite ready. If she were in Grace's position, she'd be excited to marry someone who made her laugh and had become such a friend. But wasn't he a little old? On the other hand, Grace was so out of it that perhaps an older husband was exactly what she needed to help her navigate through the intricacies of the adult world.

There was a knock at the door. Violet glanced at her watch. Who could this be calling at eight o'clock in the morning? She opened the door to find Detective Ecker standing there.

"I'm sorry to intrude Miss Violet, I know you're busy, but I have to leave tomorrow."

Violet felt the color drain out of her cheeks. "You've come to tell me about Mother."

"I've been meaning to speak with you ever since I got here." He flushed and hesitated.

She opened the door wide, and put the kettle on to boil.

"Thank you." He took a battered wooden chair. "I'm embarrassed I didn't tell you sooner, but I couldn't upset you when you were dealing with your first fashion show. And I wanted you to enjoy our evening out."

Violet turned away as she remembered the way he'd looked at her when she'd worn a blue silk gown borrowed from Camille to the ball at the Stadtschloss.

"I haven't seen you for a week," she remarked as she searched for a packet of tea.

He grimaced. "I have a large family here and many obligations. I've a married cousin who's been asking me to visit for years—I'm staying with him now. I had business to transact with the family lawyer; friends and acquaintances to look up."

Violet spooned some tea into the pot and slowly poured the boiling water over it. "I got your letter ages ago, but you didn't enclose your report."

He fixed his eyes on her as he accepted his tea. "I tried writing, many times. In the end, I decided I had to come myself."

Violet sank into her seat, tears dropping into her tea. "Mother was murdered," she muttered tonelessly.

"Her death was an accident."

"An accident?" Violet jerked up and stared at him.

He nodded.

She narrowed her eyes. "What else?"

He flushed and hesitated again. Finally he leaned towards her and whispered, "Your mother was pregnant at the time of her death."

Her hands shook so much she had to put her tea down.

"The coroner says she was about six weeks pregnant."

"She died October the twenty-ninth," remarked Violet slowly. "So that would mean she became pregnant around—"

"Around September sixteenth. Did anything special happen then?"

"I think that's when we met Mr. Russell."

He placed his hand over hers. "You're very pale. Have you had breakfast?"

"Tell me why Mother died."

He smiled wryly as he picked up his tea. "Abdominal cramps are difficult to treat. Current treatments are dangerous. Patients who have those kinds of symptoms are usually treated with mercury or arsenic, both of which are potentially lethal."

She wiped her cheek with the tips of her fingers.

He gave her his handkerchief. "I found three medical experts who testified that Dr. Jackson had done nothing wrong. Nevertheless, he has been cautioned."

"Mother died of an overdose?"

He drew the report out from his inside pocket and placed it on the table. "The medical examiner found the levels of arsenic and mercury to be high enough to cause death."

Violet turned away, wiping her eyes on his handkerchief. "I still think Mr. Russell had a hand in it."

"I had my own suspicions about Russell, so I did further research in the archives of the *Chicago Daily News*, and the *Chicago Examiner*. I couldn't find anything on him. His brother was another matter."

"Jerome?"

"Yes. It seems that before the war, Jerome Pagano practiced law in Chicago. He represented some rather crooked clients and got well-paid for his dealings with them."

"Does that prove anything?"

"Only that Russell's brother had connections with the mob."

Violet pinned her blue eyes on his face: "Do you believe that Mr. Russell was—"

"A member of the mob?" Ecker paused. "It wouldn't surprise me."

"But what about Mr. Russell and Mother? Do you think—"

"There is no evidence that he had a hand in her death. Whether he was the father of her child—" He reddened and looked down. "The only person who would know would be your mother."

"And Mr. Russell," remarked Violet, lifting her chin.

He left soon afterwards, and Violet turned to the racks of clothes again, looking for an outfit for Teresa. It had never occurred to her that Mother could have gotten pregnant, although she was a comparatively young woman at the time of her death, only thirty-three years old. Violet stopped as her sister's face came into view. Grace. She didn't know anything about this, but how could she tell her now? She put a frock back on the hanger, then froze. How could she be so blind? That was why Count von Lietzow wanted to marry in a hurry.

Violet sank down onto a stool and wept, for the wholesomeness and simplicity of their life in Georgetown. In Sin City, everything was so sordid. She dried her tears and glanced at her watch. It was getting on for nine, and she must hurry; she still had to find that outfit for Teresa.

Violet got up and looked through the racks. She hadn't gone to the trouble of making Teresa anything, knowing how difficult she could be, so Camille had told her to borrow something suitable. Violet held up a silver evening gown and considered. Teresa would kick up a fuss unless she was given something that would make her stand out in the crowd. But everyone else—apart from Aunt Paulina—would be wearing day dresses that exposed the lower leg. Would it be right to give Teresa an evening-length dress? On the other hand, it was a sophisticated creation, made out of a fashionable metallic fabric that clung to the form. It was slit at the sides, like a caftan, and revealed a powder-blue underskirt. If Teresa ruined it, it would be easy enough to make another one. The only problem was that it had a plunging neckline. Violet picked up a powder blue scarf, and packed it in tissue into a suitcase, along with the other outfits.

She was just about to lock the case shut when she remembered she hadn't chosen anything for herself. She hadn't had time to make anything, but as Grace's sister, she felt entitled to dress in something special. It took some time to decide, but Violet finally settled on a dusky rose frock that went with Aunt Paulina's burgundy red. Lastly, she added an assortment of purses, shoes and scarves, and checked her watch. It was already 9:25 and she had to get over to Aunt Louisa's. Violet shut the case, closed the shutters, locked the shop, and hailed a cab.

✠✠✠✠✠✠✠✠✠✠✠

Everything was eerily quiet when Violet arrived at Savignyplatz. No one answered her knock, and so she let herself in the front door, tiptoeing into the elegant reception room.

Quietly, Violet knelt on thick carpeted floor, opened the suitcase, and began to unpack.

"Where's Grace?"

Violet jumped and turned, dropping an armful of frocks onto the Persian rug.

Aunt Louisa stood in the doorway, her hair looking unusually disheveled.

"What d'you mean?"

"She's not in her room. I thought she had gone to spend her last night with you and Zia Paulina."

"She's not there," replied Violet, bending to pick up the crumpled clothes and hang them gently over the *Louis Quinze* chairs. "Why don't you ask Teresa?"

"Teresa was out with us last night. We went to a ball at the *Palais Beauvryé*." She paused. "Besides, she doesn't spend much time with Grace any more."

Violet glanced up. "Who does?"

"Ella. Perhaps you should talk to her, dear."

Violet finished arranging the dresses, went upstairs and knocked on the door. Ella was sitting in front of her vanity, having her hair brushed.

"I can't go downstairs, I have a bad headache." Ella put her hand to her head and turned to Anna-Maria. "Understand? It hurts here."

"Why don't you do Mrs. Philips's hair?" Violet shut the door behind Anna-Maria and turned to Ella.

"What's going on? Where's Grace?"

"I don't know. I thought she was staying with Carl."

"But he's the groom."

"How should I know? She's always with him. We don't see her now. Carl drives her off after breakfast and doesn't bring her back until supper time."

Violet sank onto a nearby chair. Her suspicions must be true. "Does she take her violin with her?"

Ella paused. "I haven't seen her violin recently. I think she must leave it at his villa." She turned away and picked up her brush. "Carl says he's been teaching her how to be a countess—'How to Count,' as he puts it."

Violet smiled, von Lietzow loved to make silly remarks. "What about Grace? What does she say?"

Ella shrugged.

"That's no surprise," remarked Violet. "She's not exactly talkative."

"No," agreed Ella, "but she seems happy."

"So you don't think she's run away, to avoid getting married?"

Ella shook her head.

✠✠✠✠✠✠✠✠✠✠✠

An hour later, Violet was in the back of Aunt Louisa's Benz being driven to Nollendorfplatz. She stared out the car window at a perfect June day. What a beautiful day to have gotten married, and now they had to break the news of Grace's disappearance to the person who loved her best in the world. What was she going to say? Violet gazed at the puffy white clouds that hung over Berlin as her mind went blank.

Where was Grace? Where could she have gone? But she didn't have time to think, for the car was drawing up outside Frau Varga's.

She followed Aunt Louisa into the dining-room parlor. There was Auntie P., sitting quietly by the window behind the *Corriere della Sera*, catching up on the latest news from Italy. Frau Varga was nowhere to be seen.

As soon as she saw them, Auntie P. put the newspaper down.

"Violetta! Luisa!" she exclaimed, kissing them. "How are you?"

"We are very well, I thank you," replied Aunt Louisa, "but we have some unfortunate news." And she explained what had happened.

"This cannot be true!" exclaimed Auntie P. rising from her chair. "You cannot have lost Grace. Where could she possibly be?"

Aunt Louisa sighed. "I wish I knew."

Violet put her hand under Auntie P.'s elbow. "Why don't you sit?"

Auntie P. collapsed into her chair, took her glasses off and wiped away tears.

Violet gave her a handkerchief.

"I can't believe she's been kidnapped," she quavered.

Violet frowned. Auntie P. had gone so white, her lips were pale. Was the shock of Grace's disappearance going to make her seriously ill?

"But she can't have gone of her own free will. Not my sweet Grace. She would never do anything like that. I hold you responsible for this, Luisa."

"How can you hold *me* responsible?"

"This would never have happened if I'd kept Grace with me."

"How do you know that? She might have behaved in the same disgraceful fashion if she'd stayed with you."

"You're not suggesting *she* was to blame?"

"She's just like her mother! Angelina ruined our lives by destroying Rosa's dress, and now Grace is destroying ours by running away."

"What are you talking about?" demanded Violet. "I've never heard this before."

"No? Well, I suppose your mother wouldn't have told you that the reason why we never grew up with our half-brothers in Chicago is because Father was so furious with her for destroying our stepmother's party dress. She cut it up, threw it on a manure pile, and got Nico—"

"You mean Mr. Russell?"

Aunt Louisa made a ladylike snort and nodded. "He must've only been four years old, but Angelina persuaded him to jump onto his mother's fancy dress. Father never forgave her, but he punished all of us." She took out a lacy handkerchief and dabbed her eyes.

Violet stared. *Thank goodness Mr. Russell isn't around; otherwise I'd think he was responsible for Grace's disappearance.*

Auntie P. sat up in her seat. "Is that why Franco sent you girls to me? I never knew."

Violet went to her and put a hand on her wrist. Auntie P. was turning yellow.

"After all I've done for her, to turn on me like this," remarked Aunt Louisa, sniffling.

Auntie P. stiffened. "How dare you say that!"

"She's probably ruined by now. She'll never make a respectable marriage."

"Does Count von Lietzow know?" asked Auntie P.

Aunt Louisa paled. "Don't you think we should delay? She might come back, after all. There'll be such a scandal—"

Auntie P. rose. "It is possible that she's with him."

✠✠✠✠✠✠✠✠✠✠✠

Violet sat stiffly between Auntie P. and Aunt Louisa on the sofa in the middle of Count von Lietzow's magnificent reception room, wondering why it was taking him such a long time to appear. She looked around. Pale flowers festooned the mantlepiece and the demi-lune tables, spilling over the windowsills. The room had a feel of airy elegance with its tall ceilings painted in white, accented by silver sconces and silver chandeliers. A sound of a stick striking marble made her turn, and Carl von Lietzow limped in. Violet couldn't help gaping. This person looked old, his cheeks hanging in jowly folds, his complexion greenish-white. Bruises bloomed under one eye. A large bandage covered a bloody wound on the side of his face, as if someone had kicked him repeatedly. He slowly crumpled into a chair as a servant scurried forward to press a glass of brandy into his hand. Auntie P. cleared her throat.

"We've come to ask you, sir, whether you know where Grace is. She disappeared and we can't find her."

He put the brandy down and slumped, saying nothing.

His silence was surprising. Violet thought he would shout and carry on. Instead, she felt as if he were dying in front of her, with the gradual realization that his plans of a life with Grace crumbling into a nothingness. The silence yawned and stretched.

"I don't believe it," he finally said, enunciating each word painfully. "I thought she'd gone home to Savignyplatz."

"I thought Grace was with you," remarked Aunt Louisa. "You called for her at your usual time yesterday, but you didn't bring her back."

Von Lietzow reddened slightly but said nothing.

"When did you last see Grace?" asked Violet.

Von Lietzow sipped some brandy and put the glass down.

"Who took her?" he said.

"We don't know," replied Auntie P.

"She may have gone by herself," put in Aunt Louisa. "She's quite capable of such disgraceful behavior. Now, my daughter—"

"Pah!" retorted Carl von Lietzow. He drained his brandy in one gulp and turned to Aunt Louisa.

"Don't be ridiculous, woman. This is not Grace. It would never occur to her to behave disgracefully. No, no, someone took her. He, because of course it was a he, either snatched her or manipulated her to go with him." He stiffly rang the bell.

A neatly-dressed gentleman whom Violet recognized as von Lietzow's agent appeared.

"Herr Nordwitz, go immediately and find an American gentleman. Let's see." He ran his fingers through his hair. "Charles Phelps and another one—a dark fellow whose name I do not know."

Hairs rose along the back of Violet's arms. How glad she was that she wasn't going to be in the crosshairs of von Lietzow's wrath.

"There were two of them, then." Herr Nordwitz made a note.

"Second, have all the ports watched. It's more than likely he's taken her to the nearest port to set sail for America. I want you to spare no expense to get her back. Go to Kiel, Hamburg, Lübeck, Rostock, Danzig, and Stettin. Get her back!"

Violet flinched. Something didn't sound right. Detective Ecker was still in town. He would know what to do.

The agent hustled off to do his master's bidding, shouting for his assistants to drop everything and help him to find the young *Fraülein*.

"Are you sure you want Grace back? Teresa would be more than happy—" quavered Aunt Louisa.

But the Count wasn't listening. Slowly, painfully, he lumbered out of his chair as his chauffeur, valet, and doctor surrounded him to prevent him from falling. Violet and her relatives watched silently as they got von Lietzow ready for a motoring trip and took him outside to a waiting car. Outside, the vehicle roared to life, disappearing behind huge plumes of smoke and dust.

Chapter Twenty-Two

Saturday, 3 June

Two trunks stood on the floor of his room at the Hotel Adlon. One, for gentlemen's clothes, the other for ladies'. A matching leather suitcase stood open beside the trunks, filled with his books and papers.

He sliced her with his glance. "Get dressed," he snapped.

Grace hesitated, but she certainly couldn't go anywhere without clothes. With trembling hands, she put on the clean underwear and cotton frock he'd produced from one of his trunks.

While she dressed, he turned away and packed with lightning efficiency."Ready?" He glanced at her, then rang a bell, summoning a porter to heft them downstairs.

Grace glared. "I'm not going with you."

"I'm taking you home to your Aunt Josephina."

Grace clenched her hands, her nails biting into the flesh of her palms. "Why are you bothering with me? You told me I was a whore, no better than Mother." She stopped as a tear squeezed down her cheek.

"Grace, I'm sorry I wounded you." He touched her arm as his voice softened. "I spoke hastily. I shouldn't have said that. I was too shocked."

She buried her face in her hands.

He pounded his fist against the bedpost. "What he did was evil."

Grace wept.

He took her hands and chafed them. "Graziella, there is nothing to be ashamed of in the pleasures of the marriage bed. But he twisted the sacrament of marriage into a perverted game."

Grace dabbed her eyes. "I can't go back to Aunt Josephina. I'm a fallen woman—like Mother."

He put both hands around her face. "Grace, you are not a tart. You've been treated abominably, but you are entirely innocent."

"But what must you think of me?" She looked away. "You saw me naked—"

"I saw a lovely young girl being tortured. It was unbearable. I hope I never have to see anything like that again. It broke my heart."

"I'll have to go back to him."

"Are you expecting a baby?"

Grace shook her head.

"You haven't missed your period?"

She bit her lip. How could she explain that her periods were so irregular, she was never sure when the next one was going to appear? It was too embarrassing.

"Perhaps it's too early to tell." He gave her a probing look. "You will have to marry someone."

Grace twisted her lips. That's what Aunt Paulina had told her. She was soiled now. "I'll have to marry him." Tears coursed down her face. "If he'll have me. I couldn't put the burden of my unborn child on anyone else."

"A man who loved you more than life itself might not care," he murmured.

She turned to him. "Do you really think so?"

"I know so." He took her hand.

She let it lie there for a minute, then gently withdrew it.

He set his jaw. "Ask yourself whether you love Count von Lietzow and whether he would make you happy." Grace relaxed as he offered his arm and took her outside, where a daffodil yellow car waited for them. Perhaps Aunt Josephina would receive her. Perhaps she could still marry Carl after all.

The porter placed the trunks in the back, tying them on with rope. Mr. Russell helped her in, went around to the driver's side, and gunned the engine. A wall of exhaustion hit her and she fell asleep.

"Grace." He shook her awake. It was a beautiful moonlit night. The silvery light outlined the jagged edges of the leaves of a large chestnut, which rustled above a quiet courtyard.

Grace climbed out of the car and swayed. "Where are we?"

"Leipzig." He wrapped an arm around her and took her inside. It was a hotel.

"Name, sir?" The manager spoke German.

"David and Gretchen Reinhardt."

"This way."

Grace's mouth opened and shut. She tugged on his arm.

"Trust me," he murmured.

The manager led them to a room with a large double bed. He left the key on the table and walked rapidly away. Mr. Russell locked the door.

Grace balled her hands into fists. "You told me you were going to take me home."

✠✠✠✠✠✠✠✠✠✠✠✠

When Phelps came to, he was lying on the ground in Jägerstrasse, not far from Weisse Maus. Someone had tied him up. Phelps wriggled, and with excruciating slowness, he forced his fingers around an end of rope and using his thumb pushed it though a loop. By shrugging his shoulders, using his teeth, index finger and thumb, he was finally able to loosen the rope and get up. As he slowly raised himself off the ground, the sun threw low beams of light onto the sidewalk. Soon it would be dark, and he must get off the street. He wobbled against a wall, putting his hand out for support as a ferocious headache pounded. His ribs screamed, he couldn't straighten his left knee, and he tasted blood. Slowly, he shambled his way down the street, hailed a cab, and asked to be taken to the Adlon. Once there, he paused only long enough to put on a set of clean clothes, intending to visit Grace's aunt. But he couldn't do it.

✠✠✠✠✠✠✠✠✠✠✠✠

When eventually Phelps rose from his bed, the light gleaming through his curtains suggested it was midday. Damn. Was he too late? He grit his teeth and forced himself up. Swaying slightly, he headed downstairs and ordered a cab for Savignyplatz.

Once there, Phelps sank into a Louis Quinze chair and shut his eyes. His headache was making his temples vibrate. What was he doing here? He should be in hospital, but he had to find Grace. He blinked as he opened his eyes into the too-bright sunshine that washed over the reception room of the mansion. Let's see, it was Sunday afternoon, not even two days after that incident at Weisse Maus. So why was the room filled with packing trunks?

A murmur of voices came from another room.

"Madam," said the maid, "there is a young man to see you."

"I'll be there in just a minute." A curtain swished, and Mrs. Philips appeared. She stopped dead.

"Oh, my. You look as bad as the Count. Surely you didn't get into a fight as well?"

"You are leaving town?"

"We think it best, given the circumstances."

"Where is Grace?"

"You don't know?"

Phelps shook his head. His headache roared. Slowly, his eyes wandered over a dozen open packing trunks that revealed more gowns than he'd ever seen in one place. The gowns were gossamer, glittering and gleaming, revealing every kind of shade, made for every kind of occasion. They were surrounded by literally hundreds of purses and shoes in matching shades.

"We've decided to summer in Évian-lès-bains," remarked Mrs. Philips.

"What about Grace?"

She shrugged her shoulders.

"Aren't you worried about her?"

"Why should I be?"

"You don't know where she is."

"True. But it is obvious what has happened."

"Obvious?" Phelps rose from his chair in one swift motion, causing the room to tilt. He sank back into his seat. Why was she so cold and uncaring? He wanted to scream.

Mrs. Philips sighed as if he were a slow child. "Detective Ecker told me that Mr. Russell was in Berlin. Grace wouldn't leave by herself; she wouldn't know where to go. So, she must have left with either you or Russell. Since you've come asking about her, she must have eloped with him."

"Why would she elope with Russell?" Phelps yanked his handkerchief from his breast pocket and pressed it to his temples. His head was exploding.

"I thought you knew," continued Mrs. Philips as if she were discussing the weather. "Russell was her suitor back in America."

"Oh, Lord." Phelps sagged into his seat.

"She's just like her mother, willful and ungrateful. I never expected she'd treat *me* like this." Mrs. Philips sniffed as she drew out a lace handkerchief from her sleeve and dabbed at the corner of one eye. "And now I must ask you to leave as I have a considerable amount of packing to do. I wish to catch the night train to Paris."

Phelps slumped into the back of a cab that returned him to the Adlon. He ran over the conversation he'd had with Russell, the day they'd met in Berlin. He'd said nothing about Grace. In fact, the infernal fellow had allowed him to babble on about her. How he must have been laughing up his sleeve, except that he looked ill, to the point of needing a doctor.

Was Russell the suitor who'd been persuaded to stay behind in America? Phelps paused, trying to remember what Violet had told him. She'd just said there were objections to the engagement but nothing else. Phelps cursed fluently. Russell must have been Grace's suitor, and now she'd gone off with him. Why? Especially as her family objected. He'd never believed that Grace could be a heartless coquette—it didn't seem like her.

Phelps wound down the window and retched. He was too late. She was in Russell's clutches now, and he would force himself upon her as soon as they reached a hotel bedroom. A cold breeze whistled through the cab. Phelps shivered, the sweat pooling around his starched collar turning icy, even as his head remained hot and throbbing. He returned to his room at the Adlon and took to his bed. The hotel manager summoned a doctor.

✠✠✠✠✠✠✠✠✠✠

Grace balled her hands into fists. "You told me you were going to take me home."

"Shut up, Grace." In three strides, he was by her side.

"But—"

"Will you listen to me first?" He grabbed her arm. "I would have explained before, but you were asleep."

She shook him off.

"We'll go to the port of Genoa, where we can take a steamer to New York. I'll escort you to Philadelphia, where you can stay with your Aunt Josephina until the rest of your family is able to come home."

"Why are we going this way? Wouldn't it have been quicker to go to the port of Kiel?"

"Because that's the obvious thing to do. That pervert will have his minions searching for us in all of the German ports between Bremerhaven and Danzig. By the time he figures out that you're not there, it'll be too late. We'll be in *Italia*."

Carl's face materialized. They would have been married today. Was he seriously injured? "What about Aunt Paulina, or Aunt Louisa?"

"They abdicated their responsibilities." Russell's mellifluous baritone was knife-cold. "They failed to protect you."

"They'll be worried."

"We'll cable them once we're in Italy."

Grace slumped onto the bed. "But how do I know—" She hesitated.

He knelt on the floor beside her and took her hand. "Grace, Grace, have I ever hurt you?"

She looked deep into his eyes, her heart thrumming.

"I pledge myself to you as your escort." He kissed her hand. "From now on, you will sleep in the bed and I will sleep on the floor. I will not touch you. Do you understand?"

"But—" Her cheeks warmed.

He kissed her forehead. "Go to sleep, Grace. You look exhausted."

Grace lay awake for a long time. Why had he gotten all those clothes for her, all the underwear, stockings, dresses, and nightclothes? And what was he doing sleeping on the floor wrapped up in that discarded cloak, when he could be in bed with her, satisfying his lust? Grace had no answers. Mr. Russell seemed to be living out a fantasy of being her knight-errant.

✠✠✠✠✠✠✠✠✠✠✠

Detective Ecker came to Frau Varga's Sunday afternoon after Mass. "Someone at the U.S. Legation received a telephone call from Phelps's lawyer," he told Violet. "Seems he may have been involved in that dust-up with Count von Lietzow."

"Where's Grace?"

"Did you know Nicholas Russell was in town?"

Of course. Violet sank onto a seat. "I had no idea."

"He booked a room at the Adlon, but the hotel manager tells me he left a couple of nights ago. In a hurry." Ecker looked at his notes. "As you know, I've done a thorough check of Russell, and he has no criminal record."

"But Mother's death seems so convenient—"

"He doesn't give me a good feeling, either. But the fact remains, I can't find anything on him. He's squeaky clean. And it is true that he was decorated for gallantry. I have the record to prove it."

Violet glanced at the piece of paper he handed her.

"I understand he plays the piano well," continued Ecker, "and Father Walsh informed me he was sure to get a position with the State Department. So, what were the objections to him as Miss Grace's suitor?"

She reddened and twisted her hands together. "Detective Ecker—"

He came closer. "Please call me Thomas."

"Thomas, then—Auntie P. wouldn't want me to discuss this because it's a family matter." She took a deep breath. "He's our half-uncle."

"No kidding?"

"Ab-so-lute-ly."

He took a step backward. "Good Lord!"

Violet looked at the floor. If Grace got snared by Russell's net, her family would have to bear this taint for the rest of their lives.

But Ecker sat down beside her. "Do you think your sister chose to go with him? Or was she kidnapped?"

"I'm not sure," said Violet slowly. "She was smitten with him and very upset earlier this year whenever his name came up. I think she truly missed him. On the other hand, I can't believe she would just leave without saying a word to anyone, especially Auntie P. There's been no note or anything."

Ecker frowned and made a note. "I understand that Charles Phelps, another of Miss Grace's suitors, visited Mrs. Philips earlier today, asking about her. So she must have left with Russell. Where would they go?"

"I don't know. But if I were to guess, I'd say he's taken her to Italy."

"Why do you say that?"

"We are from the Veneto, from a little town called Marostica."

Ecker pulled a map out of his pocket and spread it on Frau Varga's dining room table. It was a driving map of central Europe, showing parts of France, all of Germany, Switzerland, Austria and Italy, parts of Poland, Czechoslovakia and Hungary.

The door opened, and Frau Varga appeared in her pink chintz dressing gown, carrying a tray loaded with refreshments. She smiled sweetly at Detective Ecker as she set the tray down.

"How are you getting on with your researches?" she asked in German. "Have you found Fraülein Graatz yet?"

"Not yet," replied Ecker, also in German. "But we are working on it." He waved away her offer of beer and turned to Violet.

"If he took her to Italy, they might be heading to Genoa. That is the main port for steamers leaving for the United States."

"Zsa-zsa," said Violet, turning to Frau Varga. "Do you know where the Veneto is?"

"Why, it's in northern Italy. Northeastern Italy, I should say." She moved over and laid one finger on the map. "Here. It's called the Veneto, because Venice is its capital."

"Venice!" exclaimed Ecker turning to Violet. "Do you think he might have taken her there? We must go at once."

"But I can't leave Auntie P. She'll kill herself with worry."

He considered. "We should give her something to do."

"She speaks Italian fluently."

"I'll get tickets then. Do you think you could leave tonight?"

✠✠✠✠✠✠✠✠✠✠✠

They slept until late and didn't start driving until sunset.

"Aren't you concerned about the time?" asked Grace as he helped her into the car. "Won't Carl be coming for me now?"

He started the car. "Leipzig is in Saxony, so it's outside his sphere of influence."

"But I thought Germany was unified."

He looked across at her and smiled. "It is unified, but each province has different laws. That's why I drove so fast last night. I knew that once we crossed the border from Prussia into Saxony, we would be able to get away from him to a place where his legal standing is not so strong."

Grace looked at him. Why was he doing this? Especially as he'd asked her to think about whether Count von Lietzow would make her happy. Should she ask him to turn the car around and drive back to Berlin? She considered for a moment. What if he responded badly? Then she'd be in even greater danger. No. Better to play along for now. Perhaps she should get him to talk about himself.

"I never knew my father well," she remarked, "because he died when I was so young. What was your father like?"

He glanced at her as he took a deep breath. "I don't know much about him because my parents worked sixteen-hour days in a meatpacking plant on Chicago's South Side."

Grace stared. Then she turned her head away, trying to take this in. She'd no idea her grandfather had sunk so low. Aunt Paulina had encouraged her to read the newspaper regularly, so she knew working conditions in meatpacking plants were awful. What would Mother have been like if she'd been working in a meatpacking plant all day and half the night? Although she complained all the time, Mother and her sisters had been the lucky ones. Kind-hearted Zia Paulina had brought them up like ladies, so they could marry well.

"Were your parents happy?"

Mr. Russell grimaced. He pulled off to the side of the busy street and turned to her. "No, they were not." He lifted his face and looked at her. "Something must have happened, I can't imagine what, but there seemed to be precious little love lost between them."

"What did they argue about?"

His eyes lost their spark. "That's just it, they never argued. In fact, they rarely talked. I've been puzzling this out for years—"

He paused, staring unseeingly into the distance. "My earliest memories of my parents were their cold silences and glares." He frowned. "I can't put my finger on it—it's almost as if I was seeing the ashy remains—"

Grace turned to him.

He swallowed. "It was as if their marriage had been blown apart by a tremendous blazing row."

"That sounds poetic."

He smiled faintly.

"What could they have been quarreling about?"

"I have so many questions, but they are both dead."

"What did they die of?"

"Father died of a heart attack just a few months ago." He looked down at his hands."Not many people know this, but Mother had a drinking problem, which eventually killed her."

Grace studied his face. It was calm in repose, gray with sadness. His mother's name was Rosa Lotto, the much-hated stepmother Mother complained about. Was he responsible for Mother's death? A whisper of doubt crept up her spine. She must focus on getting back to Carl.

He continued to gaze at his hands, slumped in his seat. "What a family." His smile was wry.

There was a pause while Grace tried to think of something to say. Eventually, he took both of her hands in his own and gazed at her. "I have been so weak. I ask your forgiveness, Grace. I never should have pursued you. It was wrong. My brother was so very angry with me. He made me see how wrong I was."

Grace stared at him. Was he serious? Relief made her bestow a dazzling smile upon him, before she remembered to veil her eyes with her lashes. Gently she withdrew her hands before remarking, "It sounds as though you paid a heavy price. You didn't have a happy childhood."

"If it hadn't been for Girolamo, I think I might have gone insane from sheer emotional emptiness." He smiled faintly. "I know this is hard to believe, but I used to be very shy, and I lived only for my piano. Not unlike someone I know. In any event, it was my brother who went out and found a circle of friends, teachers, and other adults, who mentored us through high school and college and saw to it that we got the scholarships we needed to pursue our studies. He became a lawyer, and I worked as a translator until the war came along."

"You haven't had an easy life. First your parents, then the war. It hasn't been a life filled with joy."

He started the engine. "I'd never thought of it like that. But it wasn't easy for Girolamo either. I hope you can meet him some day. He's the kindest person I know."

Grace remained silent, secure in the knowledge that she would never have to meet him. Carl would forbid it. She slid into sleep as the car purred beneath them, picking up speed.

And that was how life was, every day spent in a hotel, every evening taken up with driving. By midnight on Saturday, they'd driven for six hours and arrived in Nuremberg. On Sunday, they drove to Munich, stopping there because the car radiator overheated. On Monday, they changed cars, crossing the Austrian border in a nondescript black car, staying in Innsbruck that night. During this time, they barely spoke. He hid behind an impenetrable wall of reserve, perhaps because he thought he'd told her too much, while Grace enjoyed her usual peace that comes with silence. From time to time, he would glance at her, but he never alluded to what he'd seen in the nightclub.

As they crossed the border from Austria into Italy, Mr. Russell leaned back in his seat and relaxed his long, elegant fingers. "We're in *Italia*." He began to teach her Italian phrases and talk about the battles that had been fought only a few short years before.

"I remember how my brother tried to dissuade me from enlisting." His expression was wry. "How I wish I'd listened to him."

"Why didn't you?"

"I wanted to fight for our country. I thought I was going home."

Grace tried to imagine it, how destroyed the landscape must have been, how loud the sounds of shells, gunfire, shouting, and groaning. Now it was a Tuesday in early June and the trees rustled gently in an Alpine wind as they passed.

"Did your brother fight?"

"Yes, but on the Western Front. His experiences turned him into a pacifist and convinced him to be a priest. He was a successful lawyer in Chicago before the war."

"How much time did this take out of your lives?"

"Lamo and I signed up as soon as war was declared."

"Lamo?"

"It's short for Girolamo, his Italian name. He calls me Nico, short for Domenico." He smiled, for the first time. "He sold his stamp collection so that I could have piano lessons. He was only twelve, I was seven."

"Mother remembered him. She talked about how he tried once to save her from a beating from her stepmother."

His fingers tightened around the steering wheel.

Grace felt a jab of annoyance. "Mother's death was a tragedy, she was turning her life around. She was going to hone her Italian and do translations."

"Are you sure?"

"You're unfair to her, Mr. Russell. Mother had her faults, but she wasn't a bad person. She cared about us."

He snorted.

"Shortly before her death, she gave me suitcases full of her old clothes. They were for me and Violet."

"So." He slowed the car as they approached a junction. "She repented."

Grace thinned her lips and turned away. What did he think of her? Was she supposed to repent too? Why did he always have to be on the right side of history? Why did she have to listen to his version of events?

"Mother had a hard time settling down in America. She missed Italy. She was always talking about the fresh mountain air of Marostica, but what she missed most was speaking Italian. She hated English."

He glared at the road ahead.

"It's strange, but it almost seems as if she was being punished for something. At least, that's the effect that coming to America had on her." Grace turned towards him. "Do you know anything about that, Mr. Russell?"

"How would I? I was only four when I last saw her, before I met her again last fall."

"You might remember the bonfire."

He was silent, his lips clamped together.

Grace compressed her lips. "So, you can't remember the pile of old-fashioned cotton dresses with large skirts, lace collars, and cuffs? And you don't want to remember the hats trimmed with ribbons, the shawls of fine wool, the photographs, and the smoke and flames as everything dissolved into heaps of ash?"

"Why are you doing this, Grace?" His voice was soft, menacing.

"Your mother burned up all of my grandmother's things. Don't you think that's cruel?"

"I remember my mother's best dress. It had been shredded to pieces by a knife wielded by your mother. She was nothing but trouble. She tormented my mother."

"*Your* mother drank."

He went white and stopped the car. "Why are you fighting me?"

"Why do you always have to be right? Why can't you imagine that Mother might have been able to turn her life around, or that I want to marry Carl?"

"You don't know what you're talking about," he spat.

"How do you know that?"

"How could a lovely girl like you possibly want to consort with the devil?"

"There you go again. You have such a simple way of looking at things. Carl is not the devil, he loves me. He designed his villa with me in mind. I have an oval practice room."

"Are you really telling me, Grace, that you want me to turn around and head for Berlin?"

She lifted her chin and gazed into his dark, flashing eyes. "Yes."

"You can't be serious."

"All my things are there, my violin, my dresses, and the wedding dress I designed myself."

"You tell me this now." He banged the steering wheel with his clenched fist.

"I told you when you hauled me away from Weisse Maus. You kidnapped me, Mr. Russell. I'm here under duress."

"You're a minor."

Grace folded her arms. "You can't just wander in and snatch up an aristocrat's fiancée without repercussions."

"I did it for you." He slumped against the wheel.

"Then why didn't you listen to me?"

"I'm not taking you back to him." He ground his teeth.

"Very well, Mr. Russell. Then you'll drive to the nearest town, one that contains a telegraph office, and you'll let me off there. I'll cable Carl and ask him to come fetch me."

"You wouldn't do that."

Grace met his gaze with a cold stare, the kind of expression Carl used when dealing with a troublesome minion. "Wouldn't I? I am the Countess von Lietzow. You will do as I say."

Chapter Twenty-Three
Monday, 5 June

As soon as they arrived in Venice, Ecker put Auntie P. to work by purchasing a selection of Italian newspapers, asking her to look through them for clues as to the whereabouts of Grace and Russell.

"I need to examine Venice thoroughly," he remarked, taking a detailed map out of his pocket. "Would you mind if Miss Violet came with me?"

A ghost of a smile flickered on Auntie P.'s pasty face. She turned to Violet.

"I would like to come with you, *cara*. But I don't have the strength."

Violet squeezed her hand and gave her a peck on the cheek.

"Don't worry Auntie P. I'm quite capable of looking after myself, and the landlady has promised to keep an eye on you."

Auntie P. flicked a glance in Ecker's direction and considered for a moment.

"Help me back to bed, *cara*," she finally said. "I'll look at the newspapers when I'm able."

And so Violet took his arm and descended the steep stairs of the *pensione* in the *Castello sestiere*, where she shared a room with Auntie P., Thomas Ecker having taken a room in the *Cannareggio sestiere*, near the train station.

"I think we should explore the *San Marco sestiere* first," she said, "because it's the tourist area with all the fancy hotels."

"It also has a number of old churches." Ecker studied his map.

And so they spent a pleasant morning looking at hotels near the *Basilica San Marco*, the Doge's Palace, the Bridge of Sighs, as well as various churches.

They ate a hurried lunch in an outdoor café in the Piazza di San Marco and then explored Cannareggio, the working-class and manufacturing district.

Violet had to hand it to him for being so focused on the task at hand. It wasn't until the sun set, melting into a soft goldenness, that he lingered by a charming stone bridge.

"What will you do when you find them?"

Violet sighed as she gazed into the still waters of a small canal.

"I don't know. My kid sister has grown up these past few months, and now she's left home. Things won't ever be the same again."

"What will you do when you get back to the States?"

"Open my dress shop, I guess," Violet stared at the water. Bother. Why were tears threatening? Shouldn't she be happy?

He edged closer. "Your family means a great deal to you doesn't it?"

Violet was silent.

"Tell me about your childhood."

"There isn't much to tell. My father was a farmer of modest means who owned a farm outside of Rockville. Mother was very young when they married. I guess she didn't know what she was getting into." Violet turned away.

He touched her arm. "Where were your mother's parents?"

"Mother's mother died young. Her father remarried. I'm not sure what happened after they left Italy." Violet bit her lip.

"Do you remember your father?"

"My father was a wonderful man." Violet smiled as she conjured up images from the past. "I was close to him. He used to come home dog-tired every evening, but he would always make time for us. I was his *bonnie blue eyes*, and Grace was his l*ittle half-pint*. I remember how he would take off his dirty overalls, wash his hands, have supper, and then he would sit down in an old leather chair, put us on his lap, and tell stories."

"What happened to him?"

"He died, a farm accident." Violet pushed away from the bridge and stood up. "It's getting late. Shall we get back?"

✠✠✠✠✠✠✠✠✠✠✠✠

Next day was the same. Thomas appeared in the morning, and they walked around the *San Polo*, *Dorsoduro* and *Castello sestiere.* Nothing, nothing, nothing. Her sister and half-uncle had vanished. By this time, it was Wednesday afternoon and they'd been searching Venice for nearly two days.

"Have you found them?" asked Auntie P. from her seat by the window, as they entered the *pensione.*

"No," replied Violet, giving her a peck on the cheek.

Auntie P's pasty face went pale.

"But where could they be? You don't think they're… they're dead?" Her voice sank to a whisper.

Violet called for the landlady to make some valerian tea, while Thomas took a seat.

"While anything is possible, it's not likely they're dead," he said to Auntie P. He had a quiet, precise way of speaking, which Violet liked because it was soothing to the nerves and because he never promised more than he could deliver.

"It's possible they haven't gotten here yet. They could be driving."

"But it's been five days since she disappeared!" exclaimed Auntie P.

"If he's coming to this region, Venice is the most likely place," argued Thomas. "After all, you tell me Russell is of a romantic turn of mind, especially where Grace is concerned. He probably wants to take her on a gondola ride at the very least and serenade her with Italian love songs."

"It's the sort of thing he would do," said Violet.

"But they're not here. They must have gone to Marostica. After all, they must be coming from that direction if he's driving, as you suggest. I shan't rest easy until I go there."

"The only sestiere we haven't seen is Santa Croce." Thomas opened his Baedeker guide.

"Let's take a look," said Violet. "If we haven't found them by the end of today, we'll go to Marostica."

And so they walked up and down the streets, crossing over canals, looking at churches.

"We're never going to find them," remarked Violet after three hours of walking. "They're forever gone." She slumped against a stone wall, wiping her eyes with the back of her hand. The water below sloshed and gurgled against the wooden pilings. Caaah! Caaah! cried distant seagulls as they wheeled overhead. "I never guessed there were so many churches in Venice. If they are marrying here, how will we know which one it is?"

Tom looked up from studying his Baedeker and smiled. "We just have to listen," he said slowly.

"Listen?"

"You tell me he is musical. He will be serenading her on their wedding day." He put his left hand over his heart, opened his mouth and sang:

Treulich geführt,
ziehet dahin,
wo euch der Segen der Liebe bewahr'!

Violet straightened. He had a smooth baritone that was richly toned. "I didn't know you could sing! What was that about?"

"Faithfully guarded, draw near to where the Blessing of Love shall preserve you!" replied Thomas. He put his arm gently around her waist and kissed her cheek.

It felt so good to be in his arms. But—Violet's cheeks grew warm as she gently extricated herself.

"It's the 'Bridal Chorus' from *Lohengrin*."

She turned from him to look around. They were standing in front of a baroque church that was surrounded by water. To her back was the Grand Canal, where several gondolas were tied up. Between the church and the canal was a small square. Picturesque Venetian buildings seemed to lean into the church from either side.

A group of women formed a semi-circle outside the front of the church. They wore peasant costumes, with white blouses, colorful vests and skirts. The central doors to the church slowly opened as two figures appeared at the head of a small entourage. Violet blinked. She'd never seen so many priests in her life. There was the priest who performed the marriage service and another priest, wearing a black chasuble, who seemed to be the best man, while others seemed to be guests at the wedding.

The bride wore a long, ivory dress of heavy satin, with an inverted tulip hem, the sort of thing Violet would design. Over her dark hair, she wore a simple tulle veil, held in place by a silver band. As she left the church, she turned to her new husband, a handsome northern Italian gentleman. There was a pause as Violet gaped, and then her face slackened. They were not Grace and Russell.

✠✠✠✠✠✠✠✠✠✠✠

They left immediately and drove north through the mountains, arriving just as the sun was setting.

As the walls of Marostica came into view, tears came to Auntie P.'s eyes.

"I cannot believe I am seeing *Marostega* again," she said, using the Venetian name for the city.

They entered the city gate and headed towards the central square, which was dominated by a bell-tower. The view was breathtaking, the hills behind the other end of the square ascending steeply into the alpine Piedmont.

Tom brought the car to a halt, and they got out.

"This air," said Auntie P, sniffing, as she looked around. "How I have missed mountain air all these years."

The little town was bustling in the evening light as the inhabitants engaged in the daily ritual of *la passeggiata,* the evening stroll.

"Paulina," a voice called. "Paulina, it is you, isn't it?"

Auntie P. beamed. "Margarita!" And she actually ran partway across the square, as if she were a young girl again.

And that is how they met Margarita Venier, Auntie P's girlhood friend, whom she'd not seen for thirty-seven years.

"We're here looking for my grand-niece," said Auntie P. to her friend in Italian.

"You must come stay with me," said Margarita, opening wide the door to her modest home.

Auntie P. sat in the place of honor, while Margarita, her husband, daughter, and granddaughters bustled around and gave them flat bread, olives, cheese, and wine.

"My grand-niece is lovely," remarked Auntie P. glowing with pride. The light had come back into her eyes, and her face had lost its unhealthy color. "She looks exactly like her grandmother, Teresa Giardini. Do you remember Teresa?"

"Of course! The loveliest girl in the village." Margarita smiled.

"But have you seen Graziella?"

Margarita shook her head. "No one has come through. I would know, because Marostega is a quiet place up in the mountains, not easy to get to. The only people who come in and out are the people who live here."

Ecker shook his head when Violet translated for him.

"We're wasting our time here," he said. "They've probably shown up in Venice by now."

Violet put her hand on his arm. "Look how happy Auntie P. is. She's glad to be back home with her friend."

His face lightened into a smile as he leaned across to give her a chaste peck on the cheek.

"You're right," he murmured. "But I'd like to be back in Venice by Friday morning."

✠✠✠✠✠✠✠✠✠✠✠

Mr. Russell wasn't well. They were staying in Trento while Grace waited for replies to her cables to Carl, Aunt Paulina, Aunt Louisa, and Violet. She insisted they sleep in separate rooms; it was important to keep a distance from him. A breeze drifted in through the half-open windows to her room, making moonlight shiver on the floor. Then she heard it, a low, long moan. Grace couldn't help herself; she opened her door. Across the corridor, his was open, the moonlight spilling out between the door and the frame, its silvery light outlining the jagged edges of the mountains outside. Mr. Russell lay in bed in a tangled heap of sheets. He was completely naked. She stared, unable to help herself. He didn't have an ounce of fat on him, and he looked so beautiful in a male sort of way as the moonlight limned his body. It had been many days since she'd sampled the pleasures of the marriage bed. Pursing her lips, Grace pulled the bedclothes up to his chin and leaned over to hear his mutters.

"I tried, but—I—could not save—them—" He drew breath and sat up. Tears bathed his face.

Grace stepped back, but he didn't see her.

"I'm a failure—" His voice was low. "I am—weak—I—have—sinned—" He lay down. "God is—punishing—me—for—pursuing—her—with darkness." More tears crept down his face.

Grace stiffened. What did he mean? In the silence, she found one of his handkerchiefs and, kneeling, slowly wiped his face and held his hand while his breathing slowed and softened. Then, she rose and closed the door quietly, keeping his tear-stained handkerchief.

Next day, Grace breakfasted alone and went out to make purchases. Mr. Russell had been generous with his money, so she bought a suitcase, a fresh set of clothes, a notebook, and two novels. She tipped a porter to take her things back to the hotel and went in search of lunch. After that, she found a music shop and spent a pleasant afternoon choosing sheet music to study.

"Signor Russell?" asked Grace as she returned to the hotel.

"*Addormentato.*" The manageress put her hands together and pillowed her head.

Grace paused outside his door, listening carefully. She knocked.

"*Si?*"

"It's Grace. May I come in?"

The door opened. He stood there, his clothes rumpled and soiled as if he'd slept in them. He held a glass of brownish liquid. "Grace," he slurred.

She walked forward and pried his fingers off of the glass. "What are you doing?"

"You're still here." He sank onto his bed, reddening.

"I haven't received replies to my telegrams." Grace put the glass on the commode.

He opened his wallet and counted out banknotes. He took one and put it in his pocket. He folded the rest and gave them to her.

"This is too much money."

"Please." He folded her fingers around it.

"You don't have much for yourself."

"So?" He smiled darkly.

"That's unfair, Mr. Russell. Of course I worry about you." She took in his room; the overflowing ashtrays, the desk piled high with dirty coffee cups, partly obscuring a litter of papers, some of which were stained.

"Is that what you've been doing, staying up late to read those papers?"

"I can't sleep, I have nightmares."

Thank goodness he didn't know she'd been in his room last night. "Do you often have them?"

"I've had nightmares ever since the war. Grace, you have no idea how horrible it was. So many lost," he shuddered, "in such hellish ways."

She looked at him as images of all those maimed young men on the streets of Berlin filled her head. She'd read about their condition in the German and American newspapers, articles that talked of returning soldiers being marked by some mysterious illness. "You have shell shock," she remarked.

He turned sharply and their eyes locked gaze. "You understand."

"I saw young men who couldn't work on the streets of Berlin. It was heartbreaking."

He nodded. "A whole generation of young men lost or maimed." He cleared his throat. "I have a choice to make. When my task is done, when I have delivered you up," he shuddered, "to your destiny, then I must decide what to do with the rest of my life."

"Is that why you're drinking?" Grace poured the contents of his glass into a cachepot containing a large basil plant and washed it out. She refilled it with freshly squeezed lemonade from the jug.

He sipped for several moments.

"What were you doing in Berlin?"

"Looking for you, of course."

"But I sent your ring back, and when you replied, you were furious."

"I was over hasty. Yes, I was furious. But once I'd cooled down, I realized you couldn't have written that letter. It didn't sound like you."

"How did you find me?"

"I have contacts at State. I traced you by your passport number. As soon as I finished the semester, I left Georgetown. I tried to come as fast as I could, but I was too late." He lowered his head. "It was my punishment for courting you."

"What were you doing in that nightclub?"

He looked at her for a long moment. "I read about your engagement in the *Berliner Morgenpost*." His jaw twitched rapidly two or three times. "I was trying to distract myself."

Grace waited.

He took her hand. "But *I* wasn't with a lady of the night. Even in my state, *I* didn't lower myself to the level of the gutter."

Grace thinned her lips. "You were sitting next to a man-woman who goes by the name of Margot. And she—he marked you with his kiss!"

"You will never mention that again. Do you understand? What happened in that nightclub is our secret, Grace."

Grace shivered as she stared into his mask-like white face, with its blazing dark eyes. He looked almost Christlike in his agony. Suddenly, his face sagged as he released her. "I had to see you one last time."

She took his glass, went downstairs, and in her elementary Italian, informed the manageress that Mr. Russell was ready to have his room made up. He required another jug of lemonade, but no more wine or bitters.

Grace stayed up late, trying to relax over *l'incendio nell'oliveto,* a novel by Grazie Deledda, but couldn't sleep. She rose from her bed. The moon sailed above, making the stone of the cathedral glow. She put a hand on her belly. It felt a little heavier, as if she could already sense the baby it must contain. She expelled the breath she was holding and looked outside. Olive trees placed in large jars around the piazza flickered in the soft breeze, their leaves alternating from green to silver. This place was ancient. People had lived and died and worked here for centuries. Their ancestors, their family.

What was he doing now? A vague warning lifted the hairs on the nape of her neck. Almost against her will, she crossed the corridor and opened his door. The moonlight glinted off a metal object on the desk. Grace drew in a sharp breath. Of course. Was it loaded? Her fingers slowly reached out to grasp the pistol.

"She—has no idea—"

She stopped and turned.

He lay in a welter of bedclothes, muttering. "She has no idea—of the lengths I went—to win her love—" He paused on a long breath. "The agony—the agony of not having—her—after all that—It is torture —" He paused on another long breath. "She scorns me—yet I love her."

He rose from his bed, straight as a lance, and made for her.

Grace backed up against the door, frozen into place. He was naked and aroused.

As his lips found hers, he kissed her extravagantly, like a bee sipping honey. Oh no. She thrummed with delight.

Grace squirmed to get free and glanced up at his face. He stared back unseeing. As his eyes gradually came to life, his face lit with a smile. "I am in heaven!" His lips brushed hers again.

"Mr. Russell." Grace pulled away. "That's quite enough. You're not decently dressed." She made to open the door, but he grabbed her arm.

"Why were you in my room, Grace?"

She turned away, her cheeks blazing.

He turned her arm over and trailed his lips along the soft skin of the inside. "Grace," he whispered. "Be kind. Stay with me before I descend into hell."

Grace wrenched away, but he tightened his grip.

"Mr. Russell, if you don't let me go, I'll scream."

He let go.

"Thank you." Grace rubbed her arm, which was getting sore from his attentions. "Now, get some sleep."

She shut his door, went to her room, and locked herself in.

Grace stayed awake, listening as night slipped toward dawn. Her stomach slowly coiled into a knot. What would happen when Carl arrived?

Chapter Twenty-Four
Friday, 9 June

GONE TO PARIS. SUMMERING IN ÉVIAN. LOVE AUNT L., UNCLE W., T., E., AND A.

LIEBCHEN: COMING IMMEDIATELY. STAY WHERE YOU ARE.

WHERE'VE YOU BEEN? AUNTIE P. AND I IN MAROSTICA. COME ASAP. LOVE VIOLET.

Grace smiled as she left the telegraph office in Trento. Mr. Russell stood outside, beside the car.

"Your task is done." She held up the telegrams. "I'll hire a cab to Marostica."

"Grace, please don't do that." Unwillingly, she glanced up at him. His face was thinner, the skin stretched tight as if he were starving, or in agony.

"I don't think—"

"It would mean a great deal to me to see you safely back to your relatives. Besides, I would like to see *Marostega* myself." His smile softened his features.

Grace sighed but acquiesced. Soon she would be with Carl, and Mr. Russell would be gone. Absent.

She allowed him to help her into the car, placing the telegrams on her lap, more for protection against roving hands than anything else, and settled down to a four-hour drive through the mountains to their ancestral home. They passed the alpine lake of Lago di Caldonazzo, hot springs at Levio di Terme, the towns of Povo, Spre, Civezzano, Selva, Malga Costa, Roncegno, Borgo, Grigno, Belvedere, Enego, Cason delle Fratte, Valstagna, Bassano del Grappa. Finally, they came to Marostica.

Mr. Russell slowed the car to a halt in the main square, and turned off the engine. His face was slack with sadness. "We come to the end of our journey." He took her hand in his and caressed it with a kiss. "I will hold you in my prayers forever."

Grace shoved down the inevitable tears as she got out of the car and retrieved her suitcase. "Goodbye, Mr. Russell." Her tone was cold. "Thank you for your help."

She turned on her heel and walked towards a house that lay at one end of the square.

✠✠✠✠✠✠✠✠✠✠✠

"Gracie! Where on earth have you been?" Violet opened the wash-house window, letting out a gust of steam.

"On a journey."

Violet peered at Grace, then disappeared. A moment later, the heavy oak door swung open, and she let her sister into the main part of the house. It was an old house with a red tiled floor, whitewashed walls, and rough wooden furniture that looked homemade.

"How did you get here?"

"Detective Ecker."

"Whatever was he doing in Berlin?"

"Visiting his cousin, a doctor." Violet flushed and looked away. "I saw him in a café."

"Did he have anything to say about Mother?"

"Yes." Violet's face grew sad. "Mother died of mercury and arsenic poisoning from Dr. Jackson's little pink pills." She swallowed. "Tom found three medical experts who testified that Dr. Jackson had done nothing wrong."

"Mother died of an overdose?"

Violet nodded. "Tom says abdominal cramps are difficult to treat. Dr. Jackson used the standard treatments, but they didn't work. He's been cautioned."

Grace sank onto a chair and let out a breath. At least he hadn't murdered Mother.

Violet touched her sister's arm. "It seems so final, doesn't it?"

Grace slumped in her seat and studied her hands.

"We took the train to Venice and spent days looking for you," remarked Violet. "Then Auntie P. got the wind up and insisted on coming up here. She was afraid of missing you. This house belongs to her old friend Margarita. They last saw each other thirty-seven years ago."

"Where is Aunt Paulina?"

"In Margarita's bedroom." Violet led her sister into a dimly lit room.

Grace entered slowly, adjusting to the gloom. Aunt Paulina lay in bed with her eyes closed, a ghost of her former self.

Violet pecked her cheek. "Grace is here."

She struggled into a sitting position with Violet's help. "Graziella," she rasped. "You've come back to us."

Grace sank onto a chair next to the bed, buried her face in her hands, and sobbed. Mother was gone, and now it seemed as if Aunt Paulina would not be here for much longer. But underneath those thoughts was the relief that comes from being finally home, from being among honest folk who worked hard, said their prayers, and went to bed each night with a clear conscience. The contrast between this life, which had been her life before Carl encircled her heart finger with that fabulous ruby ring, and her decadent life with him was too much. Grace could never tell her relatives what had happened. At least she could let them comfort her.

Haltingly, she began a story, editing it as she went along. But Grace was not an accomplished liar, and Violet kept interrupting.

"Mr. Russell." Aunt Paulina placed her hand on Grace's. "Did he make improper advances?"

Tears spilled down Grace's cheeks as she checked her need to laugh hysterically. Bless Aunt Paulina for her innocence. She had no idea that Grace had seen both suitors in the nude, or that she'd eagerly played the whore in Carl's bed.

"Mr. Russell behaved like a perfect gentleman." Grace cleared her throat. "I was obliged to spend the night with him at every hotel we stayed at because he thought it best that I pose as his wife."

Aunt Paulina's lips thinned as she plucked at the bedclothes in an effort to sit straighter.

"But he promised he would never touch me. He kept that promise."

"Mother would have been so surprised," muttered Violet.

"She was unfair to him," replied Grace. Now that she knew everything about Mother and Mr. Russell, it did seem as if they'd somehow slipped into a silly sibling rivalry the moment they met. Grace looked her relatives straight in the eye. "Mr. Russell is a man of his word."

"Where is he now?" asked Violet.

"I've no idea. I came here to see you and to wait for Carl."

"So you're going back to Berlin to marry the count?" Aunt Paulina said.

Grace nodded.

She patted her great-niece's hand and smiled. "He is acting very generously. Not every gentleman would do that."

"Did you know your disappearance caused an international incident?" Violet picked up the papers. On the front of the *Corriere delle Sera* and the *International Herald Tribune* were photos showing Grace with Mr. Russell, courtesy of *The Star,* and of Grace with Carl, courtesy of the *Berliner Morgenpost*. GERMAN COUNT LOSES FIANCÉE TO MYSTERIOUS AMERICAN blared the *Herald Tribune*.

Grace scanned the papers. "Is this going to be a big problem for Mr. Russell? What about his career?"

"Won't that depend on whether the count presses charges? It seems his lawyer is anxious to speak to Mr. Russell about an attack. The count sustained a serious concussion."

"How is he?"

"He looked pretty battered when we saw him, the day you were supposed to get married."

"I was so afraid you would have been forced to marry that tiresome Russell fellow." Aunt Paulina's eyes closed. "Wake me up when Count von Lietzow appears."

Violet and Grace helped her back into bed and kissed each cheek. Then they crept out of the room.

✠✠✠✠✠✠✠✠✠✠✠

Margarita Venier invited them to join her family for lunch and regaled them with many stories about the Paganos, who had lived at a small farm just outside Marostica. She'd been Aunt Paulina's closest friend before she married Luke Barilla in 1885 and left for America.

"I can still remember her wedding day." Margarita wiped her eyes with a linen napkin. "Your great-aunt was a handsome young woman when she was seventeen. We were so proud of her for marrying a rich American lawyer. What a shame she never had children."

"She had us," remarked Violet, taking Grace's hand.

"Indeed." Margarita smiled through her tears. "You girls meant everything to her."

Grace looked down at their interlaced fingers. How thankful she was that Aunt Paulina had no idea what had happened.

The purr of a car engine halted the conversation, and people left their seats to peer out the window. Moments later, Carl von Lietzow limped in. One side of his face was puffed up, covered in greenish-yellow bruises.

It was only a week since Grace had last seen him, yet it felt like a lifetime. She pulled out a chair and he sank into it, while Margarita bustled in with Asiago cheese, olives, ruby Bardolino wine, and freshly baked bread. She exited, leaving them alone.

Grace sat down next to him and took his hand. "Are you badly hurt?"

"Pfui, Liebchen. It's nothing."

"Perhaps we should postpone our marriage."

"Nonsense. Your Carl is well rested. He had a headache, but it's gone and his bruises are healing."

He patted her knee. "I have a plan. Suppose we marry in Venice, then we could take the train to Turkey from there."

Grace smiled and clapped her hands. "I've always wanted to go to Venice."

"Then we'll go." He kissed her hand. "I'll hire gondolas to take us around and pay the gondolieri to sing the most amorous Italian love songs!"

Grace was just about to relax into a giggle, when, from out of the corner of her eye, Mr. Russell slid into view. Her heart thudding, she turned to Carl. "Were you able to bring my things?"

"I have your violin, and Mrs. Philips was good enough to oversee the packing up of your clothes."

"What about my wedding dress?"

"I have that too." He kissed her slowly on the lips. "I can't wait, Liebchen, to start our new life together." He wrapped his arm around her as she nestled her head into his shoulder.

"What do you think you're doing?" Mr. Russell emerged from the shadows, his face a mask of rage.

Grace rose to her feet.

"Tell me, Grace dear," said Carl languidly. "Who is that individual over there? He seems to know you."

"That is Mr. Russell." Her legs shook.

Carl gave him a cold stare. "How do you know my bride?"

"I am studying to be a diplomat at Georgetown University. I have funds, and I plan on being ambassador—"

"Georgetown? I remember that name. Let me see, isn't that a Jesuit university?"

Russell smiled darkly. "A perfect place for a practicing Catholic."

Carl raised his eyebrows. "You have rather old-fashioned sentiments. My family adheres to the Protestant faith, but we don't take that sort of thing seriously these days."

"Grace is a practicing Catholic," observed Mr. Russell, coming closer.

"Pfui. This is a non-issue. If Grace wishes to practice her faith, she can have her own priest and have Mass said in one of my private chapels." His eyes narrowed. "I have seen you before. If I wasn't in such a fog, I would have recognized you sooner." He clicked his fingers, and his chauffeur presented him with a briefcase. "Thank you, Weiss, you may leave us." Carl rummaged through it and retrieved a thick legal brief. "I'm surprised you have the gall to turn up here. My lawyer has been trying to find you to issue you with papers."

Mr. Russell scanned the first page and tossed the brief on the table. "Your complaints have no standing. There is no extradition treaty between Italy and Germany."

"Not so fast, you young puppy. I know people here. I could pull strings and make a lot of trouble for you."

Russell ignored him and took Grace's arm.

"What are you doing?"

"Why are you still here?"

"Because I can't bear it."

Grace lifted her chin. "Mr. Russell, don't be silly. You survived without seeing me for several months this spring. You'll be fine when you get back to Georgetown."

"*Fine* is not a word I would choose to describe the state I was in this spring."

Grace averted her face, her heart twisting in her chest.

"I can't bear to see you swallowed up in that devil's maw."

"Are you referring to me?" Carl rose to his feet but swayed and sat heavily.

Russell took Grace's arm again and drew her close. "Don't you see how much I love you?" His dark eyes burned in his white face. "I love you more than life itself. Your marriage to that pervert is my death sentence." He prostrated himself on the floor and kissed the tips of her gray kid shoes.

"*Mein Gott!* I had no idea that Herr Russell had a taste for cheap theatrics."

"Get up, Mr. Russell, please." Grace tried to move her feet, but he'd wrapped his arms around her ankles. "You're embarrassing me."

He slowly got to his feet, drew a handkerchief out of his breast pocket, and dusted himself off. Then he put a hand in an inside pocket and drew out his pistol.

Grace flinched and backed away.

He gave a dark, mirthless laugh. "Oh, Grace. Do you truly think I could ever harm you?" His eyes kissed her with his glance. "I love you far too much for that." He put it back in his pocket and came closer. "If you abandon me, Grace, I'll shoot myself."

Grace froze. She should have laughed in his face, but she couldn't. She turned away to avoid those magnetic eyes, while everything swirled to a halt and became quiet, except for his words. Grace swallowed. She could see it too clearly, the expression on his face as he took one last, long, imploring glance at her, the crack sounding as his shot rang outside. Her heart knotted in her chest, her temples vibrated, a wave of nausea rose in her gorge. She clutched a chair and drew in a heavy breath. This insufferable, righteous, fragile man was going to kill himself. Could she ever forgive herself if that happened?

"Mr. Russell, what are you doing here?" Violet appeared.

"I thought I told you never to contact Grace." Aunt Paulina appeared on Margarita's arm. "You, sir, are completely unsuitable."

"I rescued Grace from a fate worse than death," he replied.

"Pah!" Carl waved a hand dismissively and took Grace's hand. "We should be on our way, Liebchen. It's a three-hour drive to Venice."

"I am beyond furious," said Mr. Russell loudly to Aunt Paulina, "that you handed over this precious jewel to a pervert just because he had a title to his name."

"You call *me* a pervert?" Carl rose to his feet, grasping the back of a chair.

"You deserve it."

"Mr. Russell, explain yourself, sir," said Aunt Paulina.

He cleared his throat and reddened. "You force me to be direct. When I found Grace, she was higher than a kite, and he," he jabbed a finger at Carl, "was treating her like a lady of ill repute, in public, in a seedy nightclub, watched by leering strangers."

Aunt Paulina's pupils contracted. She turned to Carl. "Is this true, sir?"

"He has misrepresented the situation." Carl's blue eyes swept Grace with a glance.

Russell cut in. "Furthermore, it was obvious that this so-called count had taken liberties with her, not just once, but many times."

"Is that true, Gracie?" Violet's question dropped into the thick silence.

Grace's face became hot. She hesitated.

"Cara?"

She looked from the fabulous ruby ring on her finger to Aunt Paulina's tired face, and the truth seeped out. "The day after he put this ring on my finger."

Carl set his jaw. He reddened as he crumpled into his chair.

"His ring was her chain," remarked Russell. "By contrast, I recently had the privilege of spending six nights with this angel. I haven't touched her once."

"I doubt that," Carl remarked. "When I last saw you, you were in this same seedy nightclub, seated next to Margot, a well-known transsexual prostitute who specializes in tying people up and whipping them."

Like a coiled snake, Russell lunged at the count. His pistol clattered to the floor.

In a sudden fury, Grace grabbed his arm. "Mr. Russell. I hold you responsible for Carl's injuries. Can't you see he's not well?"

Russell stood there, panting hard, as Grace held onto his arm. Finally, he calmed down. "You save me from myself," he remarked, his smile grim.

Grace put her hand out. "Give me that pistol."

He complied. Grace hefted it. Father had lived on a farm and shown her how to load and unload pistols. She hadn't been very old, but he'd made her do it over and over again until she could do it in her sleep. Somehow, as if she could hear him telling her what to do, Grace released the lock and pushed the barrel down to expose the rear of the cylinder. Opening her purse, she dumped the unspent cartridges into it, rotated the barrel and cylinder, locking them back into place, put the empty gun on top, and closed her purse.

Then she went over to Aunt Paulina, kneeling in front of her. They held hands and wept.

"You will have to marry." Aunt Paulina wiped away her tears with a handkerchief.

Grace glanced at her suitors. Carl slumped in his seat, his face mottled with anger. Russell stood white and taut, his eyes soft with desire. Neither of them were the gentlemen they claimed to be.

"Do you really want me to do that?"

She nodded.

Grace went to the window and gazed out into the peaceful courtyard, with its olive trees whose leaves rotated silver and green in the passing breeze. She must choose now for the sake of her unborn child. The sun drifted lower through the sky, spilling golden light that lit up the stone buildings and created shadows from the leaves of the trees. She knew exactly what life she'd be living if she married

Carl. Suddenly, it was too much like Mother's for comfort. And *he* needed her.

Grace turned. "I must marry Mr. Russell."

Everyone started talking at once.

"Don't sacrifice yourself!"

"Liebchen! He was threatening me with a pistol. He's mentally unstable!"

"He's not suitable, *cara*. You know that."

"But we can get a papal dispensation," replied Grace. "You know that too."

"What's this I hear?" roared Carl. He came up to Grace. "Are you seriously considering falling for this fellow's cheap theatrics? Are you out of your mind? He's an accomplished liar, a—how do you say it? A con artist."

Grace gazed into a pair of angry blue eyes. "But what he says is absolutely true. He *will* shoot himself—"

He cut her off with a gesture. "I have been more than generous, but my patience has now worn thin. I was willing to overlook the fact that you spent a week in this fellow's company, unchaperoned, because I thought you to be innocent and pure. I misjudged you. I am at a loss to understand your—strange taste in a husband. The fellow is quite mad." He glared.

Grace gazed back, willing him to understand. "I wish I didn't have to hurt you, Carl, but I must save Mr. Russell's soul from eternal damnation."

"The young lady is right."

"*Padre Girolamo è arrivato,* Father Jerome has arrived," Margarita called from the doorway.

"Holy cow," muttered Violet.

Father Jerome had a tensile, nervy quality to his good looks, perhaps because he was so thin. In comparison to the elegant Russell, Jerome seemed almost emaciated. Yet he exuded a toughness that his younger brother didn't have.

While greetings were exchanged in Italian, Violet came up and put a hand on her sister's arm.

"Look at Russell's brother," she whispered. "Isn't that a broken nose? Isn't that a scar running down one side of his face? You know, Gracie, he looks just like a gangster."

Grace glanced at her sister. "I have to do this."

Violet gave her sister a poke. "Wake up, Gracie, this whole show is unsavory. Tom told me he's been involved with the Chicago Outfit. How do you know he's not hiding firearms under his priestly robes?"

Grace sighed. "Violet, somehow I've acquired three suitors. None of them is really suitable."

"There's Mr. Phelps."

"But he knew Margot. I saw him introducing her—him to Mr. Russell."

"Seems like everyone knows Margot," muttered Violet.

"Indeed," replied Grace. "Including Carl."

Violet bit her lip and turned away.

Carl was the last person to be introduced. As his name was mentioned, Father Jerome's eyes flashed, making them look eerily like Russell's. He gave Grace a long look.

Her cheeks warming, Grace lifted her chin. "I'm not marrying Carl von Lietzow."

Carl came forward and took her hands, his face pale. "Liebchen," he pleaded, "you don't know what you're saying." He took her hand and led her over to Aunt Paulina.

"I am the suitable suitor. I am not mentally unstable, nor am I given to amateur theatrics when I don't get my way. I therefore ask you to give your blessing to our marriage."

Aunt Paulina smiled at him. "Graziella, *cara,* you are very lucky that Count von Lietzow still wants you after your adventure. You should accept his offer."

"If you do that," said a soft *basso profondo,* "you will kill my brother. No one loves Grace as much as he does."

"He's mad!" roared Carl. "How can you countenance that marriage as a priest?" His eyes were like sapphire daggers. "If you are one!"

Father Jerome's soft bass changed tonal color."You are an outsider," he hissed. "How could you possibly understand? Graziella and Nico will heal a family rift. Their love will nullify a terrible hatred."

"It is absurd to force a young woman to sacrifice her life for a mentally unstable fellow. He will ruin her life!"

Father Jerome stepped up to the count so that he was right on top of him, forcing him to look up. His eyes flashed blackly as he shouted, "What makes you think you are right for her? You are an aristocrat, she is not. You are German, she is Italian. You live in Berlin, she lives in America. It would be extremely inconvenient for you to spend time in America. It would take you away from your lands and sphere of influence. You would destroy Grace's ties to her family."

He paused to change volume. "Your friends will laugh at you behind your back," he remarked softly, almost silkily, "for choosing a young woman who is foreign, poor, and of lower social status than yourself. But my brother has no such encumbrances. He is her equal."

The count fixed Jerome with one of his cold stares. "I am accustomed to doing as I please."

"But I did tell you I wasn't suitable." Grace drooped in front of him. "I know nothing about being a countess."

Violet shook her head. Only Grace would say something like that.

"You are *not* one of us," continued Jerome leaning forward. His voice became louder, forcing Count von Lietzow to take a step backwards. "You cannot possibly understand. Now get out, before I force you to leave!" He drew a stiletto from beneath his robes.

The count recoiled as the narrow blade flashed in the sunlight. Swaying, he stepped forward.

"I am not accustomed to being threatened, or insulted in this fashion. As for you, *miss*," Carl turned to Grace, "you have played me for a fool!"

Grace glared back, looking unnervingly like Mother. Then she took his ring off her finger and held it out.

Her aristocratic suitor dropped his gaze first as he took his ring and pocketed it. "I leave you to your delightful relatives, and if you," he swept the Pagano brothers with a look of scorn, "ever come to Berlin again, you can expect to hear from my lawyer." He made a stiff bow and stalked off.

His dark robes flowing behind him, Jerome softly shut the door on Count von Lietzow.

Violet glanced over at Auntie P. What did she make of this apparition and the cool way in which he'd brushed aside her wishes?

But she was sunk into her armchair, her face yellow, her eyes closed.

As Russell took Grace's hand with a possessive smile, Violet rose and moved towards her great-aunt. But Father Jerome neatly inserted himself. He sat down by Auntie P. and talked in languorous Italian forever—

Chapter Twenty-Five
Tuesday, 13 June

Violet lost her best friend when Auntie P. passed away. She had no one to support her, because Thomas couldn't attend the ceremony. He'd returned to Venice to search for Grace and Russell, and when she cabled him to say they were safe, he'd cabled back saying he had to return to the States. Violet missed him more than she'd thought possible.

Grace seemed unaffected by her death, Violet couldn't understand how she could be so dry-eyed. But then, Auntie P. had died without giving her blessing. Perhaps Grace was relieved she was spared a continuing battle with her great-aunt, just as she'd been relieved when Mother died unexpectedly.

Since her adventure with their half-uncle, Grace had changed for the worse. Gone was the dreamy sweetness Violet knew so well. In its place was a wary guardedness. Grace was just as quiet as ever, but now she bit her fingernails to the quick and greeted everyone with an unsettling stare. They had frequent dust-ups.

The morning after Auntie P.'s funeral, Father Jerome found Violet by her grave.

"My daughter," he began, pitching his voice to a sweet softness, "I know your loss has been great, but I am going to ask you to set aside the past and consider the future."

Instantly she rose, folding her arms tight across her body.

He stood there silently, his dark eyes the exact same shape and color as Russell's.

Violet met his stare. This creep had a violet streak. It wasn't hard to imagine *him* sliding that stiletto under someone's ribs. How many people had *he* murdered?

Finally, she said, "What d'you want?"

"I have come to talk with you about your sister."

"You mean you've come to talk at me about your brother."

Father Jerome turned his hands palm up, in a placating gesture. "As you wish."

"But I don't wish it. He *lied* to us. He's her uncle for Pete's sake! Doesn't it bother *you* that they'd be committing incest?"

Father Jerome stood there impassively, allowing her words to die on an incoming breeze that ruffled the petals of the newly budding roses.

"Has your sister talked to you about—her experiences in Berlin?"

Violet glared. He hadn't been there when Russell manipulated her into confessing her sordid experiences to her mortified relatives. Now his brother had used his priestly authority to pry that piece of information out of her again. How dare he insinuate his way into the family like this.

"She is not happy. Indeed, she has been deeply wounded."

Violet continued to glare. Why did everyone have to go on about Grace and how sensitive she was? While no one noticed how she felt? Auntie P. used to talk about Grace that way, as if she were a fragile flower whose graceful stem might be broken, spilling pretty petals on an indifferent terrain. And how had she been repaid? Grace didn't care a straw about her death.

Violet cleared her throat. "And I s'pose you think they should marry?"

"They both wish it."

"What's stopping them?"

He stared back, unblinking.

"Okay. I get it. You mean I'm stopping them."

"It would mean a great deal to your sister if you gave her your blessing," he murmured sweetly.

"Why should I? She always gets what she wants. I don't know why she and your brother are bothering to marry. He's probably already forced—"

"I think you should be very careful what you say."

Violet flinched. Now his voice cut like a blade of steel.

He leaned forward and smiled.

"*Violetta, cara,* I understand your point of view. Indeed, I do. Of course it is unfortunate they are so closely related. But you shouldn't allow that problem to blind you to all the good that can result from this marriage. God works in mysterious ways. Graziella and Nico are deeply in love. They've seen too much evil in this world and need each other to heal. Wouldn't you like to be a part of their healing?"

Violet grimaced. Damn. Why did he have to be so persuasive?

"As the dispensation has not yet been granted, I am on my way to Rome, to use my influence there. I am going to marry them myself. We hope to perform the sacrament very soon."

"Why so soon?"

"That is something you should ask your sister. She would like you to be her bridesmaid."

Violet pursed her lips. It was just as she thought. Grace was definitely expecting. Maybe that explained her sour mood.

✠✠✠✠✠✠✠✠✠✠✠

Afterwards, Violet returned to *Zia Margarita's,* as she now wanted them to call her. The stone house welcomed her with refreshing coolness as she stepped inside. Violet went to the pantry where she selected three or four glass milk jars to arrange all the left-over flowers from Auntie P.'s funeral. If only she could have buried Mother here too, in the country she loved, surrounded by family. Mother had been the unlucky one, wrenched away as a reluctant ten-year-old. At least Auntie P. had spent all of her girlhood in this heavenly spot, choosing to leave Marostica when she was seventeen by marrying Luke Barilla, who had just made partner in a flourishing legal practice in Georgetown—

"Violetta!" called Zia Margarita.

Violet went to the pantry door and opened it.

"I've spent all morning searching for this—I couldn't remember where I'd put it." She pushed a small package into Violet's hands. Slowly, Violet unwrapped the faded linen cloth to reveal a round circle that had been oddly twisted.

"It was your grandmother's wedding ring."

Violet held the thin golden band up to the light. "It belonged to Teresa Giardini?"

Margarita nodded. "Did you know she was crushed by a cart?"

Violet stared at her. Mother had never mentioned it, but then she was only four years old when her mother died.

"It was her custom to go out every day at daybreak to get milk for her children. She was a creature of habit, never varying her routine."

"This wasn't an accident?"

"Someone interfered with the brake."

"Who?"

"No one could ever find out. But that didn't stop people from talking."

"Let me see…" Violet searched her memory. "Would this have had anything to do with Grandpa's second wife?"

"Rosa Lotto was intensely jealous of your grandmother. She had a three-year-old son to think of. No one knew who the father was, but people surmised that it must have been your grandfather because he was always giving her money."

"She got impatient waiting for Grandpa Franco to make her an honest woman?"

Margarita sighed.

"Wouldn't he have guessed who was responsible for Teresa's death?"

"Maybe. Maybe not."

"How many children did she have?"

"Only two that I know of. Padre Girolamo was the older boy. Followed five years later by Domenico."

"You mean my new brother?"

Margarita nodded.

Jerome's voice intruded, telling Count von Lietzow that Grace's marriage to Russell would nullify a terrible hatred. Was this what he'd meant?

Margarita's voice took up this thread of thought. "How unfortunate that your mother, Angelina, was blamed for creating the rift in your family. It is true that she took her revenge by cutting up Rosa's party frock." Margarita giggled. "But my belief is that it went deeper than that. I think that Franco was wracked with guilt at taking in his first wife's murderess and couldn't look his daughters in the eye."

"So he knew?"

"I think he guessed. I remember overhearing a conversation between my father and your grandfather. My father urged him to go to America to get away from all the wagging tongues."

Violet looked down at the bit of twisted metal in her hands. "Grace is marrying the son of her grandmother's murderess."

Zia Margarita covered Violet's hand. "I know your family means a lot to you. I wanted to tell you this story to help you understand why your sister's marriage is a good thing. It will heal a rift in your family." She closed Violet's fingers around the ring. "Keep it as a memento."

Later that day, at Margarita's evening meal, Father Jerome produced documents, a legal ruling stating that the Paganos had been illegally turned out of their home all those years ago. They were his wedding gift to his brother.

The villagers took them outside town to see it. Violet was glad it looked dilapidated. That way she didn't have to feel disappointed no-one thought to ask her if she'd like to have it. But Russell's face lit up as he took in his humble abode. He told everyone it would make the perfect summer home. The very next day, he showed up with some villagers and set about cleaning the place up, helped by Grace and Margarita's female relatives. Not long afterwards, a procession of villagers went to the farmhouse carrying a brass bedstead, feather mattresses, linens, flatware, pots, and pans.

A few days later, Violet paid a visit. In the early morning light, the kitchen looked like a scene from a painting. The wooden breakfast table was covered with breakfast things, wrought iron knives, spoons and forks, a basket of eggs still warm to the touch, thick and crusty slices of bread, plain white china that was chipped, and folded unbleached linen napkins, soft with use.

In one corner of the kitchen stood the butter churn. The scent of fresh butter mingled with the stronger tones of grappa. The grappa, a wedding present from Zia Margarita, wafted through the wooden floorboards from the cellar up into the quickly warming air.

Violet gazed at this scene of domestic tranquility, completed by the happy couple, her sister, and her half-uncle-and-soon-to-be-brother-in-law, surrounded by a crowd of villagers. How strange to think that Mother had been here, with Auntie Lou, Aunt Josie, Grandpa Franco, and that stepmother they'd hated, Rosa Lotto, who'd murdered their mother and given Grandpa two sons, Girolamo, or Father Jerome as he preferred to be called, and Nico, who now went by the sanitized name Nicholas Russell. He was there now, dominating the kitchen of this tiny farmhouse, giving a speech in mellifluous Italian to the assembled company.

"Tomorrow is the day when my lovely bride, Grace, and I unite in the sacrament of marriage. Since our meeting last September, Grace has been my lodestar. I feel truly blessed for the first time in my life."

Some of the women dabbed at their eyes with their handkerchiefs.

Violet remained dry-eyed.

He took Grace's hand.

"Grace and I plan to treat Marostega as our home. We will stay here until *Ferragosto*, when we must return to America, so that I can complete my degree at Georgetown University. We will come back every year for the summer."

The place erupted, and then prosecco was poured, toasts were drunk, and speeches made. Finally, Violet was able to make her way through the crowd to her sister.

"Violet. I'm so happy."

But before Violet could reply, her uncle-brother appeared, beaming possessively as he put an arm around her sister's waist.

Suddenly, it was all too much. Maybe it was the incestuous union. Or maybe it was because no one had acknowledged her claim to the farmhouse.

"You should've let Grace marry Count von Lietzow," hissed Violet. "You shouldn't have kidnapped her."

"Have you gone insane?" whispered Russell. He glanced around at the crowd, grabbed her by the arm, and ushered her none too gently into their bedroom.

Grace shut the door and stood against it, arms folded.

"You don't know what you're talking about," he said.

"He would've made a better husband than you." She drew out her grandmother's battered wedding ring and waved it in his face "After all, your mother murdered our grandmother."

His pupils contracted as he slumped against the wall. "*No, no! Questo non può essere vero!* No, no! That cannot be true! Who told you?"

As Violet watched, something happened to his face, the sophisticated mask of the man-about-town peeling away to show the uncertain boy who lay beneath, a glint of fear leaking out of his eyes. She pressed her lips together as an unexpected wave of nausea rose in her throat.

But Grace, seemingly oblivious, went to him and stroked his face. She turned on Violet.

"What are you talking about?"

"Rosa broke the handbrake and sent the cart rolling down the hill. It killed Grandma Teresa and—"

"Enough!" roared Russell. He took a handkerchief out of his breast pocket and dabbed his lips.

Grace came forward. Her gray eyes pierced Violet's.

"Does it matter? What has this to do with Nico? He wasn't responsible."

"It happened before I was born," he murmured, sinking onto the bed as the color returned to his face.

"I still think you should have married the count," muttered Violet, staring at the floor.

"Violet!" exclaimed Grace. "Why are we having this conversation? I gave my reasons. You were there." She stared at her sister, her eyes flashing.

Russell glared. "Do you feel better now that you've made my wife miserable at our engagement party?"

A sudden jolt of rage lifted Violet's head.

"She's not your wife yet, and I know what happened. You're responsible for Mother's death. You did it because you're the father—"

"Cristo Santo!" Russell retched into a nearby cachepot containing a lemon tree, then grabbed Violet's arm in a vice-like grip. "What are you talking about? Your mother died because she was being treated for stomach problems with mercury and arsenic."

"Mother was pregnant at the time of her death," spat Violet. "Were you the father?"

"Of course I wasn't!" he roared. "How dare you accuse *me* of incest, of having relations with the mother while I was trying to woo the daughter! You've got a disgusting, dirty mind!"

Grace moaned and collapsed onto the floor.

He went ashen and dropped to his knees.

"Graziella, vita mia, si torna, si torna." Grace, my life, come back, come back.

He stroked her with his elegant fingers, but she wouldn't stir. He picked up her limp body and oh-so-slowly placed her on the matrimonial bed.

"If anything happens to her," he snarled, turning to Violet, "I'll hold you responsible. *Vai a farti fottere!* Go f*** yourself!"

Outside, it was starting to rain. Violet walked to Margarita's, sat in her room, and wept. What had come over her? She should never have said such hurtful things. But she was enraged. Violet shook as she wiped her cheeks with her handkerchief. She took a deep breath and looked down at her hands. If only Thomas were here. What would he say? She looked up as a breeze stirred the olive trees outside, causing them to rotate silver-green, silver-green. He would probably say that he couldn't find anything on Russell—that she couldn't expect him to admit he'd done anything wrong. That they would never know what really happened to Mother.

She looked around the room. They were getting married soon, but she didn't have to give her blessing. Quickly, she filled a suitcase with her and Aunt Paulina's things. Then one of Margarita's male relatives drove her to Trento, where she made her way north to Berlin. At least Frau Varga would be glad to see her.

✠✠✠✠✠✠✠✠✠✠✠

Violet was in Berlin for less than a week. She was helping a customer when Mr. Phelps hobbled into Modes Camille, his face pale and bruised, his lip cut, his left knee stiff, to inform her that she had to leave immediately because thousands of people were taking to the streets and the State Department could not guarantee her safety. Foreign Minister Walther Rathenau had just been assassinated in Berlin. It was Saturday, 24 June 1922.

Everyone was so kind. Camille promised to pack up her designs and clothes and ship them to Georgetown. Frau Varga helped her pack, insisting on making sandwiches for the journey. And Phelps personally escorted her to Kiel, putting her on board the steamer that left that night for New York.

"Where will you go?" asked Violet, as they parted on the dock.

"I'm being posted to Moscow."

"Céline?"

"Never." His gray eyes flashed steel. "Grace?"

"Married. How is your family?"

"Not on speaking terms. Except with Mabel."

"I'm so sorry."

His face sagged, his gray eyes becoming muddy, and then he straightened up and touched his hat. "Keep safe, Miss Violet."

Chapter Twenty-Six
Friday, 16 June

Was Grace never going to see her sister again? She'd left suddenly, with no note or explanation, even for Zia Margarita. Unable to face the quizzical faces of the villagers, Grace asked to leave Marostica. For the rest of the afternoon, they drove mindlessly through the countryside of the Veneto.

So much had been lost. Mother was never coming back; neither was Aunt Paulina. But Violet? Would she really turn her back on her? She had always been Grace's strongest supporter, but in the eyes of society, Grace was the wrongdoer, not Violet. All Grace needed to do was ask Mr. Russell to stop the car, leave her where she could find some kind person to take her to the nearest train station, and return to Berlin. Violet would be there, and Grace could ask for forgiveness. But Grace could not do that.

The landscape became lower and less dramatic as they drove east. At length, they came to a large river, where he stopped the car.

"Where are we?"

"The Piave River." His eyes became glassy as he looked ahead without seeing. He clutched the steering wheel with shaking hands.

"Nico?" After everything they'd been through it seemed silly to continue calling him Mr. Russell. There was no response. Grace leaned over and gently pried his hands away, warming them with her fingers as he had so often done for her. Gradually, his face came back to life. "What happened?"

"A battle. I fought here. So many men lost." The words were torn from him, making a pattern that sounded like the clatter of Morse keys, or gunfire.

"Let's get out of the car." Grace opened her door, came around, and opened his.

He stood up, shaking, so she put her arm through his, and arm in arm they walked down to the river. Hesitantly, he began to tell about the horrors he'd experienced, of sleeping in muddy and vermin-ridden trenches, of never knowing when a shell was going to explode, of having the experience of dearly loved friends dissolve into pieces, never to return, of being unable to sleep, of nightmares.

Perhaps she shouldn't have let him go on and on, but Grace was young and resilient, and it was her duty to help him bear this burden. As he talked, as they leaned into one another, he calmed and became less twitchy.

"Let's eat." She pulled his arm.

"I can't eat here. It's too painful. We must leave."

This time, they headed south, in the direction of Venice.

✠✠✠✠✠✠✠✠✠✠✠✠

Coming to Venice was like coming home. The quiet waters of the lagoons gave everything an air of great peace. No wonder it was sometimes referred to as La Serenissima.

"I've cabled Lamo," remarked Nico. They sat in a café on the Grand Canal, near the church of San Stae, sipping coffee. The late afternoon sun glinted off the waters, their surface ruffled by the passage of gondolas, *vaporetti*, and fishing boats returning with a day's catch to the Rialto Market. "Last I heard, he was on his way to Venice, but he didn't say where he'd be staying." He showed her the telegram.

IN ROME. HOPE TO HAVE GOOD NEWS. ARRIVING VENEXIA TOMORROW. LAMO.

Grace curved her lips into a smile, but what she saw was Violet glaring and shouting appalling accusations at the man Grace had chosen to marry.

"He's probably arrived." He signaled the waiter. "I thought we could surprise him and enjoy our own tour of Venice." He paid the bill and put his Baedeker on the table. "We should explore the San Marco quarter first because Lamo is mostly likely to be there."

She leaned forward to look at where his finger pointed. It shook as he spoke about San Marco, the Doge's Palace, and the Bridge of Sighs. She stroked his arm. "Time to drown our demons."

He turned to her at once. "Grace, we don't have to do any of this if you're not up to it. Perhaps I should take you back to your *pensione* so you can rest."

She lifted her head. Venice gleamed in the golden light of a late spring afternoon. "But if we do that, I'll never be able to stop thinking about it." She took his arm. "And neither will you. It is such a lovely afternoon. Don't you think we should try to enjoy ourselves?"

"I do." His lips brushed hers. Then he hailed a gondola, and they set off.

It took them some time, but finally they found Father Jerome lodged in the Cannaregio *sestiere.*

Once again, Grace fell into a pair of magnetic eyes, but their tonal range was different. Gone was the softness of desire, in its place an expression of steely compassion. Father Jerome was as tough as an old vine.

As Nico appeared in the door, his sharp face lit with a smile. He gave his younger brother a bear hug and slapped him on the back. He glanced from one to the other and smiled more: *"And of his fullness have we all received, Grace for grace."*

"I am the luckiest man in the world." Nico laced his fingers through hers as a tear squeezed down his cheek, followed by another. Grace gazed, astonished. She had never seen him cry before.

He moved closer to his brother. "Lamo—"

His brother made the sign of the cross. "Welcome home, my son."

"But—" Nico stood there, shaking, his jaw twitching, his cheeks reddening under his tan. Grace took a step forward. Perhaps their visit to the Piave River had been too much for him.

Father Jerome held up his hand. *"In my Father's house are many rooms."*

Grace hesitated as nausea rose in her throat. The baby was beginning to make its presence felt. She pressed her lips together, willing away the discomfort. Perhaps Father Jerome could teach her how to ease Nico's distress.

"I am the way, the truth and the life," intoned Father Jerome. He shook his head slowly from side to side, reminding Grace of a wolf she'd seen as a child staring down its prey. *"The light shineth in the darkness,"* continued Father Jerome, his voice pouring honey into the dim room, *"the true Light, which lighteth every man that cometh into the world."*

As if mesmerized, Nico glided towards his brother, his eyes lighting with—hope?

"Cast thy burden upon the Lord, and he shall sustain thee. For by Grace are ye saved through faith." Father Jerome raised his right hand, making the sign of the cross.

As if on cue, Nico dropped to his knees and bowed his head.

"In nomine Patris, et Fillii, et Spiritus Sancti. Amen." Father Jerome placed his hand on his brother's head.

Grace bowed her own and crossed herself. In the powerful healing hands of his brother, Nico was being made whole again.

"Welcome home, my daughter." Grace started as Father Jerome took her hand and gave it a courtly kiss. "I wonder, if I might speak with you privately."

Grace recoiled. Had she done something wrong? But Nico rose to his feet, smiling at them both.

"I am not ordering you to see me." Father Jerome's smile had that quality of tenderness that Nico's possessed. "Yet we have much to talk about, and I fear *he*," he nodded at his brother, "would be in the way."

Nico opened his mouth to make a retort, then collapsed into delighted laughter, all demons gone. "Mind you don't scare my bride away."

"Would I do a thing like that?"

"I suppose."

"Let us go on a little exploration—of Venexia."

Leaving Nico to rest, Father Jerome offered his arm, conducting Grace into those quiet corners of this glorious city unfrequented by tourists. She was not surprised to see that many of these sites included churches or that Father Jerome seemed constitutionally incapable of passing a church without going inside to pray at least one novena. While they walked, they talked in a way that seemingly had no purpose. Yet there had to be one, for Father Jerome struck her as highly intelligent, with keen powers of observation.

Grace tried to relax as they wandered around that bright spring evening, Father Jerome telling many amusing stories about Nico, which made her laugh with pleasure. After a couple of hours, they paused on a charming bridge that arched over a narrow canal. "You love him very much," he remarked. It was a statement, not a question.

Grace's breath caught. She thought she'd loved Carl, and yet—

"I see it in the way you respond to my stories." His smile was wry, his tone dry, without any of its hypnotic qualities. Even the scar on his face had melted into insignificance. "You have no idea how much worry that brother of mine has caused me over the years. Well, I should say over the past five years, ever since he insisted on going away to fight in that war. I've never forgotten the day he returned to me in November of 1919. In place of my shy, sensitive brother, whose expressive face used to give everything away, there was a cold stranger with an unseeingly stare." He shuddered. "I shouldn't say this, but frankly there were times when I despaired." He glanced at her. "Especially recently."

"Aunt Paulina was cruel," Grace heard herself murmur. *Una donna malefica*, Mother had called her after one of their tiffs.

Father Jerome touched her arm. "I'm sure she was trying to protect you."

Grace twisted her lips.

"But let us look to the future." Father Jerome took her hand between his. "Believe me, I have known Nico all his life. He is a good man, a peacemaker at heart."

"He doesn't seem like that. He was always having rows with Mother—"

"Are you sure your mother wasn't having rows with him?"

"He assaulted Carl von Lietzow!"

"I heard about that." Father Jerome's expression was somber. "I am not condoning his actions, but I will merely point out that my brother was at the end of his tether. People will do all sorts of things—even behave out of character—when they are pushed too hard." He smiled faintly. "If there is one thing I've learned in this life, it is that people are uneven. Behaving badly today doesn't mean bad behavior tomorrow. Gifts, including ethical gifts, don't translate from one situation to another. People are unpredictable, saints one day, sinners the next. That is what makes them so fascinating."

Grace thinned her lips. Before Aunt Paulina had ended their courtship, she had always believed Nico to be kind, attentive, gentlemanly. "I've never seen him this way before," she remarked. "When he's with you, he seems so young, so—vulnerable."

Father Jerome took both of her hands. "That is who he really is. He needs you, Graziella. He needs your love, which I know you have for him. Of course, he has to wear a mask when he's out in the world. He's a young Italian who's going to have to compete with scions of the ruling classes for positions and promotions in the State Department. You know all the family secrets, Graziella *cara*. He has a lot to conceal."

Grace looked down at her fingers resting on the stone parapet, trying to remember what life was like before all this sordidness gushed out of the family closet.

"I know it's hard to understand," continued Father Jerome, "because you don't have anything to hide. Not yet. But you will, given time." She looked up into his twisted smile. "We all need to cultivate compassion, for ourselves and for others: *As you sow, so shall you reap*."

Grace looked down at her fingers again. Poor Mother, she'd been a helpless child when she'd been yanked away from the home she loved, here, in *Italia*. Life had not treated her well in the United States, starting with her too-hasty marriage, ending with her too-early death.

He moved closer. "You have a most interesting expression on your face, Graziella *cara*. May I ask what you were thinking about?"

She lifted her head. "Mother."

His gaze sharpened. "Nothing you do will bring her back, her death was a tragedy," his voice oozed. "Graziella *cara* for the sake of my brother, I'm asking you to let her go. You're so young. Why not seek the happiness and joy of being loved in the way my brother loves you?"

Grace averted her face. "You're asking me to abandon her, to forgive him, to forget her." The words slipped past her lips unheeded.

He was standing so close to her, she felt him tense. But he gently tilted her chin. "You can never forget you mother, Graziella. She is a part of you. But life is too short to spend it in mourning."

Grace lowered her lashes. Mother would be so unhappy, so would Aunt Paulina, so would the rest of her family. But where else could she go? Everyone was angry with her, and she was too embarrassed to ask for help.

"Do you remember what Our Lord and Savior Jesus Christ said at the last supper?"

Grace looked up.

"That you love one another as much as I have loved you." He paused. "I know my brother. His love for you is real. You hold great power in your hands, my daughter."

Grace never used to think of herself as a person with great power. But as he looked into her eyes and said those words, she knew it was true. Her life took shape once more.

As she straightened, Father Jerome smiled. "When I saw Nico just now in your company, my prayers had been answered. My brother has found himself again." He took her hand and gave it another courtly kiss. "He is a young man in love."

Grace's face eased into a smile. How wonderful to have that kind of love. Their marriage would be as harmonious as the music they would make together. She saw herself on a concert stage with Nico, a priceless violin cradled in her arms —

As her fingers touched her new leather purse, she swallowed. There was another task she must do first. She opened it, retrieving the pistol and cartridges. "I think you should have these."

His face became gray. "Nico's?"

"He knows I have them. He says I am good at saving him from himself."

He took and stowed them away. "Indeed you are. You have saved his life, you have saved his soul."

Grace nodded as the color leaked from her cheeks. She had Nico's soul in her keeping. Would she be able to bear this burden? She wiped away a tear. "Do you think we can marry?"

He placed his hand on hers. "Of course you can."

✠✠✠✠✠✠✠✠✠✠✠✠

Grace arose from her prayers and looked out the window. Dawn was breaking, bathing the still waters of Venice in a cloudy light. She crossed herself. *Today I purify myself with the sacrament of marriage.* She opened the narrow window, breathing in the moist, salty breeze. From somewhere, the dulcet notes of Corelli caught her ear. Venice was a city of violins, its sweet tranquility masking deeper passions. Grace heard them at every turn, and if she half-closed her eyes, she could almost sense the presence of Vivaldi, the red priest, with his school of girl violinists.

After a breakfast of hot rolls, cheese, and coffee, Signora da Canale, Grace's landlady, did her long brown hair into plaits, which she pulled back and wrapped around the back of her head into a chignon. Then she helped Grace into her wedding dress, an old-fashioned flounced affair made of white satin with a lace overlay. Grace looked at herself in the mirror, trying not to think of that glorious wedding dress, the one Carl had taken back to Berlin when he'd departed in a fury. Grace lifted her chin. The person who gazed back looked old-fashioned, ladylike, and very Italian. She would have to do.

A *gondoliere* arrived with his long-handled oar and punted Signora da Canale, her daughters, sisters, aunts, and Grace to church. The women fluttered and giggled as they took turns holding Grace's bouquet, making sure her skirts didn't get damp. As they alighted at the church of San Stae, the water churned and eddied against the wooden piling. Distant seagulls wheeled overhead, silent, against the gray-blue sky.

It was still early when the priest ushered them from the misty morning light into the dusk of a Venetian church. Grace shivered as she entered its cave-like interior, for it was cold and damp. Slowly, she crept along the aisle, following the priest and his acolytes, the crucifix exuding a faint gleam of dull gold.

As Grace arrived at the altar, Nico slid out of the gloom to her right, dressed in black, the white starched collar setting off his tanned face. His smile suffused his face as he kissed her hand. They took their vows in front of a crowd of curious strangers. The only person Grace was aware of was Nico. But as the rings were presented, a dim figure in priestly garb glided into view. Father Jerome was Nico's best man.

After the vows, there was the nuptial Mass, and then Nico offered her his arm, and they progressed along the aisle to the great west doors, which opened, bathing the musty interior with late spring sunshine. Bells pealed as they stepped into that dreamy Venetian light, singing surrounding them like a cloud. They were in the middle of a semi-circle of men dressed in traditional costumes with colorful jerkins over white blouses trimmed with lace. One of them came forward and bowed. Putting his hand to his heart, he sang:

E lucevan le stelle—

"How radiant the stars, how perfumed the earth, the orchard gate creaked open as a footstep creased the sand. Fragrant, she entered, and dropped into my arms—" Nico murmured into her ear. "It is my wedding present to you—"

"—Oh, sweet kisses, oh languorous caresses," continued Nico, as Grace's cheeks burned. "While feverishly I stripped the lovely form of its veils! Forever, my dream of love has vanished. That moment has fled, and I die in desperation! I die in desperation! I never before loved life so much—"

Grace remained silent as the stormy music broke over her.

E lucevan le stelle—

"It is Cavaradossi's last aria from *Tosca*." Nico leaned towards her and whispered, "He's an artist who's dangerously in love."

Grace's lips curved into the expected smile, but she shuddered as the poignant music drifted around her like a mist.

Part III

Farewell My Life

Late Summer to Fall 1938

✠✠✠✠✠✠✠✠✠✠✠

PROLOGUE

Tokyo, Japan
July 1938

"You can't mean that." Grace turned pale.

"It's my first European posting," remarked Nico.

Grace slumped into her chair, her gray eyes the color of a churning sea. "Couldn't you, just this once, do something for me?"

"*Staremo bene,* we'll be all right." He brushed her cheek with the back of his finger.

Grace shied, like a startled horse. "You know why I don't want to go. You know this is my worst nightmare."

"But they need me in Berlin. The crisis in Czechoslovakia is heating up again. British Intelligence says —"

"And I need you not to go! Don't you care about that?"

"*Vita mia,* of course I care."

"Of course you don't!" she spat, rising abruptly from her chair. Something about her manner made the hairs stiffen on his arms."All you ever think about is yourself. You don't even notice me."

"Grace, you know that's not true."

But she'd gone.

Russell stood bereft, hollow with emptiness. Worst of all was the look she threw him just before she left. Full of fury and venom, her expression was eerily exact. Russell had heard somewhere that all women became like their mothers, but he prayed on his knees every day that Grace would never become like Angelina.

What a horror that would be.

Chapter Twenty-Seven
Berlin, Germany
Friday, 5 August

The letter, when it came, was square and heavy. Grace stopped in front of the demi-lune table in the foyer of the rented mansion in Savignyplatz, Berlin and picked it up. Its thick edge made a dent in her palm. She ran the tip of her middle finger over the gold embossed characters that proclaimed the address:

Villa Lietzow, Kladow, Berlin.

His Louis Quinze furniture had gleamed gold from the light of a magnificent chandelier. *Allow me to introduce myself to you. I'm Count Carl von Lietzow. What is your name? Tell me what you think of this villa. Do you like the color of the walls? Please call me Carl, Liebchen.*

How had she, a shy girl of seventeen, managed to captivate a German aristocrat? Grace lowered her head as the familiar notes of the opening of Verdi's *Requiem* sounded softly in her inner ear. These events had taken place so long ago, sixteen years ago. Her youth had vanished like the notes she'd used to coax out of her violin, spinning like gold thread from the contact between bow and string, arcing up into the air—then gone.

Slowly, reluctantly, she turned the envelope over, broke the seal, and slid out his message. It was addressed to her, in English.

August 3, 1938

Liebchen,

A little bird told me that you had returned to Berlin. It has been too long since I've seen you, and we have much to discuss. Would you do an old friend a favor and come to tea

at my villa? I will send a car for you at three on Sunday. Do come!
Your Carl,
Count von Lietzow.

"Oh, no," murmured Grace. She held the letter up like a fan so that its soft creaminess caressed her cheek. Her lips curved as the sound of his laughter resonated within her head. *But that was then, this is now.*

The letter dropped to the floor. Grace leaned against the table, struggling to make that fizzling feeling in her chest go away. It reminded her of the way she'd felt before going on stage to play her violin to a crowd of strangers. *I mustn't.* Grace bent to retrieve his message. Without reading it again, she took the envelope between her second and third fingers so that she was barely touching it, walked from the entrance hall to the music room, sat down at the piano, and hid it within the sheets of music on the music stand. Leaning against her hand, she stared at the dark reflection that gleamed back at her from the highly-polished mahogany of the Steinway grand. Her thick, dark hair was cut so that it fell in stylish waves around her oval face. Her skin appeared flawlessly young in the veiled reflection of the piano, so that she seemed for a minute to be looking at the seventeen-year-old she'd been when she'd first met him.

Absently, she picked up the sheet music placed by the side of the music stand. There was Bach's *Preludes & Fugues,* and underneath that was Brahms's *Hungarian Dances*. Grace put the Brahms on the stand and opened it to number eight. Slowly, lightly, she let her fingers run over the keyboard. The music had a wandering quality that perfectly mirrored the state of her mind. Her life was flowing through her fingers like the rippling notes of a cadenza, but unlike it, her days were the same note, going on and on in a monotone, the daily concerns of a wife and mother trying to run a household and look after her children while moving countries every couple of years. It had been ages since she'd last played her violin, longer still since she'd given a concert. Where had her violin gone? Grace had been unable to find it when they'd packed up their belongings in Tokyo last month, to come to Berlin. Last night, she'd had one of those recurrent dreams in which she was playing to a rapturous crowd of people, a priceless violin cradled in her arms, her husband Nico Russell at her side, sensitively accompanying her on the piano.

That was how they'd met, playing a Brahms sonata. He'd been superb, she'd fallen in love. Ever since, she'd had dreams of them going through life, making music together. But Nico was a rising star at the State Department, and since the *Anschluss* and now his subsequent posting to Berlin, she'd scarcely seen her husband of sixteen years. He was putting in twelve-hour days trying to defuse another crisis, this time over Czechoslovakia. Every time she tried to discuss something, he was on the phone saying things like, *We must get Herr Hitler to see reason. We must send a note to Sir Nevile Henderson, representing to him in the strongest possible terms that Britain should not back down over the Sudetenland.*

Grace smoothed the pages of the music open. In the early days of their marriage, he would've explained these things to her. In those early days, they spent so much more time together, going to operas, concerts, and plays, just the two of them. Now, everything revolved around his career. She played slowly, allowing herself to sink into the music by accentuating the syncopated rhythms of the piece. She turned the page and played number nine. A movement caught her eye. Eight-year-old Marina danced into the room in time to the music. Grace smiled and played, fitting the music more exactly to her movements.

"You're so good, Mama!" exclaimed Marina, executing a final pirouette. "You're as good as Papa."

"No," replied Grace. "Your Papa is superb."

"But he plays only one instrument. He told me that when he met you, you dazzled him with your violin playing."

Grace smiled as she looked down into the eager face. Her arms ached for the violin.

"Oooh, a letter." Marina made for the square envelope that peeked out from behind the *Hungarian Dances*.

Grace picked it up quickly. "That's not for you. It's something your Papa and I have to discuss."

She rose, the front door opening. Nico put his head into the room. "I heard some beautiful music, *vita mia*," he remarked as he bent to kiss her.

"I told Mama she was just as good as you!" exclaimed Marina.

"But you are wrong," he said, stroking Marina's cheek. He bent and whispered, "Your Mama is so much better."

Grace shook her head as tears welled.

He shot a look at her and turned to their daughter. "Go tell Frau Hoffmann that I'm back, and we would like supper in an hour."

Marina nodded and ran off. He shut the door. "Something is troubling you."

She showed him the letter.

He put his briefcase down, took his spectacles out, and scanned briefly. "When did this arrive?"

"Just now."

He grunted. "He presumes you'll say yes to his invitation." He glanced at her. "Do you want to go?"

She flushed.

"I see."

She shook her head. "No you don't. You don't see at all. This is why I didn't want to come to Berlin."

"We've been through this before. This is my first European posting. There's a crisis on in Czechoslovakia. They need me here because I can speak German."

You want to be ambassador to Rome. She lifted her head. "You always put your career before your family."

His face lost its expressivity, becoming blank and mask-like.

Grace hugged herself. "I've never forgiven him for what he did. But now I have to see him."

His dark eyes blazed. "If you do that, you'll be playing into his hands. Of course he wants to see you. He's hoping that he can persuade you to give up Peter."

She sank down onto the piano bench. "I don't want Peter to know," she murmured.

"Ignore it, then."

"But I can't do that."

"Then tell Peter. He's fifteen."

"But what will he think of me?" Her stomach roiled.

"You are his mother."

"But will he be able to forgive me?" She glanced at Nico, but he'd turned his back to gaze out the window. How could she tell her son he was illegitimate? It would ruin him. Besides, Nico had been so good. He'd gallantly taken her on, marrying her in Venice, even though he knew she was soiled goods. She'd never heard one word of complaint. *But he's never warmed to my son.*

A likeness that made her shiver slid into the dark gaze of the mahogany piano. How like Carl he looked.

"Father?" Peter looked quizzically at his parents.

"What is it, my son?" Nico made a small movement with his mouth, a suggestion of a smile.

Peter dropped his eyes. "Nothing."

"Well I have some news to discuss." Nico withdrew a letter from his briefcase. "I applied for you to attend the Technische Hochschule in Berlin."

"Why didn't you tell me?"

"Even though Père Moreau from St Joseph's in Yokohama wrote a glowing report, you didn't get in."

Peter flushed and looked down.

"It's time to think about getting you into a top-notch place," continued Nico. "I've hired a tutor to work with you this fall on calculus, differential equations, and linear algebra. You'll reapply in the spring."

Peter looked up. "You mean I'll have no time to adjust to a new city?"

"Your future is at stake. I expect *you* to get into MIT, or the California Institute of Technology."

Peter stood there silent, his lips pinched together.

"Well? Aren't you grateful? I hired an expensive tutor. He is a PhD candidate in mathematics here at the University of Berlin—"

Grace rose, pasting a smile on her face. These kinds of altercations were becoming all too common between her husband and eldest son. She placed a hand on Nico's arm. "Of course, he's grateful," she murmured. "He's just surprised. Let's discuss over dinner."

✠✠✠✠✠✠✠✠✠✠✠

He declared himself entirely at her disposal: The adventure struck him as diverting.

A shadow slid across these words. *"Liebchen?"*

Grace tensed, clutching the book so hard her nails became white. Without looking up, she slipped *The House of*

Mirth into her purse. Slowly, unwillingly, she turned. A pair of bright blue eyes smiled down at her.

He sat next to her at the café table, placing his hand on hers. "At last, after all these years." The last sixteen years had not changed him, except for his hair, which was now iron gray.

He hung his eagle-headed cane on the chair next to him. Its ruby eyes glinted, reminding Grace of that fabulous engagement ring he'd given her. Now, Carl took her hand and kissed it slowly. "*Gnädige Frau*," he murmured, making her tingle.

Grace frowned, withdrew her hand, and shifted her seat to sit as far from him as she could.

He signaled to the waiter. "Some champagne, if you please."

The waiter blinked and hurried off. Grace had only just arrived, but even she was aware of the shortages—sausages stuffed with bread, watery milk, butter made of whale blubber.

"You will join me, will you not?"

"It's only ten-thirty in the morning."

He laughed. "You Americans, I see that you still live under the shadow of prohibition. But you will join in my little celebration? Yes?"

"Celebration?"

He squeezed her hand. "Of course it is a celebration when I behold my *Liebchen* again."

Her cheeks flaming, she withdrew her hand. "I don't think—"

The waiter appeared with the champagne, which he poured into two bowl-shaped glasses. Von Lietzow raised his high. "To our future happiness."

Grace eyed the scene before her, noting the other café-dwellers who were beginning to turn and stare. She picked up her champagne glass, sipped, and put it down again. "You shouldn't be here."

He turned his eyebrows into zigzags as he smiled at her. "You did not answer my invitation. I was forced to find you."

She remained silent, compressing her lips. How that expression had amused her as a child. How much he'd made her laugh. But she couldn't fall for those tricks now.

He held his glass up to the light. "Ah! Champagne!" he declaimed. *"Nur der Champagner war an allem Schuld!"*

"Only the champagne was to blame," said Grace to herself. She remembered the line from *Fledermaus,* and how Carl had taught her German by studying the libretto with her.

"There's nothing like it for lifting the spirits." He put his glass down, his eyes twinkling. "Do you not agree?"

Grace frowned, compressing her lips again. "Why are you here?"

He sipped slowly for several moments before placing his glass on the round marble table. He claimed her hand again. "I am not going away."

She tried to withdraw her hand, but he gripped it tight. "You look wonderful, not a day older than when I last saw you. And your figure is just as lovely as ever. How do you manage that with four children?"

"I—How do you know?"

"I make it my business to keep well-informed." He picked up his glass with his other hand and twirled it. The light, golden liquid swirled inside the bowl, gently releasing bubbles. "It is very useful, this American custom of making birth certificates publicly available, do you not agree?"

She shivered.

"Where is he?"

She thinned her lips and stared at the black marble table.

"He is *my* son."

"You don't know that."

He leaned in and whispered, "I know you were a virgin when you came to my bed on the twenty-first of April, 1922. I also know that I made love to you every day, several times a day."

Grace shrank into her seat as heat seared her cheeks. *Was that all he'd cared about? Her virginity? But he'd been so gentle. She hadn't known what he was doing to her until too late. He'd been so affectionate afterwards, telling her with tears in his eyes how much he'd loved her. But did he really love her? Nico had furiously insisted she'd been raped.* "You've no right to speak about such matters in a public place."

"But I do have a right to be heard," he replied in a low tone. "I am forced to talk with you in a café since you would not come to my villa. Now where was I? You probably want to know why I made love to you before marriage."

She tried to draw away, but he clung to her hand.

"*Liebchen*, don't make a scene. This is important. It was a large part of our relationship, and it is why we are where we are today. I spent a sleepless night arguing with myself about that. But I'd seen so many terrified brides being led to the altar, I told myself I would be doing you a kindness. That way, you would know what to expect on our wedding night. But perhaps you disagree?"

"Disagree? You never *asked* my opinion!"

He zigzagged his eyebrows again. "Hush, *Liebchen*, or I'll be forced to put you in my car and carry you off to my villa."

Grace glared, then burst into laughter.

His answering chuckle made the grayness of her life lift. He rubbed her palm with the pad of his thumb. "You enchanted me. Ah! I could not get enough of you. And then—you disappeared. On June the third."

She pulled away. "I married Nico—Nicholas—shortly thereafter."

He put his mouth close to her ear. "You were pregnant before you disappeared. Don't you remember how sick you were every time you came to lunch? Don't you remember how I noticed your breasts changing when I kissed them? I called them my little spoons."

She stood. "Do not talk to me like this. I am not your wife."

He grasped her hand and turned it over. Nico's pearl and amethyst engagement ring nestled behind her wedding band and her diamond encrusted forever ring. "Do you remember you promised to marry *me*?"

That was true. She'd promised to marry him. And would've done so if Nico hadn't appeared and—interfered. She stared into his eyes, which had hardened into ice, and sat.

"*Liebchen*, be reasonable," he said, smiling again. "You have wronged me greatly, but I am willing to forgive you."

She fastened her eyes on the marble table. It was the kind of black marble with veins of gray running through it.

"I never married," he continued. "You see, I was unable to forget you, and I could never bring myself to give up the hope that I might see you again. I knew your husband was well-placed in the American State Department. With his command of German, I reasoned that he might be posted to Berlin one day. Especially in view of the recent interesting political situation."

She lifted her lashes.

He leaned forward and put one finger under her chin. "You are so lovely that even when you stare at the table, you look like one of Raphael's *Madonnas*. But it is your eyes that give your face such life. They're gray but fiery. How do you have such an effect on me?"

She pulled away and stared at the table again. "What are you going to do?"

"Ah, now we come to the point. As I said, I never married, and consequently I have no heir. Your eldest child, Peter Russell, is therefore my heir. I propose that he come live with me and be groomed to be the next Count von Lietzow. First, I think we should get rid of that silly name. He should be named after his father. His rightful name is Count Carl von Lietzow. Do you not agree?"

"His name is Peter Russell."

"Peter Carl Russell. An interesting middle name, don't you think?"

She hung her head to avoid his gaze.

"*Liebchen*, you chose his name. Admit it. You know perfectly well I am his father. Why, I'm told he looks exactly like me."

"Who told you?"

He leaned back in his chair and smiled.

She flushed and turned away.

"Do turn towards me, *Liebchen*. You look uncomfortable like that."

"I am his mother!"exclaimed Grace, turning to face him.

"No one is disputing that. But *I* am without a countess." He leaned forward. "My offer is still open. Why don't you get rid of your husband and marry me?"

"Get rid of Nico?"

"I mean, of course, you should divorce him."

"I couldn't do that!"

"Why not? It would keep your children together, under one roof."

"Out of the question!"

He put his hand on his cane. "Think about it, *Liebchen*. It would solve many problems. For one thing, you would not be tied down by your children because I would be able to provide adequate staff to see to their needs."

"I don't need—"

"I think you do." He took her left hand and turned it over, then brushed his thumb over the padless tips of her fingers. "When did you last play your violin?"

"I—That is none of your business!"

"The happiness of *my* son's mother is *my* business."

She remained silent.

He smiled. "Having settled that, I just wish to point out that the estimable Mr. Russell is a busy man who does not have time for his lovely wife. Whereas I'm in a position to give *my* countess *my* undivided attention."

Grace picked up her purse.

He put a hand on her arm. "I have a beautiful villa that I decorated to suit your tastes. Don't you remember the yellow room that reminded you of D-sharp?"

She sank back into her seat.

He leaned forward to brush away a sudden tear that slipped down her cheek. "You would have a home of your own, for yourself and your children. No more running around from one place to another every two years."

"I couldn't—"

He put a hand on her thigh. The warmth of his hand penetrated the thin silk of her dress. Grace closed her eyes and shuddered.

"I adore you," he murmured, his warm breath buffeting her cheek. "I would take care of you. You could have a career as a violinist."

She rose abruptly, causing the other patrons to eye her over the tops of their newspapers and coffee cups.

He clung to her hand, but she wrested it away. As she turned to leave, she could hear him chuckle softly. She glanced back as he kissed his hand to her. "Farewell, my life. Until next time."

Grace gripped her purse, stiffened her spine, and marched off back to her family. She'd made her choice. She wasn't going to fall for one of his ploys.

Chapter Twenty-Eight

Tuesday, 9 August

"I adore you," he murmured, his warm breath on her cheek.

She turned her head, and his lips fastened on hers. He kissed her, like a thirsty man taking deep draughts—

"Grace! Grace! What is this?"

She felt as if she were underwater, his voice a long way away. Slowly, she surfaced to see her husband standing in the doorway. His stood stiffly to attention, his face pale, his lips compressed, making those vertical lines that framed his nose more pronounced. Silently, he handed her a letter.

Grace slid into a sitting position in their plush bed, with its drapes and innumerable pillows. She eyed the document, her eyes blurry with sleep. It was long and complex and her thoughts refused to coalesce. She looked up.

Nico stood next to her, a pillar of black, topped by his starched white shirt collar. As usual, he was immaculately dressed for the office even though dawn was only just breaking. He frowned. "This is a legal brief from von Lietzow. His lawyers are demanding that we go to court to answer questions about Peter."

She flinched, trying to reconcile the blissful dream she'd just had with the crisp document that now lay in her lap.

"I thought you'd settled things with him." His tone of voice was one he'd been using more and more frequently of late, when berating her for forgetting to tell the housekeeper, the tutors, or one of the nursemaids something. *I hire these people to help you,* he'd say, his tone laced with scorn. *But you have to communicate your wishes to them. I don't have time to deal with this.* Now he looked at her, his dark eyes cool. "You told me he'd been charming and friendly."

She flushed as she recalled the heft of his hand on her thigh. His fingers had hovered over, but not quite touched, the skin above her stockings.

"Grace?" His voice cut across her thoughts.

"I thought we'd sorted things out," she murmured.

"Well, now he wants us to go to court. A date has been set for August the nineteenth." His face set into its handsome lineaments. His generous mouth, which used to curve at the corners, was now hardening into a thin line.

Grace turned away. "I suppose we'll have to go, then."

"What? You can't imagine I would ever allow that fellow to pick and prod his dirty way through our private lives." He came closer and nailed her with his dark gaze. "You must be out of your mind!"

She stared up at her husband, her head thrown back by the force of gravity emanating from his eyes.

"Grace! Grace!" His tone hardened as he sucked in breath through his teeth. "What have you taken? You're in one of your fuzzy moods. Don't you understand how important this is?"

She looked down at her lap.

He sat down beside her, and sighed, crossing one elegant leg over the other. "Didn't you get enough sleep last night?" He caressed her hair with his long fingers.

She closed her eyes and leaned into him. But the magic was gone.

"We should go away somewhere," he murmured, kissing her cheek.

She peeked at him through her lashes. His mouth had relaxed into a gentle smile.

"*Luce mia*, it's been too long since we—"

Oh no. Of course he wanted that, but she didn't know if she could satisfy him after so long. It had been, what? Five years since the birth of her youngest child, Benny, when the doctor had taken her husband aside and told him that there could be no more pregnancies. She was saved by a familiar voice.

"Mama!" Marina peeked around the door.

Instantly, he rose. "Ignore that court appointment," he whispered, pecking her on the cheek. Then he ruffled his daughter's hair. "I'll be late this evening. Don't wait dinner for me."

Grace watched him through the lace curtains as he strode down the pathway and disappeared. She glanced at her watch. It was only seven o'clock.

"What are you going to do, Mama?"

"I don't know." Perhaps the best thing was take Nico's advice and ignore Carl—

"Is it about that funny man?"

Grace jolted awake. "What funny man?"

Marina fidgeted, wrapping long strands of her dark brown hair, the exact same shade and consistency as Grace's, around her fingers. "That man with the funny walking stick. He let me look at the bird. Did you know its eyes were made out of real rubies?"

"What?"

Marina eyed her mother. "We had a long talk. He was nice. He came with a box of chocolates for you, but he let *me* have one." She let her tongue touch her lower lip. "He asked for you, but you were out."

How had Carl managed to get hold of a box of chocolates? Grace put both hands on her daughter's shoulders. "What did you talk about?"

Eight-year-old Marina gazed back at her, eyes wide. "Everything. I told him all about Stacy and Benny." She counted off her siblings on her fingers. "And Peter."

"Did he see Peter?"

Marina shook her head.

Still holding her daughter's shoulders, Grace knelt on the floor, her stomach roiling.

"Did I do something wrong, Mama?" Marina put her small arms around her mother's neck and touched her cheek to cheek.

✠✠✠✠✠✠✠✠✠✠✠✠

"Why do I need a new frock?"

During the three or so weeks since receiving that legal brief, Grace had languished in bed, the curtains drawn, pleading a headache, in effect taking Nico's advice and ignoring Carl. She'd even missed that court date set for August the nineteenth. In return, she'd been met with an ominous silence.

Now, the first Friday in September, Grace met Stacy's inquiring stare as they stood in the foyer of the Savignyplatz mansion they now called home.

"Your father has invited a number of guests for Sunday lunch. It's the first time you've attended a formal party. Don't you want to look good for his sake?"

"I s'pose," Stacy mumbled, her dark-gold curls hiding her face as she stared at her shoes.

Grace's shoulders slumped as Frau Hoffman closed the front door behind them. Keeping a wary distance, Grace and her daughter walked down the white marble steps to the car. The child had just turned thirteen and seemed to be getting more difficult with every day that she aged.

They sat in the backseat while the chauffeur took them through the strident hustle of Berlin to the Ku'damm, its smartest shopping street. Through the half-open window Grace was assaulted by the spicy aroma of pretzels, the cries of newspaper boys, the squeals of bicycle brakes, the fumes of motor cars, the stink of hot oil, the brassy honks of automobile horns. Eventually, they arrived at the fashionable boutique

Aunt Louisa had patronized all those years ago. *Modes Lillas* was still there after sixteen years.

Grace closed her eyes. Since her marriage to Nico, she'd lived in Turkey, Trans-Jordan, Greece, and Tokyo, with a couple of tours of duty in Washington DC. The tours of duty in the District had been the hardest, because Violet lived in Georgetown. Grace had made several attempts to ease things, but relations with her sister remained strained. To keep her husband and sister apart, Grace had rented a house on the other side of town, on Capitol Hill. Cousin Ella was the only one who kept her informed, and it was through her that Grace had learned of the deaths of many of her relatives, Uncle James, Aunt Josephina and Uncle William. It was Ella who'd told her that Violet had married Detective Ecker a year after her own marriage to Nico, and she now had three boys. It was Ella, who lived in a New York walk-up with a lady friend, who was the only one who truly welcomed Grace and her family.

Stacy nudged her. "Come on, Mother. We don't have all day."

They exited the car and went inside the plushly appointed shop. Waving away the blandishments of a bevy of young female assistants, Grace rummaged listlessly, while Stacy hovered nearby, biting her nails.

"Here are some frocks I'd like you to try on."

"But those dresses look so babyish!"

Grace sighed and looked at the garments draped over her arm. They were in pastel colors, suitable for late summer. "Why don't you show me what you'd like?"

Stacy flitted around the shop, choosing with an unerring sense of style that Grace had never possessed.

"Let's get this," she remarked, emerging from the fitting room dressed in a sophisticated chocolate dress which molded her body in finely knitted wool. Grace cringed, but tried to see it from Stacy's perspective. It was fashionable and the color suited her daughter.

"You have your Aunt Violet's eye for color," she remarked as her daughter preened in front of the mirror. "But don't you think it's a little too revealing?"

"It shows that I don't have any boobs yet," Stacy remarked with a pout.

"Stacy!" Grace tried to sound outraged, but a smile broke through."In any event, it's too old for you. It won't go with your socks and shoes."

Stacy stabbed her mother with a sherry-colored glance. "I don't want socks and flats, Mother. I want nylons and high heels." She disappeared behind a rack of party frocks.

A thread of tension wound up Grace's spine. She didn't enjoy being addressed as *Mother* rather than the more affectionate *Mama*. And she didn't like the edge to her daughter's voice. She examined another frock. It had a pattern of green and violet flowers on a white background, and came to just below the knee. It was pretty and appropriate, but Stacy, or Anastasia, as she now wanted everyone to call her, would hate it. Perhaps she should get her daughter something more sophisticated.

As she turned to the rack to choose another dress, a hanger caressed her bosom. Grace closed her eyes. It had been so long since any man had touched her in an intimate way.

"Mother?"

Grace whipped around.

Stacy stood there in a purple velvet robe with a plunging décolletage. It made her look much older than thirteen.

Grace shook her head. "Your father won't like that."

"Why not?"

Because it makes you look exactly like my mother. "You can't possibly wear that, Stacy. Whatever would your father say? It's not ladylike."

"He's not here. Besides, I like it, Mother."

Grace grabbed the dress hanging in front of her. Too late, she saw that it was a confirmation dress, its collar and cuffs edged in lace.

"That's so boring!"

"That's enough, young lady. You'll wear something that's appropriate and be grateful. There are plenty of other girls your age who can't have nice clothes."

Stacy knitted her brows together, reminding Grace again of Angelina when one of her fiery outbursts was about to erupt. Grace massaged her temples with the tips of her fingers. *Dear God, I hope Stacy—Anastasia—isn't going to take after her grandmother. Or me.* "I don't know what's gotten into you."

"I'm thirteen."

"That's not enough to choose your own wardrobe. When I was your age, I had to make do with Aunt Paulina's hand-me-downs and anything else your Aunt Violet was able to make me. We couldn't afford to buy new clothes."

Stacy rolled her eyes. Now she looked exactly like her Aunt Violet when she was about to let fly one of her sharp-tongued retorts.

Grace thinned her lips, picked up the white dress, and another one of a similar style in cream-colored fabric. For good measure, she added a dusky pink. "We'll try these on, you will pick one, and then we're going home."

But Anastasia emerged from the dressing room in an olive-green number that was in a satin fabric, cut on the bias. It had a gently scooped neckline and came down to below the knee, but was also fashionable and slinky. Her daughter was growing up and the dress suited her.

"What do you think?"

"That one suits you."

"What's wrong, Mother?"

"You're growing up and I'm going to lose you soon." Grace eased a tear away with the tip of her finger.

✠✠✠✠✠✠✠✠✠✠✠

The distinguished gentleman with white hair rose to his feet as soon as Grace and her daughter returned to the elegant mansion.

"Good day to you, Madam," he said in heavily-accented English.

Grace stiffened. Stacy leaned in close. "Who is he, Mother?"

"My name is Herr Weinstock, and I am the lawyer for His Excellency Count Carl von Lietzow," he replied, bowing his head.

As Grace stared at this elegantly-dressed lawyer, her stomach tightened into a knot. This was why she hadn't wanted to come to Berlin. She handed the shopping bag to Anastasia. "Go upstairs, *cara*. I must speak with this gentleman."

"But Mother—"

"Do as you are told," said Grace, quietly shutting the door behind her. Letting out a breath, she sat down. "Please excuse me. My daughter is young and doesn't understand."

Herr Weinstock cleared his throat as he picked up the document lying on the coffee table. "I am sorry to tell you, Madam, but His Excellency has advised me to instruct you that he will issue legal sanctions if you do not keep your court appointment."

✠✠✠✠✠✠✠✠✠✠✠

"He said what?" Nico was standing before his mirror removing his cufflinks. This was perhaps the most beautiful bedchamber that they'd ever shared, with its high ceilings, high windows, and French doors leading onto a trellised balcony. At night, several gilt mirrors enhanced the glow from the sconces.

Grace sat on the stool in front of her vanity, drooping, after yet another endless evening of dinner-party small-talk in the service of her husband's career. "He told me I had to go to court to answer questions about Peter, or the count would issue legal sanctions."

"And you actually agreed?"

The sarcasm of his tone was like a too-bright light shining into her eyes. Grace looked away as she took off one brown high-heeled shoe and massaged her foot. "Not exactly."

He eyed her. "I refuse to let my wife be dragged through this mess in a public proceeding."

She turned away and unzipped the back of her evening gown. It was chocolate brown with short sleeves, pointed revers in the front, and a fashionably low back. "It won't be a public proceeding. The count invited me to his villa, and I accepted his invitation."

"What?"

Grace glanced at her husband, the heavy satin of her evening gown sinking to the floor as she took it off. "What choice do I have? The options seem to be either a public proceeding or a private meeting."

He frowned, staring into his dressing mirror as he removed his starched collar. "You should take a lawyer with you."

"I don't want to do that," she said, unfastening her stockings and rolling them slowly down each leg. "I don't know anyone here. I don't feel comfortable."

He looked at her in his mirror. "You don't mean to tell *me* that after all he did to you, you trust him?"

Did she trust Carl? She slid into her silk nightgown, the voluptuousness of the fabric making her tingle. That thought hovered as she threw a quick look at Nico from under her lashes. He stood there, nailing her with his cool stare, his white tie dangling from his hand. Whatever she felt about Carl, she didn't want Nico's interference. Peter's parents should decide his future together.

"Of course I don't trust him," she remarked. "But I have to see him. I've told you this before, and it's true. I know you don't like it."

He turned back to the mirror and ran his hand through his hair. It was still thick, still dark, although he was graying at the temples. "I would go with you, if I could, but I cannot get away. There is too much going on with this whole business over Czechoslovakia." He looked at her again in his mirror: "*Starai bene?* Will you be all right?"

Grace smiled as she enveloped herself in a dressing gown of matching black silk. Her heart skipping, she turned away from him and discreetly removed the rest of her underclothes. "I'll be fine," she murmured as she sat before the vanity and applied cold cream.

Chapter Twenty-Nine
Wednesday, 7 September

"I'm telling you. Ignore it."

"But I can't do that." Grace clutched the latest legal document from Carl von Lietzow, instructing her to appear in court next Friday. She wore a frock of gray silk with matching high heels, all bringing out those wonderful gray eyes. Her hair was done and her face made up, almost as if she were about to go out herself. He was surprised. Grace didn't usually rise until late in the morning.

He finished knotting his tie. "Peter is an American citizen. I am a diplomat. I can provide diplomatic immunity for my family."

"You've never said that before," she murmured, her long lashes veiling her eyes.

"You know that!" He sighed to keep himself from dressing her down. He loved his wife dearly, but her vagueness about important matters drove him to distraction. He took a deep breath. "I thought you'd explained that to him."

Her head sank forward on her graceful neck, like a flower wilting under a too-hot sun.

"What have you been doing? You've had every opportunity to make him see that he can't touch Peter."

Grace turned away, her cheeks flaming.

He put on his wrist watch. "I must go." As she followed him downstairs, he said, "I'll be late this evening. Don't wait dinner for me." He pecked her cheek, put his hat on, picked up his briefcase, and left.

If this were a normal capital city, Russell would enjoy his walk to the U.S. Embassy, for it was a glorious morning in early September, the dew heavy on the well-tended lawns that nestled beside the Savignyplatz mansions. But Berlin was like a patient in a dentist's chair. Russell stepped over planks laid over newly dug holes, passing heaps of bricks. If only he had more time to attend to this matter over Peter. The trees with their turning leaves vibrated, not to the dulcet breezes of the season, but to the judder of drills and the din of cement mixers as the Nazis erected yet more monumental buildings to celebrate the new world capital of Germania. Something wasn't right. Grace was never the most assertive person at the best of times, and clearly von Lietzow required a firm hand. But why was she acting more scatterbrained than usual?

Russell paused on the corner of Budapeststrasse and Kufürstenstrasse to allow a military procession to pass, the soldiers goose-stepping energetically. On the other hand, she seemed happy here. Her eyes were bright and she held her head up, just as she had when they'd first married. *Santa Maria*, but he was a lucky man. She was still *bellissima*, and even when he was annoyed with her, as he had been just now, he longed to take her in his arms and make love to her. He crossed the street, making his way towards the Landwehr Canal. It had been years since they'd done that, not since the birth of Benny five years ago. Grace had had a difficult time, obliged to spend most of the pregnancy in bed. The doctor had shaken his head and murmured that so many pregnancies weren't good, that it was too much to have four children and three miscarriages in ten years. So he'd been celibate for the good of her health. This last year he'd made several gentle attempts, but she never seemed to be in the mood. And latterly he'd been too busy.

He emerged onto Bendlerstrasse, the nerve-center of the German High Command, and nodded to the guard at the entrance of Bendlerstrasse 39, the temporary home of the U.S. Embassy. The guard gave him the Nazi salute as his radio blared the thoughts of Hitler and his propaganda minister, the word *Juden* hissing like a profanity over and over again. Russell frowned and tightened his hold on his briefcase as he went through the iron-barred gates. He'd done brilliantly in his career, and there was talk of promoting him. His dearest wish was to be made U.S. Ambassador to Rome. But ambassadors were nominated by the president and confirmed by congress. He was going to have to play his cards extremely carefully as there were many who would jockey for that plum, especially as he didn't have the patrician background that went along with such an august posting. On the other hand, he had an outstanding military record, having been decorated with the Congressional Medal of Honor. *Grazie a Dio* he'd Anglicized his name all those years ago. Without that English veneer, he'd have no chance at all.

"Once this mess with Czechoslovakia is cleared up, we'll be able to send you back to Washington, D.C., where you can act as undersecretary of state for a couple of years," Ambassador Wilson had said to him last Friday.

"But won't you need my services here?" he'd asked. "Isn't there going to be a war?"

"I don't think it will come to that. Not with our best fellows on the job, eh?" And Wilson had cracked a smile and given Russell a friendly clap on the back. "And undersecretary would be perfect for you. Your wife is from Georgetown isn't she? She could go home, and it would be good for your career. It's what Phillips did before he became ambassador to Rome."

I could go home, Grace would be happy, I could see Lamo—except I can't. At the thought of his brother, tears pricked. Lamo had died of a heart attack a year ago, at the age of forty-eight. Lamo's absence was profound, overwhelming. Russell pushed that thought away. *Why hadn't he told Grace they might be going home soon? Because he never seemed to have much time for her these days.*

"Ah, there you are, Russell," said Ambassador Wilson. "Early, I see. That's good, because I need to talk to you about Czechoslovakia."

"What has happened?"

"You're usually the first to know. But of course, I gave you the weekend off to be with your lovely wife. How is she?"

Russell murmured something. "What happened?" he said again.

"Things are escalating. There have been a couple of German deaths in Mährisch Östrau, in the Sudetenland. And an editorial in the London *Times* has suggested that the best way of solving the Czech crisis would be if the Sudetenland were incorporated into the Third Reich."

"Oh, Lord." Russell took the paper and scanned quickly. It was well-known that *Times* editorials reflected the opinions of the British government. "Herr Hitler will definitely march on Prague now."

"Maybe. But I believe he can be controlled. It will certainly give the American press, controlled by the Jews of course, the perfect ammunition they need to sing a hymn of hate against the Nazis, while Herr Hitler makes every effort over here to build a better future."

"Do you believe he is building a better future for the Jews, sir?"

"The Jews need to be taken down a peg or two," replied Wilson, jabbing a finger at Russell. "Otherwise they'll end up controlling everything. Look around you. You were here back in '22. Can't you see how much better things are? Herr Hitler has led his people from moral and economic despair into a state of pride and very evident prosperity." He leaned closer and scrutinized Russell's face. "That counts for something, don't you think?"

Russell kept the muscles of his face still. *Should he say something? What about all the food shortages, the sludgy "coffee," the wurst filled with stale bread?* "What do you wish me to do about this latest crisis, sir?"

"Ah, I almost forgot. How good is your Czech?"

"Not wonderful."

"You're too modest, my dear fellow. You're one of our best linguists."

"I haven't had much time for study."

"I need you to get on the next train to Prague. Find out what the Czech fortifications are like and what Prague intends to do about this. Antonia has your tickets for you." He checked his watch. "Your train leaves in a couple of hours."

✠✠✠✠✠✠✠✠✠✠✠

As his footsteps faded away, Grace sagged against the front door. He was so consumed with his work, he'd forgotten her birthday. Today, Grace turned thirty-four, making her older than Mother had been when she died. Slowly, she closed the door, walked upstairs and entered their bedroom. Picking up a bottle of pills, she swallowed two. She'd spent the last several days rehearsing what she was going to say to Carl. She stood in front of the mirror to put on her hat, a gray pill-box with netting. As she did so, a warning whispered up her spine. Nico didn't want her to go, preferring to shield her behind their as-yet-unhired lawyers. But what about Peter? Grace remembered too well how her relatives had fought over her marriage, battling Nico at every turn.

She grimaced at the memory of Mother's shouting matches with him and took a deep breath. The fact was, she needed to answer these legal briefs, and a private visit seemed the best way. She opened her eyes and straightened her spine. She would explain to Carl that Nico was offering their son a brilliant future in the United States. Picking up her purse and gloves in matching gray leather, she made for the stairs. She must see him now—

The front door bell clanged, making her jump. Who could it be at this hour? She listened intently as Frau Hoffmann shuffled toward the door and greeted a man who spoke German.

"Frau Graatz," the housekeeper called. "A visitor."

"I'll be down soon," she replied before closing the bedroom door. He was here already.

Her stomach clenched into a fist. Quickly, she took off her hat and gloves, placing her purse on the vanity. *I must get to him before he meets Peter.* She ran a brush through her hair. *At least Peter would probably be on his way to school.* Checking that her wedding ring, engagement, and eternity rings were prominently displayed on her left heart finger, she forced herself to walk slowly down the stairs.

"Liebchen!" His eyes ran over her like a caress. "How becoming you look this morning." He kissed her hand with a flourish.

"Mother?" Peter lifted his head from a pile of photographs he'd been studying.

Grace froze. Oh no. How had Carl known what time he left each morning? As she drew closer she could see that the photos were of a young man in officer's uniform. The likeness was uncanny.

Grace's cheeks warmed. She cleared her throat. "This is Count Carl von Lietzow."

Carl smiled at their son. "Your mother and I were great friends sixteen years ago, in Berlin."

Grace winced as he let his voice linger on the word *sixteen*.

Peter's blue eyes hardened and became the color of ice. How like his father he was. Peter had Carl's build, his blue eyes, and his round face. Had he been happy in the home she'd tried to make for him? He'd been a stocky blond in a family of slender Italians. "Why didn't you tell me?"

Grace's cheeks fired up, the flush spreading all the way down her neck.

It was that simple, the shattering of a secret.

She supplicated, extending her hands. "I wanted to protect you. Your father—that is, your stepfather, can give you diplomatic immunity. You are an American citizen, Peter."

"Does Father—Mr. Russell—know?"

Grace nodded.

"I'm surprised at you, Mother. I never imagined you would allow—such things to happen. I always thought you were a lady."

Carl frowned. "You should not talk to your mother in that way. It was not her fault. She was very young, only a couple of years older than you when it—happened. You see, I was going to marry your mother."

Peter's face softened.

Carl sat next to their son. "You may have noticed that your mother is a very beautiful woman. She acquired many admirers here in Berlin. Her relatives, her uncle and aunt, her great-aunt, even her sister Miss Violet, were all in favor of *our* marriage. What I hadn't realized is that the very persistent Mr. Russell decided to visit her in Berlin as a way of making one last plea for his suit. He arrived in Berlin and—-spirited your mother away."

"Why didn't *you* prevent that from happening?"

"That is my greatest regret. I have to say that in that case, Mr. Russell bested me." Carl looked down. "He knocked me out in a fight."

Peter stared at his father. "I never imagined Father—I mean Mr. Russell—could be violent. He doesn't seem like the kind of person who would do that. I mean he's a diplomat and all…"

Carl smiled grimly. "Believe me, he went for me in a furious rage. I still have the headaches to prove it."

Peter studied Carl with some awe. "And what about you, Mother?"

"I was planning to marry Carl."

"So why did you marry Mr. Russell?"

"I had to." Grace turned away, Russell's voice telling her yet again that if she abandoned him, he'd shoot himself.

"But now that your mother is back in Berlin, we have a chance to rectify things. I intend to make her my countess and —"

"Is he the evil man Papa told me about?"

Peter grimaced.

"Benedetto!" exclaimed Grace.

"Father says my name is Benny. He doesn't like Italian names."

Carl zigzagged an eyebrow. "Why not? He is—you are all Italian, are you not?"

Benny cocked his head to one side. "Sort of."

"Can you tell me your age, young man?"

"I'm five years old."

"When is your birthday?"

"November the ninth."

As Carl put her youngest at ease and Peter returned to those photographs, Grace deliberated. How could she explain about the intolerance Italians faced in the United States? It had been eleven years since the execution of Sacco and Vanzetti, and feelings against Italian-Americans ran so high that most were obliged to hide behind Anglicized names, which is how

Graziella and Domenico Pagano had become Grace and Nicholas Russell. How lucky they were that Domenico—Nico—was able to take their family abroad so very frequently, so that they could enjoy their Italian heritage. At least in the privacy of their home.

She came to as Benny giggled. Carl was turning his stick so that the rubies flashed in the morning sunlight.

"Can I do that?"

While the child, entranced, made those rubies sparkle, Carl leaned forward and whispered conspiratorially. "And what is your real name?"

"My real name is Benedetto Girolamo Domenico." Benny jumped up and handed the stick back. "But I'm only allowed to tell that to family members," he remarked, before skipping out of the room.

Carl chuckled. "It seems I've been promoted. What an Italian accent he has."

"His father made him repeat it until he got it right," said Grace, her smile relaxing the muscles of her face.

"Speaking of birthdays, I wish to present you with a small gift." Carl fumbled in his jacket pocket and produced a jewelry box.

"Carl—You know I can't possibly accept—"

"Why don't you open it and see?"

Slowly, Grace undid the clasp. Inside was a silver collar set with semi-precious stones. Peter came forward. "Here, Mother, let me." He clasped it around her neck.

"What do you think?" Carl drew her towards the large mirror that hung over the fireplace. The stones were opalescent, catching the light in her eyes.

The door opened."*Tesoro mio*, I have to leave for Prague immediately. Could you—?"

Nico's dark gaze skittered around the room, taking everything in. He stiffened. "I see you have company."

"This is Count Carl von Lietzow."

"I can see that for myself. What are you doing here?"

"I've come to meet my son."

"Why didn't you tell me who my father was?"

Russell's cheeks turned dull red as he glanced at Peter. "I was hoping that your mother and I wouldn't have to." He swept von Lietzow with a glare. "Clearly, circumstances have forced our hand."

Peter's pale blue eyes fastened on Nico's dark brown ones for a long moment, Peter's youthful face mimicking Nico's immobility until there was a slight softening around the jaw line.

Nico stuck his chin out and returned Peter's gaze without blinking, as if he were dealing with a tiresome dinner-party acquaintance.

"It's true then." Peter moved away from Nico. "I'm illegitimate. My life is ruined, Mother—and it is your fault."

Carl rose to his feet. "Young man, you must not speak so disrespectfully to your mother. You are my heir. I have great plans for you—"

"Peter is an American citizen," said Nico between clenched teeth. "I have diplomatic immunity. There's no way in which I'm going to give up my son—"

"But you have just admitted that he is not your son. Why should you care? I have a perfect right to invite *my* son to *my* villa at Kladow—"

Nico compressed his lips. "I'm afraid that's not possible."

"But we'll have to visit Carl now," remarked Grace, "now that Peter knows who his father is."

Nico paled. "I absolutely forbid it. I will not have my family involved with that—*quella figa,* that p***y."

Carl went white. "You cannot hide behind your language of origin, Herr Russell. I understand Italian perfectly well. And you have just insulted me. I demand an apology."

Peter raised his head. "I have a right to see my father, Mr. Russell." There was an edge to his tone Grace had never heard before.

Nico glared back unblinking. Slowly his cheeks reddened. "Damn him," he muttered under his breath. "I don't have time to deal with this, I'm on my way to Prague." He banged up the stairs.

"Oh dear." Grace sank onto the loveseat.

"Liebchen, don't worry. I can handle your husband."

Grace raised her tear-stained face. "I think you should go, I have to help him pack."

"You think I'm going to leave without our son?"

"He's very upset," she whispered, glancing at Peter. "They both are. We need time to get used to this. Please go now."

"If you—insist."

She nodded.

"Very well. I am at your service Liebchen. For now." He kissed her hand, then turned to Peter. "We should get to know each other. No? You are not illegitimate. You are my son and heir."

Peter responded with a faint smile.

"I invite you to my villa at Kladow to talk things over, with your mother. Would you like that?"

Peter smiled more. "Yes, sir."

"Capital. Expect to hear from me soon." Carl offered his arm to Grace, and they walked outside. Just before he stepped into the waiting limousine, he kissed her gently on the lips.

"You are as lovely as ever. And that necklace suits you, it belonged to my mother." He kissed her more slowly. "Auf Wiedersehn, Liebchen."

Grace wobbled back to their rented mansion, her senses reeling.

"He's gone?" Nico stood just outside the front door, holding a small suitcase.

Grace's cheeks flamed.

He shot her a searching look. "You're rattled. Perhaps I shouldn't go to Prague. I don't like seeing you like this."

Grace pressed her lips together and held her tongue.

Nico sighed as Anastasia appeared, holding Benny's hand.

"I'll be back in a week."

Grace allowed him to pull her close, but when his lips claimed hers, she turned her head.

She felt him stiffen. "What is this?"

Grace extricated herself from his arms.

"Grace! Are you refusing your husband? Are you refusing *me*?"

She glared back. "Is it too much to ask you not to make a scene in public?"

He lunged at her, his dark eyes blazing.

She stepped back, shielding the children.

"Clearly, I should stay," he snarled as the limousine from the embassy drove up and purred at the curb, "but I have to go." He gave a hiss of exasperation through his teeth. "If you wish to spend your time with that—*stronzo*, a**hole, I can't stop you," he spat. "But understand this, if *he* makes threats, *you* behave inappropriately, or *our* children are dragged into this mess, I will fight him!" His face was so close, drops of spittle hit her face.

Grace flinched as Marina skipped across the lawn. Keeping her head bent, she held the folds of her voluminous skirts that came down to just below the knee.

"I heard voices. I'm sorry I'm late but I wanted to show you my new dress, the one with the birds." She came forward, smoothing out a blue satin frock showered with white embroidery around the neckline, depicting birds of various kinds. "There's a thrush, a lark, a wagtail, and a warbler. How do you say it in German?" She raised her head and stopped. "Papa! Where's the funny man?"

Nico gave Grace a look of pure loathing. "*Così. E 'stato qui prima,* he's been here before."

Grace didn't answer.

The waiting limousine honked politely.

"*Cazzo!* F***!" Nico shot her a thunderous look and left.

✠✠✠✠✠✠✠✠✠✠✠

As they entered the mansion, Anastasia turned to her mother. "What was that about? You've never mentioned your boyfriend—"

Grace sagged against the doorway. "Anastasia, I need you to help the little ones get ready. I must visit Count von Lietzow. Frau Hoffman will help you." Slowly she walked upstairs, opening the white-paneled door to the bedroom while Anastasia's question reverberated in her head.

Carl had managed to outmaneuver them all. Why hadn't she seen that coming? More to the point, why hadn't Nico seen that coming? He was usually a superb strategist. *Because he doesn't have time,* the voice in her head reminded her. Picking up a bottle of pills, she stared at it for a moment, put it down, and stared unseeingly out the bedroom window. The rising sun warmed her face but offered little comfort. Should she visit Carl? She shoved the memory of his kisses aside and forced herself to concentrate. What would happen if she didn't go? There would be more threats, more difficulties. Did she really want to face a phalanx of German lawyers, who might say indelicate things about herself and Nico? Her reputation, as well as his gosh darn-it career that she had sacrificed so much for, would be in ruins.

Absently she wiped her clammy hands on her dress, then frowned as she saw faint marks of moisture on the gray satin.

Grace went over to the armoire and rummaged. She couldn't go in that ruined frock, she needed something fresh. One with three-quarter sleeves would do nicely. She flinched as she dropped a powder blue number onto her bed. Blue always reminded her of the color of her sister's eyes. Where was Violet now? What was she doing? She wished she could just pick up the phone and ask her sister for advice, but they never reconnected, not since Violet had left abruptly all those years ago. That memory caused Grace to pause, as she re-experienced the pain of that rejection all over again. Tears welled, and she pinched herself in frustration. *Why was she always on the verge of tears these days? Thank goodness she'd managed not to cry in front of the men. How stupid that would've been.*

Grace glanced at the clock that squatted on the bedside table next to her side of the bed. It was already quarter to ten. She must go—before she talked herself out of it. She must return that necklace.

Chapter Thirty

Wednesday, 7 September

The train left the Berlin *Hauptbahnhof* at ten precisely, heading due south in the direction of Prague. Russell sat in his first-class compartment, a map of Czechoslovakia spread before him, a Czech phrasebook at hand. The Sudetenland was the German-speaking part of Czechoslovakia that lay in the western and northern parts of the country, forming a crescent around Prague. He set his jaw and concentrated on the task at hand. The fortifications that the Czech government was putting in place were along the border that faced north towards Ratibor and the Cosel region of Upper Silesia, where Adolf Hitler's Second Army was waiting. Russell planned to spend a day or two in Prague, then find a way of somehow slipping into the Sudetenland to spy on those fortifications. He didn't have much time; Berlin wanted him back in a week.

He looked out the window as he sipped his coffee, forcing himself to think about something innocuous. After his sojourn in Tokyo, Russell had been looking forward to his return to Berlin and its famed cafés. It should have been the perfect place for coffee, but it was now so expensive that most establishments served ersatz blends with the bitter taste of chicory. This coffee was unexpectedly flavorful, smooth, complex, dark. It had mysteriously appeared, like *il cazzo*, that prick von Lietzow. Russell's fury mounted, threatening to choke him. His hands shook with rage, causing precious drops to slide down the outside of the bone china cup. He put his cup and saucer down. He'd never known his wife to rebuff his advances. He eased his fingers under his starched shirt collar. Surely she didn't prefer her rapist to her husband? His cheeks thudded with heat. How could she do that do him, when he'd taken her on so gallantly, marrying her so that her reputation would remain unsullied? She was just like her mother.

As if on cue, Angelina's face materialized in his mind's eye, her lips twisted into a delighted smile.

Russell lowered his face into his hands. Was this truly the end of everything he'd possessed with Grace? It was hard to believe their marriage, their passion for each other, could dissolve so rapidly. When he insisted on going to Berlin, he never imagined he might lose his wife. Jagged chunks of ice slowly filled his stomach. There was absolutely nothing he could do. He had to swallow his emotions and get on with the commission given by Wilson. He couldn't fail State now, not when the stakes were so high.

Russell ground his teeth as his headache pounded. What was Grace doing? He had to reach her somehow, if only to prevent the frail thread of their marriage from snapping. Promising himself that he would call or telegraph frequently, he shoved his emotions away and picked up his Czech phrasebook.

The train rolled smoothly out of the Dresden Hauptbahnhof. Russell kept his head down, compelling himself to conjugate irregular verbs in Czech. A shadow crossed his map of Czechoslovakia. A well-dressed fellow with intense eyes stood in the doorway. He looked vaguely familiar.

"I see you don't remember me."

Russell frowned.

"Carl Friedrich Goerdeler at your service."

Russell stood, shook hands, and invited him to sit down. As the new foreign officer at the U.S. Embassy, he'd been approached by Goerdeler shortly after arriving in Berlin. Russell had been surprised to have his lunch at the Casino Club interrupted by a German civil servant who warned him about the aggressive and dangerous foreign policy of the Nazis. Why had Goerdeler been telling him that? His colleagues at the embassy had laughed it off, saying that Goerdeler was known to be eccentric and indiscreet. *I wonder if there is more going on.* Russell ordered another cup of coffee for his companion.

"I was hoping you'd be on this train," said Goerdeler in English. His clipped accent might have sounded British, except for his vowel sounds and intonation, which were entirely German.

"How did you know?"

"Do you remember a chap named Phelps?"

"Charles Phelps?" That was a name from a long time ago. He'd also had a promising career at the State Department, but their paths had never crossed. Russell made sure of it. "I haven't seen him in years."

"Well you wouldn't have. He's been posted to Moscow. I know his sister Mabel. She's on her way back from seeing her brother. Their parents are dead and I understand they've inherited quite a fortune."

"What does that have to do with me?"

"It turns out that she knows everyone at the embassy, and people do talk. Even at the American Embassy." He looked up, his bright gray eyes flashing beneath heavy brows. "She knew I wanted to see you, and so she was good enough to let me know your whereabouts."

A prickle of unease made the hairs on the backs of Russell's arms tingle. Was this story true? It seemed unlikely. The foreign service officers he'd met were dedicated to their work and not likely to casually mention the whereabouts of their colleagues, for loose talk cost lives. He took a cigarette from his monogrammed case and offered one to Goerdeler, who accepted with thanks. "You didn't come here to tell me this."

Goerdeler brushed his mustache with the back of one finger. "Do you know a fellow named Oster?"

Russell shook his head.

"But you've heard of the *Abwehr*?"

"Of course." The Abwehr was the German intelligence-gathering organization.

"You have connections there?"

"I always make it a rule never to discuss my connections with people I don't know well."

"That's very commendable. I see I need to establish my *bona fides*." He felt in his pocket and produced a crumpled piece of paper. It was a letter of introduction to various people in England signed by Admiral Wilhelm Canaris, head of the Abwehr.

"You visited England in the past year?"

"I tried to warn them about Herr Hitler's foreign policy. I told them he was dangerously out of control."

"What did they say?"

"Not much."

I'm not surprised. Russell inhaled deeply on his cigarette as he regarded Goerdeler. *They were probably perplexed by such talk*. He remembered seeing a note from Sir Nevile Henderson, Great Britain's ambassador to Berlin, that had shared some details on Goerdeler. Sir Nevile had concluded his summary by saying something like, "I am inclined to be chary of uninhibited advice from Germans."

Goerdeler returned his stare. "I went to see them again this spring."

"You did?"

"I told them that if Herr Hitler hadn't manipulated the timing of the *Anschluss*, the army would have got rid of him and his Nazis in a *putsch*."

"You mean to say that Herr Hitler suspected this? That he deliberately made sure that his top commanders were in the field for the Anschluss to *prevent* this coup d'état from occurring?"

Goedeler smiled faintly.

"Who are these people involved in the *putsch*?"

"They're called *Die Schwarze Kapelle*." Goerdeler leaned forward, his intense eyes meeting Russell's, as his voice sank to a thread of whisper.

The Black Orchestra? Russell scrutinized his face. *Was this really true? If so, who was the conductor?*

"Oster is their leader," remarked Goerdeler.

"The fellow you mentioned earlier?"

"You don't miss much. That's good. When you return to Berlin, look up Obersleutnant Hans Oster. You'll find him in the *Abwehr.*"

"But why would the army launch a coup? Don't most of them support Hitler? Haven't they taken an oath of allegiance?"

Goerdeler leaned forward and spoke under his breath. "It's a long story that goes all the way back to *der Nacht der langen Messer*, the Night of Long Knives, when two senior army generals were murdered. But if I had to summarize it in one sentence I would say that we are all motivated by fear that the Austrian corporal's raging thirst for war will lead to another humiliating defeat for the German army, and the ruination of our beloved fatherland." He rose abruptly and went to the door.

"You are leaving?"

"Did your colleagues at the American Embassy mention a Colonel Stronge?"

Russell shook his head.

"He's in Prague. Colonel H.C.T. Stronge British military attaché. He's a good fellow. I know him personally. He'll have something interesting to tell you." Goerdeler opened the door and said in German, just as the waiter arrived with lunch, "Please give Fräulein Mabel my warmest greetings and tell her I'm looking forward to another *tête-à-tête.*"

While the waiter set the table and poured wine, Russell grabbed his notebook, and wrote down in code:

Meet Colonel Stronge in Prague. Military expert.

Meet Lieutenant Colonel Oster in Berlin. Black Orchestra.

Invite Mabel Phelps over for tea.

He sank back in his seat. There was something familiar about that last name. It had something to do with Grace, which was surprising as she didn't make friends easily. Grace depended on him for everything, and these days he no longer had the time to make her happy, something which that sonofabitch had noted and was using to his own advantage. *Dio serpente,* he'd even remembered her birthday. He put his hand in front of his face to blot out thoughts that were causing his stomach to roil with rage. He must focus. Of course. He knew that name because Mabel Phelps was the one friend Grace had made all those years ago. In Berlin.

✠✠✠✠✠✠✠✠✠✠✠

As the sound of the taxi vanished down the drive, Grace stood in front of the door of Count von Lietzow's villa in Kladow for a long moment, for the memories were painful and plentiful. How naïve she'd been as a seventeen-year-old, so naïve that she hadn't realized that he was proposing marriage to her. *How had he put it?* He'd talked about his newly decorated villa, and the practice room he'd had installed for her. Why didn't she connect the dots and understand that he wanted her to be his wife? Then, before she'd had time to draw breath, he'd talked to Aunt Louisa about it, and she couldn't disappoint her family by backing out. *Except that she'd disappointed them anyway, by marrying Nico.*

Grace stared at the door. It was painted silver gray and had an art nouveau flourish around its edge. She'd never actually rung the bell before because she'd always been accompanied by someone. The door would open, and one of his flunkies would bow and murmur a greeting as she'd entered, escorted either by her relatives or by the count himself. Now she was totally alone, and—where was he? He had an uncanny habit of anticipating her next move. She hadn't announced her visit, but might he be waiting for her behind that closed door?

She clenched her jaw and pressed the buzzer. A loud clang resounded within. There was a pause, then the door opened. Count Carl von Lietzow stood there by himself.

"*Liebchen!*" he exclaimed, his face brightening. "I wasn't expecting to have the pleasure of your company so soon. I take it your husband has gone on his errand to Prague?"

Grace nodded.

Carl chuckled. "Come in, come in. Make yourself at home."

She followed him into the reception room. He sat on a Louis Quinze sofa and patted the space next to him. She found an upright chair opposite, sitting stiffly with her knees together.

"Can I offer you anything to drink?"

She shook her head. The furnishings were much as she remembered, Louis Quinze in white-painted wood with blue silk toile. She turned her gaze back to him. He'd taken out a pipe and was lighting it.

She studied the carpet. It was in matching colors of cream and blue with a wavy rococo border. *Would Peter be happy here? Would Carl be able to give him opportunities that, perhaps, couldn't be expected of Nico?* It hadn't occurred to her when she married Nico that he might have a hard time dealing with his rival's son, that he mightn't have been able to be impartial or fair when confronted with the child. Now Peter had failed his entrance examination to the *Technische Hochschule* and was being punished with months of intensive study. If he didn't get in a second time, what would Nico do?

Carl puffed on his pipe as he sat near that beautifully carved mantlepiece she'd admired all those years ago. "I've imagined you sitting here with me for so many years, Liebchen. It is a real treat to have you here, at last."

Grace turned her head to wipe away an inevitable tear.

"I've never forgiven him for what he did," he threw out, his voice hard. "I am not the most moral person in the world, but I would never have told a vulnerable seventeen-year-old that I would kill myself if she refused to marry me. If that is not moral perversion, then I don't know what is."

Grace dabbed her eyes, continuing to study the carpet, noting that it was dusty and faded. She could have been here and taken care of everything. She should have been here. She would have been here, if Nico hadn't blackmailed her. Grace flinched. What an ugly word that was. Her insides twisted. She'd made a terrible mistake. Naïvely, she'd believed Nico would help her with her career. It had never occurred to her that he would be so self-centered, so consumed with ambition, that he would break his implicit promise to her.

"I did not know that he and his brother—that *soi-disant* priest—would prove to be such tough adversaries. I had no idea I would be dealing with members of the Chicago mob—

what do they call themselves? Ah yes, the Chicago Outfit. I would have brought along reinforcements—"

She cleared her throat and looked him in the eye. "We need to talk about Peter."

"My life was empty without you," remarked Carl, "and so my thoughts turned increasingly to how I could help my country. I was concerned about the way Germany had been treated. The DNVP was against the Versailles *Diktat* and wanted a restoration of the monarchy. I helped out by giving money and organizing events."

"Why are you telling me this?"

"Because it's important for you to know these things, as the mother of the next Count von Lietzow." He sucked on his pipe, causing a billow of smoke to unfurl. "Have you been keeping up with German politics?"

She remained silent.

"The DNVP is the *Deutschnationale Volkspartei,* the German National People's Party if you like. When Kuno von Westarp left in 1929, I followed. The next four years were chaotic for Germany, politically and in many other ways. Then, in 1933, political parties were banned."

"After Herr Hitler came to power?"

A smile lit his face. "So you have been keeping up with what has been happening in Germany, *Liebchen.*"

Grace studied him. He must have thought of leaving, many times, but he came from a family of Prussian aristocrats that went back centuries. He would see it as his duty to serve his country. *What exactly had he been doing? And what did it mean for Peter?*

"What can you do if political parties have been banned?"

"Much. Political activity has gone underground since the ban, but it is not dead. Many people in my position are trying to do something for the country that we love. My greatest friend—Ah! But I cannot talk about that to *mein Liebchen*, much though I would like to."

She stared at him.

"You are American, and that husband of yours is in the State Department. These matters are too dangerous to speak about." He knocked the ash out his pipe and got up. "May I offer you something? A sherry? Tea? Champagne? It is your birthday today."

He must have stockpiled his luxuries. "What about Peter? You're not suggesting that I should leave my son with you and expose him to danger?"

"*Liebchen*, what do you take me for? He is *our* son, and my heir. Of course I'm not going to expose him to unnecessary danger." He moved towards the door.

Grace rose to her feet. "You can't expect me to hand him over without more assurance than that!"

He smiled. "I admire your attitude, *Liebchen*. Truly I do. But let's talk it over calmly. Would you like champagne?"

Grace narrowed her eyes.

"It is true the situation is not what I would wish. It may require you to make some sacrifices."

She drew in a deep breath. "I'd like some tea, please."

"Capital! I won't be long." He disappeared, leaving Grace by herself in the dilapidated grandeur of his reception room.

Grace sat there her eyes half-closed. As the minutes ticked by, the room settled, becoming quieter. Where were his servants? Was he so poor that he was reduced to getting her tea by himself? But that didn't make sense, because his villa was on his ancestral lands near the village of Kladow, where he was well-known. She remembered a conversation they'd had about the German economy sixteen years ago. The mark had been falling through the floor, and everyone was worried about money. When she'd pressed him, Carl had assured her that he'd invested in American Steel, and that she shouldn't worry. Perhaps his investments hadn't been enough.

The mid-morning sunshine slanted into the silent room, bearing the shadow of a large tree outside. A crunch of gravel made her glance up. But there was no one there. The room settled back into its quietude. The crunch sounded again. Grace got up and peered out the window. The crunch paused, letting in a flood of birdsong. Then it started again. It stopped and a soft tendril of air blew a low murmur of voices to her. Grace craned her neck but could see nothing. The footsteps disappeared, melting into the gentle sound of autumnal breezes.

After several more minutes he returned, bearing a tray of tea-things. He poured hers with a flourish, handing it to her in an elegant cup that Grace recognized as the fine Meissen porcelain they'd chosen together all those years ago.

She sipped her tea in silence, inhaling the aromatic blend of finely-selected leaves mixed in with bergamot.

He patted the seat beside him. "Why don't you come sit here so we can chat more comfortably?"

She picked up her teacup.

"*Liebchen*, you would make an old man very happy."

She glanced at him. His smiling eyes suggested the still waters of a summer-afternoon lake. *How much more pleasant things would be if she just did what he wanted. But she wasn't here to flirt.* She put her cup and saucer down. "I'm here to talk about Peter. Someone has just paid a surreptitious visit to your house."

"Ah! So my *Liebchen* heard that."

"Is that why you left to make tea? I need to know exactly what is going on."

"And so you shall. When you become my countess."

"You're not suggesting—"

"I'm not suggesting anything. I told you a few moments ago that you would be required to make sacrifices for our son. You don't want to leave him with me. Very well. Then why not divorce Russell and become my countess? That way, you can be actively involved in our son's life."

"You know I can't do that. Nico would never let me go." She rose and held out the jewel box. "I really cannot accept your present."

"*Liebchen*, surely you're not telling me that you allow that husband of yours to control every aspect of your life."

"We took our vows before a priest."

"Ah! Those Catholic marriages. I take it then, that you go to church regularly?"

An image of the dark interior of a church filled her mind, candles glinting from its dark corners, the sweet woody smell of incense, disembodied ethereal voices. How she loved *a cappella* singing. Grace put the jewel box on an occasional table.

"Has your religion helped you with your life?" His words intruded, an uncomfortable reminder that it had been so long since she'd been to the confessional because she had nothing to tell, so long since she'd prayed to God and the Virgin Mary because they'd stopped talking to her. She couldn't remember when she'd stopped her private observances. It had something to do with Nico. He was the pious one in the marriage, and so, one day she'd stopped praying just to see if he'd notice. He hadn't.

"You don't have to allow old-fashioned ways to shackle you."

"But I have a duty to my family."

"You have a duty to your children."

"There's no way Nico would allow me to have custody of them."

"Are you sure? He's too busy to look after his children."

"He's very fond of Benny. I think he has plans for him to join State, eventually."

"Benedetto is his son and heir. What about his daughters?"

A thread of pain wound around Grace's forehead. She wasn't a good mother. She'd allowed herself to become too preoccupied with Anastasia, her prickly adolescent, at the expense of the others. Marina and Benny deserved better than to be left to shift for themselves, caught between an absent father and a preoccupied mother. Even Peter, her firstborn, had been left too much to himself. He had a tendency to wander off and get into scrapes. He needed a strong hand.

The silence drew out as her tears spilled down her cheeks.

He patted the seat beside him. "*Liebchen*, why don't you come here so that I can dry your tears?"

Slowly, Grace drifted over to where he sat on the Louis Quinze sofa.

He took her hand and kissed it. "That's better." He held her hand for a while, interlacing his fingers with hers. "Losing my *Liebchen* was the worst thing that ever happened to me."

She turned away.

He leaned closer, his breath hot on her cheek. "I took infinite pains to make you happy. Don't you remember one special afternoon? And how afterwards, you laughed? You told me you'd never expected to be so happy. Those were your exact words."

She looked down, her cheeks warming. *It was true, Carl had been a skillful lover, better than Nico if she allowed herself to think about the difference. But it had been so long since she'd made love with her husband, she could scarcely remember it any more.*

When she looked up, she found his blue eyes boring gently into hers. He took her hand and kissed it, then put one arm around her, causing her to melt into the warmth of his body.

She veiled her eyes with her lashes. She was aching for intimacy and didn't pull away. He raised his head, gazed into her eyes, and then lowered his head, thrusting his tongue into her mouth.

Her eyes opened.

He kissed her slowly, luxuriating in the movement of his mouth against her lips, while his hands slowly slid down her back.

She stared at the wallpaper, at the scenes of shepherds and shepherdesses etched in white over a background of Prussian blue, the color of his eyes.

He sighed as he settled her legs across his lap. Kissing her hand, he took one high-heeled pump off. He lowered his lips to her mouth, while his fingers wandered up her stockinged leg.

Grace tensed and closed her eyes. It was almost as if his kisses had anesthetized her, destroying any will power she might possess. As his fingers reached the bare skin of her thighs, she moaned. He rested there for a moment, the tips of his fingers burning her cool thighs while he made small circles on its delicate skin. Then he slid under her panties, into that warm, wet place between the legs.

She gasped and arched, contracting around his fingers.

"Liebchen," he murmured, a smile in his voice, as he eased off the slip of silk.

I must stop. I must think about Anastasia, and Marina and Benny—

But he came inside, and then it was all over. She lay slumped on his elegant sofa, her legs spread apart, while her body thrummed. She'd forgotten how alive he could make her feel. Finally, she'd come home.

Chapter Thirty-One

Wednesday, 7 September

Arriving at the British Embassy, Russell found Colonel Stronge in the lounge. At first reluctant to talk, Stronge opened up when Russell provided the State Department papers, explaining how the Czech High Command had issued the unusual invitation of letting him take a three-day tour of the fortifications.

"It's not just a wall." Stronge gulped his beer. "It's a whole system of defense."

"I suppose there is no chance I could get an invitation." Russell sipped an iced tonic topped by a swirl of lime.

Stronge tapped the side of his reddish nose. "The Czechs don't want this to get into the wrong hands. They want to give the krauts a nasty surprise. You'll have to snoop around by yourself, old boy."

Hurrying next to the American Embassy, Russell presented himself to Ambassador Wilbur J. Carr. A balding bespectacled gentleman in his sixties, Carr looked up from a neat pile of papers as Russell entered his office, a smile warming his face.

"Mr. Russell, I'm glad to see you, sir. Come in, come in. What can I get you? A drop of bourbon on ice? Or the local slivovitz? Or would you prefer a mint julep?" He held up his highball.

"I'll take just a splash of bourbon—with plenty of ice, sir."

"There's nothing like a bourbon for restoring the nerves," remarked Carr in his soft-spoken way as he added a generous amount to the glass.

Russell permitted himself one abstemious sip before placing the drink on one of the occasional tables that dotted the room.

Carr sat on a loveseat, waving Russell to sit next to him. "I've heard a good deal about you, sir," he said slowly, crossing one leg. He glanced at the abandoned drink. "Not a heavy drinker?"

Russell flushed at the slight edge to Carr's mellow voice. "Can you tell me more about the Sudetenland?"

Carr laughed. "We'll have time to discuss that at dinner."

"But time is of the essence—"

Carr waved his objection aside and leaned forward. "You're highly regarded, I hear." His light-colored eyes probed Russell's.

Russell stared back, silent.

Carr leaned back in his seat. "I'm told you're a gifted linguist."

"You're too kind, sir," replied Russell, tightening his jaw.

Carr took a final swallow of his mint julep and rose. "We have seven acres of gardens here. I'm fond of gardening, it was hard for me to leave my home on Wyoming Avenue in the District. Do you like gardening much yourself?"

"There isn't time," replied Russell, thinning his lips as a vision of Grace assaulted him. She'd been so young and so happy when they'd first married, taking a picnic to him in their vineyard in the Veneto where he pruned the vines every day. She hadn't known anything about farming or setting up house, but she'd been so willing to learn.

A glint of amusement lit Carr's face as he put a hand on Russell's shoulder. "You'll appreciate the view, then."

The gardens stretched before them, running uphill to a belvedere, where the flat white walls of Prague Castle, topped by the fairy-tale towers of St. Vitus Cathedral, soared above them.

"Can't complain about the digs either." Carr gestured behind him. "The Czechs have given us a hundred-and-forty-room palace to go along with these magnificent gardens." He leaned against a column that formed an elegant arcade, the very picture of a southern gentleman on his plantation.

"You're very quiet," smiled Carr. "Is something bothering you?"

How Russell ached for her presence. How he lusted after her. Even her hands had power, for no one could soothe away his headaches the way she could. Yet those hands had been used for other things, like coaxing sounds out of her violin. But she no longer played. Something in his gut clenched as he wondered why not. He raised his head.

"A lot bothers me these days," he snapped. "I am bothered by Hitler and his régime. I am bothered by the Nuremberg Laws, which deprive Jews of their citizenship and bar them from voting, holding office, practicing medicine—"

"But they're just *kikes*," drawled Carr. "They're filthy and often dangerous in their habits."

Russell glared for a flicker of an instant, before hastily casting his eyes down. *He is exactly like Wilson*. Ambassador Wilson's continual endorsement of the Nazi régime was a thorn in his side. Why hadn't he spoken up more forcefully the other day? *Because you want that ambassadorship to Italy*, the voice in his head remarked.

Carr retrieved a cigarette case from his inside pocket and held it open. Russell shook his head, watching in silence as Carr nonchalantly lit up.

Why was State packed with people who were so anti-Semitic? Couldn't these people appreciate what was happening in Germany, or were they so blinded by their own prejudices? Couldn't Secretary Hull see how this was going to hamper the ability of the U.S. to help the Jews, who, even now, were clamoring for visas?

Are you going to speak up? asked the voice in his head. He cleared his throat. "I'm concerned about this crisis over the Sudetenland. It wouldn't surprise me if this were a set-up so that Hitler could march into Prague."

"You don't believe that!" Carr turned to him sharply, before his face relaxed into a smooth smile.

"One of my sources told me recently that the *Anschluss* was timed so that all the generals would be in the field and thus unable to participate in a coup d'état against Hitler."

Carr eyed him over his spectacles. "Are you sure? I haven't heard anything like that."

Russell remained silent, his throat clenching.

"How reliable is this source?"

Russell hesitated.

Carr exhaled, enveloping himself in a cloud of smoke. "Sounds like a tall tale to me."

"It sounds just crazy enough to be true. Hitler may be mentally unstable, but he seems to have an uncanny instinct for survival."

Carr stubbed out his cigarette. "I'll have someone show you to your rooms. We'll be dining at eight. It's white tie, of course."

Russell followed him back to the mansion. "I wonder if I could meet with Mr. Beneš. Tomorrow morning, if possible."

Carr chuckled as he patted him on the back. "Wouldn't you like to look around Prague first?"

✠✠✠✠✠✠✠✠✠✠✠

"Frau Graatz!" called Frau Hoffman. "A visitor. His Excellency awaits below."

Grace sagged in front of her vanity, cheeks flaming. It was early morning, not quite seven, and she'd just climbed out of bed. Quickly, she grabbed her dressing gown, tying it into knots.

"Tell him I'll be down soon." She hurried along the corridor and knocked on Peter's door.

It had been two days since their last…meeting. She closed her eyes, feeling his fingers on her nipples. After that initial encounter on the loveseat, he'd picked her up and taken her into his bedroom. Grace's cheeks burned. Whatever had possessed her to fall into bed with him like that? She must have been out of her mind. A shiver of guilt wriggled its way up her spine, while her heart clenched in her chest.

"What is it, Mother?"

"There's a visitor downstairs. Your—father has arrived."

Peter straightened and opened the door wider. He was still in his pajamas, his dirty blond hair mussed and untidy.

Grace resisted the urge to smooth his hair. "Can I come in?"

"Sure thing, Mother." Peter grinned. "There's no one here. No girls—yet." It was eerie looking into her son's face. Now he was making little jokes, just the way Carl did, with similar facial expressions to accompany them.

Grace sat on his bed and leaned forward. "Peter, we need to talk. What do you think about your father? He has plans to—"

"I know. He visited yesterday, when you were out."

"What?" Grace's heart lurched in her chest. "Why didn't you tell me?"

"You weren't there."

"What did he say?"

Peter's eyes shone for a moment, then his face assumed its usual stolidity. "He's going to give me riding lessons and enroll me in the Prussian Military Academy as soon as my German is good enough."

"He can't do that."

"Why not?" Peter's mouth quirked at the corners. "He's my father. Why did you never tell me that I'm exactly like him, Mother? I know I look like him, but I didn't realize we had similar personalities and interests. We had such a long talk, I think he was waiting for you. He's quite a character. Very friendly and charming, despite the fact he's an aristocrat and all. I feel at home with him already—"

"Peter, you're not exactly like him. You're your own person." She paused to draw breath. "How do you feel about all this? Don't you want to stay with us?"

Peter's face sobered. "I'm not sure Mr. Russell wants me around."

Grace recoiled. "But I must see you! I couldn't bear to lose you!"

"Don't worry, Mother. Father has it all figured out. He said that you and the others—well not Mr. Russell, of course, but you and Stacy and the little ones could come visit him as often as you liked."

How easily he uses that word father *to refer to a stranger he scarcely knows.* Grace stared at her son, and as she did so his face shifted so that sometimes he was her golden-haired boy and sometimes he was Carl. She rose to her feet. "Peter, this is important. Promise me that you won't say anything about this to anyone."

He drew himself up. "Mother, what do you take me for? I'm not a tattling child." His mouth quirked as he kissed her on the cheek.

Grace returned to her room. Not only had Carl beguiled her into his bed, but he'd persuaded Peter he was better off living with him. Grace began running a brush through her hair. If she were fifteen years old, which would she prefer? A course of advanced mathematics to satisfy a cold stepfather, or a spell of horseback riding and German to please a warm and attentive father?

But what was best for him? Grace's heart squeezed tears. She couldn't do it. She couldn't give up her son, her first-born. The others would have to adjust. Marina and Benny would be happy no matter who they were with. Talkative Marina always made friends easily, and Benny was such a charmer. But what about Anastasia? Grace squirmed. Her elder daughter was becoming a young woman. Even Mother, with all of her gentleman friends, had kept them away from her daughters. But perhaps that was because Aunt Paulina had insisted.

Grace rested her head on her left hand. How could she reconcile the competing claims of Peter and Anastasia? A headache threatened from behind her temples. She glanced at the clock. Carl had been waiting for half an hour, and already she could hear her children's voices wafting upstairs. While she dithered, they were renewing their acquaintance with him. She rose to her feet. She must dress at once.

✠✠✠✠✠✠✠✠✠✠✠

As expected, Carl was in the elegant reception room, chatting to Marina and Benny, ensconced in Nico's favorite chair, while Frau Hoffman shuffled in and out bringing refreshments.

"Liebchen!" Carl rose to his feet, smiling. "How becoming you look this morning." He kissed her hand as always, but his eyes roved over her with anticipation.

Grace's cheeks warmed.

"When do you expect the industrious Herr Russell to put in an appearance?"

Grace coughed to clear her throat. It was now Friday. "Next Wednesday."

Carl chuckled. "While the cat's away, eh?"

"What exactly do you mean?" Anastasia entered the room, scowling.

"Ah, I see we have the pleasure of your company, Miss Anastasia." Completely unfazed, Carl took her hand and kissed it with a flourish.

Her face softened, just a tad, but that didn't prevent her from raking him with her bright eyes.

Still smiling, he said, "And how old are you?"

"I'll be fourteen next year."

"And can't wait to grow up, I see. Wishing your youth away." He turned to Grace and zigzagged an eyebrow. "They say youth is wasted on the young."

Grace's face eased into a smile. How well he was handling her tricky daughter, much better than her own father, who was too quick to become coldly disapproving when Anastasia let fly one of her barbs. Perhaps Anastasia would be all right with Carl. Her smile faded as she cleared her throat. "We need to discuss Peter."

He took her elbow and bent towards her, saying in an undertone, "Liebchen, surely you don't want a fight in front of your children?"

"No," she murmured as he drew her into a corner. "But I understand you've been telling him you're going to give him riding lessons and enroll him in the Prussian Military Academy."

Carl drew himself up. "I merely wish our son to follow in the family tradition."

"But you can't do that," whispered Grace. "Peter is an American citizen. Nico is never going to allow it."

"You think so?" Carl raised an eyebrow. "I can be very persuasive when I choose."

The hairs on the back of Grace's arms prickled. Just then, Peter appeared.

Carl moved towards their son and clapped him on the back.

Peter responded with a broad smile. In all these years Grace had never seen him look so relaxed and happy.

"I propose a little experiment, Liebchen," remarked Carl. "Why don't you move to my villa while your husband is away and see what you think?"

Grace's throat clenched. "I'm not sure that's appropriate."

"But I have many rooms, plenty of space for you and your children." He smiled at Peter. "Our son would have his own room. I could tell him about the family history. We could talk over things."

"Oooh. Did you say we would be going to Kladow?" Marina danced over.

"Would you like to go there, Miss Marina?"

"I've been *dying* to go there ever since you told me about it."

Sighing, Grace turned towards their son. His lips twitched in amusement. "Why not give it a try, Mother?"

✠✠✠✠✠✠✠✠✠✠✠

Russell was obliged to wait until the beginning of the next week before President Beneš would see him. While he waited he occupied himself by visiting the Picture Gallery, touring Vyšehrad, and taking communion twice a day at the Cathedral of Saints Vitus, Wenceslaus, and Adalbert. On Wednesday and Thursday, he'd called home. Grace took his call on Thursday, but not Wednesday. When he eventually talked to her, she sounded cold and faraway, making conversation difficult. On Friday, Frau Hoffmann informed him she'd left with the children to visit a friend in the country. Russell's whole body locked up. It was obvious who the friend was. If only he could get this commission wrapped up, he could return home early.

Finally, early on Tuesday morning, Beneš received him in Prague Castle, in a room with worn drapes and a threadbare carpet. But the shabbiness masked magnificent bones, rather like a beautiful woman grown old. A sudden image of Grace, her hair white, her face emaciated, flashed through his mind. His stomach churned.

"Would you care for a glass of our local Riesling?" asked Beneš.

Russell twisted his lips into a smile.

With careful courtesy, Beneš, poured the pale gold liquid into a cut glass, which sparkled in the rising sun. Russell swirled it gently before taking a sip. *Perfetto*. It was not too dry, not too sweet. Should he offer to speak French with Beneš, who had studied at the Sorbonne? But he didn't want to seem condescending. Instead, he proffered his most expensive cigarettes and thanked him for allowing the Americans to have the use of Schönborn Palace with its magnificent views.

"But of course," replied Beneš. "We want our American guests to be happy. We Czechs are great admirers of your constitution."

"That is most gracious of you, sir."

"You have been in Berlin for a short time only?" remarked Beneš, sitting next to him, in a dusty Louis Quinze chair.

"Yes, I arrived there from Tokyo. About a month ago."

"Ah! So you have not been—marinated in European politics. You are an outsider."

Russell set his jaw. "I do my best to provide good service."

"I'm sure you do, my dear fellow. I did not mean that in a bad way. Being an outsider is sometimes a good thing. You can see things that others miss. So tell me, what is your frank opinion about Herr Hitler's speech yesterday?"

Russell sagged in his seat. Hitler had given a much-anticipated speech at the Nazi Party rally in Nuremberg yesterday evening, in which he complained that Prague wanted to annihilate the Sudeten Germans. In response, riots had erupted in the Sudetenland.

"It is hard to reason with someone who incites violence."

Beneš stared into his wine."That is the nub of the problem. We had to impose martial law to quell the disturbances. I have a bad, bad feeling about this. My question to you is, what do the Americans intend to do?"

Russell dropped his gaze to the faded carpet beneath his feet. How could he explain that the American Congress was unlikely to do anything because the isolationists continued to drag their heels in the belief that their government shouldn't get involved in foreign quarrels? He cleared his throat as he studied the glass of wine in his hand. "The United States has always been a supporter of democracies."

"But what about your American Congress? I understand that there are some in your country who are not—partial—to foreign matters."

Russell pinched his lips together. *Of course Beneš would know all about American isolationists; he'd been the foreign minister of Czechoslovakia since the Great War, giving it up only a couple of years ago to become president of Czechoslovakia upon Masaryk's retirement.* He looked Beneš in the eye.

"I wish we didn't have to deal with those isolationists," he said slowly. "I wish the United States would buttress Czechoslovakia's claims in this matter. I am most concerned about the Czech people and the Jews, but we live in a democracy, and disagreements are just a fact of life." He inhaled deeply on his cigarette. "However, I will do everything I can to help. When I type up my report for Ambassador Wilson, I'll do my best to convey the urgency of the situation."

Beneš patted his arm. "You are a good man, Mr. Russell. Is there anything I can do to help you with your report?"

And that was how Russell got an invitation to visit the Czech border fortifications. As Stronge had said, they were well-constructed, consisting of low-lying concrete bunkers protected by the ever-present Czech hedgehogs, those angled bits of iron that looked like large three-dimensional crosses, very effective at preventing tanks from getting through a line of defense. They even had ventilation systems with filtration so that chemical attacks would not affect the defenders. The Czechs had done their work well and had seemingly thought of everything. But was it enough? Russell stood there, a cool wind from the north ruffling his hair. The biggest problems were that these fortifications were unfinished, and that the border between Czechoslovakia and Germany was long, five times as long as that between France and Germany, which had been protected by the famous Maginot Line during the Great War. If France didn't honor its agreement to support Czechoslovakia in the event of a German invasion, the Czechs would be thrown to the wolves.

✠✠✠✠✠✠✠✠✠✠✠

The days at Kladow passed easily, like golden beads strung on a necklace. The weather was beautiful, warm for the time of year, and so Carl took them around. They picnicked on his lawn, boated on his lake in his boat, motored to pretty villages in his car. Grace, seeing how happy their son was and how contented the other children seemed to be, relaxed, sleeping long and peacefully.

"You have given me a great gift, Liebchen," he remarked one morning at breakfast, "and for that I thank you from the bottom of my heart. I, in turn, have a gift for you. Miss Marina, would you be so good as to bring that package lying on the piano? Perhaps you could open it for your mother."

The package contained a violin case. Slowly, Grace moved towards it, undid the clasps, opened the lid, and gently drew the instrument from its silk wrappings. It gleamed softly, its polished wood giving it a smooth, satiny sheen.

"Oooh," squealed Marina. "A violin for Mama!"

Carl chuckled and patted her cheek. "So you approve, eh, Miss Marina?"

"Mama has been lost without her violin," observed Marina. She jumped up and angled her head to look at the priceless instrument that lay lightly between Grace's hands. "Can I see?"

But Grace didn't hear her. She held the violin up to the light and peered into its f-hole to examine the luthier's signature. Suddenly, a cold thread wound up her spine. Why was Carl doing this? He had a knack for anticipating her wishes, even before she knew she had them, and his timing was impeccable. The one person who might have protested, Anastasia, was absent, as she usually didn't come down to breakfast, preferring to sleep instead.

"It's the *Folinari Guaneri del Gesù,"* remarked Carl with a smile, as he watched her face come alive.

"What are you going to play?" asked Marina.

Grace's mouth drooped as she slowly returned the violin to its case. "Carl, I don't think—That is, it's very kind of you, but—"

"Why don't you play something, Mother?" said Peter.

"Do any of you play the piano?" Carl turned to the other children.

"I can." Five-year-old Benny stood. "Papa says I'm very good."

"He's only just started and his feet don't reach the pedals," remarked Marina with all the gravity of her eight years. "I can try, as long as it's not too hard."

"Capital! How about some Mozart?"

✠✠✠✠✠✠✠✠✠✠✠

"What will Father say?" asked Anastasia. "You can't take that violin home."

Grace remained silent, taking in the soft evening light that filtered through the lace curtains of the pretty bedroom Carl had given them. Of course she couldn't take that priceless instrument back to Savignyplatz—she shouldn't have accepted it in the first place. But Carl could be so persuasive, and she didn't want to make a scene in front of her children.

"And you shouldn't let Uncle Carl kiss you, Mother," remarked Anastasia. "He's getting too familiar."

"It was only a peck on the cheek." Grace bent her head as if examining a piece of lint on her skirt. "He was just being friendly."

"Well, you shouldn't be so friendly with him. Especially if you don't plan on seeing him after this week."

Grace looked up. "What makes you think that?"

"You'll have to go home when Father returns, and Father won't allow—"

"Anastasia—"

"I wonder what Father is going to make of this," she muttered, letting her hair fall in front of her face.

"Anastasia! That's enough."

Her elder daughter folded her arms. "I worry about you, Mother. I don't want you to get into a scrape. Father might become very angry—"

Grace stared at her daughter, surprised. Anastasia was so prickly, it was hard to see past how difficult she was. But now her young features were arranged in an expression of genuine concern. Grace put her arm around her daughter and held her close. "I will handle your father," she said softly. "This is between us. It is not something for you to worry about. Do you understand?"

Anastasia gazed at her for a moment, her eyes bright. She was the first to break gaze. "Okay," she muttered, turning her face away. "But I still think you're going to be in a real fix."

Chapter Thirty-Two
Monday, 19 September

Frantic, Russell had been trying to reach Grace for nearly two weeks. Every time he believed he could leave, something got in his way. It was Kafkaesque.

His visit with Beneš had been delayed until the following week, and so he hadn't gotten to the Czech fortifications until a week after he'd left Berlin. It had taken him a couple of days to look around, and then just when he was on the point of returning, Wilson had ordered him to Berchtesgaden to find out what Prime Minister Neville Chamberlain's surprise visit to Hitler meant for the Czechs. It had taken him two days to get there, and when he arrived Chamberlain was long gone, back in London consulting with his cabinet and with members of the French government, while Hitler remained in his eyrie at the Berghof, venting to the Berlin correspondent of London's *Daily Mail*. Yesterday, the last train to Berlin had been cancelled, and he'd been forced to cable Grace to tell her he had to spend yet another night away from home. When he arrived back in Berlin the next morning, a telegram was waiting for him from Wilson telling him to come to the Embassy immediately. After an endless morning of briefings Russell still couldn't leave because Wilson wanted his report.

He closed his eyes for a moment to shut out his desk with its clutter of papers and memoranda. He felt utterly drained, dark waves of exhaustion threatening to overwhelm him. He straightened his spine. His trip would have gone well, if only Chamberlain hadn't taken it into his head to visit Hitler. What could the British leader mean by it? Russell leaned back in his chair and stared at the typewritten page before him. Surely he wasn't going to give into Hitler's demands and just hand over the Sudetenland. Russell hit the carriage-key return and continued typing his report. A short while later the secretary put his head around the door.

"Miss Mabel Phelps to see you, sir."

Russell stared at the gaunt young man with the thin brown tie. Mabel Phelps? Who was she? Then everything cleared as his memory plugged in the connections, almost like an invisible operator at a telephone switchboard. Of course, Miss Phelps was that friend of Grace's that she'd met all those years ago in Berlin when they were both students at the music school. She was the person Goerdeler had mentioned on the train to Prague. Russell had written, asking her to stop in for tea whenever convenient, and then promptly forgot about her. Was she responsible for all that loose talk that Goerdeler claimed was going on in the American Embassy? He should really try to find out. He scrawled a quick note on his legal pad so that he wouldn't forget where he was and rose to his feet.

She must have been around Grace's age, but she looked older, perhaps because she was plump, in contrast to Grace's youthful slenderness. Everything about Miss Phelps was brown, from her woolen suit to the curls that framed her face, to her eyes.

"We'll take refreshments in here," Russell told his secretary. Then he deftly adjusted his tie, came around his desk, and advanced to shake her hand.

"Miss Phelps. How good of you to call."

She fixed her large brown eyes on his face and gave him a smiling blush. "I came as soon as I got your note. How is Grace?"

"Fine. She's fine." He indicated a club chair and they sat facing each other in silence as the secretary served tea on the *moderne* glass coffee table that Russell had recently purchased.

Miss Phelps crossed her ankles and accepted his offer of a cigarette. They traded observations about life in the foreign service until the secretary quietly closed the door behind him.

"My brother sends his kind regards," observed Mabel, leaning forward to pat ash into the ashtray.

Russell paused in sipping his tea. "I haven't heard from him in years. He never replied to my letters."

She glanced at him through her lashes. "It was a bit awkward—"

Why was Miss Phelps telling him this? "Have you come here to discuss Grace?"

She looked away. "No, no, of course not. It's just that I've returned from visiting my brother in Moscow. He looks broken, old before his time."

The now-familiar fury stirred. Grace had a devastating effect, or rather, her absence did on these men. Was this meant to be some sort of warning?

"What does this have to do with me?" His tone was sharper than he'd intended, but she raised her eyes and look squarely at him.

"Grace never said anything?"

He nailed her with a stare. "In all the time I have known Grace, I don't believe she's mentioned your brother once."

Her normally pleasant face hardened, her expression becoming pinched. She shifted in her seat, unconsciously copying his posture.

His eyes narrowed. Why had she come here? They sat like that for a while until Russell cleared his throat.

"The reason I asked you here—to tea—was not to talk about Grace. Though I daresay she would wish to see you." He coughed to clear his throat again. "It was about another matter. How shall I put this?" He drew another cigarette out of the pack he carried in his inner pocket and tapped it against his monogrammed lighter. "A rather bizarre incident happened when I was traveling on a train recently. A fellow put his head into the door of my compartment, and on ascertaining who I was, started to talk about you."

"Me?" She gave him a swift glance, then continued smoking composedly, using her right hand, while her left arm folded itself around her rather ample middle.

Russell smiled. "I wondered if you could enlighten me."

She smoked thoughtfully for several moments. "How very odd. No, I don't believe I can, Mr. Russell. Not unless you give me a few details."

He hesitated. Should he ask her straight out if she were a spy? But the thought of his professional life descending to the level of a cheap thriller. made him cringe.

Her soothing contralto interrupted. "Are you going to tell me who the gentleman was?"

"I was traveling to Prague. When the train got to Dresden, a fellow got on the train, opened the door to my compartment, and introduced himself as Carl Friedrich Goerdeler." When he pronounced Goerdeler's name, her eyes widened slightly. "He said he knew you, and that *you* told him I would be on that train. Is that true?"

She smiled and shrugged. "Of course I know Goerdeler. Everyone does, he's a very sociable fellow."

"How do you know him?"

"I met him at the Adlon, of course. At the time, I was working as a journalist."

"Am I to take it that you did this work under an assumed name?"

She sat back in her seat, cigarette held lightly in her fingers, and laughed at him.

He compressed his lips. "Miss Phelps, disturbing reports have reached my ears about loose talk at the American Embassy. I trust you realize how serious this is?"

"Of course," she murmured, veiling her eyes with her lashes in a way that reminded him of Grace at her most aloof.

He leaned forward. "Are *you* responsible?"

She smiled at him, a faint pink tinting her cheeks. "A tragedy is about to happen to the Jews in this country unless we stop it." She stubbed out her cigarette. "Are you interested in helping?"

He stared back, unblinking. How typical of a woman to change the subject like that. Yes, he knew that Jews accused of violating the marriage laws were imprisoned, and now that they had served their sentences, they were re-arrested by the Gestapo and sent to Nazi concentration camps. Every time he walked to and from the U.S. Embassy, he was a witness to abuse heaped on that people, the daily taunts from members of the SS, the daily humiliations. By now it was almost impossible for Jews to find a country that would accept them. Even when the search was successful, Jews were forced to give up ninety per cent of their wealth in "taxes" upon leaving the country.

But why would Miss Phelps be interested in helping the Jews? He thought the Phelpses were wealthy WASPs from Connecticut.

"Well?" Her voice sharpened, breaking into his thoughts.

"I am not sure it is part of my brief."

She picked up her teacup and sipped. "And what exactly is your brief?"

"I am not at liberty to tell you."

She laughed again, making a deep sound that gurgled up from the back of her throat. "It's not that hard to guess, Mr. Russell. You were plucked from your posting in Tokyo and set down here in Berlin just as this latest crisis over Czechoslovakia heated up. Events are moving rapidly. State needs someone in Berlin who's a competent linguist." She cocked her head and smiled at him under her thick, dark lashes, her best feature in a rather plain face. "Am I right?"

Was she flirting with him? Russell allowed himself to feel flattered for just one moment. At forty-four, he didn't attract this kind of attention as often as he had earlier in life. Or rather, he had been much readier to notice that sort of thing before he claimed Grace as his bride.

"We need someone who is fluent in all the major European languages," she continued. "Someone who possesses excellent powers of surveillance."

He rose to his feet and stood next to her, looking down from a height of about six feet, and said softly, "Miss Phelps, this is neither the time nor the place—"

"You're a practicing Catholic, Mr. Russell. How are you going to feel if *you* don't save innocent people from their deaths?" She fluttered her lashes. "The Nazi régime is against your moral code."

He stiffened. She had no right to say such things in his office. If someone overheard, he could get into trouble. He didn't like this woman, she was indiscreet. Perhaps she was adept at beguiling men with her feminine wiles. *She* must be the source of all this loose talk around the embassy Goerdeler had alluded to.

"You're a good man, Mr. Russell," she continued, smiling up at him coyly. "Now is your time. You cannot hesitate. You must use your gifts to save others."

He made a dismissive gesture with his hand. "You cannot expect me to give you an answer without a great deal of thought."

She put her teacup down and leaned forward. "A man who is willing to put his career on the line to speak up for the Jews is the kind of man Lieutenant Colonel Oster is looking for."

That name again. Russell had never heard of Oster before Goedeler mentioned him. Miss Phelps was working for the German Resistance then. But, more to the point, someone had overheard his conversation with Ambassador Wilson the week before, when he'd asked whether Hitler was building a better future for the Jews, and had repeated it to her. Who?

She tilted her head up. "Think it over if you must, Mr. Russell, but don't hesitate too long. Every day counts."

He glared at her. How dare she talk to him in this fashion. He walked towards the door.

"If for no other reason, give your considerable gifts to our cause in memory of Professor and Mrs. Rosenthal."

He froze, still facing the door. How the devil did she know about the Rosenthals? No one knew about them. They were long dead, and it had all happened several years ago when he'd been only seventeen years old, the new student in Professor Rosenthal's German class at Northwestern University. Russell had become his best student that semester, and a friendship had blossomed over dinner at the Rosenthal's comfortable home and through piano duets in which Mrs. Rosenthal had participated. Russell's parents had been absent, uncaring, and the Rosenthals had treated him like a son. He'd never forgotten their kindness, the warmth of their home life, or the way they'd gently broken through the brittle shell of a very shy young man. But he never talked about them. Except —he might have mentioned them to Grace, when they were courting. Miss Phelps's information must be sixteen years old.

He pivoted on the ball of his foot and moved swiftly towards where she sat at the coffee table. He must have looked furious, because she rose, and with a quickness that belied her plump figure slipped away from him, opening the office door wide.

"How—"

"Thank you for tea, Mr. Russell. And please give your wife my fond regards. Tell her I'll call soon."

She waved to him and walked away down the long corridor. He watched her sashaying hips until she disappeared around a corner.

Merda. He shut his office door. Had he said too much? He didn't think so. But how did Miss Phelps know about his exchanges with Wilson? Goerdeler's voice intruded on his thoughts. *People do talk*, he'd said. *Even at the American Embassy*. But who? Who could it possibly be? He should investigate. Russell wrote a note to himself in a small notebook he kept in his breast pocket.

He sank into his seat and massaged his forehead with the tips of his fingers. Now she wanted to recruit him when just entertaining the possibility would destroy his career.

His throat felt sandpaper dry, so he leaned forward and poured himself a glass of water from the ever-present carafe on his desk. After sipping, he went to the window and looked down at Bendlerstrasse as cars rumbled below, carrying their distinguished guests. He was at the nerve-center of the Nazi government, and maybe some of those limousines contained the princes of Hitler's empire, perhaps Himmler, perhaps Goering or Goebbels. Did Hitler himself have any idea about this? Suddenly the glass of water he held in his hand felt cold, almost icy to the touch. He placed it quickly on his desk and sat down again, massaging the lids of his eyes with the backs of his hands. Where was his bottle of aspirin? He rummaged in his drawer, swallowed two, and returned the bottle.

If the organization that Miss Phelps belonged to was that good at gathering information, maybe it was worth looking into, if only to find out who was leaking information from the American Embassy. But what was he going to do about Ambassador Wilson, who was such an admirer of Hitler? Should he risk his career to join this conspiracy and save the Jews? If Wilson found out, all of Russell's efforts in becoming the next ambassador to Rome, the long days, the sleepless nights, the sacrifice of his marriage to his ambition; all of that earnest striving for the past sixteen years would dissolve into a nothingness.

Russell sat down at his desk and steepled his fingers to stop them from shaking. He'd worked in surveillance as a young man during the Great War. He'd been sent to the Italian Front because of his gift for languages and mimicry. From now on, he must never write anything down that could possibly link him to this conspiracy. His jottings in his diary and on his notepad must be designed to throw others off the scent.

He fumbled in his breast pocket and fished out his notebook, tearing out the pages into which he'd written various notes to himself. He read them carefully, wrote some of them down in code, and tossed the rest in the waste basket.

The first thing he needed was to gain access to Hans Oster, the head of this conspiracy, to ascertain how serious it really was. Of course, he could call Oster up and talk with him under an assumed name. But any contact with Oster was going to be risky. He might have only one shot at it before he got found out. Russell drew in a deep breath. He would have to go there himself. One could tell so much by gazing into someone's face, hearing them talk, and taking in their surroundings. The minutiae of everyday life, the books, the knickknacks, even the furniture could speak to him, conveying so much about a person.

Russell gazed around his corner office. His desk backed into a dark corner that was illuminated from behind by a large floor lamp. To his right was the door to his office, and next to it on a blank wall was a large mirror in a gilt frame. To his left, were three large windows that formed a bow, with a leather-covered window seat. Next to the door, away from his desk stood three large steel file cabinets. On top of these cabinets were various large dolls, dressed as characters from Japanese Noh theater. Opposite his desk was a large painting in oils, a copy of *Girl with a Mandolin* by Picasso, done during his Cubist period. In the large space between the cabinets and his desk stood his glass coffee table with three leather club chairs arranged around it. On top of the table sat a Japanese tea service. Behind his desk were four bookcases filled with books on various languages, history, geography, politics, anthropology, and physics.

What did his room tell him? The inhabitant was male, with a taste for dark furniture in modern lines and modernist paintings. He studied languages, history, and politics but had other interests as well. He had recently been to Japan and had an appreciation for the Japanese aesthetic. He was obsessively neat, as the surfaces were mostly clear. The only exception to this was his desk, which was piled high with papers. Given the neatness of other parts of the room, this suggested the inhabitant had been away recently on a longish trip and had not yet had time to clear his desk.

Yes, he would have to meet Oster in person. But how? He couldn't simply wander over there, even though the

Abwehr, was located at Tirpitzufer 76, just five hundred meters away, a six-minute walk from Bendlerstrasse 39, where he sat now in his office. It was too risky.

But, maybe— For the first time in a long, long while, he smiled. An idea stirred in the recesses of his mind. Most people would glance at Russell's well-cut suit and imbibe the impassive demeanor he'd cultivated over the years as a foreign service officer, dismissing him as yet another stiff board. But Russell had discovered as a young man at university that he had a talent for acting. He'd gotten involved in the drama club when he gained a reputation for making others laugh with his ability to mimic the professors. In his senior year, he'd actually landed the part of Jaques in *As You Like It.* How hard he'd had to work to convey Jaques's cynicism, at a time of life when he was imbued with youthful idealism. Ah! What he wouldn't give to have those carefree days again.

Russell was well aware that many regarded him as proud and prickly, so his best course of action was to do something that would be completely out of character. Abruptly, he rose to his feet, went to the wastebasket and retrieved the screwed-up bits of paper. Methodically, he tore them into little pieces. He had diplomatic immunity. He had a flawless record of sixteen years of service. He had the Congressional Medal of Honor, awarded for his services during the Great War. He wanted to help the Jews, and now he was looking for that loose talker. Yes. That is what he would say if anything went wrong. Now was the time to act.

Ignoring the exhaustion that lapped at the edges of his consciousness, Russell took a deep breath and picked up the telephone.

✠✠✠✠✠✠✠✠✠✠

There was a noisy bustle as Grace and her children entered Carl's lemon-walled drawing room that had reminded her of D-sharp all those years ago. It was late afternoon, and the place swarmed with children of all shapes and sizes. In no time at all they'd gathered Marina and Benny into their games, but Grace found herself sitting off to the side flanked by Peter and Anastasia, an English-speaking enclave against a German sea. How wonderful to know someone like Carl, who had such a wide social circle. He'd wanted to "honor her presence," as he put it, by throwing a tea party for herself and her children. If only she could speak German. Grace took in the lively throng, straining to catch a word or two. Anastasia and Peter shouldn't be standing here with her, they should be making new friends. How could she persuade them to leave?

"Miss Anastasia!" Carl suddenly appeared, kissing her daughter's hand with a flourish, which drew a reluctant smile to her lips. "I see you have quite the eye for fashion." He took in her satin dress that was cut on the bias, the new leather high heels, and the stockings she'd insisted Grace buy her. "Let's see if I can guess. Your mother bought those beautiful shoes in Helgas Schuhladen. And your charming frock comes from that boutique your Aunt Louisa patronized. Now what was its name?"

Anastasia folded her arms and smiled. "It begins with an *L*."

"Let's see—Lotte?"

Anastasia shook her head.

"Leonore?"

"No." A dimple appeared at the corner of her mouth.

"Leopoldina? Lorelei? Lovisa?"

"No, no, no!" Anastasia laughed. "It's Lillas."

"Modes Lillas!" Carl clapped a hand to his head in a dramatic fashion. "How silly of your Uncle Carl not to remember. Now what was I going to tell you? Ah, yes. There are other young ladies here who share your interest in Berlin fashion. Would you like me to introduce you?" Soon, Anastasia was surrounded by a group of giggling girls.

Carl reappeared. "Did you enjoy your riding today?" he asked Peter.

"Yes, sir." Peter's usually stolid face shone.

"Your instructor tells me you are doing very well. It's time to buy you a horse. There are some young men here, the cream of the crop from the Prussian aristocracy. I know all their parents. Would you like me to introduce you?"

In no time at all, Peter was dashing off to the stables with his new friends.

Grace smiled at Carl as he came to sit on the sofa beside her. "Thank you," she murmured. "I want them to make friends and enjoy themselves."

"Of course, Liebchen." He kissed her cheek. "Now, it is your turn. I have some friends I'd like you to meet." They went next door to his library-cum-office, which Grace always thought of as his C minor room. As he opened the door, Grace became aware of four men seated around a table with a large map spread in front of them. They were discussing something in low tones, in English.

"His Highness Prince Wilhelm is an upright, sincere, and courageous soldier," said one.

"A constitutional monarchy?" said another

"Who is going to arrest—him?" said a third.

"Heinz and Liedig," said the last voice, which had a lilt. "They should form the assault group—"

"Liebchen, allow me to introduce you to my comrades-in-arms."

The men froze for an instant as Carl moved forward. Then seeing who it was, they relaxed. General Erwin von Witzleben, Captain Friedrich Wilhelm Heinz, Naval Officer Franz-Maria Liedig, and Lieutenant-Colonel Hans Oster rose and kissed her hand with the kind of unwelcome flourish she'd come to expect.

"I can quite see the attraction," murmured Lieutenant-Colonel Oster as he gently squeezed her hand. "Carl, you lucky devil, you didn't tell us your lady friend was *ravissante*."

"Grace has only recently arrived from Tokyo."

"Indeed?" Captain Heinz went to the sideboard and handed her a glass of chilled white wine. "And what was such a lovely lady doing in Tokyo?"

"Grace's husband is American, a rising star in the State Department."

"And may one ask where he is now?" Lieutenant-Colonel Oster's eyes twinkled.

Grace looked down at her wedding band and hesitated for a fraction of a second. "Prague."

"Interesting," said General von Witzleben. "Is he still there?"

Grace nodded.

Captain Heinz offered her a Senoulli cigarette, which she declined. "I don't suppose your husband is six feet tall, with thick, dark hair, and rather intense eyes."

Grace stiffened. Who were these people? She thought back to the day of her encounter with Carl, and his furtive visitor. The sound of gravel crunching under hesitant footsteps occasionally haunted her dreams.

"You are pale, Liebchen," remarked Carl. "Is something the matter?"

"No, no really. I—" Grace's cheeks warmed. Was Nico still in Prague? He'd cabled last night to say he'd be back today, but were these people holding him somewhere?

"I don't suppose you happen to recognize the description?" Naval Officer Liedig remarked.

"He sounds rather like the hard-charging Herr Pagano who has the good fortune to be my Liebchen's husband."

"Pagano?" Heinz frowned. "He's Italian?"

"Italian-American." Carl handed him a sherry. "He's a high-flyer at the American State Department who wants to be ambassador to Rome. He hides his origins under the name *Russell*; it's rather like the common Italian name *Rossi*. Italian-Americans are not treated kindly in the United States."

The skin at the back of Grace's neck crawled.

"That explains the accent," remarked General von Witzleben. "There was a definite lilt to it."

The others guffawed.

Carl touched her arm. "You've gone white, Liebchen. You should sit." He pulled out a chair for her and stood behind it. "How did you meet him?"

"We experienced a rather bizarre incident this afternoon—with a cleaning lady," said Oster.

"A *soi-disant* cleaning lady," put in Liedig.

"Yes, well. The lady in question—what was her name? Lena?"

"Liszka," replied Heinz. "She—he was attempting to be Hungarian."

They laughed again.

"In any event, we were sitting in Heinz's office." Oster sat down next to Grace. "It was toward the end of the day, quiet you know, and we were studying a map—"

"When suddenly, in walks a cleaning lady," put in Liedig.

There was another spate of male laughter.

"Except that this one was six feet tall, and had no feminine curves," said Oster.

"He clearly wasn't German," remarked General von Witzleben.

"It was very clear that he was a spy," said Heinz.

"I don't suppose *you* happen to know who he was?" Oster leaned towards her, causing their thighs to nearly touch.

Grace's cheeks flamed as she stared at her heart finger, encased in Nico's rings. She forced back a wave of nausea as she tried to picture her dapper and immaculately attired husband posing as a woman. She hadn't known he had those kinds of proclivities. Except—what exactly had he been doing with Margot all those years ago in that sordid nightclub? When she'd asked, he'd gotten extremely defensive, insisting it was their secret and ordering her to tell no one. Grace's stomach churned.

"I had no idea," she replied faintly. "I cannot believe he would be so stupid—"

"When did you expect him back?" asked Heinz.

"Last night, but he cabled to say his train had been cancelled and he had to spend another night in Prague."

"Hmmm, he must have had time to return to Berlin, find some cleaning lady's clothes, and spy on us. We arrived here about fifteen minutes ago," said Liedig.

"Yes, but why?" asked Oster.

"He's a talented linguist," remarked Carl. "And he's done quite a bit of spying for the American government."

Grace stared at Carl. How did he know that Nico had acted as a spy on the Italian Front?

"How interesting," said Heinz.

"But this whole thing was so amateurish," said General von Witzleben. "If the Americans have spies like this, heaven help them. He was too obvious. Why take such a risk if he is such a high-flyer?"

Why indeed? Grace stared at his rings. She'd sacrificed her whole life for his career. A slow welling of anger coursed through her. How could he throw it away just like that? Didn't he know better? Didn't he care?

"I think we should bring him in," remarked Oster. "We should take a good look at him and find out what's going on."

He looked at Carl, who gave a small nod.

Grace turned icy cold. He disgusted her. How could she be married to a man who liked men? She'd always thought his very frequent absences were due to his work, but maybe he'd had numerous male lovers in the numerous places they'd been forced to call home. She wanted nothing more to do with him. Her children were happy here with Carl. She was not going back to Savignyplatz.

Chapter Thirty-Three
Monday, 19 September
Evening

Their rented mansion in Savignyplatz seemed quiet, almost too quiet.

"Frau Graatz is out, sir," the housekeeper told him. "With the children."

Russell gave her his hat and coat, and went to the hall table. There was no note, nothing.

"Frau Graatz said to let you know she will be back this evening," Frau Hoffmann continued. "For dinner."

Russell glanced at his watch. It was nearly eight in the evening, the soft twilight outside the window making the blossoms on the trees gleam in the creeping darkness.

"She's late," he said.

The housekeeper shrugged as she hung his hat and coat on the hatstand and melted away in the general direction of the kitchen.

Russell put his suitcase down, went into the front parlor where the piano perched, opened the keyboard cover, and ran his fingers over the keys. They were dusty. He looked at his fingers with distaste, withdrawing a spotless white handkerchief from his breast pocket, wiping the piano keys. The silence was deafening, nearly unbearable. How he longed to play the piano; it had been too long since he'd allowed himself that pleasure. But if he did, he would miss the click in the lock announcing her return.

He looked around. The room was curiously untidy. The sofas had been pushed out of their customary positions, leaving impressions in the thick carpet. There was a red stain on one of the antimacassars that covered the arms of the chairs, probably red wine. There were crumbs on the seat.

Russell bent down to examine them. They looked like the remnants of crackers, yes with flakes of hard cheese. There was a small dish on the occasional table nearby. It contained an olive pit with a bit of green skin still attached.

Russell wrinkled his nose and absently wiped his hands on his pants. Why wasn't the housekeeper cleaning? He knew the answer only too well. Grace hadn't given any instructions, and like many a servant before her, Frau Hoffman was taking advantage of the lack of direction.

The wind, wafting through the half-open window, brought the faint sound of a well-calibrated motor. He walked over and peered out. A limousine with von Lietzow's crest emblazoned on it idled at the curb. The chauffeur stepped out and opened the back door. Grace emerged, dressed in a becoming shade of olive green that brought out the color of her chestnut hair. The chauffeur touched his cap and murmured something in German, which Russell was just able to catch. He sucked in his breath. Were his ears deceiving him, or had the fellow actually had the gall to refer to his wife as *gnädige Gräfin*, gracious countess? Compressing his lips, he curbed his feelings because his children were there, tumbling out of the car, Marina and Benny talking all at once, Stacy glancing at her mother, Grace silent.

After supper, Grace excused herself and spent longer than usual going through her night-time ritual with the children. Russell walked into the front parlor, smoking while he waited. Surely a husband can expect more from his wife, he thought, irritated, as he pictured the well-run households of his colleagues. *But you didn't marry a manager*, the voice in his head remarked. *You married a shy, dreamy girl with a passion for her violin*. He sighed as he stood against the mantlepiece, leaning his head against his hand. That was what he loved about her, always would. Life wasn't fair, and it hadn't been fair to the superbly talented violinist he'd fallen in love with, who was now a harried mother of four. Grace had never complained, but then she wasn't good at expressing her feelings.

Well, he had tried. He'd hired a succession of nannies for the younger children, tutors for Peter, governesses for Stacy, to deal with the not-infrequent occasions when Grace would just collapse and be unable to cope. She never gave him any warning, never said anything. She would disappear into her room, overwhelmed, while chaos erupted. When she recovered, she would get rid of all the people he'd hired, insisting that no one cared about her children the way she did. Things would go back to normal, until she collapsed again. What was he to do? How had this latest crisis come about?

A shadow made him turn. She appeared in the doorway.

"Well?" he asked.

She detached herself from the doorframe and sat in one of the chairs, one of the clean ones absent of crumbs or wine stains. Silence emanated throughout the disheveled room.

"I don't understand," he finally said. "I go away for a couple of weeks, and when I come back it's as if everything has fallen apart. Look at this room, it's dirty and untidy. There are crumbs everywhere. There's dust on the piano keys. The furniture is disarranged."

She shifted in her seat. "I haven't been here much."

Pezzo di merda, she'd been with Il Cazzo, that prick. He glared.

She leaned back in her chair and regarded him with an expression he hadn't seen before. It was a new expression, a cool expression, as if she were holding him up to a microscope and finding him wanting.

"I want my life back," she remarked. "I no longer want to move around every couple of years. I want to put down roots somewhere, make friends, and provide a proper home for the children. I want a husband who hasn't forgotten about me."

Filaments of steel radiated from his heart, traveling along the backs of his arms, up his neck, down his spine, into his limbs, seizing up his muscles, turning him into a man of stone. "Grace, what are you talking about?"

She looked up, her gray eyes unfriendly. "You don't have time for a five-year-old boy who's struggling to learn to read. You don't have time for an eight-year-old girl who's easily distracted. You don't even have time for Anastasia, who will come out in a few years."

He recoiled as his prickly daughter's face filled his mind. Truth was, he didn't care for the child; she reminded him uncomfortably of his long-dead mother-in-law. Grace had him there.

"You never told me this before."

"You never asked," she replied coldly. "You were too busy worrying about whether the entertainments I held for all of your foreign service colleagues were suitably lavish and elegant so that *you* would receive a good review."

"That's the system. I didn't ask the State Department to require wives to contribute towards their husbands' promotions."

She regarded him with a kind of unflinching flintiness he'd never seen before, looking exactly like her mother at her most confrontational. "How do you think I've felt, having my conduct watched, my clothes scrutinized, my receptions critiqued, my life disrupted? How do you think I've felt trying to cope with four children and three miscarriages when you were absent so very frequently? Where has my life gone?"

"I had no idea you were so upset."

"Of course you didn't, you never bothered to notice."

She rose and stalked towards the door.

He grabbed her arm. "Where is Peter?"

She shook him off.

"Grace?"

She looked up, stabbing him with a pair of cold gray eyes. "He's with his father."

"What?"

She glowered.

"You don't mean to tell me you're consorting with von Lietzow!"

"Why not?"

"Because—Because he's the cad who raped you all those years ago."

"So *you* say."

"Grace!"

She paused in the doorway. "Peter's place is with his father."

"What kind of mother are you? How could you just hand over *our* son to that scoundrel?"

She stared back at him, unflinching. "Carl is not a scoundrel."

"That's not what you told me all those years ago!"

Grace folded her arms. "I remember things very differently. I remember I was on the point of marrying Peter's father when you kidnapped me and spirited me out of Berlin against my will. When I finally succeeded in seeing Carl again, *you* refused to let me go."

"You came to me with a sob story about being pregnant!"

"You blackmailed me into marrying you."

"I took you on!"

"I should've laughed in your face and gone off with Carl. I've sacrificed my entire life to your career, and now I hear you've thrown it away."

"I saved your reputation!"

"Carl introduced me to a number of people tonight—"

"I saved you from being a fallen woman!"

"They were laughing over the antics of a cleaning lady who was clearly a spy. The description matched you exactly. How could you be so stupid?"

"I saved you from being a whore, like your mother!"

But she didn't seem to hear. "It's bad enough to hear that your husband of sixteen years has had a secret life as a cross-dresser," she snapped. "It's quite another to hear that he's just thrown away his career by prancing around as a maid in front of General von Witzleben and Lieutenant-Colonel Oster."

He blinked. What had she just said?

She moved closer. "What is Ambassador Wilson going to say when he hears about that?"

Russell's cheeks prickled as they drained of color. What had she been talking about? How could Grace, who never met anyone, have met the very people he'd been spying on just this afternoon? Did she say they'd been laughing at him? If they had, then von Lietzow must have been gloating in triumph. Russell felt his throat close as his cheeks fired up. He'd been humiliated, in front of them, in front of his rival. Most of all, he'd been humiliated in front of his wife. But before he could open his mouth to shape a response, Grace slipped away, disappearing into the waiting limousine.

He collapsed onto a seat, dark thoughts roiling. It was only later he noticed that she'd taken the children.

✠✠✠✠✠✠✠✠✠✠✠

Russell paced around the elegant waiting room, with its oil paintings of various landscapes, its ticking clock, its striped silk wallpaper. Herr Böhm had been highly recommended by Ambassador Wilson as a lawyer who specialized in family matters, especially German inheritance laws. But Russell couldn't relax. Did Wilson know about his embarrassing escapade? He hadn't said anything. Russell's mind churned away like the blades of a ship's motor, going down and up, down and up, dredging a life's worth of broken fragments to the surface.

He stopped in front of an oval mirror surrounded by rococo bows and chubby putti. A stranger, taut of mouth, with dark patches under the eyes squinted back. Where was Grace? It was Wednesday, the twenty-first of September, and he hadn't seen her for two days, not since that row over Peter.

Russell was beyond exhausted, but he couldn't sleep. His bed was so cold, so uninhabited. How could she leave him after sixteen years of marriage? She couldn't just have walked off like that, could she? Not his Grace. Not the wife he loved so much.

Grace was not good with words, she'd told him as much at their first meeting, or rather, the first time they'd walked out together. A sharp pain twisted his insides as he recalled the way she'd spoken to him then, how she'd tilted her head shyly, how an enchanting dimple appeared as her lips formed each word. He'd been hopelessly in love with her even then, with a girl-child of seventeen who had no idea of the power she wielded over him.

Somehow, he'd lost the knack of reading her silences because Grace did not communicate with words, but with posture, with the way she walked, how she sat, the quality of her silences. He sighed as he rubbed his left hand across his eyes, his wedding band cold and unforgiving. Grace's rebuke was justified, the press of work had made him absent so very frequently, and he'd forgotten her—well, not forgotten, exactly. He could never forget Grace. But he had not given her the attention she deserved.

And now, in this too-silent waiting room, images from his past attacked him: Grace's stark face pleading with him yet again not to go to Berlin, Angelina's dead eyes staring at him in surprise, a soldier's body bloating in the cold waters of the Piave river. Russell clenched his jaw as a satisfied smirk appeared on Angelina's face. Almost unconsciously, his fingers throttled a plump cushion in the lawyer's waiting room. She should be punished, he would make her suffer.

The well-appointed room paused breathless, like a nervous junior officer late for a meeting. Russell picked up the *Berliner Morgenpost* and scrutinized the news item on Czechoslovakia. That whole mess pitched his stress levels to such a height, he sometimes felt it would be better if the Nazis just marched in and got it over with. He opened his silver monogrammed cigarette case and lit up. Of course, that is what Herr Hitler wanted. He was the master manipulator of the psychological state.

"Herr Russell?"

A short gentleman with finely made bones and gray hair gestured him into his wood-paneled office.

"How can I help?" he asked as they sat across from each other.

"It's—delicate."

"I can assure you that everything you say is strictly confidential."

Russell patted the ash off his cigarette. "When my wife was very young, scarcely more than a child, she was engaged to be married. Her fiancé was a cad of the lowest sort who took advantage of her innocence. She became pregnant."

"He intended to marry her?"

"Yes. Well—That is an interesting question."

"Did they marry?"

"No. I found her in a—compromising situation, in a Berlin nightclub."

The lawyer paused, his pen suspended about his notes. He frowned. "I believe I've heard something like that before. Didn't some jumped-up nobody appear, and in the resulting melée attack a very august gentleman?"

Russell tapped his left ring finger on the polished mahogany.

The lawyer continued. "The lady vanished, if I'm not mistaken. Many say she'd been kidnapped—"

Russell thinned his lips. That story must have been swirling around Berlin for the past sixteen years. Many, like this lawyer, must have dined out on it.

"I found her in a sordid Berlin nightclub, in tears, attired very scantily." He inhaled on his cigarette. "I took her away. Only later did I discover she was expecting. So, I offered to marry her."

The lawyer looked up from beneath his bushy eyebrows. "You can produce a marriage certificate?"

Russell placed the document in front of him.

"In the fullness of time, Grace gave birth. The child, a son, was born in the United States." He leaned down and retrieved another document from his briefcase. "This birth certificate lists me as the father."

"But you are not?"

"I wanted to protect my wife's reputation."

"Ah, I see."

"And now, von Lietzow has issued a paternity suit, claiming the boy as his own."

The lawyer leaned forward. "So you were the fellow who…"

Russell stared back, unblinking.

"My dear sir, what are you doing here? Don't you know His Excellency could sue you?"

"I am a diplomat, I have immunity. Besides, it happened sixteen years ago."

"Nevertheless—"

"I am not here about that. I am concerned about my son, Peter. Unfortunately, my wife visited von Lietzow recently—against my wishes, you understand—and took it into her head to hand the boy over."

"Where does he live now?"

"With von Lietzow."

"I see. And what does the boy—I mean, your son—look like?"

Russell sighed. Slowly, reluctantly, he retrieved a photo from his coat pocket.

The lawyer scrutinized it for a moment.

"This is a recent likeness?"

Russell nodded.

The lawyer gently placed the photo on his desk. "My dear sir, you have no case. This young man resembles His Excellency."

"I am listed as his father."

The lawyer shook his head. "We have special laws in this country concerning such matters, the *Ius Sanguinis* laws. You understand that we Germans attach great importance to bloodlines? You cannot get around the fact that this young man is a younger version of Count Carl von Lietzow. Any lawyer in this city, indeed in this country, will tell you there's not a judge in this land who will ignore that kind of evidence. There is not a shred of doubt that His Excellency is the father, as he himself says. It is an open and shut case."

"Peter is an American citizen."

"My dear sir, we are sitting at table in Berlin, where Count von Lietzow wields enormous power. He is a scion of one of the oldest Berlin families, and that counts for a great deal around here. Even if your son did not look so much like him, you would have a hard fight ahead of you—"

"I am determined—"

The lawyer shook his head again. "You would be wasting your money. In any event, the deed is done. You say your wife took him to His Excellency?"

"Yes."

The lawyer spread his hands. "I am sorry, but I cannot help."

A shiver ran through the hairs on the back of his neck. For the first time Russell wished he had not come to Berlin.

✠✠✠✠✠✠✠✠✠✠✠

What was so odd was that Grace knew the fellow. Russell had gone from his morning's meeting with the lawyer to his office, where he'd put in a full day's work. The British Foreign Office had sent around a note summarizing an Anglo-French plan, which called upon the Czechs to surrender large parts of their country to the German Reich. Not surprisingly, the Czechs were not happy. However, when they resisted, the British and French told them that if they didn't accept the plan, they'd be abandoned to fight the *Wehrmacht* alone. Meanwhile, Hitler had ordered several towns in the Sudetenland to be occupied. At the request of his British allies, who wanted to maintain calm while these fragile negotiations ran their course Beneš had not yet expelled the German *Freikorps*.

Russell returned late to Savignyplatz to find his wife waiting for him in the front parlor, after a couple of days' absence, attired in a blue satin gown, its elegant lines set off by an elaborately beaded jacket. As he washed his face and changed into white tie, Russell wondered where she'd found her outfit but had no time to ask as the limousine was waiting downstairs.

Tonight the American Embassy was packed with the local Prussian aristocracy, high-ranking ministers, and members of the German military. Russell's cheeks warmed as he took in General von Witzleben, Admiral Wilhelm Canaris, and Lieutenant-Colonel Hans Oster, who flashed a smile for Grace as he kissed her hand, holding it far longer than necessary.

As Russell glowered, he remembered Oster had been demoted a few years ago because of an affair he'd had with a brother officer's wife. Yet his colleagues must have thought highly of him to have placed him in the Abwehr. Rumors whispered he was Canaris' second in command.

Eventually, Grace withdrew her hand and, scarcely glancing at her husband introduced them all, her German pronunciation perfect.

"Tell me, Mr. Russell," piped up one young blade. "I understand you are an expert on Berlin cleaning ladies. The floor in my office is very dusty—"

Russell tightened his jaw while the youngsters guffawed and their elders barely contained their smiles. Grace had been right. His attempts at getting close to Oster had been noticed—by everyone.

A not-very tall fellow with a roundish face and Polish eyes, the lids slanting slightly down, came forward. "Gräfin?" he murmured, his eyes fixed on Grace. Then he glanced at Russell and clicked his heels. "Mrs. Russell." He kissed her hand with a continental flourish.

Russell expected his wife to withdraw. Instead, she held her head up. "*Graf von Kleist, erlauben Sie mir, mein Mann Nicholas Russell einzuführen,* Count von Kleist, permit me to introduce my husband, Nicholas Russell."

The fellow shook hands and started making small talk, while Grace drifted off. It was only then that Russell realized she'd introduced her friend in German. But he had to be polite, as now the fellow wanted to know about the visit to Prague.

Russell frowned. How had that gotten out? Then he remembered Goerdeler.

"Prague is a beautiful city." Russell twisted his lips into a smile. "While I was there, I took the opportunity to visit the picture gallery, and I was duly impressed."

"I've been to Prague many times myself. I was born in Brünn, you know, or Brno if you prefer the Czech version of the name." He steered Russell into a corner. "Many of us have relatives in that part of the world. For example, I have a close friend whose parents were married in Prague. His mother was a von Welchau, his aunt married into the von Graslitz family. Both had estates to the west of Prague."

Russell nodded politely, hoping that the wine he was sipping wouldn't send him to sleep.

"What's happening in Czechoslovakia hits—how do you say? It hits close to home."

"What do you expect me to do about it?"

"My dear fellow, I expect nothing. Rather, I was hoping I could interest you in our little scheme."

"What do you mean?"

"We need to protect our families. We must prevent war. Are you interested?"

✠✠✠✠✠✠✠✠✠✠✠✠

Russell had no intention of acceding to von Kleist's request. He couldn't afford to alienate Wilson still further by engaging in risky, undercover activities whose outcome was unclear. But as Grace abandoned him yet again to that too-quiet mansion near Savignyplatz, Russell found himself reconsidering. Nearly a week had gone by, and Wilson still hadn't said anything and likely never would. Count von Kleist must know Il Cazzo, so perhaps his little scheme would bring Russell closer to Grace. Not seeing his wife was the worst thing that could happen to Russell as it robbed him of the power of persuasion. If only he could talk to her, she would forgive him, as she had done so many times before. Also, he missed his children, more than he'd thought possible. Their constant chatter, the debris they left in their wake, were former annoyances he now longed for.

And so Russell found himself four days later on a Sunday afternoon in late September, in a chauffeur-driven limousine, escorted by von Kleist to a villa on the outskirts of Berlin, the home of his dear friend code-named *Taube,* or Dove, who had Czech relatives. Taube must be the code-name for a woman. As they drove along, Russell tried to picture Frau or Fraülein Taube.

"How old is she?" he asked von Kleist.

"She?" Kleist smiled faintly. "She is a lady in her fifties."

Russell resumed his ruminations. Frau Taube was probably a matronly lady, her figure thickened by child-bearing and too many marzipan confections, sweet breads, and *Kaffee mit Sahne.* He tried out one or two Czech phrases in his head:

Good afternoon. *Dobré odpoledne.*

I am pleased to meet you. *Rád tě poznávám.*

Lovely weather for the time of year. *Jsme s krásné počasí na ročním období.*

He glanced out the window. It was a glorious afternoon, the trees changing color, their leaves glowing in the sunlight. As they turned south near Pichelsdorf to edge around the western side of Lake Wannsee, through Gatow and Hohengatow, multi-colored leaves drifted lazily down as cooling breezes came off the lake. Finally they came to Kladow, a pretty village with a church. Nearby, up a winding drive stood a pale green stucco villa, pavilion-like, very much the summer house, a Sanssouci in miniature. They exited the car and entered the foyer, which was palatial and ornate.

A stocky man with iron-gray hair turned his head, and Russell found himself looking into a pair of icy blue eyes.

He recoiled. What was he doing in the home of his arch-rival?

Carl von Lietzow gave him a feral smile. "At last, the industrious Herr Russell has spared enough time from his busy schedule to come to my door."

Of course he'd been expecting him. Russell glared at von Kleist who smiled back. He had fallen into a neat trap.

"Let me introduce my friends and comrades-in-arms: General von Witzleben, and *Obersleutnant* Oster."

Merda. It never occurred to him Il Cazzo could be involved in the Oster conspiracy.

"I gather that you have gone to a great deal of trouble to meet them," continued von Lietzow. "But I know them all personally. You had only to ask, my dear fellow."

Russell glared into their smiles.

"What would you like?" von Lietzow snapped his fingers, and a flunky scurried forward.

"Nothing," muttered Russell.

"Oh come now, my good fellow," remarked von Lietzow, smiling. "You need a little something to relax the nerves. We are not the Borgias, you know."

Russell stiffened. How dare Il Cazzo cast slurs upon his Italian heritage! How dare he suggest—Russell's cheeks prickled as his face drained of color. What *was* he suggesting? Surely he didn't know about Grace's mother—

"You seem upset," remarked von Lietzow. "I have just the remedy. How about a little Armagnac from Condom? I am told it is one of the best."

Russell glared again. When the brandy arrived, he pursed his lips to take the smallest of sips. Il Cazzo was right, it was excellent. But how had he managed to acquire such a luxury?

"Why a cleaning lady?" asked Oster, an annoying grin plastered across his face.

Russell remained silent, his cheeks warming.

"You do realize there are laws in this country against men dressing as women?" Il Cazzo gave him a wolfish smirk.

Russell drew himself up. "I have diplomatic immunity. My war record is superlative. I received the Congressional Medal of Honor—"

"You are not at the American Embassy," remarked Oster, smiling.

"If we reported this to the Gestapo…" said Il Cazzo.

Russell froze.

Il Cazzo laughed in his face. "Come! Let us sit down so that we can chat more comfortably." Between them, they herded Russell to a sofa that was penned in by a coffee table. Il Cazzo sat down next to him, putting his boots upon the white marble table-top.

"I know you do not believe me, Herr Russell, but I am a gentleman. As a proud Prussian aristocrat, I do not allow my guests to be—how do you put it? Ah yes, to be roughed up."

The others chuckled.

"But we wish to warn you," said von Witzleben. "Don't ever do that again."

"We cannot be responsible for the consequences," said Oster.

"Believe me, you do not want to make the acquaintance of the Gestapo," remarked Il Cazzo, smiling.

Russell's hands shook as he contemplated the white marble table. It was a handsome piece veined with gray. The *Geheime Staatspolizei* or the German Secret State Police was known for its brutality. It had the authority to investigate treason, espionage, sabotage and attacks against the Nazi Party. Of course these conspirators were not going to report him to the Gestapo, they must live in fear of it every day themselves. They had just been playing with him, and he hadn't understood because he was worn down with exhaustion. He should never have come here—but where was Grace? Peter?

Von Kleist sat on his other side. "I have a commission for you, if you are interested."

Russell rose to his feet. "I am not interested in your games. I wish to speak to my wife and son."

"All in good time." Il Cazzo bared his teeth into a smile. "First, we would like your assistance."

"It is a pleasant task, I assure you," remarked Kleist. "It concerns a lady."

Russell's cheeks flamed. He was utterly in their power, and that lava-like fury he curbed with an iron bit so that it only emerged during those dark hours when his head touched the pillow and he could not sleep, that fury threatened to erupt as he realized they would not stop in their efforts to humiliate him.

"Her name is Mabel Phelps," said Oster.

Russell winced. How did they know about her? Did they know about that indiscreet meeting in his office?

"We want to know if she is a double-agent," said von Witzleben.

Russell picked up his goblet and took a long swallow of his brandy. "Why me?"

"Well," drawled Il Cazzo, "your English is good—"

"And we have reason to believe that she…fancies you," remarked Oster.

Russell bit his lip. *Dio Cane*. Someone must have given them a thorough report.

"A little harmless flirtation, eh?" Il Cazzo zigzagged his eyebrows as he raised his brandy glass.

"But—"

"Why not invite her out for coffee, you know, that sort of thing?" remarked Oster, with a smile that would have been charming if the fellow were not so irritating.

"What happens if I refuse?"

"I think you know the answer to that," replied General von Witzleben.

Chapter Thirty-Four
Tuesday, 27 September

Somehow he stumbled home from Il Cazzo's blasted villa. Somehow he appeared at work each day, even though his colleagues looked at him cross-eyed as rumors about the precarious state of the Russell's marriage began to swirl. He would never get that ambassadorship to Rome now, he would always be a junior attaché, a paper-pusher, a flunky.

A couple of days later, a woman appeared as he sat at a café across from the Reich's Chancellery, not far from the American Embassy. She looked vaguely familiar, but he was in such a fog of despair, he couldn't recognize her.

"I see you don't remember me, Mr. Russell. I'm Mabel, Mabel Phelps. Don't you remember? I had the pleasure of meeting you a while ago." She leaned in closer and extended a hand. "I'm the person you're supposed to be spying on." Her laughter tumbled out of her throat.

Ignoring her hand, he sagged in his seat. Here was someone else come to make fun of him. He was almost getting used to it. At that moment, a unit of troops marched in front of the Chancellery. Russell narrowed his eyes as he took in the scene. There must have been around two hundred people standing in the square, their faces taut, as an uninterrupted procession from Unter den Linden passed, a whole army in flow, with horses, tanks, cannon, baggage wagons, and soldiers, endless numbers of them, their steel helmets low across their foreheads.

The balcony door opened and Hitler walked out, bareheaded, moving quickly to the railing. Russell glanced around. There were no cheers, no raised arms. Instead, people tightened their lips, stared at the ground, frowned. The tanks rolled past the silent populace. The Führer, un-cheered, vanished from the balcony, white-gloved SS men shutting the doors in his wake, drawing the curtain inside the window.

"Goodness," observed Miss Phelps. "They really don't want to go to war."

Russell nodded. He had never seen the German people react that way before.

"Did you hear Hitler's speech on Monday night from the *Sportpalast*?"

He shook his head.

"The speech degenerated quickly into a series of shrieks and shouts. I could barely understand what Hitler was saying, and my German is very good. Bill Shirer, who reported the story, told me he'd never seen anything like it. He told me that for the first time in all the years he's been reporting on him, Hitler seemed to have entirely lost control of himself."

Russell remained silent, suddenly wishing he could leave this accursed city, where violence was now so ubiquitous one seemed to breathe it in every minute of every day.

Miss Phelps signaled a waiter and ordered coffee and sandwiches for both of them.

"I don't like the way you look, Mr. Russell. When did you last eat?"

He couldn't remember.

"What about sleep?"

"I don't sleep," he replied through gritted teeth.

Somehow she managed to coax him to eat half a sandwich.

"I think you should take the rest of the afternoon off, and—spend some time with me."

"I couldn't do that."

"Why not?"

He was too tired to explain about all the work piling up on his desk.

"Let me put it another way. I have a commission for you."

He groaned. "Not again. I'm too depleted—"

"But I would be there with you. I think you need a complete break. How about flying to London with me?"

"Wilson would never permit that."

"He would if I explained that the only way to find out what's happening between Hitler and Chamberlain would be to go to London, pose as journalists, and find out from the British Foreign Office what is going on."

Russell peered into the depths of his coffee, too exhausted to react.

"Hitler and Chamberlain had that spat in Bad Godesburg a week ago. Now relations seem to be improving. Meanwhile, our friends Oster and Kleist are having to sit here in Berlin, biting their nails. No one expected Chamberlain to fly to Berchtesgarten in mid-September." She leaned forward and lowered her voice. "I understand that Oster was just about to arrest Herr Hitler and set up a constitutional monarchy when Chamberlain surprised us all by his willingness to appease Hitler. He wants to avoid going to war over the Sudetenland."

"Are you working for Oster?"

"Of course I am."

"I see. I was given a different impression."

She trilled out a laugh. "You were asked to spy on me, by that prankster Hans Oster. He was playing with you. Didn't you understand that?"

Russell put a hand to his temple, where the inevitable headache throbbed away.

"I'll talk to Ambassador Wilson myself." She rose, smiling.

He followed her back to the embassy.

"Don't move," she instructed as he opened the door to his cluttered office. "I'll be back in two shakes of a lamb's tail."

Russell slumped in his seat, returning to the Czech newspaper he'd been translating in a desultory fashion so that Wilson could be apprised of the latest events coming out of the Sudetenland. What was Grace doing now? He'd read in the Berliner Morgenpost that she was engaged to her rapist, who was introducing her into Berlin high society. As he pictured her lying naked in front of *quella figa*, that p*ssy, his fury mounted in his chest, vibrating against his ribs. He closed his eyes, ground his teeth, and shoved it deep down into his sore stomach.

He returned to the translation. He'd never imagined he'd miss his children so much, especially the two youngest. How he missed Marina's sweet ways and Benny's high spirits. He tried not to think of the two eldest, of Peter whom he'd unwillingly accepted as his own, or of Stacy, who was becoming unnervingly like her grandmother. As if on cue, Angelina's face materialized, her lips together in a coy smile. How she loved gloating over him. Savagely, he thrust her away, returning to the translation.

✠✠✠✠✠✠✠✠✠✠✠

In a London hotel, in the early hours of the morning on September the twenty-eighth, Russell heaved and tossed in a welter of bedclothes, unable to sleep. The other inhabitant of the large, curlicued bed, Miss Phelps, asked him in a whisper if he wouldn't mind lining up for tickets to the House of Commons Stranger's Gallery, so they could take in the first debate of the season. Given the current crisis, the gallery would be jammed, and so Russell left immediately, walking over to the Palace of Westminster. It was still dark, only three in the morning. By nine, he was in possession of two much-coveted tickets. He returned to the hotel where Miss Phelps greeted him with smiles of delight. Against his protests, she ordered a large breakfast. Afterwards, they walked around Whitehall and took in a lunchtime concert at St John's Smith Square before making their way to the House of Commons. They were among the first to take their seats. While members of Parliament listened attentively to Prime Minister Neville Chamberlain's account of the past two months, the Stranger's Gallery slowly filled with ambassadors, clergy, members of the royal family, and other famous people. A nondescript fellow stood at the back of the chamber, waiting.

Miss Phelps nudged him. "That's Sir Alexander Cadogan," she remarked. "He's permanent undersecretary for foreign affairs. I wonder what he's doing here."

Sir Alexander produced a note that was handed around, gradually making its way through the labyrinth of back benchers to Sir John Simon, the chancellor of the Exchequer, who sat next to Chamberlain.

Sir John took the note and with a small gesture, tried to attract the prime minister's attention, but Chamberlain continued speaking. It was only when Sir John rose to his feet that Chamberlain paused.

There was dead silence as the Prime Minister read the note.

"Shall I tell them now?" he whispered.

Sir John nodded.

Chamberlain turned to face the house.

"I have now been informed by Herr Hitler that he invites me to meet him at Munich tomorrow morning. He has also invited Signor Mussolini and Monsieur Daladier. Signor Mussolini has accepted and I have no doubt Monsieur

Daladier will also accept. I need not say what my answer will be—"

"Thank God for the prime minister!" shouted one of the members of parliament.

Chamberlain smiled his thanks. "We are all patriots, and there can be no honorable member of this house who did not feel his heart leapt that the crisis has been once more postponed to give us once more an opportunity to try what reason and good will and discussion will do to settle a problem which is already within sight of settlement. Mr. Speaker, I cannot say any more. I am sure that the house will be ready to release me now to go and see what I can make of this last effort. Perhaps they may think it will be well, in view of this new development, that this debate shall stand adjourned for a few days, when perhaps we may meet in happier circumstances."

The house rose as one, with the notable exception of three people. Miss Phelps peered down. "That's Sir Anthony Eden, Sir Harold Nicolson, and Leo Amery. They're all firmly anti-appeasement." One other was silent and seated, his head sunk into his shoulders. "Why, that's Sir Winston Churchill," she remarked. "I'd recognize him anywhere. I interviewed him a few years back."

Russell squinted down as the prime minister moved to the back of the chamber, about to pass an honorable member who so clearly disagreed with him. But Churchill rose, and shook hands. "Godspeed," he told Chamberlain.

✠✠✠✠✠✠✠✠✠✠✠

The next couple of days passed in a blur, as the world held its breath awaiting the news from Munich. Russell tagged along after Miss Phelps, who insisted that he call her Mabel, doing the usual sorts of things, lunching at the Author's Club in Whitehall, visiting art galleries and museums, taking in a play or two. But he just couldn't focus. He seemed to have lost control of his life completely. How had that happened? The last time he'd been in such a fog had been the spring of his first year at Georgetown University, for the same reason: Grace, or rather her absence. Grace, Grace, Grace taunted his headache as he peered into luxury shops in London's Mayfair district, reluctantly accepted a scone from Mabel as they took tea at the Ritz, slumped on a bench at the National Gallery, drinking in *The Virgin of the Rocks* by Leonardo da Vinci. Grace.

Her absence left him numb, affectless. Everything seemed so drab, the colors muted and dull. He was dimly grateful for Mabel's solicitations, her concern, but he just couldn't summon up enough energy to thank her. The days stretched long and murky. For the first time since he could remember, he had no plans because he had no hope. Eventually, on Friday September the thirtieth, news came that Hitler's conference in Munich had ended. Mabel immediately found transportation to Heston Aerodrome so they would witness Prime Minister Chamberlain's return from Germany.

When they arrived, it was pouring rain, but that didn't stop crowds of British people from standing stoically at the aerodrome, heads up, peering out from under their umbrellas, looking for the machine as it came in through the clouds.

Russell checked his watch as it circled around in the dirt-washed sky. The prime minister had made this journey in a little under three and a half hours, as the wires had reported the machine had taken off from Munich at 2:20 PM. Slowly, he scanned the document that Mabel had obtained for him. Titled "The Munich Agreement," it showed that Great Britain, France and Italy had signed a settlement permitting Nazi Germany's annexation of the Sudetenland, those parts of Czechoslovakia that were mainly inhabited by German speakers.

Russell glanced up as the machine rolled to a stop, and the Prime Minister of Great Britain unfolded himself from his aircraft seat. All the men doffed their hats. "Hooh-raay! Hooh-raay! Hooh-raay!" cheered the crowd as they clapped.

Smiling and beaming, Chamberlain greeted his Foreign Secretary Lord Halifax, the French Ambassador, and representatives of the German Embassy.

Russell glanced at the document again. The Sudetenland was of immense strategic importance to Czechoslovakia as it contained most of its border defenses and heavy industries. Even worse, representatives of the Czech government were absent from the list of names who signed the agreement that dismembered their country. Russia had not been invited, either. That could spell trouble.

Someone jogged his elbow as the crowd streamed past the barricades. "Hip, hip hooray!" they shouted.

"There's only two things I want to say," remarked Mr. Chamberlain. "First of all, I've received an immense number of letters during all these anxious times. So has my wife."

Russell winced.

"Letters of support, and approval, and gratitude. And I can't tell you what an encouragement that has been to me. I want to thank the British people for what they have done."

"We want to thank you!" remarked a young woman.

Russell examined the Munich Agreement again. Why such humiliating terms? Chamberlain had given Hitler everything he'd asked for. This document was almost identical to the Bad Godesberg memorandum of the previous week.

"And next, I want to say, that the settlement of the Czechoslovakian problem, which has now been achieved is, in my view, only the prelude to a larger settlement in which all Europe may find peace."

The only difference was that Hitler had actually made a slight concession. Instead of invading the Sudetenland on October the first, he had postponed it until October the tenth. Russell frowned. That made no sense. Then he spotted the piece of paper that Prime Minister Neville Chamberlain was now flourishing.

"This morning, I had another talk with the German Chancellor Herr Hitler, and here is the paper which bears his name upon it as well as mine."

"Hooh-raay!" cheered the crowd.

"Some of you, perhaps, have already heard what it contains but I would just like to read it to you:

> "We, the German Führer and Chancellor, and the British Prime Minister, have had a further meeting today, and are agreed in recognizing that the question of Anglo-German relations is of the first importance for the two countries, and for Europe. We regard the agreement signed last night, and the Anglo-German Naval Agreement, as symbolic of the desire of our two peoples never to go to war with one another again."

The crowd roared.

"We are resolved that the Method of Consultation—"

"Hear, hear," murmured some people near Russell.

> "—shall be the method adopted to deal with any other questions that may concern our two countries. And we are determined to continue our efforts to remove possible sources of difference, and thus to contribute to the peace in Europe."

The crowd roared again.

Just then, Mabel nudged him. "I've been looking for you everywhere," she said, struggling to make herself heard above the crowd.

"Well done, Mr. Chamberlain!" said a middle-aged gentleman standing nearby.

"Three cheers for Neville!" said the young man next to him.

Russell and Mabel struggled through the massive crowd to a cordoned-off area, which penned in members of the press.

"This is disastrous news for Hans Oster and friends," she remarked, when they got there.

He nodded. How ironic that their best hope for overthrowing that tyrant Hitler has been destroyed by this weak, well-intentioned man. Oster and his friends could never launch their coup and arrest Hitler now; he was just too popular. They would have no support from the German people. Hitler had done it again. His instinct for survival was uncanny.

"Good old Neville, for he's a jolly good fellow, for he's a jolly good fellow, for he's a jolly good fellow, and so say all of us. And so say all of us, and so say all of us, for he's a jolly good fellow, for he's a jolly good fellow, for he's a jolly fellow, and so say all of us," sang the crowd as the prime minister was ushered to his car, which drove off in the direction of Whitehall.

"We should go to the Foreign Office to learn more," said Mabel. "I hope they're still open. I'll find someone to give us a ride."

✠✠✠✠✠✠✠✠✠✠✠

The Foreign Office was not as deserted as Mabel had feared. Upon hearing their request to meet with Lord Halifax, the Secretary of State for Foreign Affairs, a punctilious junior officer, ushered them up its imposing staircase to a plush waiting room. Even though it was now early evening, there were many waiting there to speak with him.

Mabel furnished Russell with her copy of *Paris Soir* while she left the waiting room in search of coffee.

LA PAIX! proclaimed the newspaper, which went on to describe how Édouard Daladier, the French premier who'd signed the Munich Agreement along with Chamberlain, Mussolini and Hitler, was acclaimed by a cheering crowd all the way form the airfield to the center of Paris.

Russell glanced up as the door opened, expecting to see Mabel's cheerful face. Instead, a coolly elegant vision of loveliness materialized.

"This way, please, Madam." The punctilious young man bowed low.

Russell dropped his newspaper as he leapt to his feet, his heart thudding in his chest.

She took a step backward and gave him a long look, but it was impossible to read her expression through the thick netting that veiled her elegant hat.

"Grace!" he whispered. "What are you doing here?"

The young man paused, his hand on the door leading to Halifax's private chamber.

"Do you know that gentleman?"

"No." Her voice was as cold as the freezing waters of the Piave River.

Russell came closer. "I must speak with you—"

The door opened and the lean figure of Halifax appeared.

"The Countess von Lietzow." The flunky bowed again.

"Enchanté," replied Halifax, folding his tall frame into a low bow as he kissed her hand. He glanced at Russell.

"I'll be with you shortly, my dear fellow. Ladies first, you know." As Halifax ushered her into his office, the sleeve of Grace's blue moiré jacket brushed against Russell's arm.

The door shut.

Russell sank back into his seat. The brush from her jacket was almost a caress, except it was not. He bent down to retrieve his newspaper, glancing up to see people's faces tilted towards him, their expressions ranging from pity to contempt. Russell's cheeks fired up. *Porco dio*, that scoundrel must have sent her here. His cronies in that Black Orchestra would also want to know what had happened in Munich. She was on the same mission. His thoughts revved up. Where was she staying? Was there any hope he could see her?

"Here we are." Mabel sat next to him in the seat he'd saved for her, handing him a cup of black coffee. "What's wrong?"

He remained silent.

She leaned in. "You look as if you've received a dreadful shock."

He turned away to hide the lone tear leaking down his cheek.

"Is Grace here?" Mabel cocked her head towards the closed door of Halifax's office.

He nodded. "She arrived just now." He swallowed. "She wouldn't even look at me." He gazed into his bitter brew: *Schwartz we die Nacht, Heiß wie die Hölle, Süß wie die Liebe*, Dark as Night, Hot as Hell, Sweet as Love, sang the advertising jingle in his head.

✠✠✠✠✠✠✠✠✠✠

Of course. He was waiting for her outside. Grace stiffened as Russell came silently towards her. Thank goodness Carl had insisted on her taking an entourage to London. As he appeared, Carl's minions formed a semi-circle around her.

"How could you?"

She stopped.

"You are my wife."

Grace remained silent.

"I demand that you return to Berlin with me."

Grace continued silent. Something told her that the only way to get out of his clutches was to refuse to engage, which meant refusing to speak. He could do nothing to her, the children were back in Berlin, staying with Carl's Great-Aunt Sidonie.

"Grace!"

She lowered her eyes. Over the past month, she'd forgotten how magnetic he was. She'd forgotten that she couldn't be completely unmoved by his naked pain. He was so thin, he seemed almost famished. His emaciation had the effect of making his eyes larger, and it was the light in those eyes that sent a whisper of fear coiling up her spine.

"Grace." His voice kissed her. "You cannot do this to me. You cannot be so cruel." He came closer. "You are torturing me—"

"Gräfin." Herr Nordwitz, Carl's personal secretary, stepped forward. "We must leave." He offered his arm.

Grace allowed him to escort her away.

"Noooo!" A cry of agony burst from Russell's lips. "Grace, you cannot abandon me. I am in the fires of hell. *Graziella, vita mia, si torna, si torna*—-Grace, my life, come back, come back—"

Somehow, Grace kept moving without looking back. She hadn't known she could be so cold, so unmoved by his pleas. Sixteen years ago, she'd been unable to ignore him. Now she knew better. Grace wrinkled her nose. She knew all his dirty secrets. If only she'd listened to her relatives all those years ago.

"Nearly there, Gräfin." Herr Nordwitz steered her into the waiting limousine that took them to a discreet hotel near Covent Garden. As they drove away, Russell's keening cries washed over her, making the hairs on the backs of her arms prickle.

✠✠✠✠✠✠✠✠✠✠✠

On the first Tuesday in October, Violet stood close to the window of her boutique in Georgetown, holding up a piece of fabric for the sun to shine through so that she could check the weave of the silk for evenness. Dorothy Taussig Willard, Edith Taussig's daughter, was getting married. She was a little younger than her mother had been when she'd attended that party seventeen years ago, the one Auntie P. had thrown for Grace to gauge everyone's reaction to her suitor. Violet frowned as she pictured her half-uncle Domenico Pagano, the *soi-disant* Nicholas Russell, playing piano with Grace. It was remarkable how one person could get their way over the objections of everyone else. No one had wanted that marriage, not Auntie P., not Mother, not Violet. Yet, somehow, he'd managed to circumvent them all. *If I were living in the Middle Ages*, muttered Violet to herself, *I'd say he'd bewitched her*. Not for the first time, she wondered when his spell would ever be broken.

She moved away from the window, laid out the fabric on her cutting table, and with tape measure and tailor's chalk began to mark it up. Life had been good. She had a supportive husband, three wonderful sons, and work she loved doing. Tom had helped her get a bank loan so that she could turn the small house on Beall Street into *Modes Pauline*, named in honor of Auntie P. He'd bought her a car so that she could travel from their home in Petworth to the shop in Georgetown, where Violet specialized in custom evening wear, wedding dresses, and accessories for her wealthy clientele.

There was a knock on the half-open door, and the postmaster stuck his head around.

"Mrs Ecker, this telegram has just come for you. Says it's come all the way from Berlin—Deech-land."

Violet took it. "Deutschland. It's from Germany—Jeepers creepers! It's from von Lietzow."

"Who's he?"

"A count, or something." Violet hastily scanned the message, asking her to call immediately. She looked up. "He's an aristocrat."

"My, oh my! What fancy friends you have, Mrs. Ecker."

She picked up her hat and put it on. "I'm going to have to use the telephone at the telegraph office."

✠✠✠✠✠✠✠✠✠✠✠

"Violet?"

"Gracie!" When silence reverberated from the other end, Violet's stomach dropped. "Are you all right?"

"I—I'm fine. I didn't expect to hear from you, Violet."

"I'm calling because I got a telegram from Carl von Lietzow. This is the right number?"

"Yes—I'm staying at—" The years slipped away, and Grace slid back into her niche as the dreamy younger sister.

"What's wrong, Gracie?"

Grace fingered the opal necklace Carl had given her for her birthday. What should she say? How could she tell her sister that their half-uncle was becoming unhinged, that she couldn't bear to be with him any more? Violet would start on again about Mother, and Grace didn't think she could bear to hear that, not when the disturbing light in those dark eyes haunted every moment, day and night. Had he looked like that when he'd—been with Mother? She should tell her sister she was expecting another child, Carl's child, but she couldn't do it. Not yet. It was too embarrassing. She took a deep breath and blurted out the first thing that came to mind.

"It's Carl—Count von Lietzow. He wants Peter."

"Well, he can't have him."

"I don't know—"

"Gracie! You weren't thinking of handing him over?"

Tears trickled down Grace's cheeks.

"Grace! You can't do that to your own son!"

"But he's Carl's son."

"I realize that, but—I assume Mr. Russell doesn't agree with you?"

Grace wiped away tears with the tips of her finger. "I wish I hadn't gotten myself in such a mess."

"Don't cry, Gracie. I'll come as soon as I can."

"Thank you," sobbed Grace.

"Just hang tight, and whatever you do, do *not* go and see the count."

"Why ever not?"

"Isn't it obvious? Because he's a manipulative bastard who will winkle that boy out from under your fingers before you have time to say Jack Robinson."

Grace smiled, despite herself.

"Gracie? Are you still there?"

"I'm here. We're staying in a mansion in Savignyplatz, I mean—" Grace paused. She really should tell her sister to come to Kladow.

"Sah—what? Oh, never mind. Don't worry, I'll find you. Bye for now and keep your chin up. And promise you won't visit him."

Violet put the phone down and exited the telegraph office. She was busy now that the Christmas season was coming on, her boutique churning out frocks for Georgetown's wealthy ladies. She didn't have time to go to Berlin, but—wait a minute, why had Gracie been talking about Carl von Lietzow as if he were the problem, when the telegram she'd received had come from von Lietzow himself? That whole thing about Peter couldn't be right, or if it was, it couldn't be the most pressing issue. And the odd thing was, Gracie hadn't mentioned her husband or the other children once. Why not? Why had Carl von Lietzow appealed to her, Violet, Grace's estranged sister?

It had been ages since she'd heard from Grace. Of course, they exchanged birthday and Christmas cards, but they'd only had one or two tentative visits over the years. The truth was, Violet couldn't bear her half-uncle-brother-in-law. He was thoroughly untrustworthy, and hiding something. Russell reciprocated by being distant and prickly. Their visits were awkward and brief. So for von Lietzow to actually ask her for help—Gracie must be in quite a pickle.

Violet checked her watch. It was four o'clock on a Tuesday. If she hurried, she could leave, maybe, on Thursday, which would get her to Berlin by the end of the following week. She'd have to make sure her assistants could cover for her while she was away, and perhaps hire a new girl. Violet crossed the busy road and made her way back to her boutique. She had to go, and the sooner the better.

Chapter Thirty-Five
Thursday, 13 October

The rest of the fall was just as disastrous as his marriage. On October the first, the Munich Agreement forced the Czechs to give up the Sudetenland to the Nazis. On October the second, the Poles occupied Teschen and Freistadt. On October the third, Hitler toured the Czech defenses that Russell had seen for himself a month before.

Russell wandered along Bendlerstrasse, so tired he couldn't sleep, so on edge that everything was too much, the corners of the buildings too sharp, the sunlight too bright, his starched shirt too scratchy. He needed a doctor. He wasn't getting any rest, but even in his current state, Russell drew the line at using drugs. He drank far too much black coffee in the mornings, then tried to induce sleep by downing too many scotches on the rocks in the evenings. But the alcohol woke him too early, before he'd had a chance to catch a deep sleep. Most of all, his rage had nowhere to go. It detonated in his too-quiet bedroom as he went to bed. It revved him up during the early hours, as he paced, smoked, drank. It slid into his thoughts at awkward moments during the day. It choked every breath. And sometimes it seemed that every time he drew breath, his chest threatened to explode. This couldn't be good for his heart. If matters didn't improve, he could find himself in an early grave, like Lamo.

Russell paused for a moment. How he missed his brother, how he longed for his advice. Lamo's absence was profound, deafening. Now that this mess over Czechoslovakia was over, he could leave Berlin and head home. But he couldn't go without his children, he couldn't depart without his wife. Grace was still his wife, wasn't she? Russell had heard nothing, seen nothing, since that encounter with Grace in London.

Feeling nauseous, he pushed his way up the steps of the American Embassy, forcing himself along the dim corridor towards his office. Slowly, he grasped the brass knob and opened the door. A figure was sitting in a club chair in front of his coffee table, powdering her face. Angelina raised her head and twisted her lips into a ghastly smile.

✠✠✠✠✠✠✠✠✠✠✠✠

Violet had arrived early that morning, changing trains in Hamburg. She went straight to the American Embassy, inquiring for Mrs. Russell. The young man behind the counter carefully wrote the address on a strip of paper. Violet grabbed a cab and made for Savignyplatz. How cold and grand these frozen mansions seemed, reminding her of Aunt Louisa's lodgings in Berlin. She glanced at the piece of paper. She was going to Mommsenstrasse 1, on the corner of some other street whose name she couldn't make out. The taxi cab stopped, she paid him off, and went up to the front door. Grace had come up in the world to live in such a fancy mansion. Violet pressed the bell on the front door. How was Frau Varga? She must go over to Nollendorfplatz and find out. The house exuded silence. Violet frowned and pressed the buzzer again. No response. She stepped down the marble steps and walked around the back of the house. Everything seemed untended, the grass overgrown, the roses blowsy with neglect.

Violet walked to the Ku'damm and hailed a cab, returning to the embassy to ask, this time, for Mr. Russell. She was directed to a reedy young man who favored skinny ties.

"I'm looking for my brother-in-law, Mr. Russell."

The young man blinked. "I didn't know he had family."

Violet stifled a retort. "*Bitte,*" she said. "I've come all the way from America to see him."

"Ah, I see." He opened the door to a large and well-furnished corner office. "May I offer you refreshment?"

He brought coffee in a gilded china cup with matching saucer and minuscule teaspoon, offering cream and sugar.

Violet took a sip and grimaced.

"Es tut mir leid, wir haben nur Kaffee-Ersatz, I'm sorry we have only fake coffee."

"I thought things were improving."

The secretary looked down and fiddled with his tie, explaining that the German people were required, by their Führer, to make sacrifices for the good of society.

Violet rolled her eyes. "Tell me about Mr. Russell. How is he?"

The young man glanced up. "Do you really want to know?"

Violet blinked. "Of course I do. I'm his—-how do you say sister-in-law? Schwägerin?"

The secretary nodded as he hovered near her seat and licked his lips.

"You look uncomfortable, please sit down."

"I'm not sure Mr. Russell would approve."

"He's not here, is he? Besides I asked you to sit."

The young man closed the office door oh-so-quietly and perched himself on the very edge of a Louis Quinze chair. He leaned forward. "I'm quite worried about him." He lowered his voice. "He's been acting strangely recently. He keeps falling asleep at his desk."

"So he's been working too hard. Is that surprising?"

"No, but—" He twisted his fingers. "He eats—nothing. Well—not much."

"Why is that?"

"I don't know, but it is said that Mrs. Russell spends a great deal of time these days with Count von Lietzow at his villa in Kladow."

Oh. So that would explain von Lietzow's telegram. But why hadn't Gracie said so?

Violet put her cup and saucer down and asked the secretary to give her directions, which he wrote down for her in large spidery handwriting.

She pocketed the note. "What else?"

"Well—" He fiddled with his tie again. "One day, it must have been a month or so ago, I opened his door. You understand he instructs me to open it very quietly so I don't disturb him when he's working. And he was walking—I don't know the word in English."

"Show me."

The secretary rose, stuck out his derrière, and pranced around the room, taking mincing steps.

"Are you sure?"

"*Jawohl*. Later that day, he returned to the office. It was very late, you understand, around seven in the evening. He carried a bag with him, and in it was a wig. A lady's wig."

Before Violet could ask more, a telephone rang. The secretary made his excuses and scurried off.

Goodness, gracious, she had no idea that Russell had those kinds of interests. She'd no idea he was a pervert. Did Grace know about this? Is that why she was spending time with von Lietzow?

She'd just opened her powder pack to refresh her face when the door opened. As Russell's eyes locked onto hers, his pupils dilated, and his face drained of every ounce of color. He grasped at the door knob as if to stop himself from falling.

"Surely you remember me. It's Violet."

Slowly, the color returned to his face. "*Maledizione*, Damn," he muttered.

"Thanks," returned Violet. "Same to you too."

He glared, then laughed reluctantly.

Violet scrutinized him. Outwardly, he seemed normal, immaculate in an expensive suit, shirt, and silk tie, with one of those irritating matched silk handkerchiefs. But he was too thin, his skin stretched taut over high cheekbones. He must have lost at least twenty pounds.

"Mr. Russell, I'm concerned about you."

"You may call me Domenico." His tone was gently reproving.

"Sorry. May I call you Dom? Your name is a bit of a mouthful."

"You may call me Nico." His face sagged as he shut the door behind him. "It's what my brother called me when we were young."

"So, Nico. I'm concerned about you. You look exhausted, and you're making mistakes."

He sat behind his huge desk, and compressed his lips. "Who says so?"

She leaned forward. "Now, don't go all prickly on me, I know I'm offending your pride by saying so, but this is dangerous. Someone spotted you with a lady's wig."

He paled.

"I had no idea—"

"It's not what you think," he replied between gritted teeth.

"How is Grace?"

"That is none of your business."

Violet folded her arms. "I come all this way to Berlin, at Grace's request, and the first thing I hear is my brother-in-law has been seen going around as a drag queen. Naturally, I have a few questions."

He made exasperated clicking noises between his teeth.

"What on earth were you doing in that getup?"

"I really cannot tell you."

"Okay. So you're a spy."

"Will you please keep your voice down?"

"Okay, okay." She lowered the volume. "I don't mean to blow your cover. I'm concerned, that's all."

"You say Grace asked you to come."

"We talked over the phone."

He frowned.

"She didn't tell you?"

"No."

"Well that's a pretty pickle. She sounded really upset."

"What about?"

"She was crying because Count Whatsit wants to take Peter away from her."

"Oh. That."

"Yes, that. Has she been to see him?"

He took a cigarette out of his monogrammed case and offered her one, which she declined. He lit up with a matching monogrammed lighter

"You're not sure?" she asked.

"Don't look at me like that."

"How am I supposed to look? You're married to her, aren't you?"

There was a pause. "Indeed I am. Thank you for reminding me." He curled his lips, baring nicotine-stained teeth. "Please tell your sister, when you see her, that I expect her to return home, to me, immediately."

The expression in his dark eyes made her shiver. Violet rose. "I don't think—"

"I do not care what you think," he snapped. "Your sister is *my wife*. Her duty is to *me*."

"Okay, okay. Keep your hair on. I'll go see her right now."

Violet exited the room before he could say more, the hairs on the back of her neck prickling. Never before had her fussy, irritating brother-in-law creeped her out quite like this, even though she'd privately called him a creep more than once. What on earth was going on?

✠✠✠✠✠✠✠✠✠✠✠

"Fraülein Violet? How nice to see you." Carl von Lietzow looked much the same as he had sixteen years ago. "I expect you'd like to see your sister and your nephews and nieces. But first, what can I get you?"He snapped his fingers and a flunky appeared. "Would you care for a sherry or some tea?"

Violet ordered tea and perched on the edge of a grand curlicue of a chair in his elegant reception room.

He lit an ornate pipe, settling down opposite her. "You're looking very well, and you're married I hear. Who is the fortunate gentleman?"

"His name is Tom. Tom Ecker. He's a detective."

"Ah yes. I remember the name. I believe he was involved in your mother's case."

"You keep yourself informed."

"Indeed, I do. Anything concerning my wife and our son is my business."

"Grace is not your wife."

"Not yet."

"You seem very confident."

He leaned back in his seat and smiled.

"You mean to sit there and tell me that you're going to cross swords with Mr. Russell—and win?"

"Why not? Mr. Russell may have many good—aspects, but he's not invincible."

"He usually gets his way."

"Does he now?"

"I don't understand."

"I see you are not familiar with German law. In this country, we take bloodlines very seriously. There is not a judge in this land who will ignore that kind of evidence, even if our son did not bear such a marked resemblance to me."

"That's interesting. What are the laws in Germany regarding cousins?"

"Marriage between first cousins is perfectly acceptable here, not so in Austria."

"How about half-uncles?"

"Why do you ask?"

"You haven't heard?"

"What haven't I heard?"

"Did you know that the name Russell is an alias?"

"Yes. I did know that. Unfortunately, his alias is a common name in the United States. I had the Pinkertons searching records at Northwestern, and we could not find him. We had to find him through his brother. Fortunately, there was only one person during the year of 1910 who had the name Girolamo Pagano. Their addresses matched."

Violet was silent. She had no idea that over the years, Carl von Lietzow had been spying on her sister, or the family.

"This is important isn't it? I can tell from the expression on your face."

"Mother's maiden name was Angelina Pagano."

"*Wirklich?* You mean that the illustrious Herr Russell is related to your mother?"

"He is her half-brother."

He whistled. "I didn't know that. So that is why you ask about half-uncles. *Heiliger Strohsack*, why didn't I know before?"

"I guess our family is good at keeping secrets."

"Why did no one stop them from marrying?"

Violet sagged in her seat.

"My memory of that time is hazy. I was knocked out you know. The doctor said I had concussion. All I clearly remember is that *mein Liebchen* seemed to think it was her duty to marry him."

"No one in our family wanted them to marry, but it's not prohibited in Leviticus."

"Aha! Yet people will hear the word *uncle*. It doesn't sound good. I can—how do you say it Fraülein Violet? Ah yes, I can make hay out of this. *Vielen Dank*. A most useful piece of information." He chuckled as he placed his pipe on a marble table, and rose. "Fraülein Violet, you've been most helpful. Now, I expect you wish to see your sister."

✠✠✠✠✠✠✠✠✠✠✠✠

Grace, when she found her, was pale and drawn. Violet hugged her close. "What's wrong?"

Tears streamed down Grace's face. "I've made such a hash of things—"

Violet gave her a handkerchief. "Are you living with Carl?"

Grace nodded.

"What about Mr. Russell—Domenico?"

Grace wiped her eyes. "I can't live with him any more. I just can't."

"What does Carl say?"

"He keeps telling me not to worry. He says he has Nico well in hand."

"What an ugly name Nico Russell is," murmured Violet. "It doesn't suit him at all. Which…Grace, I went to see him—"

Grace went white. "You didn't. Oh, Violet, I should have warned you—"

"Warned me about what?"

Grace turned her head away. "I don't know,"she mumbled. "He hasn't been himself lately. He's becoming—deranged."

"You sound like Mother, Gracie."

Grace slumped. "If only she were here, if only we hadn't lost her too soon—"

"You've never said that before."

"I often wonder what would have happened if she hadn't gone."

"You wouldn't have married Mr. Russell, or whatever he calls himself."

"I wouldn't have gotten pregnant,"murmured Grace.

"You would have been free to pursue your career as a violinist."

"Don't, Violet." Grace grimaced as if she were in pain.

"I'm sorry Gracie, I'm just trying to make you see—"

"Make me see what, Violet? Exactly what is it you're trying to say?"

"He was responsible for Mother's death."

"You don't have a shred of evidence for that."

"Doesn't Mother's death seem too convenient?"

"You're saying I married a murderer. But that doesn't make sense. In all the years I've known Nico, he hasn't seemed the least bit violent."

"He didn't have to once he'd gotten you. But he did threaten violence once, didn't he? Don't you remember how he threatened to shoot himself if you didn't marry him?"

"That's different."

"Is it? He threatened violence when he saw he was going to lose you. Mother stood in his way, so he removed her."

Grace looked as though she were about to throw up. "Don't, Violet. I can't bear it."

✠✠✠✠✠✠✠✠✠✠✠✠

"I am not divorcing my wife," said Russell softly. "How many times do I have to repeat myself?"

It was less than a week after his encounter with Violet, only the third week of October. Yet, despite the glorious sunshine outside, Russell felt cold to the bone. He'd been working in his office when he'd received a summons from a Berlin judge. When Wilson saw it, he told him to go at once. "He's the most esteemed fellow in the country. You don't have to obey this summons as you have diplomatic immunity. All the same, I think you should go to hear what he has to say." So Russell stepped into the waiting limousine, which drove him to a palatial building in Wilhelmstrasse, the diplomatic nerve-center of Berlin.

"I see I must offer you an inducement, my dear fellow," remarked Il Cazzo. "I can produce witnesses who will testify that Grace's relatives were most unhappy with her choice of suitor."

Russell tightened his jaw.

"Let me see…there is Mrs Philips, Grace's Aunt Louisa, who was most put out when the expensive wedding she'd planned for her niece came to nothing. There is the Marquise de Chabrillan, Grace's cousin Teresa, who will verify this. And there is our star witness, Violet Ecker. She is, I believe, your sister-in-law."

Russell glared. He might have known that interfering bitch would stir up a hornet's nest. How blithely he'd gone against Grace's relatives, her aunt, cousin, and sister, never imagining they could do anything against him.

"She is my wife. Our union was sanctified by God—"

"And your brother," interrupted that scoundrel von Lietzow, a smirk on his face. "If that isn't nepotism, I don't know what is. Your marriage was a rushed affair with your brother as the officiating priest."

"My brother was my best man," hissed Russell.

Von Lietzow sighed as he clasped his hands over his stick, whose ruby eyes glinted malevolently at Russell. He glanced at his lawyers.

"I was hoping I would not have to do this, but you give me no other—option. I have heard that Mrs. Philips, the Marquise de Chabrillan, and Mrs. Ecker were not the only ones opposed to your marriage with Grace. There was Mrs. Barilla, Grace's great-aunt Paulina, who'd taken care of her in her own home since the age of six. Then there was the well-known opposition of Grace's mother, Mrs. Angelina Miller." Von Lietzow paused, fixing Russell with a pair of icy blue eyes. "What happened to Mrs. Miller?"

Russell stared back, unblinking. He couldn't know, he couldn't possibly know, except—

"I don't know what you mean." Russell forced words through lips stiff with cold.

"You don't? Your sister-in-law Violet Ecker is married to a well-regarded detective in Washington. They've had suspicions for years. After all, Mrs. Angelina Miller was a young woman when she died, only thirty-three years old. Her daughter Violet is willing to swear that her mother didn't look ill. What do you have to say to that?"

Russell fumbled in his coat pocket for his silver cigarette case, retrieved it, opened it, slid a cigarette out, and struggled for several moments to light it.

The nicotine hit relaxed him. "You are talking of matters that happened years ago, sixteen years ago. There was an inquest into the death of Mrs. Miller. The verdict was death by accidental causes. You cannot overturn that."

"There is no statute of limitations on heinous crimes in the United States, is there, my dear fellow? Such as first-degree murder?"

Russell glowered. Damn him, he was good.

Von Lietzow smiled and cracked his knuckles. "If I made it known that Grace's uncle kidnapped her on the eve of her marriage to me—"

"Half-uncle," responded Russell automatically, before doing a double-take. What had he said? How did he know? *Dio merda,*

"Do you really think the public will care about that distinction?"

"It has Biblical import."

Von Lietzow rose. "I can ruin you. I can have this story all over the German and American press tomorrow. How would you like to read *The New York Herald* and see a front-page headline that says: INCEST! UNCLE KIDNAPS MINOR, FORCES HER INTO HIS BED. What does that do, my dear fellow, to your chances of becoming ambassador to Rome?"

Russell winced. His chances of becoming ambassador were gone, already flushed down the toilet by his disintegrating marriage. But could he bear the agony of flashing bulbs? Could he stand up to months of impertinent questions? Von Lietzow was threatening to torture him with the drip-drip-drip of his unsavory past.

"On the other hand, if you agree to divorce Grace, I promise you my silence."

"What about the children?"

"Peter, or rather Carl-Peter von Lietzow is my heir. He stays with me. As for the others, that is for their mother to decide."

"No! I insist on having the younger children."

"But not Miss Anastasia, your eldest, eh? Perhaps she reminds you too much of your long-dead mother-in-law."

Russell rose to his feet swiftly, but not swiftly enough. He found his arm pinioned behind him in an excruciating grip.

Von Lietzow stood there, smiling, from under his bushy eyebrows. "That reminds me, I could sue you for assault and grievous bodily harm. Ordinarily, the statute of limitations should have passed, but I have influence here in Berlin."

Russell remained silent, gritting his teeth as the pain in his arm radiated out to his elbow, shoulder, neck, and upper back.

Von Lietzow stepped close, so close Russell could smell his breath, a rank mixture of beer, tobacco, and other unidentifiable odors. "If you ever attempt that again, I will have you thrown in jail. Now, do we have our agreement?"

Russell swallowed. He really had no choice. He managed a small nod.

Il Cazzo handed him a pen. "These are the divorce papers. You will sign them. Now."

As Russell exited the lawyer's offices, a burning stew of jealous rage roiled his gut. He wasn't going to put up with this. He marched back to his office, where he spent hours pacing, unable to work. He should be exhausted but his rage was giving him an inhuman amount of energy.

✠✠✠✠✠✠✠✠✠✠✠

In the ensuing days the Berliner Morgenpost teased him with snippets of Grace's life, how her cousin the Marquise de Chabrillan arrived from France with her daughters to stay at Kladow, along with Il Cazzo's aunt Gräfin Sidonie von

Graslitz. How that bitch Violet Ecker acted as maid of honor at the wedding that duly took place. The photo above the front fold the following Monday showed his wife looking ethereally lovely in a wedding dress she'd apparently designed back in 1922, surrounded by their children. He couldn't understand it. She'd seemed so happy in the early days of their marriage. It had never occurred to him that she might be pining for her rapist, or for the life they'd planned together in Berlin. Russell staggered to his feet and spent several moments retching into the commode.

The worst thing was that their wedding had taken place on October the twenty-ninth, the anniversary of Angelina's…death. Everyone, including Grace, knew. What was he going to do?

Chapter Thirty-Six
Wednesday, 9 November

It began with a small thing, a lost dog, a stuffed animal only six inches high. But Benny wanted it, and it was his birthday.

How strange children are, thought Grace. After months of not noticing they'd left behind this much-hugged toy in their haste to leave, six-year-old Benny was now clamoring for it. As they turned into Mommsenstrasse, Grace told herself they would be safe, for Carl's minions kept her apprised of her ex-husband's whereabouts. He was taking his yearly vacation in Paris, and wasn't expected back for another week. Grace intended to stay at Savignyplatz only as long as it took to find the toy. But as she walked up the steps to the mansion, her stomach clenched, then went into spasms.

Oh no. Grace was too familiar with the symptoms of miscarriage, and she didn't want to alarm her children, who were now roaming around, looking for Benny's little friend. But she needed privacy, and almost without thinking, she slowly mounted the stairs, clutching at the bannister, making her way to her former bedroom. As she arrived at the top of the stairs, she paused, the silence of upstairs engulfing her.

Slowly she pushed open the door. As her eyes settled on his things, she recoiled. She couldn't be here. She took in his hairbrush, his comb, his shaving brush, all neatly placed on the toilet stand. Then she noticed bottles of face cream, littering the vanity he'd given her. Underneath the drapes that concealed the vanity's drawers peeped a pair of pink satin slippers.

She shouldn't be here, it was an intrusion. Turning to go, Grace put one hand on the bedroom door, while her stomach knotted up. If only Carl were here, he would know what to do, but he was gone for the day, rushed to the bedside of Aunt Sidonie, who was dangerously ill. Grace headed for the stairs, but waves of nausea assaulted her. She felt ghastly. Blindly, she turned back, re-finding the door to the room that had been theirs, and collapsed onto the bed.

✠✠✠✠✠✠✠✠✠✠✠

Russell exited the taxi and walked slowly toward the rented mansion in Savignyplatz. Mabel had persuaded him to keep it on in case his children needed him. That way, they would know where to find him. Mabel, Mabel, Mabel. She meant well, but he resented the way she'd taken control of his life. She'd even had the gall to move into this mansion with him, then set about erasing all memories of Grace. It would have been bad enough if she'd been a married woman, or a divorcée, but living with an unmarried woman, even if she was well into her thirties, was something he could no longer countenance. He would have to ask her to leave.

He put his suitcase down and fumbled for the key. His vacation in Paris had not gone well. Naturally, it had been Mabel's idea to go there, and normally the loveliness of that gray European capital in early autumn would have charmed him. But he didn't enjoy Mabel's company. She bored him, and when she didn't bore him, she annoyed him. After one particularly tense exchange, he'd packed his bags and taken the next train to Berlin.

As he pushed open the front door, he could hear children's voices within. Russell stilled. Was he hearing things? If the children were here, that must mean Grace was here also. His heart thrummed, making him feel alive for the first time in weeks. He left his suitcase by the front door, and put his hat on the hatstand. Swiftly, he mounted the stairs, and very gently, using only the pressure of his fingers, opened their bedroom door. He drew in his breath. Afternoon light filtered past the heavy drapes making it just possible to see a form under the bedclothes.

She was here.

Silently, he shut the door and descended the stairs.

"Papa!" Benny barreled into him. "Have you seen my toy? The little dog with the bell?"

Russell's face cracked open with a smile as he looked down at his son's eager face. Things were going to get better, he could feel it.

"Where are your sisters?"

Benny made a dismissive gesture. "They're around somewhere."

Taking his youngest's small hand, he walked outside. Marina was skipping on the lawn with a jump rope she'd found somewhere.

"Papa!" She threw the toy down, her face lighting up. "Where were you? I've missed you."

"I've missed you too," he replied, kissing her soft cheek.

He glanced up to see his eldest, his too-thin teenaged daughter raking him with her gaze.

"Where's Mother?"

"She's upstairs, but too ill to be disturbed." He moved forward and pecked her on the cheek. The child was coiled as tight as a length of barbed wire, the sort that he used to get caught in during the Great War. This child would interfere with his plans, his need for privacy, his craving to spend some time alone with Grace. He needed to send his children away, somewhere. Now.

Leaving them to occupy themselves, he walked back to the house, deep in thought, ideas coming to him with their old fluency. One benefit of his trip to Paris with Mabel was that she'd taken him around various French boarding schools.

"You never know what might happen," she'd remarked when he asked why. "Carl von Lietzow may tire of your children—after all, they're not his. You should look for a suitable place for your daughters. You can think about Benny when he's older." He went into the hall, picked up the phone and called an agency. Within the hour, Nanny Fawcett, a no-nonsense British woman corralled the children together and escorted them onto a train bound for Paris. She was going to act as chaperone until they arrived at the École Sévigné in Neuilly, a smart suburb of Paris.

With the children gone, he went upstairs to visit Grace again, but she was wan and unresponsive. Alarmed, he called a doctor. When he came, he spent a considerable time with her.

"What is wrong?"

The doctor paused, the back of his hand slowly closing the door to the darkened room. "You should ask your wife."

Russell paid him and went back up to their bedroom, but she was fast asleep. He sat there staring at her motionless form. He should have been furious at the way she'd abandoned him, but all he could feel was love. Russell sat there, drinking her in, the sound of her breathing soothing him as nothing else could. Their marriage stretched before him, a countryside of emotions. They'd begun in fields of ripening corn. Now, they were in arid land surrounded by thorns. He cursed that prick Il Cazzo yet again. If only he could have been the first to make love to her, she would not have become pregnant with his rival's son, and the fissures between them would never have happened. How he ached to have his wife back. He would do anything to make a happy home with her again. Russell fell to his knees and made a private vow to win her back and keep her forever.

Something made her startle, and she opened her eyes. They rested on him for a moment, then flicked away, as if in distaste. When she spoke, her voice was low and cool.

"Where are the children?"

As he explained that he'd sent them off to Paris with a chaperone, she moved her head restlessly from side to side.

"How dare you. I'm their mother."

"But Grace, you're not well."

She sat up, her face pasty-pale. "I must go."

"Grace, don't you remember the doctor? He just came to visit you. He spent a considerable amount of time—"

She yanked the bedclothes to the floor.

"Where are you going?"

"To see the children, of course." She lurched towards the armoire.

Russell's gut coiled into knots. "Grace—"

But his fragile-seeming wife knocked his hand away and yanking open the door, threw a pile of left-behind dresses onto her bed. She scrabbled though them, sorting haphazardly, then stood up. Grabbing a chair, she scrambled up, swaying as she stretched her hand towards a suitcase.

He held the chair for her, helping her get the suitcase off the top of the armoire and down onto the floor.

She flung her dresses into the suitcase, piled on a drawer full of more stuff she'd left behind, underthings, followed by shoes, hats, purses. Finally, she sat on the case, struggling to close the lid.

"Would you please call a taxi?" Her voice lacerated him like a whip.

His neck stiff, he left. As he hurried downstairs towards the phone, he wondered why he did her bidding without question.

Eventually, she staggered downstairs, clothed in fresh garments, dragging that suitcase behind her.

"Grace—"

But she pushed him away and opened the front door.

"Grace!" He grabbed her arm. "Surely you're not going to take off and leave *me* like that—"

She ignored him, and with a superhuman strength picked up her suitcase just as the taxi rounded the corner. Suddenly, several month's worth of pent-up fury surged forth. Striding down the path, he got in front of her.

"Let me pass."

"I am never going to allow you to leave me again."

A look of contempt punched him. "You disgust me," she hissed. "How can you look at me with those sheep's eyes, when you've had male lovers for years?"

He halted, allowing her to push past him. Where had she gotten that idea? Yes, he'd been propositioned by several men over the years. But he'd been faithful to her since the day he'd fallen into her silver-gray eyes. He'd been chaste for the sake of her health for six years.

"*Sei una fica!* You c**t!" The words sprang forth before he could stop them. He'd never sworn at his wife.

She didn't even pale. "*Sei uno finocchio!* You faggot!" she spat in return.

Through a dark haze he lunged at her, his fingers closing around her throat. Eyes widening, she collapsed. He sagged on top of her. What had he done? "*Graziella, vita mia, si torna, si torna,,* Grace, my life, come back, come back," he murmured over and over again, uncaring at the commotion that erupted, as the taxi driver called for help, as von Lietzow's flunkies descended, bundling her lifeless form into a hearse.

Someone handcuffed him and threw him into the back of that taxi. As it took him out of Berlin, white faces peered from behind the flimsy safety of their drapes, while dark figures darted, smashing shop windows on Kantstrasse. The taxi jerked along unlit city streets, past shouts, jeers, and signs. The letters crowded in upon him, JUDEN AUS alternating with THE LADY VANISHES, the latest Hitchcock movie.

As they left the city, turning into that silent country road that strung together the villages of Pichelsdorf, Gatow, and Hohengatow, an orange glow throbbed from the direction of Berlin, nearly obliterating the faint stars.

The taxi slid to a stop, someone shoved him out, he collapsed onto a heap of broken leaves, mud, and dead twigs in front of a pair of feet, encased in thick, leather boots. Slowly, he strained his neck and looked up.

His rival glowered down at him. He moved his mouth, he roared, he spat, he barked orders, but Russell was beyond hearing. Yet he understood perfectly. Yes, shooting was too good for him. Yes, he should hang for his crimes.

A rope looped high around a branch in an ancient linden. Someone fashioned a noose from the other end, putting it around his neck, dragging him to the tree, forcing him up a ladder.

The murky November scene before him had a particular odor, something dark, and sharp, like petroleum. A bonfire burned in a brazier, the flames coiling, leaping into the freezing air.

Only one thought revolved in his head.

Grace.

How perfect she had been for him, coming into his life like a miracle, when he'd been a shell-shocked war veteran.

When he'd tumbled into her eyes, he'd known then that he would claim her as his wife. It was extraordinary how certain he'd felt.

And now she was gone.

Endlessly absent.

If only she could come back, even as a shadow, even in a dream—

A blow bit into the back of his neck as someone kicked away the ladder.

A light brighter than white exclaimed.

The linden tree creaked as his broken body swung in arcs.

✠✠✠✠✠✠✠✠✠✠✠

They buried her in marble, in the family crypt, in Kladow.

They obliterated him, pouring a libation of petroleum, annihilating him with fire.

Acknowledgments

This book took me ten years to write. I could not have done it without the help of many people. The first person who deserves thanks is my fabulous editor Catherine Adams, founder of Inkslinger Editing, for her work in giving this manuscript what I hope is a polished, professional feel. Any mistakes are my own.

I was privileged to take classes with many excellent teachers during my journey with *Farewell*. I wish to thank my mentors at Lesley University: Rachel Kadish, Christina Shea, and Tony Eprile, who demanded that I make this manuscript the best that it can be. I also would also like to thank A. J. Verdelle for giving me the tools to polish this manuscript via her class on manuscript revision, given at Lesley during the June 2014 residency.

I also wish to thank Ann Hood, author of *The Book That Matters Most* for her discussion of Italian-American families at the 2016 VCFA Postgraduate Workshop; Tayari Jones, author of *An American Marriage*, for her incisive reading of the novel during the 2012 Napa Valley Writer's Workshop; Elise Capron from the Dijkstra Agency for her suggestions at the 2015 Squaw Valley Workshop; Jon Sternfeld, then of the Irene Goodman Agency, for his astute comments on the first thirty pages of the manuscript during the 2011 Unicorn Writer's Conference; and Terri Valentine, author of *Louisiana Caress*, for her class "Revision and Self-Editing," given during the spring of 2011.

I would like to thank my wonderful friends, Beth Franks and Robin Schuster for offering their wisdom on various aspects of this novel, Nick Dennerly of Nick Dennerly Designs for the original conception of the cover, Pegg Nadler of Pegg Nadler Associates for the final design, and Sophie

Spinelle of Shameless Photography for the final editing of the cover image.

Richard Wetzel and the staff of the Goethe Institut of Washington, D.C., initiated my research on Berlin in the 1920s, and my friend Jeremiah Riemer, helped with the timing of my novel, so that poor Grace would not have arrived in Berlin in 1919 just as the Spartacists were shooting at everything in sight.

I received a great deal of help and kindness from various people whom I met in Berlin during a research trip made in May-June 2012. They include the staff of the *Grisebach Villa* on Fasanenstrasse in Berlin for giving me a copy of their catalog and for allowing me to visit and take photographs, as well as the staff of the *Universität der Künste* Berlin (formerly known at the *Hochschule Für Musik*), who answered numerous questions and also allowed me to walk around and take pictures so that I could accurately depict Grace's music school.

The following writers deserve thanks for reading the manuscript and making useful suggestions: Kristin Abkemeyer, Dena Afrasiabi, Michael Badger, Sally Bensusen, Adam Brickley, Peter Brown, Andrea Caswell, Sara Clark, Marina Cobbs, Emily Cohen, Valerie Cousins, Katie Cotugno, William Craig, Shane Delaney, Stephane Dunn, Curt Eriksen, David Everett, Kendra Fish, Christian Garbis, Chuck Glenn, Ruth Hanham, Samantha Heuertz, Chas Jackson, Michael Jeffrey, Rebecca Jeschke, David Langness, Gene Leutkemeyer, Dulce Lopez, Sage Kalmus, Jill Kelly, Michelle Kouzmine, Anu Krishnaswamy, Katherine Lim, Tina Manousakis, Phil Margolies, Michelle McGurk, Angela McIntyre, Celeste Mohammed, Joe Oppenheimer, Jodi Paloni, Dave Powers, Julia Rappaport, Laura Remington, Linda Stewart, Steffanie Triller, David Tucholski, Gina Ventre, Whitney Watson, Ben Werner, Margaret Wilkerson, Tom Wood, and Monica Zarazua.

Trudy Hale of the Porches Writing Retreat in Nelson County, Virginia, welcomed me and gave me space in her charming cottage to write the ending of the novel.

Last but not least, I wish to thank my husband, Georges Rey, for prodding me to continue with Grace and for giving me the space to work.

Below is a partial list of books I used in researching *Farewell My Life,* followed by a family tree.

Books

Baignet, Michael and Leigh, Richard. *Secret Germany: Stauffenberg and the True Story of Operation Valkyrie.* Skyhorse Publishing, 2008.

Carrier, Thomas J. (1999). *Washington DC: A Historical Walking Tour*. (Images of America). Arcadia Publishing and The History Press, 1999.

Chernow, Ron. *The Warburgs*. Vintage Books, 1994.

Churchill, Winston S. *The Second World War* (6 vols). Houghton Mifflin, 1948.

Craig, Gordon A. and Gilbert, Felix (Eds.) *The Diplomats 1919-1939*. Princeton University Press, 1994.

Enzensberger, Hans Magnus. *The Silences of Hammerstein*. Seagull Books, 2009.

Flesch, Carl. *The Memoirs of Carl Flesch*. Rockliff, 1957.

Friedrich, Otto. *Before the Deluge: A Portrait of Berlin in the 1920s*. Harper Perennial, 1995.

Gay, Nick. *Berlin, Then and Now*. (Then and Now, Thunder Bay). Thunder Bay Press, 2005.

Gilbert, Martin. *Churchill: A Life*. Henry Holt, 1991.

Gisevius Hans B. *To the Bitter End: An Insider's Account of the Plot to Kill Hitler, 1933-1944*. Da Capo Press, 1998.

Gordon, Mel. *The Seven Addictions and Five Professions of Anita Berber, Weimar Berlin's Priestess of Depravity*. Feral House, 2006.

Gordon, Mel. *Voluptuous Panic: The Erotic World of Weimar Berlin*. Feral House, 2008.

Hoffmann, Peter. *Stauffenberg: A Family History, 1905-1944*. McGill-Queen's University Press, 2008.

Isherwood, Christopher. *Christopher and His Kind*. Farrar, Straus & Giroux, 1976.

Jones, Nigel. *Countdown to Valkyrie: The July Plot to Assassinate Hitler.* Frontline Books, 2008.

Kessler, Harry. *In the Twenties: The Diaries of Harry Kessler*. Holt, Rinehart & Winston, 1971.

Large, David Clay. *Berlin*. Basic Books, 2001.

Leary, Josephine Davis. *Backward Glances at Georgetown, with Anecdotes of Famous Washingtonians and Their Georgetown Homes*. The Dietz Press, 1947.

Lesko, Kathleen M., Valerie Babb, Carroll R. Gibbs. *Black Georgetown Remembered: A History of the Black Georgetown Community from the "Town of George" to the Present Historic District*. Georgetown University Press, 1991.

Lubrich, Oliver (Ed.). *Travels in the Reich, 1933-1945: Foreign Authors Report from Germany.* The University of Chicago Press, 2010.

Kirke, Betty. *Madeleine Vionnet*. Chronicle Books, 1998.

MacDonogh, Giles. *1938: Hitler's Gamble*. Basic Books, 2011.

Madsen, Axel. *Chanel: A Woman of Her Own*. Holt, McDougal, 1991.

Magida, Arthur J. *The Nazi Seance: The Strange Story of the Jewish Psychic in Hitler's Circle.* Macmillan/Palgrave, 2011.

McDonough, Frank. *Hitler, Chamberlain and Appeasement* (Cambridge Perspectives in History). Cambridge University Press, 2002.

Metzger, Rainer. *Berlin: The Twenties*. Harry N. Abrams, 2007.

Mitcham, Samuel W. *Why Hitler? The Genesis of the Nazi Reich.* Praeger, 1996.

Neffe, Jürgen. *Einstein: A Biography*. Johns Hopkins University Press, 2007.

Norton, Robert E. (2002). *Secret Germany: Stefan George and His Circle*. Cornell University Press, 2002.

Parssinen, Terry. *The Oster Conspiracy of 1938: The Unknown Story of the Military Plot to Kill Hitler and Avert World War II*. HarperCollins, 2003.

Pearson, Drew and Robert S. Allen. *Washington Merry-Go-Round*. Horace Liverlight and Company, 1931.

Post, Emily. *101 Common Mistakes in Etiquette and How to Avoid Them*. A. D. Steinbach & Sons, 1939.

Reck-Malleczewen, Friedrich. *Diary of a Man in Despair.* Paul Rubens, 2000.

Roth, Joseph. *What I Saw: Reports from Berlin 1920-1933*. W. W. Norton, 2004.

Roux, Edmonde Charles. *Chanel and Her World*. Vendome Press, 2005.

Sereny, Gitta. *Into that Darkness*. Vintage Books, 1983.

Vassiltchikov, Marie. *Berlin Diaries 1940-1945*. Vintage Books, 1988.

Notes

Chapter One:

Italians mostly refer to *Venice* as *Venezia*. But the people from the Veneto call it *Venexia* in their local dialect.

The piece that Russell plays on the piano by himself is the *Italian Concerto* by J. S. Bach.

The music that Angelina and Russell dance to is *Tango* by George Gershwin, composed 1915.

The music Grace and Russell play at their first meeting is Violin Sonata No. 2, in A major by Johannes Brahms, Opus 100, composed 1886.

Known in English as *Raphael*, *Raffaello Sanzio da Urbino* (1483-1520) was a painter of the Italian Renaissance.

Chapter Two:

The piece that Grace practices in her bedroom as she thinks of Russell is the *Siciliana* from Violin Sonata No. 1 in G minor, BWV 1001 by J. S. Bach composed 1720.

Chapter Three:

The piece that Professor Burneys want Grace and Russell to try is Violin Sonata No. 3, in D minor by Johannes Brahms, Opus 108, composed between 1878 and 1888, First Movement.

Chapter Five

The pieces that Professor Burneys wants Grace to learn are Violin Concerto in D Major by Johannes Brahms, Opus 77, composed 1878; and Violin Concerto in D Major by Ludwig van Beethoven, Opus 61, composed 1806.

Chapter Six:

Grazia Deledda (1871-1936) was an Italian writer who received the Nobel Prize in literature for writing that captured the struggles of the people of Sardinia, where she was from. *La Grazia* was published in 1921.

Alma Moodie (1900-1943) was an Australian violinist, regarded as the foremost violinist of her generation during the 1920s and 1930s. She won a scholarship to the Brussels Conservatory when she was a child. In 1919, she met Carl Flesch who took her on as his pupil. Flesh was later to write 'amongst all the pupils in my course I liked Alma Moodie best.'

Institute of Musical Art in New York City, the predecessor to the Julliard School, was founded in 1905. The Juilliard School was not created until the mid 1920s.

Gazette du Bon Genre was a fashion magazine published in France from 1912 to 1925 and distributed in the United States by Condé Nast. The title roughly translates as "Journal of Good Style."

Chapter Seven:

The music Grace plays when she's left alone at home, while Zia Paulina and Violet go to the funeral parlor is Quartet, Opus 33, No 3, by Josef Haydn, beginning, 1st violin part. Part of a series of six string quartets called the "Russian" quartets, it was composed in 1781.

Carl Flesch (1873-1944) was born in Hungary, began the violin at the age of seven, continued his studies in Vienna and Paris, and taught in a variety of places including Bucharest, Amsterdam, Berlin, and Philadelphia. In 1934, after Hitler became Chancellor of Germany, he settled in London. He published a number of instructional books, including *Die Kunst der Violin-Spiels* (*The Art of Violin Playing*, 1923) and *Das Skalensystem*, (*The System of Scales*) published as a supplement to *The Art of Violin Playing*. Among his pupils were Bronislaw Gimpel, Ida Haendel, Alma Moodie, Ginette Neveu, Yfrah Neaman, Max Rostal, Henryk Szeryng, Roman Totenberg and Josef Wolfsthal.

The Spartacist uprising, also known as the January uprising, was a general strike in Germany from 4 to 15 January 1919. Similar uprisings occurred and were suppressed in Bremen, the Ruhr, Rhineland, Saxony, Hamburg, Thuringia and Bavaria, and another round of even bloodier street battles occurred in Berlin in March, which led to popular disillusionment with the Weimar Government. Russell's news is about three years out of date.

Chapter Ten

The pieces that Grace plays for her audition with Professor Flesch are *Adagio* from Violin Sonata No. 1 in G minor, BWV 1001 by J. S. Bach composed 1720; Violin Sonata No. 3, in D minor by Johannes Brahms, Opus 108, composed between 1878 and 1888; and First Movement.*Rondo alla Turca* from Violin Concerto No. 5 in A major, K. 219, by Wolfgang Amadeus Mozart, composed in 1775.

Lette-Verein, where Violet goes to learn fashion design, means Lette Society. Pronounced LET-tuh ver-RYN, it was founded in 1866 in Berlin by Dr. Wilhelm Adolf Lette, as a technical school for girls. There were classes for dressmaking, machine-sewing, the cutting-out of linen, the manufacture of artificial flowers, glove-making, millinery, and hair-dressing. The Lette-Verein received the support of influential members of German society, beginning with the Emperor and Empress. It is still located at Viktoria-Luise-Platz.

Kalócsa, pronounced kah-LOTCH-ah, is a town in the Southern Great Plain of Hungary, known for its paprikas.

Chapter Twelve

Otakar Ševčík, pronounced Oh-tah-kah SHEV-chick, (1852-1934) was a Czech violinist and influential teacher. He studied at the Prague Conservatory and began his career in 1870 as concertmaster of the Mozarteum in Salzburg. From 1875 to 1892 he was professor of violin at the Russian Music Society in Kiev. In 1892 he became head of the violin department at the Prague Conservatory. In 1909, he became director of the Violin Department at the Vienna Music Academy, until 1918, when his nationality forced him to leave his position.

Rodolphe Kreutzer (1766-1831) was a French violinist, teacher, conductor, and composer. Born in Versailles, he was initially taught by his German father, who was a musician in the royal chapel. He became one of the foremost violin virtuosos of his day, and is best known as the dedicatee of Beethoven's Violin Sonata No. 9, Op. 47 (1803), though he never played the work, declaring it unplayable and incomprehensible. He was a violin professor at the Conservatoire de Paris from its foundation in 1795 until 1826. He was co-author of the Conservatoire's violin method with Pierre Rode and Pierre Baillot, and the three are considered the founding trinity of the French school of violin playing. He was well known for his style of bowing, his splendid tone, and the clearness of his execution. His best-known work is the collection of *42 études ou caprices* (*42 Études or Capriccios*, 1796) which are fundamental pedagogic studies.

Professor Josef Wolfstahl (1899-1931) taught at the *Hochschule Für Musik* (*Technical School for Music*) in Berlin. Not much is known about his life, except that he produced a beautiful sound, and that he died tragically young of an operation gone wrong. It is possible that he did not become a professor at the Music School until the late twenties, but I couldn't find anything definitive about that. I decided to give him a cameo role in my novel because he taught my own violin teacher, Nannie Jamieson.

Professor Wolfstahl speaks French to his students. Even German professors would have had a smattering of French to deal with the international students, which was the diplomatic language of the day. After the Second World War, English became much more prevalent.

The music is Quartet Opus 33, No. 6 by Josef Haydn, composed 1781.

Chapter Fifteen

Graslitz, Bohemia, now Kraslice in the Czech Republic, is one hundred miles west of Prague.

Welchau, Bohemia, now Velichov in the Czech Republic, is eighty-two miles west of Prague.

Posen, Prussia, now Poznań in Poland, is about 170 miles east of Berlin.

Chapter Twenty

Louis XV, King of France reigned from 1710 to 1774. The Louis XV style, or Louis Quinze, is a French rococo style of furniture, decorative arts, and architecture.

Chapter Twenty-Three

L'incendio nell'oliveto: *The Fire in the Olive Grove*, a novel published in 1918 by Grazie Deledda.

Chapter Twenty-Six

All biblical quotations are taken from the King James bible.

And of his fullness have we all received, Grace for grace. John 1:16.

In my Father's house are many rooms. John 14:2. King James says: "In my Father's house are many mansions," but I have kept the more modern translation, as it makes more sense.
I am the way, the truth and the life. John 14:6.
The light shineth in the darkness. John 1:5
The true Light, which lighteth every man that cometh into the world. John 1:9
Cast thy burden upon the Lord, and he shall sustain thee. Psalm 55:22.
For by Grace are ye saved through faith. Ephesians 2:8.
As you sow, so shall you reap. Galations 6:7.
That you love one another as much as I have loved you. John 13: 34-35.

Chapter Twenty-Seven
The Sudetenland comprised the northern, southwest, and western areas of Czechoslovakia, specifically those border districts of Bohemia, Moravia, and parts of Silesia, which were originally part of Austria-Hungary until the end of the First World War and were therefore inhabited by people of German ancestry who spoke German.
Technische Hochschule: Literally translated as "Technical High School", this was actually a university-level technical institute, comparable with MIT.

Chapter Twenty-Nine
The Blücher Palace on Pariser Platz, was purchased in 1930 as a new and permanent home for the U.S. Embassy in Berlin, but before it could be converted for embassy use, a fire damaged the building. Money shortages in America, due to the Depression, and soured relations with the Nazi régime (after 1933) delayed its refurbishment. In fact Ambassador William Dodd (1869-1940), assigned to Berlin

from 30 August 1933 to 29 December 1937, asked the State Department not to rebuild on the site because Hitler used Pariser Platz as a Nazi showcase for rallies and marches. In the meantime the embassy operated in the Tiergarten area on Stauffenbergstrasse (then known as Bendlerstrasse). The temporary location was Bendlerstrasse 39, just down the street from the Bendler Block (Bendlerstrasse 13-14) where the *Oberkommando der Wehrmacht* (Supreme Command of the Armed Forces), the *Oberkommando des Heeres* (Supreme Command of the German Army), and the *Abwehr* (German Intelligence) were located.

U.S. Ambassador Hugh R. Wilson (1885-1946) was stationed in Berlin from 3 March 1938 to 16 November 1938. Hitler was delighted when Dodd left and Wilson was appointed in his place, as he knew Wilson to be an admirer. Wilson also coined the phrase 'a pretty good club' when describing the Foreign Service.

William Phillips (1878-1968) was assistant secretary of state before being posted to Luxembourg, and under secretary of state before being posted to Rome. He was the American ambassador to Rome from 4 November 1936 to 6 October 1941.

Mährisch Östrau or Moravian Östrau, is now a city in the Czech Republic called Ostrava.

Chapter Thirty

Ratibor is Racibórz, in Silesia, Poland.

Cosel is Kędzierzyn-Koźle in Poland.

Carl Friedrich Goerdeler (1884-1945) was a monarchist conservative German politician, executive, economist, civil servant and opponent of the Nazi régime.

Nevile Henderson (1882-1942) was a British diplomat and Ambassador of the United Kingdom to Nazi Germany from 1937 to 1939.

Anschluss is the takeover of Austria by Nazi Germany in March 1938.

Hans Oster (1887-1945) was a general in the Wehrmacht of Nazi Germany who was also a leading figure of the German resistance from 1938 to 1943.

der Nacht der langen Messer is the *Night of Long Knives*, 30 June 1934, when Hitler launched a purge, in which he murdered around eighty-five people, to consolidate his hold on power.

Austrian Corporal refers to Adolf Hitler, who was born in Braunau am Inn in Austria-Hungary (present-day Austria). He moved to Munich as a young man, and due to an administrative error, served in the Bavarian army rather than the Austrian army during the First World War. He was decorated for bravery, receiving the Iron Cross First Class in 1918.

Chapter Thirty-One

Wilbur J. Carr (1870-1942) was U.S. Ambassador to Prague from 13 July 1937 to 6 April 1939.

Edvard Beneš, pronounced BEH-nesh, (1884-1948) served as President of Czechoslovakia from 1935 to 1938. Before that he was Minister of Foreign Affairs.

Chapter Thirty-Two

Erwin von Witzleben (1881-1944) was a German officer and army commander in the Second World War.

Franz-Maria Liedig (1900-1967) was a Kriegsmarine officer and member of the military resistance against Adolf Hitler.

Chapter Thirty-Three

Ewald von Kleist-Schmenzin (1890-1945) was a German lawyer, a conservative politician, and opponent of Nazism.

Chapter Thirty-Four

William Shirer (1904-1993) was an American journalist and war correspondent. He became known for his broadcasts from Berlin, from the rise of the Nazi dictatorship through the first year of World War II.

Neville Chamberlain (1869-1940) was a British Conservative politician who served as prime minister of the United Kingdom from May 1937 to May 1940.

Benito Mussolini (1883-1945) was an Italian politician. Known as *Il Duce* (*The Leader*), Mussolini was the founder of Italian Fascism.

Édouard Daladier (1884-1970) was a French politician and the prime minister of France at the start of the Second World War.

Anthony Eden (1897-1977) was a British Conservative politician who served three periods as Foreign Secretary and then a relatively brief term as prime minister of the United Kingdom from 1955 to 1957.

Harold Nicolson (1886-1968) was a British diplomat, author, diarist and politician. He was the husband of writer Vita Sackville-West.

Leo Amery (1873-1955) was a British Conservative Party politician and journalist, noted for his opposition to appeasement.

Winston Churchill (1874-1965) was a British statesman who was the prime minister of the United Kingdom from 1940 to 1945 and again from 1951 to 1955. Churchill was also an officer in the British army, a non-academic historian, and a writer (as Winston S. Churchill). He won the Nobel Prize in

Literature in 1953 for his overall, lifetime body of work. In 1963, he was the first of only eight people to be made an honorary citizen of the United States.

Edward Wood, 1st Earl of Halifax (1881-1959) was one of the most senior British conservative politicians of the 1930s. He held several senior ministerial posts during this time, most notably those of viceroy of India from 1925 to 1931 and of foreign secretary between 1938 and 1940.

Chapter Thirty-Five

Teschen is divided into two towns, Cieszyn, Poland and Český Těšín, Czech Republic.

Freistadt is Fryštát in the Czech Republic.

Chapter Thirty-Six

Kristallnacht (*The Night of Broken Glass*) was a pogrom against Jews throughout Nazi Germany on 9–10 November 1938. The name Kristallnacht comes from the shards of broken glass that littered the streets after the windows of Jewish-owned stores, and synagogues were smashed.

JUDEN AUS: JEWS OUT

The Lady Vanishes is a British thriller directed by Alfred Hitchcock. It was released in London on 7 October 1938.

The Paganos

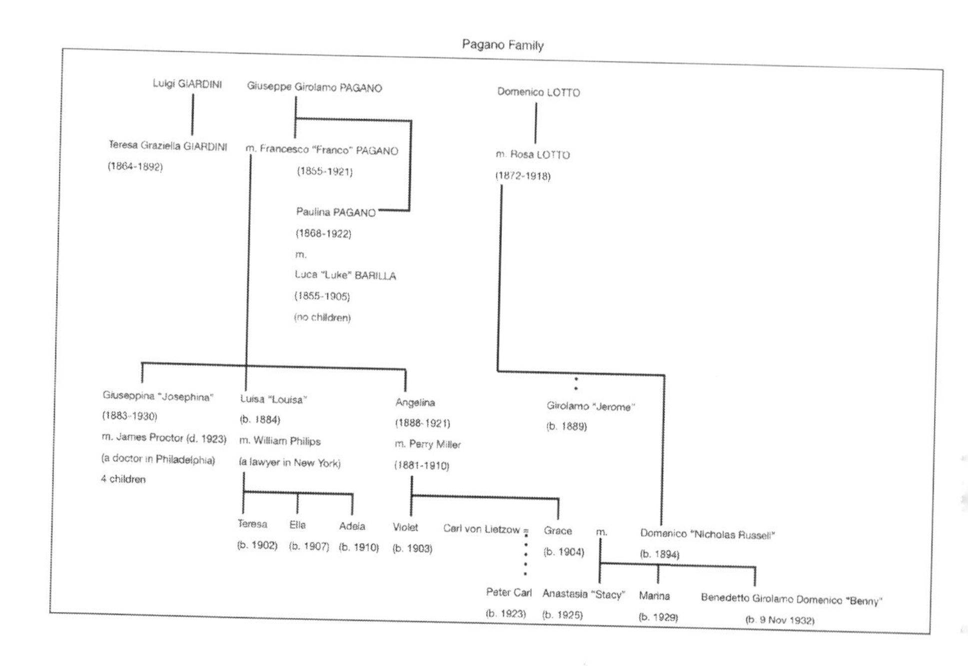
Pagano Family
Luigi GIARDINI
Giuseppe Girolamo PAGANO
Domenico LOTTO
Teresa Graziella GIARDINI
(1864-1892)
m. Francesco "Franco" PAGANO
(1855-1921)
m. Rosa LOTTO
(1872-1918)
Paulina PAGANO
(1868-1922)
m.
Luca "Luke" BARILLA
(1855-1905)
(no children)
Giuseppina "Josephina"
(1883-1930)
m. James Proctor (d. 1923)
(a doctor in Philadelphia)
4 children
Luisa "Louisa"
(b. 1884)
m. William Philips
(a lawyer in New York)
Angelina
(1888-1921)
m. Perry Miller
(1881-1910)
Girolamo "Jerome"
(b. 1889)
Teresa
(b. 1902)
Ella
(b. 1907)
Adela
(b. 1910)
Violet
(b. 1903)
Carl von Lietzow =
Grace
(b. 1904)
m.
Domenico "Nicholas Russell"
(b. 1894)
Peter Carl
(b. 1923)
Anastasia "Stacy"
(b. 1925)
Marina
(b. 1929)
Benedetto Girolamo Domenico "Benny"
(b. 9 Nov 1932)

Made in the USA
Middletown, DE
19 January 2020